SHADOWS OF THE DEAD

Spencer Kope

MINOTAUR
BOOKS
—
NEW YORK

First published in the United States by Minotaur Books, an imprint of St. Martin's Publishing Group

SHADOWS OF THE DEAD. Copyright © 2020 by Spencer Kope. All rights reserved. Printed in the United States of America. For information, address St. Martin's Publishing Group, 120 Broadway, New York, NY 10271.

www.minotaurbooks.com

Library of Congress Cataloging-in-Publication Data

Names: Kope, Spencer, author.
Title: Shadows of the dead / Spencer Kope.
Description: First edition. | New York : Minotaur Books, 2020. |
    Series: Special Tracking Unit ; 3
Identifiers: LCCN 2020010732 | ISBN 9781250178343 (hardcover) |
    ISBN 9781250178350 (ebook)
Subjects: GSAFD: Suspense fiction. | Mystery fiction.
Classification: LCC PS3561.O63 S53 2020 | DDC 813/.54—dc23
LC record available at https://lccn.loc.gov/2020010732

Our books may be purchased in bulk for promotional, educational, or business use. Please contact your local bookseller or the Macmillan Corporate and Premium Sales Department at 1-800-221-7945, extension 5442, or by email at MacmillanSpecialMarkets@macmillan.com.

First Edition: 2020

10 9 8 7 6 5 4 3 2 1

For Lea and the girls.

ACKNOWLEDGMENTS

I want to say a huge thanks to my editor, Keith Kahla; my assistant editor, Alice Pfeifer; and my agent, Kimberley Cameron. This would be a lesser book without their tremendous expertise and dedication.

I'd also like to thank the men and women of the Whatcom County Sheriff's Office who provide an endless supply of ideas and inspiration. They represent the real law enforcement that I try to portray in my books.

Finally, thanks to my wife, Lea, for putting up with me when I disappear into my study for hours on end. After thirty years she certainly knows what it means to be an author's wife.

SHADOWS OF THE DEAD

PROLOGUE

Six months ago . . .

Music would've been nice.

Guns N' Roses, Nirvana, Korn, perhaps a little Pearl Jam . . . but . . . she shakes her head. No, those aren't right; they don't fit. Something softer is called for, something melancholic. "My Immortal" by Evanescence comes to mind. It's close but lacks the precise ambience that she's looking for.

"The Dance," she suddenly whispers to the quiet. Yes, "The Dance" by Garth Brooks; it had always been a favorite of hers, though she hadn't heard it in years. It was perfect. It fit.

Even the thought of it rests soothingly at the edge of Melinda's consciousness, a welcome change from all the other things—the bad things—that have occupied her mind of late. She lets go a little more, loosens up, begins to slip away, losing herself in the embrace of the warm bath.

An empty wineglass stained with a California merlot sits on the floor, while a dozen candles of varying sizes festoon the wide lip around the foot of the tub, casting their feeble light against the wall of the bathroom. It's almost primal; flames against a cave wall.

Fire and the shadow of fire have always had a mesmerizing effect on humans. Perhaps the pulsating glow of embers stirs something in our DNA, something that tugs at the shadowed corners of our brain, saying here is safety, here is warmth.

Something stirs inside Melinda.

Is it regret?

She opens her eyes and a single tear breaks free and flows down her wet cheek. It doesn't matter, she thinks. None of it matters. It's just her and the quiet bathroom now; her and the candles and the empty wineglass, and the dark water in the darkened, primal room.

The hour is late.

It's likely no one will see her Facebook post until morning. Better that way, she thinks, sinking farther into the tub, farther into the warmth. Not exactly the way she wanted to deal with the situation, but it's done. There's no taking it back.

Not this time.

She lifts her hand and wipes her face. The water gives off a reddish hue in the flickering candlelight, as if, instead of drinking the last of the merlot, she'd poured the entire bottle directly into the tub.

"The Dance" plays in her head, melancholic and final, the kind of song you cry to after drinking too much merlot. A song you may have heard a hundred times before, but never with more meaning and emotion than at this exact moment, even though it's only in your head.

The moment doesn't last.

A different song soon begins to play, distant at first, but drawing nearer.

It's familiar, but unpleasant. She struggles with the sound, her mind almost lost in the warmth, unable to recall. And then she remembers: a siren.

The harsh tone interrupts the song in her head, and she

tries to push up in the tub, but she can't. Her hands grip the sides, dripping merlot water, straining, and then she just gives up and sinks back into the blissful warmth.

It'll be over soon, she thinks.

She isn't taking any chances this time. She did it just like the website showed, long cuts from her wrist to her elbow; guaranteed results. Still, the blade hurt. Even with the wine in her, she may not have cut deep enough. It would get the job done, she was sure of that, but would it get the job done in time, before the siren arrived?

Now she regrets the Facebook post.

It was a stupid impulse, a final goodbye.

Drumming now, the hammering of fists at the front door; the water so warm; the scented candles so far away, like stars now, twinkling in the night sky; a hurried riot of sound drawing ever closer.

Crashing; a door giving way; shouts and shadows.

They're here.

Time's up.

CHAPTER ONE

And into the forest I go, to lose my mind and find my soul.
—John Muir

Sunday, December 14

The dogs sit alert and rigid at the cusp of twilight, unmoving silhouettes cut from stone. Their breathing has settled after the miles-long chase through the woods, and they pay no mind to the keening wind overhead, the whipping treetops, the winter storm that has finally caught us.

Here, in the deep woods of the Olympic Peninsula, one might be forgiven for mistaking them for wolves, these hard hunters with bodies so similar to those of their wild ancestors. One might even feel a chill, a touch of terror at their presence, if not for the quiet presence of their handlers crouched next to them.

With unimaginable discipline, the heads of the police K-9s remain fixed and unflinching as their sensitive noses sample the air, smelling the runner, smelling his nervous fear. Their eyes never leave the rectangular shadow resting among the trees ahead, a place of humans, though long abandoned.

With their handlers—their alphas—beside them, the exhausted dogs feel peace and satisfaction—even joy. The long hunt is almost over. Their prey lies just ahead, injured and exhausted. They smell the blood. They wait now for the command, the human word that will send them to finish the hunt.

Like coiled springs they sit, patient and focused.

The cabin is ancient, a relic from a different era now battered and decrepit.

From our concealed position a hundred feet behind it, I can see the thick green blanket of moss draped over the roof like a half-made bed. The empty window casings are hollowed out, resembling the sunken eyes of an ancient man looking upon his final days. The remnants of wooden shutters, where they still exist, hang at an angle, reduced by time and weather. Even the planks used in the construction of the cabin speak of a different era, a time when sawmills ripped lumber into long wide slabs that both sealed a building and served as siding.

The thickness of the slabs is likely the only reason the cabin still stands.

"One room, maybe a hundred and fifty square feet at most," whispers Detective Sergeant Jason Sturman as he studies the dark openings through the thermal scope of a borrowed sniper rifle. "Probably an old hunting cabin from the thirties or forties."

Despite the storm, we keep our voices low, knowing the howling wind could ebb at any time and catch one of us in midsentence, giving away our presence.

"Do you think it's his?" asks my partner, FBI Special Agent Jimmy Donovan. "Or did he just stumble upon it?"

"Stumbled upon it would be my guess," Jason replies quietly. "If it was his I'd expect it to be in better shape." He gestures at the structure. "One heavy snow and it's going to be nothing but a crumpled pile of mossy tinder. The only reason anyone would hole up inside is if they had nowhere else to go. Desperation makes you do stupid things."

"Sounds like our guy," I mutter.

My name is Magnus Craig, but everyone calls me Steps, even my mom. I'm a man-tracker for the FBI's Special Tracking Unit, and my partner and I have done four searches here in Clallam County: two missing hikers, a bank robber, and a bona fide murder suspect. The last search was eight months ago—the bank robber—and I only remember *that* because it was part of the briefing before we left our office at Hangar 7 in Bellingham this morning.

I have a hard time with names and faces.

We travel to so many places and meet so many people that it really is impossible to keep them all straight, at least for me. Faces blur together; names morph; personalities flatten out. Or maybe my mind just processes information differently and anything deemed no longer of value gets purged, a scrubbing of the hard drive, so to speak.

Jimmy always remembers names and faces.

When Detective Sergeant Jason Sturman and Detective Nathan Critchlow met us on the tarmac this morning as we disembarked from Betsy, the Special Tracking Unit's Gulfstream G100, Jimmy immediately recognized both Nate and Jason, and greeted them with genuine enthusiasm. We've worked with these guys twice before, and they're hard not to like.

The Clallam County Sheriff's Office only has four detectives, so the odds of us ending up with Nate and Jason again were fifty-fifty. I like to think they volunteered when they heard we were coming.

Our impromptu tracking party includes two state troopers and three Clallam County deputies. With Jason, Nate, Jimmy, and me, that makes nine bodies in all—eleven if you count the dogs.

"What do you think, Steps?" Jason asks, turning from the cabin. "Is he inside?"

"The trail leads in that direction," I confirm. "We're going to have to check it out, either way." I glance back at the faces clustered in a half circle behind me. "Anyone want to hike seven or eight miles back to civilization and fetch a tactical robot?"

The words bring weary smiles and a couple chuckles.

"Guess we'll have to do it the hard way, then," I say, and turn to Jimmy. "Why don't you and I take a nice wide stroll around the cabin?"

"Perimeter check?"

"Only way to be sure. If we find any tracks leading away from the cabin, we'll know he's still on the move. And if not . . ."

"Yeah," Jimmy says. "*If not*, then we have a whole new problem on our hands." He glances at the cabin and then at the darkening sky. "Namely, how to get him out of an old, rotting cabin without collapsing it on top of him or setting it on fire with a flashbang."

I pat him on the shoulder. "You'll figure it out."

Our circuitous reconnaissance takes us in a counterclockwise direction around the shack, our movements hidden by trees, distance, and understory vegetation.

We start in a northerly direction, moving by steps, careful not to create any more noise than necessary. In a wide-arching sweep, we soon find ourselves heading to the northwest, then westerly, and so on, until we're 180 degrees from where we started and two hundred feet west of the cabin.

Jimmy and I now have a clear view of the front door—or, rather, we can see the gaping black hole in the empty place where a door once stood, eons ago. I can barely see Jason and the others hunkered down in the trees on the east side of the cabin. Most are just shadows upon shadows.

"Front door is missing," Jimmy whispers into the mic attached to his portable radio. "No movement. We're going to sit here a moment and see what happens."

We don't have to wait long.

A massive gust, perhaps sixty or seventy miles an hour, viciously bends the treetops and creates what in eons past might have been mistaken for a dragon's roar. Twigs and branches snap and crack and tumble to the forest floor, stirring up their own cacophony.

This draws out our suspect.

Curiosity is a powerful thing, especially in the face of nature. I see him first, a dark shape stepping out from the left side of the doorway, brushing his pants off as if he'd been sitting. He walks with a heavy limp.

"There he is!" Jimmy hisses as the figure steps fully into the frame of the door and pokes his head out, looking skyward.

Perhaps it's the trees he fears?

This, after all, is the witching weather of widow-makers, massive tree limbs sheared off in such weather and sent hurtling to the ground to smash anyone and anything foolish enough to get in their way. They can send you from this life to the next in an instant. Such a limb falling from such a height would crush the old cabin as surely as a boot on an eggshell.

As the trees continue to sway to this new, more violent song, the occasional smaller branch does indeed break off, tumbling to the forest floor with mixed results: some are muted by the storm, while other, larger specimens give an audible accounting of their arrival.

"We have confirmation," Jimmy whispers into his mic. "He's in the doorway."

In that instant, the figure looks our way.

A chill runs down my spine and I remain perfectly still, afraid even to breathe. There's little chance he can see us, but perhaps he heard something, or imagined he heard something.

He stares for a long time, his face a mask of shadow. At last he retreats back into the cabin, disappearing to the left, returning to whatever old chair or spot on the floor that he came from.

Jimmy and I exhale in unison.

Getting my attention, he taps the bud in his ear, and in a breathy, barely audible voice says, "They're putting together a plan. They want us to stay put and keep eyes-on."

That's fine by me. We've got the perfect location to watch the coming takedown, a spot with little chance of stray rounds spinning our way. The wind can't reach us, and though we're lying on the ground I haven't felt this warm in hours.

It's almost pleasant, and a sense of peace begins to settle over me.

That's when Jimmy's phone rings.

There are some things that are almost always loud and crystal clear. One is the sound of a toddler using a curse word in front of his grandparents, another—to put it crudely—is a fart in church, and still another is the sound of a cell phone going off in the middle of a supposedly empty forest while a dangerous fugitive rests in a nearby cabin. Admittedly, the last example is far less common than the first two, but now we know it happens.

With shrill tones strung together like pearls, one of Jimmy's special ringtones issues forth, piercing the encroaching night and seeming to amplify the sound twentyfold, carrying it through the trees with the force of a Chinese gong.

Just like that, everything changes.

It's the spoiled appetizer before the soup sandwich.

A world of fumbling and grabbing ensues as Jimmy searches his pockets, finally remembering he placed his phone in the zippered inside pocket. He kills the call before it gets halfway through the third ring.

For a moment he just stares at the phone in his hand, a look of shock and horror on his face. It's a rookie mistake, and he knows it. When he finally looks at me, the shock has changed to embarrassment, and all he can say is, "Damn."

That's about as vulgar as it gets for Jimmy.

When his earpiece comes to life a second later, startling him, he has to live the moment again as he explains to the others what happened.

More embarrassment.

Meanwhile, my heart still drums in my chest and pulses in my neck. It's so loud I fear the sound of it will carry to the cabin and set its walls to trembling. The thought is preposterous, I know, but still I fear.

A minute passes.

I'm waiting for something to happen, some reaction from the cabin, perhaps an attempt to flee. He had to have heard the ring. It was impossible to miss. My attention is so completely focused on the slouching old hovel that I nearly cry out when I feel Jimmy prying at the fingers of my right hand. That's when I realize that I've clamped down on his shoulder, my knuckles white from the pressure.

Releasing, I give him an apologetic look and he tries to smile. It's a tense smile, but the effort is appreciated. I exhale to the count of four, and then inhale to the same count, repeating the cycle several times. It's a calming technique Jimmy taught me years ago, a way to reclaim control of my body when adrenaline threatens to take over.

My eyes are off the doorway mere seconds, but when my gaze returns a chill electrifies me and I freeze as if turned to stone, as if Medusa herself looked out upon me. Breath is once more stuck in my throat, unable to enter or exit.

There, in the doorway, at head-height, a sliver of face with a single, probing eye peeks out from the left side of the opening, unmoving, staring into the darkening forest.

The plan is simple.

"He's in the front corner," Jimmy whispers to Jason over the radio. "He was just left of the doorway a moment ago—my left, not yours." There's a short pause. "No, no gun. Not that we saw, anyway." Another pause. "We're good for now. Have everyone spread out and move up a bit for containment. The perimeter's going to be tight in these trees, but we don't have a choice. As soon as it's a go, we need to tighten it up further."

As the next words come through Jimmy's earpiece, he glances at me apprehensively and then looks way. "Are you sure?" he asks.

The response appears to be in the affirmative, because his next words are tight and to the point: "I can do that. When?"

I don't hear Jason's reply, but Jimmy nods in the darkness. "You got it. Make sure the dogs are ready to give chase, just in case."

When he ends the transmission, he sits silently for a moment, eyes on the dark shadows overtaking the cabin. "Are you ready?" he asks at length.

"Ready? Ready for—"

Apparently it was a rhetorical question, because before

I can finish, Jimmy calls out in a loud voice, projecting the usual challenges: *We know you're in there; Come out with your hands on your head; You're surrounded,* that sort of thing. Experience tells me to expect two possible reactions: silence or profanity. On rare occasion, gunfire decides to join the party.

We get none of these.

Instead, from the blackness of the cabin issues a quiet, hysterical laugh, and the words, "He's going to be so mad." After a short pause, the words come again, louder: "He's going to be so mad!"

The eye has retreated to the back of the cabin now and I can see him pacing back and forth, his mantra growing louder and more desperate with each passing moment. As he moves, he alternates between clasping his hands together in front of him and pressing them to the top of his head. Whether this is to keep the demons out or trap them in, I cannot say. These actions would be irrelevant but for the fact that they show me he doesn't have a gun in his hand, a fact I pass on to Jimmy with some relief.

"He's going to be so mad!"

The wretched voice rises with each repetition until it's almost a scream, the cry made hideous by its implicit despair. All the while, the suspect continues to pace a trench into the floor at the back of the cabin, back and forth, back and forth.

Jimmy updates me on the plan, occasionally pausing to call out to the suspect, urging him to surrender. There's little chance of this happening, but the FBI voice calling out from somewhere in the woods is simply to distract the suspect, keep his attention at the front of the cabin.

On Detective Jason Sturman's side of the forest, orders are already being executed.

The search team moves forward and fans out, encircling the rear and sides of the cabin. The dogs move into position fifty feet to the left of the open doorway, ready to give chase if the suspect decides to run.

A lot of suspects wisely surrender at the first sight or mention of police K-9. The jaws of a fully grown German shepherd can be persuasive that way.

The key to this plan rests with Detective Nate Critchlow, who moves up behind the cabin, ducks low, and then moves forward along the side until he's under an empty window frame. In his hand is something I can't see, though I have a pretty good idea what it is.

When everyone is in place, Jimmy runs through a mental checklist and, satisfied, keys his mic. He utters but a single word repeated three times: "Go, go, go!"

The night turns to chaos.

CHAPTER TWO

I never asked to be the lead man-tracker of the FBI's elite Special Tracking Unit, nor could I have envisioned the events that brought me to this point.

Sometimes things just happen.

Cosmic forces conspire, or perhaps God just decides to correct a mistake . . . or make a new one. A boy takes a wrong turn in the woods, which leads to a string of wrong turns. Soon he's lost, and the forest grows tall around him, hovering above, menacing and impenetrable. The whole thing turns into one big gut punch from Mother Nature when a blizzard rolls in and the snow piles deep. The boy dies, taken by hypothermia, though he is only eight.

I was only eight.

It was my father and a team of searchers who found me and revived me. How long my heart had been still is hard to say. It was likely just minutes, but dead is dead, and no one comes back from such an experience unscathed. I was no exception.

Jimmy says that Mother Nature doesn't gut-punch little

boys, but I'm not so sure. Regardless, something touched me that day, and in the aftermath there lingered . . . well, an aftermath: a blessing, a curse. Your guess is as good as mine.

Jimmy says it's a gift, but he doesn't see what I see.

He doesn't see the neon glow of the blood. He doesn't see where it landed, where it dripped, where it dried. He doesn't see the hands on the throats.

It's been almost twenty years since that day in the woods when I was eight, when death took my hand and then reluctantly let me go. Despite the years, I've never fully come to terms with what came next.

My "blessing" started the moment they revived me, and while it's fair to say that *everything* is mysterious when you're eight, this was different.

At first I thought the cold had done something to my sight, perhaps casting a film over my eyes, because a slight haze had invaded my vision. I noticed the palest shades of color beginning to appear in blotches and smears on the walls, floors, cabinets, seats, and counters. I tried to blink it off, as any eight-year-old would, but to no avail.

In the weeks and months that followed, the hints of color became more pronounced, taking on richer hues, each remarkably distinct. In time, the vivid forest of neon began to assault my senses, splitting my head with migraines that may as well have been brought on by an ice-pick massage directly to the brain, hammering, hammering, hammering.

It was maddening.

The glow was everywhere and on everything.

More importantly, I could now see the cause. That pale grime of color that had first plagued me was now manifest in footsteps, handprints, and the smudge of color on the wall where someone leaned into it with their shoulder.

Though young, I started to understand.

There was nothing wrong with my eyes. That part should

have been a relief, but the truth that came with it was perhaps more terrifying. What I was seeing was, in fact, some type of human residue. Like the glow of a lightbulb after the switch has been turned off, only this glow never completely dies. The intensity dims over time, but never disappears entirely.

The colors I see are endless in tint and combination, and beautiful to behold if not for the fact that you can't turn them off. Woven throughout is an equally endless variety of textures that lie over the color, merging with it, giving it dimension and luminosity. Some of these textures are like sandpaper or pebbles, while others might be pulled wool, beach wood, or the rough skin of an alligator.

The combinations are singularly unique.

At the time, I explained what I was seeing to my dad, fearing he'd think me crazy. He didn't, of course, and it was he who helped me through those first difficult years. He helped me learn to control the flood of color, to dampen and suppress it, so that it wouldn't overwhelm me.

Dad called it *shine*.

He later suggested that the color was the *essence* of a person, unique to them, perhaps representative of their very soul—though my father wasn't a particularly religious man.

Unfiltered, the shine comes at me from a thousand directions, as if I have the eyes of a dragonfly and every one of them sees something different. You don't realize how much we interact with our environment until you see it in bold colors. Imagine if, for a day, everything you touched, everywhere you sat, every spot you placed your foot, and even the spray of your sneeze was displayed in bright glowing red.

Imagine this and you begin to understand shine.

Now multiply that by every person you encounter, every person who's walked the same path in the last hundred years or touched the same faucet in a public restroom. Even my own shine invades my sight, though, oddly, it's less pronounced. Motel rooms are a particular nightmare, and I've taken to bringing my own sheets and pillowcase whenever I travel.

With shine, the world is a billion-hued kaleidoscope—beautiful and horrifying in the same glance, an onslaught of color that gives me piercing headaches if I indulge it too long. It's why, as a boy, I first learned to love reading. The pages of books, even used ones, are rarely touched except at the edge or corner. New books are a particular delight, their virgin pages filled with beautiful letters and words and not a hint of neon.

To this day, books are a blessing, as are the sky, lakes, and oceans.

It was a life-changing turn of events when I discovered, quite by accident, that lead crystal completely blocks the neon glow of shine. And it was my father who secretly ordered the manufacture of a special pair of lead-crystal glasses from a glassblower in Seattle. These days I keep at least two pairs of glasses handy at all times. They block the shine when I don't want to gaze upon it, and I can take them off when I must.

We never told Mom.

Not even a hint of it.

I didn't understand this as a child and took it as evidence that my father was embarrassed or afraid of my special dilemma. As I grew older—perhaps a bit wiser—I came to realize that my dear, sweet, stern Norwegian mother would not have taken kindly to the news that her eldest son could see the subliminal leavings of humans as they went about their daily business.

My mother clings to the superstitions of her upbringing.

As a boy, I remember her loudly proclaiming, "Hallo! Hallo!" upon entering the house after an absence. This was usually after we'd been gone the better part of the day, and especially if we'd been on vacation. She's a bit nuts—in the good way—so I always assumed she was just happy to see the house again, giving it a proper greeting and all that.

As I grew older, I learned that she did this so our sudden reappearance wouldn't upset any gnomes or dwarves who might have taken up residence during our absence, kind of like clapping your hands to shoo the rats away before walking into a dilapidated old building.

Such are the superstitions of Norway.

Whether she actually believes any of this is debatable, but she clings to the tradition nonetheless, much as an American might avoid walking under a ladder or opening an umbrella indoors, even while proclaiming the superstition preposterous.

So, we didn't tell Mom about shine.

Over the years, I've gained a certain mastery over my bane, much like the beekeeper who masters the hive but doesn't yet know the purpose of the veil. It's a painful learning process.

I've often wondered what life would be like without shine—what it would be like to be normal, or at least the common perception of normal. In quiet times, when I indulge this fantasy, I imagine myself working in a bookstore, one that specializes in rare and collectible works. Such is my passion.

But life isn't fair, nor is it easy.

I learned long ago that what we want for ourselves and what we get are often at odds. To some degree, I made peace with my curse long ago, though I suppose *peace* may be a misnomer, as it's more akin to mutually assured destruction, a nuclear détente of sorts. Now I use the duality of the curse and the gift in the best way I know how: finding the missing, finding the dead, and finding their killers.

Since shine is much like DNA or fingerprints in that no two combinations of essence and texture are alike, I'm in the unique position of being able to walk onto a crime scene and see every touch, every footfall, every drop of cast-off saliva, blood, or semen. If the suspect hid the murder weapon, his glowing footsteps lead me right to it. As to ferreting out the identity of the suspect, well, that's another matter.

Despite my unique position at the FBI's Special Tracking Unit, my secret remains closely held. In addition to my dad, the only other people who know about shine are my partner, Jimmy, and the director of the FBI, Robert Carlson, who served with Dad in the Army during the Cold War.

It's fair to say that my dad was the architect of the Special Tracking Unit, but it was Robert Carlson who made it reality.

CHAPTER THREE

My morning had started as all mornings should, yet rarely do. I was lounging on my living room couch with a good book in my hands as horizontal rain pelted the row of bay windows. Indeed, a howling torrent blew outside, blurring the world into vague outlines of hills and horizons, of sky and sea. The perfect weather for reading.

Straight out the windows to the west, the Puget Sound was heaving and churning, as if some great leviathan were just below the waves, wrestling in its slumber, throwing up immense whitecaps as it turned in fits and starts. Not a day for sailing. Not a day for *any* outdoor activity here in the Pacific Northwest. There's a certain sense of inner peace on such days, when the storm is outside, and you are inside, comfortable and content.

That was supposed to be my day.

My entire day.

———

I'm ashamed to admit that I've never read *The Lord of the Rings* trilogy or *The Hobbit*. I was never much for the fantasy genre but having seen the movies repeatedly it seems a bit unfair to ignore the original material—unfair to both Tolkien *and* myself. So far, I haven't been disappointed. In *The Fellowship of the Ring*, the first book in the trilogy, I've already discovered the mysterious and enchanting Tom Bombadil, who was completely ignored in the movies.

It was just the book for such a day. The wind outside stirred my imagination as I turned the pages, and the violent rain against the windows set the mood, as if even from this world something lashed at the heels of our heroes, setting them to flee into darker and darker territory.

When the phone rang, I gave a start.

I glared at the rude device; my first impulse was to ignore it, and I did. My mind was fully bent around the pages of the secondhand, dog-eared paperback, and I wasn't about to let the phone break me from the fantasy, at least not while Frodo and the hobbits were in peril.

I didn't answer.

I refused.

It was Sunday. It was stormy. I deserved a good book and the warmth of my living room and some rum eggnog in a hot mug. I didn't *really* have a mug of rum eggnog, but that was beside the point.

"No," I said firmly to no one.

The phone stopped . . . only to start up again thirty seconds later.

Picking up the handset, I glanced at the caller ID and muttered, "Of course." As if suddenly emboldened, the wind lashed ferociously at the wall of windows as I pushed the talk button. A harbinger, I supposed. It seemed fitting.

"Yes, Diane," I said in measured words upon hearing her

heavy breathing on the other end. "What are you doing in the office on a Sunday?"

"I'm not," she replied shortly. "Not yet, anyway."

Diane Parker, the third member of the Special Tracking Unit, serves as our intelligence analyst, the puzzle master who tries to sort things out and dig up information as each case progresses. At fifty-four, she reminds me of an older version of Janine Melnitz from *Ghostbusters*, complete with the short hair and the glasses resting on the tip of her nose.

She needs to work on the voice a bit.

Diane is also our self-appointed janitor, receptionist, travel adviser, and den mother. She embraces these duties as if they were a badge of martyrdom.

"We just got a call," Diane explained. "You need to come in. Jimmy's on his way, same with Les and Marty."

"Where are we going?"

"Olympic Peninsula," she replied, grinding the words through her teeth like wheat through a mill. "You fly into Port Angeles and then drive south a half hour or so."

"What's the case?"

"Police pursuit gone bad. Driver crashed near Sequim and fled into the woods."

"How does that warrant our attention?"

"I wondered the same thing, but it seems when they popped the trunk on the stolen car, they found a woman inside, bound, gagged, and unconscious. I'm not a crack *tracking* expert like you, but I'm guessing she didn't get there by herself. To complicate things, she didn't have any identification."

"Anything else?"

"Nothing that won't wait—well, except a trooper was injured during the pursuit. He's going to be fine, but the state patrol really wants this guy."

"Who's lead, state or county?"

"County. I'll have more by the time you get to the hangar."

"No dead bodies?"

"Not this time."

The no-dead-bodies pronouncement is always a good thing. Jimmy and I can't seem to get away from bodies of one sort or another: dead bodies, ripe bodies, missing bodies, found bodies, parts of bodies, staged bodies. Most of our ops involve the dead and the dying.

As we spoke, my eyes took in the blurred-out windows, and my ears absorbed the howl of the wind and the drum of the rain as it punished the glass. "What about this weather? What did Les and Marty say?" I asked, referring to the pilot and copilot of the unit's Gulfstream G100 corporate jet. "Are they okay taking off under these conditions?"

"Marty says it's just fine."

"Yeah, well, I want a second opinion from the *sane* member of the flight crew."

Diane gave a chuckle, caught herself, and said, "You can ask Les when you get here."

Oddly, the phone went mysteriously dead. I spent a brief moment trying to delude myself into thinking the connection was bad, that somehow the weather took out the phone lines. The truth was, Diane hung up on me before I could ask more questions that she didn't have the answers to.

I imagine she got a chuckle out of that.

As I stared at the dead phone, the whipped and flurried rain outside the windows took on a more ominous tone, a chipping sound, like a thousand chickens pecking grain from the same tin trough. Only one type of rain makes that sound, though, and it's a rain that hurts.

"Great," I muttered, "sleet."

Perfect flying weather. I could already imagine the obituary. No doubt the words "crashed on takeoff" and "too stupid to come in out of the rain" would appear someplace above the paragraph telling people where to send flowers.

CHAPTER FOUR

It's been just seven hours since I was relaxing on my couch
with a good book, enjoying all the pomp and circumstance
of a winter storm without the unpleasantries. It was supposed to be my morning, my afternoon, and my evening, an
entire day of blissful reading.

Seven hours.

It seems like days.

Time is funny that way. And while I've never been much
of a believer in luck or fate, as I stand in this dark, frigid forest in the midst of the storm I thought I had avoided, and on
the edge of a possible gunfight, one question keeps knock-
knock-knocking at the hollow place at the back of my skull:
Why does this keep happening to me?

The events at the cabin unfold in slow motion, traced out in
striking neon.

On the *Go!* command, Detective Nate Critchlow rises
slightly from his crouched position next to the empty win-

dow frame and tosses something through the opening. Quickly, he stumbles backward through the dark and takes cover behind a thick fir that's so tall it disappears into the gloom above.

It takes the suspect a moment to realize what just happened.

He likely heard a flutter as the canister passed through the air; it's a certainty he heard it thud and roll as it bounced off the wall and settled in the corner. Yet, it's the third sound that likely concerned him the most: a slow hiss, like a pissed-off snake.

Make that a furious snake.

It takes the runner—the kidnapper—a few seconds to process this information, during which the gas begins to fill the cabin. The unbearable sting in his eyes answers all questions. Holding his breath for as long as he can, he finally exhales with a rupturing sound. Unable to stop himself, he inhales deeply, sucking gas into the well of his chest.

His lungs suddenly ache and burn, as if consuming him from the inside out.

A roar rises from the cabin.

It's nothing short of animalistic, the howl of one cornered and beaten, without options. And then the gas *really* starts to go to work. The roar rises to a wail, painful now, and then devolves into a coughing cry of despair. Pain sears his eyes, blinding him temporarily.

Tears flow.

Mucus runs.

Through the dark of night, through the cabin door, and through the spreading toxic mist, I watch as the kidnapper thrashes about, covering and clawing at his eyes, bashing his head against the timber walls. Stumbling and choking, he begins to search for the doorframe, one arm outstretched. A moment later he finds it and pulls himself forward, pulls himself through the opening and into clean air.

Modern tear gas may have had its birth in the trenches of World War I, but its legacy is much deeper. There is evidence that the Aztecs and Mayans both burned chili peppers during warfare, creating smoke and fumes to weaken and disrupt their enemies. Reportedly, the Aztecs even punished children by holding their heads over chili peppers burning in the fire. The Chinese, for their part, would grind cayenne peppers into a fine powder that could be propelled into the faces of their opponents.

The Latin term for tear is *lacrima*, which is why tear gas was originally referred to as a lacrimatory agent or lacrimator. There are a wide variety of lacrimators, some more dangerous than others, some more effective than others. Some just cause the eyes to tear, while others irritate the lungs, throat, and skin.

Law enforcement agencies use either CS or OC gas—which aren't really gases at all, but solids or liquids that have been turned into aerosols. The Clallam County deputies are equipped with the OC variety of tear gas, which, taking a cue from the Aztecs and Mayans, is derived from chili pepper oil, or *oleoresin capsicum*, hence the OC designation. Civilian versions of pepper spray generally contain a less potent mix than that used by police, sometimes significantly less potent. The law enforcement version is equivalent to bear spray.

Needless to say, it's extremely debilitating.

For a cabin this size, one canister is more than enough.

As the suspect stumbles from the cabin, six powerful halogen beams light him up. It takes only a fraction of a second to assess the situation: no gun in his hand; no bulges under the arm concealing a weapon, no bulges around his waistband, front or back.

Two figures move swiftly from the left and—in the vernacular of law enforcement—escort the suspect to the ground.

It's not a soft landing.

The wail that rises as he struggles with the deputies is chilling as it echoes through the dark forest. It's not just the sound of it, it's the words that come with it, mournful cries of, "He's going to be so mad," and "I did it just like you said," and "I'm sorry." The last two clearly directed at some person, real or imagined, who is not present.

A thorough frisk turns up a wallet in the suspect's back pocket, but there's no identification, nothing that gives a hint as to who this guy is. He's no help either. When asked his name, all he'll say is Faceman, sometimes uttering it slowly as if it were two words, other times running them together as if it's a single name, like Batman or Superman.

"Okay, Faceman," Jason says, easing the cuffed suspect to a sitting position, "let's see about cleaning off some of this OC." Retrieving his canteen, he starts by flushing out the man's eyes. A half dozen additional canteens are soon stacked before them as others contribute their water to the cause. One of them suggests stripping off the suspect's tainted clothes and wrapping him in a thermal blanket while they try to air out his shirt and pants.

I suspect this is more out of self-interest than concern for the prisoner. We're going to have to walk this guy out of here, and it's going to be pretty unpleasant if OC is bleeding off his clothes during the miles-long journey.

One of the state troopers with our tracking party suggests rubbing Faceman's clothes in dirt, believing it'll help soak up or wipe away the OC. It's a bit like dry cleaning, I suppose, but with dirt. I've never heard of such a thing, so I watch with curiosity—and from a distance—as the trooper recruits an idle deputy and the two of them go to work on the garments, giving them a good dirt-scrubbing.

After a few minutes, they shake the earth from the fabric

and then beat the shirt and pants against a tree for the better part of a minute. They remind me of old-school lumberjacks, only instead of axes they wield clothes.

When they're satisfied with their work, they carry the "clean" garments back to our still-unidentified suspect. I have doubts about the efficacy of the dirt bath, which is reinforced when my eyes begin to burn as they pass.

I suppose it doesn't matter. The suspect's hair and body are just as contaminated, and we can't exactly hose him down in the middle of the forest with temperatures now dipping into the high thirties. It's going to be a long walk out of here for all of us.

I plan on staying upwind.

While the cleaning process continues, Jimmy, Nate, and I check out the cabin. We quickly find a blue-and-gray Dakine backpack stuffed into the front corner, partially covered with old leaves and other debris, a hurried and poor attempt at concealment.

Setting it on the ground before us and snapping on a pair of gloves, Jimmy reaches into the backpack slowly, delicately, his movements bearing the practiced caution of one who has discovered too many used syringes, open blades, and other hazards among the possessions of the people we hunt. A moment later he has something, and with equal patience he pulls a thin gray rectangle from the backpack and hands it to Nate.

"One Dell laptop," he announces, and then reaches back into the bag. Next, he extracts a yellow-and-black handheld device that I initially take for a walkie-talkie, but then realize my mistake.

"One Garmin GPS," he says, handing this to Nate as well. These are quickly followed by a half-used roll of duct tape, a pair of handcuffs with the key still in the lock, a four-inch folding pocketknife, and two bottles of water. Finally, from the very bottom of the bag, he extracts a factory-sealed sack of something called Mirror Image.

"Alginate impression material," Jimmy reads from the package. "Mint-flavored." He holds it up. "Any idea what this is?"

I take the package from him and turn it so that Nate and I can get a better look. After a moment, I flip it over and read from the back label: "Distributed by Consortium Dental Supply, Lansing, Michigan."

Jimmy's brows scrunch together. "Dental supply?"

"That's what it says."

"Probably what they use to make molds of your teeth," Nate offers. "I got a crown last year and they filled the back corner of my mouth with the stuff. I don't remember the mint flavor, though."

"If this creeper turns out to be a dentist . . . !" I say, leaving the rest unspoken.

"Let's not jump to conclusions," Jimmy says. "I'm sure there are plenty of places you can buy this stuff, maybe even on eBay. It doesn't mean the suspect's a dentist—or even a dental assistant."

"Agreed," Nate says, "but then, what's he need it for?"

It's a question with no answer.

Nate disappears momentarily and returns with some plastic bags and evidence tape. We go through the process of identifying, dating, and sealing each piece of evidence in individual bags, and then Nate signs his bold signature across the taped seam of each bag in thick black Sharpie. This ensures that if anyone tampers with an item it'll be immediately apparent. Standard evidence-handling procedure.

After stuffing the bagged items back into the Dakine pack, Jimmy starts to swing it over his shoulder. Nate stops him.

"I can take that," he offers. "If our psycho poster child has any accomplices, you don't need that getting in your way."

Jimmy doesn't argue.

"Besides," Nate says, "if the bullets start flying I can use it as a shield. Who needs body armor when you have a laptop and some algae molding crap?"

"Alginate," Jimmy corrects, smirking at the detective.

With the cabin and surrounding area searched and our prisoner cleaned up to the best of our ability, we turn our attention to finding a way out. Between the intermittent GPS signal and a compass, we plot a course north-northwest and start off through the swaying timber.

Night is fully upon us.

With stealth no longer a concern, everyone has their flashlights out, and I notice that the beams frequently rise to the treetops, apprehensively searching for widow-makers among the swaying branches. I find myself doing the same thing. It's always best to find widow-makers before they find you.

Much of the walk out is single file along animal trails, so Jason walks in front of Faceman, his Taser drawn and at the ready. The suspect's hands are still cuffed in front of him, but Jason has strung several sets of handcuffs together to create a sort of chain, which he clings to with his free hand. Jimmy walks directly behind, his hand constantly on the suspect's right shoulder, reminding him that he's there.

Before starting the hike back, Jason gave Faceman a wet, folded cloth to wipe his eyes with as the need arose. He promptly lost this along the dark trail and took to using his bare hands, which only exacerbated the problem because they still had some lingering residue of OC, despite repeated washings.

Due to Faceman's mental state, we decided back at the cabin that we'd wait to interview him once clear of the forest and in a stable, more appropriate environment. Despite this, the guy won't shut up. It's a nonstop parade of:

"My name is Faceman.

"I'm a fixer.

"Where is Eight?

"He's going to be so mad.

"My name is Faceman.

"Where are we going?

"Am I in trouble?"

It's a maddening barrage that never seems to quit, at times rising to a pitiable wail. You'd think the guy was being tortured.

These outbursts are accompanied by a heavy amount of blubbering and drooling as he constantly wipes his nose on his OC-contaminated sleeve.

When we emerge from the forest thirty minutes later, we're exactly where we intended: on an isolated road more than seven miles from where we started this morning. An aid car and several patrol units have responded to the area and are waiting nearby as we stumble from the tree line, exhausted and cold.

I can only imagine how we look.

Leading Faceman directly to the nearby ambulance, we finally get our first good look at him in the full light of the waiting emergency vehicles.

He seems to have two states. In one, he's distraught and talking nonsense; in the other, he's constantly grinning, almost comically, as if this has all been a great game and he enjoyed the chase, even though he lost. Sometimes he mixes the two states, wailing in distress and grinning at the same time. The effect is disturbing and suggests he's even less stable than we first imagined.

If I had to guess his age, I'd say midtwenties, maybe a

couple years younger than me. It doesn't take long to figure out that the path that brought him to this moment, through the long months and years of his life, had been a very different path from my own.

On the surface, he's weak—a victim. He has small hands that are almost delicate, and a pockmarked face from an ongoing battle with acne. Yet there's a hard edge to him . . . and something else, something I can't place.

It's in his empty brown eyes.

I've seen more life in the gaze of a corpse.

On the way to help retrieve our search party, the patrol sergeant made a stop at one of the local coffee shops and bought the biggest container of hot coffee they offered, a box that held twelve cups. When he told the barista what it was for, she squeezed in an extra cup.

I'm not much of a coffee drinker, but I choke down a cup despite myself. Anything to drive the chill from my bones. Jason and Jimmy, meanwhile, look like a couple addicts after a dry spell. They sip at the coffee sparingly but constantly, their cups never drifting farther than four or five inches from their lips.

Nate is standing guard at the ambulance as the medics determine Faceman's condition, but when Jimmy holds up a paper cup with steam rolling off the top, he immediately heads our way, chin tucked low against the chill wind.

"He's cuffed to the gurney," the detective says quickly, anticipating Jason's question. "Medics say he's got a seriously sprained ankle and two cracked ribs from when he wrecked the car. He's also got a slight case of hypothermia, so they want to transport."

"How long before we can get a fit?" Jason asks, referring to the fit-for-jail determination needed from a hospital before an injured or sick arrestee can be booked.

Nate shrugs and shakes his head.

"Well, that's just great," Jason mutters in a tired voice, not looking forward to the prospect of babysitting Faceman at the hospital while they wait for a decision.

"He *did* say something interesting," Nate adds, offering up the words like someone who's privy to a tantalizing secret and dying to tell.

"Yeah, what's that?"

"Well, you know how he kept going on about how someone was going to be mad at him?"

"Please, don't remind me," Jason moans.

Nate grins. "I know—like listening to an endless game of *ninety-nine bottles of beer on the wall*, only you're sober. Anyway, when I kept asking him who 'he' was, he finally says, 'It's okay,' which I take to mean, you know—okay, like everything's copacetic, only that's not what he means." Nate drops the last words in a slowing cadence and then pauses, as if for dramatic effect. Jason's too tired to play along, and just lowers his head slightly and lifts an eyebrow.

"It's O-K," Nate says, a little disappointed. "OK is an acronym."

"An acronym?" I say. "For what?"

"Not *what*," Nate quickly corrects, "*who*." He rubs his hands briskly together to get the blood flowing and then stuffs them back into his coat. "He said that OK stands for Onion King—or *the* Onion King, I suppose. He rambled on at one point that the Onion King was a master; used words like *brilliant* and *genius*, but then he shut down instantly, like he just remembered that he wasn't supposed to talk about it—or at least that's what I took from it. You should've seen his face when he realized his mistake: I couldn't tell if he was happy or scared to death." Nate shakes his head with deliberation. "Dude freaks me out."

"The Onion King?" Jimmy says thoughtfully. The coffee cup begins to drift precariously away from his lips but quickly recovers. "Is this Onion King supposed to have something to do with the woman in the trunk?"

"Stands to reason," Nate replies. "He was so worked up about this Onion King being upset with him, it's likely that he failed at something; something big." He looks at me, then at Jason and Jimmy, each in turn. "I'm guessing he was following orders from this Onion King. He was taking her somewhere . . . for some purpose."

It's a dark thought, a disturbing thought, and it carries with it a sober mood that settles about us like vultures on carrion.

The medics finish their evaluation and wave us over for an update. Faceman is tucked into the back of the ambulance, cuffs still in place, looking like a weathered scarecrow that someone threw out. As we approach, however, he seems to gain new life.

With a sudden jerk, his upper body rears to a sitting position like some undead thing out of a horror film. His eyes sweep over those gathered, including the deputies and troopers behind us, seeing and not seeing, yet it's in that moment that I feel he's looking only at me, his dead eyes singling me out.

"She is Eight," he proclaims loudly, as if announcing a prophet or queen. "Call her Eight."

Then, with a weary sigh, he falls back and wilts into the gurney.

CHAPTER FIVE

Entering Port Angeles from the east, we continue along Highway 101 until it morphs into Front Street. A few blocks later we turn right onto North Washington Street and find the Olympic Medical Center lying just ahead. It's a squat building, unimpressive at first glance, but it's situated on a bluff overlooking the tempestuous Strait of Juan de Fuca, a ninety-five-mile stretch of water that connects the Salish Sea to the Pacific Ocean.

The view is breathtaking, a feature of the hospital that's often lost on the patients. I mean, who cares if whitecaps dot the strait and birds glide overhead if you just stroked out and your blood pressure is too high?

Jason drew the short straw when it came to the question of who was going to ride with Faceman in the ambulance, much to Nate's relief. By the time we park, he and the EMTs are wheeling our peculiar suspect through the emergency room entrance. Even from a distance I can tell that he's calmed down a bit during the drive, either because the OC is finally out of his eyes, or the warming blanket is putting him to sleep; maybe both.

Jason and the EMTs are gone by the time we enter the emergency room. A pleasant nursing assistant directs us down a hall to the left and we catch up to them just as they're parking the gurney behind a cloth partition tucked away in the corner, away from other patients. The attending nurse, obviously briefed by the EMTs while en route, doesn't say more than ten words before opening and spiking a new IV bag, which she hangs next to the gurney.

"Gentlemen, give us some room," she says briskly, shooing us from the curtained cubicle. She doesn't ask what Faceman's crime was, nor does she show any fear as she manipulates his forearms and hands in search of an adequate vein.

It's not her first shift among the wicked.

Detective Sergeant Jason Sturman double-checks the handcuffs that secure the unhinged kidnapper to the gurney and then steps grudgingly away, waving for us to follow. Once out of earshot of the nurse and her patient, he turns and says, "This Onion King might just be in his head. He was saying some pretty outlandish things on the way here."

"Such as?" I press.

"Well, he kept repeating what he said earlier, about her being Eight, as if that's her name, and how he was going to fix her."

"*Fix* her?"

"Yeah, I pressed him on that and all he'd say is that she's broken, that she's ruining her life somehow and he can fix it."

"How far gone is this guy?" Jimmy asks, tapping his right temple with his index finger.

"He's pretty baked. Probably should be institutionalized—and I'm guessing he will be after this little episode."

"Did he give you a name?" Nate asks.

"No, but we can't keep calling him Faceman. I think he likes it." He unzips his jacket and lets his body breathe. "I talked to the jail ten minutes ago and they're sending someone over with one of the mobile fingerprint scanners," Jason continues. "If he's ever been booked—and I'm betting he has—we should have an identification shortly." His eyes are suddenly drawn to movement at the end of the hall. "And speak of the devil, here comes our scanner."

Lumbering down the hall in a Clallam County corrections uniform that must have been carved from a sultan's tent is the biggest man I've seen since serial killer Pat McCourt leveled a double-barreled shotgun at me almost three years ago. He's easily six-eight and three hundred pounds, though not an ounce of the man appears to be fat. His uniform ripples and stretches with each movement, as if holding back a nest of coiled car springs. Lieutenant bars adorn his oversized collar, looking small by comparison.

"Now, there's a man who's never lost a fight," I mutter to Jimmy.

Jason greets the lieutenant with a handshake that looks like a botched mugging, and then turns our way. "Oak, meet Jimmy and Steps," he says by way of introduction. "They've been wandering the woods with us half the day trying to find this guy. You ever need someone tracked down," he adds, wagging a finger my way, "Steps is your man. I don't know how he does it, but he's scary-good."

We shake hands all the way around and I say, "Oak? Is that your first name or last?"

"Just a nickname," the giant replies. "Steve McKenna's my given name, but no one calls me Steve, not since I was in middle school." He eyes me. "How about you?"

"Me?"

"Yeah, Steps isn't exactly . . . well, it's not really a *name*, now, is it?"

"Came with the job," I say. "That's what happens when you follow footsteps for a living." I could give him the long explanation, but I'm tired of the telling. I've recited the story so many times at so many crime scenes that I'm starting to hate my own sad history.

Oak just chuckles and doesn't push it any further.

In the lieutenant's right hand is a smartphone with an attachment at the bottom that adds four or five inches to the phone's length. Closer examination reveals a small glass screen in the center of the attachment that's not much bigger than a postage stamp.

"You want to scan him," he asks Jason, holding out the unit, "or can I do the honors?"

"Oh, please," the detective sergeant says, sweeping him forward with a gesture. As the big guy makes for the curtained partition, Jason adds, "Try not to scare him too badly." Oak casts a glance back over his mountainous shoulder and grins.

I suddenly pity Faceman.

Less than a minute later and without a peep from behind the curtain, the lieutenant emerges, his eyes fixed on the smartphone screen as he waits for a digital return.

It doesn't take long.

"Murphy Haze Cotton," Oak reads off the screen. "Twenty-seven years of age, last known address is on Down Street in Bremerton. No felonies, but several misdemeanor convictions for shoplifting, harassment, and threats."

Jimmy scratches out some notes as the lieutenant rattles off the info, which also includes an FBI number assigned to Murphy years earlier, and other data pulled from the National Crime Information Center, or NCIC, the national database that tracks criminal history, warrants, no-contact orders, and other crime-related information.

"The guy is a nobody," Oak says in summary.

Jimmy finishes writing and mutters, "That may be about to change."

"Murphy Cotton—sounds like a brand of underwear," I say, "or bedsheets or something."

Jimmy looks at me.

"Murphy Cotton," I repeat, stressing the words, but he still doesn't get it.

Retrieving the phone from his jacket pocket, Jimmy dials Diane. She answers on the first ring and in two condensed sentences he gives her Murphy's horsepower—his identifying info, such as date of birth, height, weight, FBI number—and asks her to dig up as much as she can. He ends the call, stuffs the phone into his pocket, and stands there staring at me.

"It does sound a bit like underwear, doesn't it?"

CHAPTER SIX

An hour later we're still waiting for the fit.

Most jails have strict policies regarding an inmate's condition at booking. Basically, they don't accept ill or injured arrestees, particularly those who have blood seeping from wounds, are hypothermic, or have other conditions that may cause them to . . . you know . . . die.

You don't have to work in law enforcement long before you realize that the ridiculous mountain of policies and regulations one must abide by are there for a reason. In this case, aside from concern for the well-being of the inmates in their care, the jail doesn't want the unpleasantness of a death investigation on the cell block, or the unwelcome attention of a press eager to exploit tragedy for the sake of ratings, or the lawsuit from estranged family members that is inevitable in such situations.

Because of Murphy's cracked ribs, sprained ankle, and borderline hypothermia—attested to by his chattering teeth when we walked him out of the forest—we have to follow procedure and wait for hospital staff to declare him fit for jail, which also limits our access and ability to fully question him.

"He's fit," Nate mutters to himself halfway through the first hour. "Wrap his chest, wrap his ankle, and let's go already." His frustration is aimed at the hospital staff, though they're just doing their jobs and he knows it. After you've done your share of fits, you get a feel for how it's going to go.

Murphy's fit for jail.

It's a no-brainer.

But it's policy, so they go through the motions.

A young nursing assistant arrives with a tray of food: chicken noodle soup, a can of ginger ale, bread, and cubes of raspberry Jell-O, which she sets on a table next to Murphy before hurrying away.

Margaret, the hard but fair attending nurse, has by this time learned that Murphy Cotton had something to do with the young woman brought in earlier that morning, the woman who now occupies a bed in the intensive care unit and only recently regained consciousness.

How she came across this information is a mystery, and to protect that mystery, she and I are careful not to make eye contact when she suddenly announces that it's okay to interrogate Murphy right there in the hospital.

"No waterboarding," she says as she walks away. Without a backward glance, she adds, "At least not while I'm around."

CHAPTER SEVEN

The interview is frustrating.

Jimmy seems to take it well, but I'd rather listen to a five-year-old try to explain the complexities of cold fusion than listen to Murphy's ramblings for one more minute.

As I stand at the curtained entrance to his semiprivate space, I'm struck by how different he looks after a little cleaning up. His eyes are still bloodshot from the OC, but his face is no longer stained by dirt and ugly tear streaks, his previously disheveled hair is surprisingly in order, and his disposition is relatively calm: no longer the wailing, blubbering mess that he was in the woods.

Murphy's appearance is unusual in other ways.

Taken separately, his features would be of little note, but combined in the whole, they create the image of a slightly odd figure. Jimmy once mentioned a guy in his squadron whom the other airmen referred to as "Spare Parts" because nothing about the guy was symmetrical. One leg was longer than the other; one shoulder seemed to ride higher than its counterpart; one eye loomed larger; and even his hair seemed to favor one side of his head. It was as if someone took apart ten dolls and used one piece from each to build a wholly new doll—a Frankendoll.

Jimmy assured me that Spare Parts wasn't *that* odd, it's just that subtle discrepancies add up, and you could tell at a glance that one thing wasn't like another.

Murphy gives off the same impression.

His face is pockmarked, which isn't all that unusual, and he has one prominent gray tooth at the front of his mouth that stands as a tombstone every time he smiles—and it's a disquieting smile. His thin lips seem to pull tight and stretch over the rows of teeth like taut canvas as it reaches its breaking point. I half expect them to snap like rubber bands. And when they're not stretched over his teeth, they're constantly twitching, so much so that he seems incapable of giving them pause.

Murphy's ears are too big by half and his hands are remarkably small, the hands of a child. His hair is brown, and if the eyes are the window to the soul, then Murphy Cotton has no soul, for when I look into those dark wells, nothing looks back. They're simply empty pools of infinite black.

A soul could not survive such a place.

As Jimmy patiently weaves his way through their convoluted conversation, Murphy interrupts constantly, insisting that he needs to take Eight to his shop, so he can fix her. By this time, we know that the girl in the trunk is actually Charice Qian, recently reported missing out of Tumwater.

When Jimmy tells Murphy her name, there's no reaction.

"I can't help Eight until I take her to the *shop*," he insists, injecting anger into the last word. "That's where all my equipment is. If the conditions aren't right I could make a mistake; I can't have that. Eight is very important."

Jimmy raises an eyebrow. "How so?"

"She's an even," Murphy replies, shifting uncomfortably in the bed and then yanking on the handcuffs almost comically, as if he expects them to give way. "Odds have to be balanced with evens," he finally says, settling back down.

"Odd and even—as in numbers?"

"Yes! Of course numbers!" He seems suddenly irritated, as if the question is silly or nonsensical. "Seven is an odd; that can't stand. Everything has to be balanced, like a ledger."

Jimmy nods briskly, as if he knew that all along, and lets the question lie, shifting to another. "You mentioned equipment; I bet a guy like you has some pretty amazing stuff."

Murphy's eyes brighten and his face bends into a proud smile. "You should see it," he replies with childlike glee. "I had to do some serious hunting to find the right chair. Everything else I found on eBay and Amazon, but that chair . . ." He shakes his head to emphasize the scope of the challenge.

"What do you use it for?"

Before answering, Murphy glances around. Then, lowering his voice, he says, "It reclines. That's very important to the process." He nods, his features now serious. "OK says Eight is broken, and only I can fix her; it's because I figured it out. I know how to make people better, even when they're so broken they're almost gone."

"What do you mean by broken?" Jimmy asks.

"Broken," Murphy snaps, as if the answer is self-evident. "Not the people they're *supposed* to be." He taps the side of his head sharply with his index finger. "They've chosen destructive behavior. Not thinking straight; not taking the path."

"The path?"

"The *life* path! The right path. The path we all take, broken and unbroken, until we reach the door. Choices!" He nearly shouts the word. "We all make choices, only some make the wrong choices and have to be shown the way. Sometimes their choices have to be simplified, and then life becomes easy. Friends, limited choices, joy—these are the path to the door."

"What the *hell* is he talking about?" I hear Nate mutter to Jason. They're just outside the curtained partition behind me, watching the interview in amazed horror.

"Right, right," Jimmy says, as if this were obvious. "But how do you fix someone like Eight and get her back on the path?"

He moves closer to Murphy and drops his voice. "It would take a person with some amazing skills to do that. I just don't think it's possible." His posture, words, and mannerisms are those of a confidant or devotee, one mesmerized by the suspect's every word. If it weren't for the handcuffs and Murphy's hospital gown, they could pass for close friends talking in conspiratorial whispers over a beer in the local pub.

"Oh, no!" Murphy says with a guarded laugh and a wave of his finger. "You want me to give away secrets, and I can't do that; it's all part of the transcendence. Besides, it would be cheating. OK told me—"

"OK? You mean the Onion King?"

"Yes," Murphy says, drawing out the word. He scrunches up his nose. "Easier to call him OK, don't you think? Besides, he doesn't seem to mind."

"Why's he called the Onion King, anyway?" Jimmy asks casually, studying his fingernails intently, as if the answer carries no importance other than the weight of idle chatter.

The corners of Murphy's mouth suddenly shoot up into an exaggerated, impish smile, revealing large dimples for the first time. "He's the king of Onionland." The words burst from him as if born of electricity, sparked from the core of his tongue.

"Onionland," Jimmy says in an enchanted voice that almost goes too far. "I like the sound of that. Is that where you meet to do the fix?"

"Oh, no. I've never met the Onion King three-dimensionally."

"Three-dimensionally?"

"You know, face-to-face, like you and I." He smiles. "It won't be long, though. I think we're almost ready for the revelation, and then I'll finally meet him for the first time. I'll stand beside him as we explain the process, and he'll give me most of the credit—because that's the way he is. In truth, I had most of it figured out before he provided the final piece."

"So, you've never been to his house?"

"Oh, no," Murphy says with a chuckle.

"But he must live close, right?"

"I suppose. We're not really supposed to talk about stuff like that." He gives a knowing nod. "For security reasons, you know?" He lowers his voice and leans toward Jimmy. "He *has* mentioned a few places in the Seattle area, so I guess I always thought he lived there."

Murphy looks suddenly startled. "I shouldn't have told you that." The timbre of his voice changes and he says, "He warned me to always be careful." His face contorts into a tortured mask. "I tried. I did!"

"To be careful?"

"Yes, to not let it out; to not give it away."

He sighs, his breathing now short and shallow. "I'm always careful—doing it just the way he told me, borrowing cars and always driving the speed limit." He grows quiet a moment and turns to the side, rocking his body side to side as his mind begins to race. The smile is gone now, replaced by a dour face and eyes watered in misery.

"He said to be careful. I try to be like him, but I'm not." A small portion of the smile returns, and he gasps, "He's *so* smart."

The words are reverent, worshipful.

He shrugs his shoulders lightly. "It's not that I'm stupid, least not compared to most people, but everyone's stupid compared to the Onion King. I came up with most of the fix myself, even ran some early tests, but OK helped me make it better."

"Early tests?" Jimmy asks, hiding his sudden alarm. "On other victims?"

"They're patients," Murphy snaps. "And of course not. I'd never experiment on humans. The only reason I can use the process on Eight is because I know it works."

Turning his body again, he leans closer and lowers his voice. "I'm not a *real* doctor," he says, "but I consider myself a metaphysician. I'm still learning, reading books, that sort of thing, and my research helped me come up with the fix . . . to help people."

"So, you care that people are hurting?"

"I care that they're broken."

"What's the difference?"

Murphy shrugs. "I'm good at fixing things—computers, game consoles, TVs, just about anything, and now even people." He smiles and tries to extend his uncuffed right arm to show Jimmy the watch he fixed, but then realizes it was booked into evidence after his arrest. The smile fades; the arm drops to his side; the room grows quiet.

"I like to fix things," he says at length.

"I don't know," Jimmy says skeptically. "Computers and TVs, sure, but people are complicated. I don't see how anyone could fix them once they're broken, not really. You'd have to be a real genius to do that." His voice rises with these last words, as if the mere thought is ludicrous.

It has the desired effect.

"There's a kind of rot that runs through people, you know, that corrupts them and takes away what they are and what they could have been. It's usually just their *minds* that are broken," Murphy insists. "Well, sometimes their bodies, too, but the real person, the soul or the entity, isn't in the mind *or* the body, it's in the face."

"In the face? How so?"

Murphy shifts on his raised bed, pressing forward, as if enjoying the discussion and eager to share his wisdom. He takes a drink from his ginger ale and then sets it back down. "When you look at me," he says, "do you look at my hands, my arm, my left foot?" He pauses, but only for a moment. "No. You look at my face, don't you? You're doing it right now."

He points an index finger at Jimmy, then at his own face. "We greet each other, acknowledge each other, recognize each other by our faces because we know instinctively that the mind, the soul, the entire being is centered in the face."

"What about the eyes?" Jimmy says. "Some people say the soul is in the eyes."

Murphy waves this away as an afterthought. "The eyes are in the face. It's all the same." Still determined to prove his point, he asks, "If you saw a picture of my hand, would you recognize me?"

"No," Jimmy concedes.

"Exactly. Because this"—he flops his right hand around in the air like a limp fish—"isn't me." He points to his face with an index finger, hand cocked like a gun. "This is me. My soul is in my face: my mind, my being, my personality, it's all there." He seems almost euphoric as the words pour from him. "Everything we are, have been, or hope to be is in the face. There is nothing else; never has been."

"I see," Jimmy says soothingly, admiringly. "So, what does the fix do?"

When Murphy starts to protest, Jimmy quickly adds, "I don't want to know *how* it works. OK knows better than both of us, and if he wants it kept secret for now, we need to just trust him, right? It's just . . . I never heard what the fix does to make someone like Eight better."

Murphy grimaces and starts to shake his head.

"Please?"

Murphy's body sags, and for a moment he looks like a scarecrow again, his head hanging low. When he glances up, his words come in a whisper: "This is just between us, right?"

"Just between us," Jimmy whispers.

Murphy pauses, staring at the cooling soup on his tray. "The ancients believed that the heart was the seat of consciousness; did you know that?"

"No, I didn't," Jimmy lies. "How interesting."

"It's only more recently that people started thinking the brain was the seat of consciousness, the place where the soul resides, but, as I said, I know better. It came to me one day when I was putting a new hard drive in an old computer. That's when I had my revelation—about the face. That's when I first had the idea about the fix."

Jimmy puts on an intentionally perplexed look, and says, "But why the face?" As the words roll off his tongue I'm suddenly struck not by his verbal communication, but by the irony of all his nonverbal communication: the lifted brow, the puzzled eyes, the skewed mouth, the pinched forehead—all of it projected by his face, as if making Murphy's point.

"It's mostly the eyes, as you said," Murphy whispers, "but also the nose, the tongue, the ears, the skin. All the senses are represented: sight, smell, taste, hearing, touch. Without them we may as well be a hard drive connected to nothing. Everything we are and everything we perceive," he continues, his eyes growing wild, "is driven by our senses, and they all converge in the face. That's the key." He slaps the mattress. "That's everything."

Jimmy forces himself to smile slowly, as if a great revelation were overtaking him. "That's why he calls you Faceman, isn't it?"

Murphy smiles—and my blood runs cold.

"So that's the key to fixing them," Jimmy whispers

urgently, leaning in close to Murphy. "It's all in the face and the senses, so . . . what? You do something to make their face better?"

Murphy shakes his head. "Once they're broken, they're broken; you can't fix the old face, you have to—" He suddenly catches himself. "No, no, no," he says in rising alarm. "It's not safe yet. The timing's not right. OK will be upset. He said we can't talk about it except to each other." And then he seems to remember something else OK said. Lowering his eyes, he says flatly, "I need a lawyer."

Just like that, the interview is over.

CHAPTER EIGHT

With Murphy Cotton invoking his right to counsel, Jimmy, Nate, Jason, and I raid the vending machines in the dining area and then make our way to the hospital lobby. As I emerge from the hall, the first thing I notice is the water wall dominating the north side of the room, opposite the main entrance. The trickling, gurgling water brings with it a sense of serenity, and I can almost imagine myself sitting down next to it and forgetting this long, hellish day.

A busy information island occupies a large square in the center of the lobby, so we drift to a cluster of empty chairs against the sidewall—well away from inquisitive ears—and begin to put a plan together.

"So, how do we figure out if this Onion King is real or imagined?" Jason asks.

"Two suspects?" Nate says in disbelief. "That elevates things from criminal to four-alarm creepy. It's not exactly the kind of problem we see out here on the peninsula."

Jason lets out a long sigh, something obviously weighing on him. Before he can put it to words, his phone gives a sharp chirp, startling him. He scans the newly arrived text and shoots off a response. "Sheriff's on her way down."

"She's here?" I ask.

"Yeah, she heard that Charice regained consciousness and wanted to take a run at her, see if she could tell us anything. The boss is a thousand miles away from sexist, but she knows that women are more likely to talk to other women, especially in a case like this."

"Pretty hands-on for a sheriff," I say.

"You have no idea," Nate mutters. The words are meant to sound disgruntled, but there's a certain pride running through them that can't be disguised, and when I look at him he just grins and shrugs.

Angela Eccles is an attractive woman by any measure.

With long strawberry-blond hair kept neatly in a low bun, penetrating green eyes, and a swimmer's physique, she hardly looks her forty-seven years.

Jimmy would remind me that forty-seven barely qualifies as middle-aged, but I think that has less to do with Angie's appearance and more to do with the fact that he's in his early thirties and starting to feel the inevitability of time.

With twenty-three years in law enforcement, Angie has a reputation honed on competence, fairness, and the ability to scrap with both crooks and members of the county council . . . which can sometimes seem like one and the same. It's this experience and punch that got her elected to her first term as sheriff of Clallam County just four years ago.

Her campaign promised a no-nonsense approach to crime fighting, an expansion of mental health services at the county jail, and a new commitment to intelligence-driven policing. There were other promises, of course, promises she did her best to keep, even if she didn't always succeed. Still, her job performance was more than adequate, convincing the good citizens of Clallam County to reelect her over-whelmingly just last month.

The first four years were tough on the new sheriff.

Perhaps her second term will be better.

Angie emerges from the main hall and strides forcefully across the lobby, barely slowing before plopping down in a chair next to Jason and stealing a Dorito from his half-eaten bag.

"What's the story, boss?" Jason asks.

Angie finishes chewing, swallows, and says, "Well, her condition has certainly improved since this morning; I barely recognized her as the same woman. There's even talk of re-leasing her sometime tomorrow, but she doesn't seem all that eager to go. In fact, I think she's scared to death."

"Of Murphy?"

"No," Angie replies in an ominous tone. "Get this, she says she never saw Murphy until this morning. It was this other guy, the Onion King, who kidnapped her. He grabbed her as she was walking up the front steps of her house in Tumwater and held her for probably two weeks. We're not exactly clear on the time frame because the missing person report wasn't filed until later."

"So he's real?" Jason says, looking a bit dismayed.

Angie just nods . . . and takes another Dorito.

"When Murphy came along and found her tied to a tree in the forest," the sheriff continues, "she just assumed he was a hunter or hiker. After he cut her loose, they walked from the forest side by side, like nothing was wrong. By the time they reached Murphy's car, Charice had figured out that the guy wasn't all there. He kept calling her Eight and telling her how special she was. Then things turned ugly, and you pretty much know the rest."

"Car chase, girl in trunk, pursuit through the forest,

tear gas, hypothermia," I summarize, using all five fingers to count them off.

That draws a round of chuckles.

"Even at that," Angie says, "Charice hardly gives Murphy a second thought. It's the Onion King who scares her. You should see the look on her face when she talks about him."

Angie shakes her head. "It all sounds pretty depraved, to hear her tell it. The Onion King insisted she call him *husband* during her captivity. Her recollection is a bit fuzzy, but she said there was a *Fifty Shades of Grey* aspect to the whole thing—her words, not mine. He kept her for almost two weeks and only raped her the one time."

"When was that?" Jimmy asks.

"Last night, after which he put her in the car, drove an hour or so, and left her tied to that tree." She looks at me, then at Jimmy. "After raping her, he slipped a single red rose into her hand. Can you believe that?"

I want to say, *Yes, we can*, but decide against it. Angie has enough to digest right now; she doesn't need to imagine or contemplate the long list of horrors that Jimmy and I have experienced in almost six years together.

As she sits staring at the half-eaten Dorito in her hand, I can tell there's more. I can see it in her face, some disturbing aspect beyond rape and roses, beyond Angie's will to even confront.

"Just before Murphy knocked her out and stuffed her into the trunk," she says at last, her voice uncharacteristically subdued, "he told Charice that . . . that the other seven were waiting for her, that they'd all be just like sisters."

It takes me a moment to process this, but then I just stare at her, stunned.

A murmur sifts through our small gathering, but not of words. It's the soft rustle that occurs when feet and hands are set into motion, when the weight of disbelief bears down and dislodges bodies from their comfortable positions, forcing them to adopt a new stance, as if a change of posture will help one grasp the horror of what's just been laid out before them.

"Steps and I have run into our share of ritualist killers, psychos, and sadists during our years with the Special Tracking Unit," Jimmy says. "If this information is true, then experience tells me this will likely end one of two ways: either we rescue seven or bury seven." He grows quiet and glances around, taking in each face. "Which of these it will be," he continues, "has probably already been decided."

This brings an unsettled silence, and it falls to me to ask the inevitable question: "So, where are the other seven victims?"

CHAPTER NINE

As must happen, the unpleasant conversation eventually returns to Murphy Cotton, the mental train wreck who began all this drama and who will surely be the key to its unwinding.

"How'd the interview go?" Angie asks.

"Dude's a psychopath," Nate replies immediately.

Jimmy purses his lips and tilts his head slightly to the left.

"You don't agree?" Angie says, interpreting the expression correctly.

Jimmy hesitates a moment before answering. "I'm not qualified to diagnose him," he says by way of caveat, "but I think Murphy's the real deal."

"A psychopath!" Nate repeats.

"No," Jimmy replies. "That's a common misconception. Psychopaths know the difference between right and wrong, they just choose to ignore it. They don't empathize with others like you or I would, so the harm they inflict doesn't matter to them."

"And psychopath doesn't automatically mean killer," I add.

Jimmy directs his index finger at me as if to emphasize my point. "That was made clear by a recent study where they determined that as many as one in five business CEOs are actually psychopaths." He raises an eyebrow and adds, "We've all had that boss, right?"

Jason chuckles. "You have no idea."

When Angie gives him a look, he waves her off, saying, "Different job; different time. You're only a psychopath when you have to deal with the county council."

Nate nods his agreement a little too vigorously and Angie concedes the point.

"As I said, I'm nowhere near qualified to diagnose him, but I'd say Murphy suffers from a rare form of psychosis known as delusional disorder."

"How rare?" Angie asks.

"It accounts for between one and two percent of patients admitted to mental facilities. Like people with other forms of psychosis, those suffering from delusional disorder are unable to distinguish between what's real and what's imagined. The difference is they have an unshakable belief in something that simply isn't true, and no amount of argument or reason will dissuade them. Often it's something that could theoretically be true but isn't. For example, they may believe that someone is poisoning them, or conspiring to get their job, or even that some celebrity is in love with them.

"In Murphy's case, he seems to be suffering from a variant called grandiose delusional disorder, distinguished by the subject's overinflated sense of importance or knowledge. His belief that he's made some great discovery—this *fix* he keeps talking about—is what convinced me. There's absolutely no doubt in his mind that the fix works, and there's nothing that you or I could say to convince him otherwise."

"What if the fix involves hurting them?" I ask.

"Even then."

Angie shifts in her seat, a grave expression clouding her face. "And this delusional disorder is the type of mental illness that would cause him to kidnap and rape?"

"That was the Onion King," Jimmy reminds her. "As far as we know, Murphy's not aware that they were kidnapped—despite finding Charice tied to a tree. To him, they're just broken. He doesn't even seem to know their names. No, as hard as it is to say this, he may be as much a victim in this as the women."

"See, I have a big problem with that," Nate blurts. "Guys like Murphy run around creating all kinds of havoc, only to claim some mental incapacity when it comes time to stand tall before the judge. I don't see how someone can be sane one moment and some kind of psychopath the next. No offense, but it just doesn't wash."

"I agree," Jimmy says. "The idea of temporary insanity is a real problem; sanity isn't something that just comes and goes randomly. On top of that, you have psychologists and defense attorneys concocting a long list of designer defenses to get their clients off: the Twinkie defense, steroid defense, mob mentality, and, most recently, affluenza, to name a few. In almost every case the suspect was fully aware of what he or she was doing, knew it was wrong, and acted willfully and with intent."

"But if Murphy doesn't know the difference between right and wrong," Angie argues, "why did he run?"

"To protect the secret," Jimmy replies. "The Onion King told him no one could know about the fix, at least not yet. He probably told him that if anyone caught him he was to run, even if it was the police."

"He told you this?"

"Not in so many words, but yes."

Nate's still skeptical. "He's got to know it was wrong. No

one runs that far with a banged-up rib cage and a sprained ankle unless they're scared—*really* scared."

Jimmy pushes forward in his chair and spreads his hands wide in front of him, palms up. "Imagine for a moment that you have an internal road map," he says. "Let's call it a morality map, for lack of a better name. And let's imagine that, like traditional maps, it has destinations and routes, with perhaps a thousand different ways to get to where you want to go. Unlike traditional maps, you're not looking for the shortest route, but the correct route—the moral route.

"Fortunately, our morality map—yours and mine—has a bright yellow line that shows us the way, and as long as we don't stray from that optimized path, all is well. Now"—here he points at Jason—"let's suppose that Jason is a psychopath. He knows the difference between right and wrong and is in complete control of his actions, so when he looks at his morality map and sees a bright yellow line leading him in one direction and he chooses to go in another, he's well aware that's he's embarking on a path that others will find concerning, reprehensible, or even criminal."

He points to me next. "Now, Steps here is our psychotic."

"Thank you," I mutter.

"Let's say for argument's sake that he suffers from delusional disorder like Murphy. He has a map just like you and I, and just like Jason. The difference is that, for Steps, there is no yellow line to ignore. It's completely absent from the page. At any given moment he could be on the right path or the wrong path and he has no way of knowing the difference. It's all the same."

Jimmy lets that sink in for a moment before continuing. "We don't know who this Onion King is, but clearly he's aware of Murphy's condition and is taking advantage of it. He's our real psychopath, the one we need to be concerned about."

There's a long moment of silence, and then Angie asks, "How does Murphy go through life not knowing right from wrong? I mean, if he's at the store and he sees something he wants, doesn't he just take it and then get arrested for shoplifting?"

"He does," Jimmy replies, "and he learns from it. He learns that he can't take things without paying for them, not because it's wrong, but because something bad will happen to him if he does."

He gives Angie an odd smile. "Our locals once had to deal with this guy who was constantly getting arrested for exposing himself and masturbating in public. No one really bothered to find out what this guy's issue was until one day when a corrections deputy sat down next to him and asked him if he knew why he was in jail. He had no clue, he just knew that the police didn't like him, and they kept putting him in jail."

"How do you *not* know what you're arrested for?" Nate says. "They have to list your charges when they book you."

"True, but remember we're talking about mental illness here. Just because they *tell* him his charges doesn't mean he understands them. Fortunately, the corrections deputy in this case recognized that something wasn't clicking, and she explained to him that there are things you do in private and things you do in public, and that he couldn't be exposing himself like that in public because it alarmed and offended people."

"And that did it?" Angie says.

Jimmy gives a long shrug. "Seems so. They never booked him again, at least not for indecent exposure. Once he understood the reason for his repeated arrests, he knew what to avoid. I don't know that he suddenly understood that it was wrong, not in the way you and I would, but he understood the consequences. Sometimes that's enough."

"I guarantee you," Nate persists, "every wienie-wagger out there knows perfectly well that what they're doing is wrong; they just like it. It shocks people. It's how they get off." He quickly grimaces and adds, "No pun intended."

Jimmy chuckles. "I get your point, and I know that mental illness is an easy scapegoat when someone gets caught, but not everyone is using it to beat charges. There are some folks out there with some serious issues." He pushes back in the chair. "I don't know if you're seeing the same thing in Clallam County, but mental contacts have shot through the roof all across the country. If it was hereditary I'd expect it to be more consistent. This is something else."

"Drugs," Jason says.

"Yeah, meth in particular," Nate adds. "Fries the brain. I'm seeing guys who I arrested ten years ago who are now twenty-five or thirty years old and they're having audible and visual hallucinations like you wouldn't believe. And it's not from the meth they're doing now; it's from the stuff they did ten years ago. The damage is done."

"Job security, I guess," Angie says resignedly.

"I'd prefer shoplifters and bicycle thieves," Jason mutters.

The heartbreaking futility of our jobs settles over us and leaves us quiet. The soft gurgle of water trickling down the north wall coalesces with the indistinguishable voices of people scattered about the large room and the hum of cars passing on the street outside, creating a pleasant murmur.

I almost wish I could bottle the sound and take it with me.

"Friggin' Onion King," Nate finally says, breaking the silence. The randomness of it sets us all to smiling.

"So, what's our next move?" Jason asks.

"It's your investigation," Jimmy replies. "We're here to follow your lead. If it was me, though"—he turns to Angie—"I would try to keep Murphy's name off the jail roster when he gets booked."

She immediately understands his intent. "You want it kept out of the press?"

"If we can, at least until we know what we're dealing with."

"That shouldn't be a problem. We can book him as a John Doe, but that's only going to be good for seventy-two hours, give or take. Will that work?"

"Perfect." Turning to Jason, he asks, "How's your relationship with Bremerton PD?"

The detective sergeant shrugs. "We occasionally have crossover—some of their bad guys coming up here, and vice versa—but it's not common enough to build first-name relationships. Fortunately, I went to the academy with one of their detectives: Jan Pique. She's good people. Why do you ask?"

"It's Murphy's last known address. Might as well start at the beginning."

"Right."

"Do you think your detective friend would mind driving by the place, see what it looks like, maybe make contact if it looks safe? Call it a welfare check or a knock-and-talk; whatever works. We need to know if the other seven women could be there. Make sure she takes backup. In the end, we'll probably need a warrant to do a proper search."

"You really think he'd keep the women in town like that?" I ask.

"No, but we can't afford to be wrong either."

"Why not see if Murphy will give us consent to search the place?" Nate suggests. "It's a lot easier than trying to get a warrant later, and, well, he's right down the hall."

Jimmy shakes his head. "Normally I'd be right there with you, but in his mental state I can see a defense attorney using that against us."

"I see your point."

———

Twenty minutes later, Detective Jan Pique calls with mixed news. The residence on Down Street is actually owned by Murphy's mother, Gloria Cotton, who lets him live in a run-down fifth-wheel trailer in the backyard.

"We peeked through the windows," Jan says, "but I couldn't see much." Her words sound tinny and truncated as they issue from the phone's speaker. "The trailer looks like it's been there for years. Every tire is flat, and it has enough moss on the roof to start its own ecosystem. You want us to try for a warrant?"

"That would be great," Jason replies. "I'll have someone email the particulars."

"Does that mean you're headed our way?"

"It does, and we're bringing company."

"Yeah, who's that?"

"A couple guys from the FBI's Special Tracking Unit."

"Feds," Jan grumbles in a disenchanted voice. "That's just great."

"You're on speaker," Jason reminds her.

"Yeah, yeah! Why do you think I'm behaving myself?"

The phone goes dead without a parting word or even a click.

"I think we just found Diane's long-lost sister," I whisper to Jimmy.

"I like her already," he replies.

CHAPTER TEN

It's after nine when we step out of the hospital and into the dark and cold of the December night. The northeaster that had plagued us throughout the day seems to have settled and lost some of its bluster. It's now just a gusting breeze, though it still carries winter's bite. I turn my collar up against it.

We make a beeline for Nate's SUV and pile inside, Jason riding shotgun.

"What's the drive time to Bremerton?" Jimmy asks.

"About an hour and a half—provided we don't get stuck at the Hood Canal Bridge," Nate says, referring to the floating drawbridge that connects the Kitsap Peninsula with the Olympic Peninsula. "If they have to open, we'll be stuck for a while, maybe a half hour to forty-five minutes. But I doubt there are many boats on the water right now, and the submarines out of Bangor only transit during daylight . . . or at least that's what I've heard."

Jimmy leans purposefully forward between the front seats, resting his elbows next to the headrest on either side. "So . . . have you guys ever ridden in a Gulfstream?"

When Betsy lands at Bremerton National Airport twenty-five minutes later, Detective Pique is waiting for us just off the tarmac. Introductions are made, and I get the sense that the Bremerton detective is sizing us up, perhaps deciding whether we're worth the time and bother. The answer remains shrouded behind her brooding eyes, and she doesn't seem impressed by the Gulfstream.

"The house is ten minutes from here," Jan says, motioning us into her vehicle: an unmarked gray Crown Victoria. "By the time we get there we should have a telephonic."

A telephonic is a search warrant obtained over the phone. It's an expedited way for an officer to get a warrant after hours or when she can't appear before the judge in person, usually because she's at the scene of the crime.

In such a case, she'd prepare her warrant affidavit describing the purpose of the warrant and the location to be searched, just as she would with a regular warrant, but instead of coming before the judge, it would all be done by telephone. After being sworn in, the officer would read her affidavit to the judge word for word. This testimony would likely be recorded and later transcribed, becoming part of the case report.

Procedures vary from state to state, but if the judge finds probable cause to issue the warrant, he directs the officer to sign the judge's name to either the warrant or a duplicate, including date and time. After that, the warrant is valid and ready to be executed.

"Since it's just a fifth-wheel, I'm guessing the five of us can handle it," Jan says with only a hint of sarcasm. "If something comes up and we need extra bodies, I can pull a couple officers from patrol. Detective Sawyer is also available." She shrugs. "He's our newest detective; doesn't actually start in his new position until the first of January." In a guiltless monotone, she adds, "I kind of promised him that he could tag along if he did the warrant paperwork."

"You're bad," Nate says with an appreciative shake of his head.

"Only on Sundays," the detective shoots back.

The single-story home on Down Street is dated but well maintained. The lawn is cut and edged, the paint is several years old but still fresh, and the whole place has a well-scrubbed look and feel, as if it had just been photographed for an edition of a vintage homes magazine.

After we ring the doorbell and present the warrant, Gloria Cotton escorts us around the side of the house, through the cedar gate, and into a world very different from the one at the front of the house. The fenced and gated backyard is clearly the realm of Murphy Cotton, and the embarrassment on his mother's face is prominent and without excuse.

"The boy's a slob," she says flatly.

After pulling a long drag from her cigarette, she drops the spent butt to the ground and grinds it out with her heel. "God knows I've tried," she adds, leaving some question as to *what* she tried. Perhaps she tried teaching him how to clean up after himself, or how to water the grass, or put the trash in the trash can. Perhaps she tried teaching him to be responsible. Or maybe what Gloria really meant was, *God knows, I tried teaching him not to lock strange women in his trunk.*

Without further comment, she leaves us to our task, apparently uninterested in what we'll find in her son's trailer. She turns on the outside light and enters the house through the back door, letting the aluminum screen door bang closed behind her.

Murphy's world is one of bare earth marked with the occasional patch of dead grass. Scattered about are empty beer cans, a well-used burn barrel, and mounds of junk electronics separated into piles: two piles for old CPUs, one for old-school boxy monitors, one for keyboards and speakers, and one for miscellaneous items like old Xbox units and DVD players.

Along the fence on the south side of the backyard, lined up as if still taking up space on the floor of a busy arcade, are seven coin-operated video games. From the look of them, they've been there for years, and are ruined beyond repair due to prolonged exposure to the elements. Behind the trailer is a 1991 Dodge pickup, and, like the trailer itself, all the tires are flat and moss has collected on the roof and in the corners of the bed.

There's more, of course, tossed here and there and stacked in corners: bicycle frames and old toasters and forty-year-old generators.

"What a dump," Nate mutters.

"I was going to say junkyard," I offer, "but dump works just fine."

Murphy's world is a solitary dump. Aside from Detective Pique and presumably her partner, the only recent shine I can see is that of himself and his mother, and she never seems to venture very far from the back door. The rest of the tracks are old, from maybe five or six years ago. If Murphy *has* friends, they haven't been to visit in at least that long. More importantly, if he's holding seven women captive, he's either keeping them elsewhere or he brought them here long ago.

Still, we have to check.

Rattling the battered door handle to the fifth-wheel, Nate finds it locked. "Boss," he says to Jason, "you got your kit?"

The detective sergeant moves forward while fishing a soft vinyl case from his pocket. He extracts a tension wrench and rake pick from the lock-picking kit and goes to work on the pin tumbler in the trailer's door. Twenty seconds later he gives the handle a twist, and the door pulls open.

"Open sesame," Nate mutters with a little awe. Before entering, he makes the sign of the cross, as if blessing the trailer or warding off evil spirits, then he steps through the door—and immediately retreats, gagging. "Holy hell!" he barks, gasping for breath and waving his hand in front of his mouth and nose, as if that's going to help. "Smells like month-old garbage in there."

"Move over," Jason grumbles, pushing past Nate, who's now bent over with both hands on his knees looking like he's about to dry-heave. Positioning himself in front of the open door, Jason takes three deep breaths and holds the last. Rushing into the trailer, he slides open the side window to the right of the door, and then another farther down. As he's working on the window on the opposite side, we hear him exhale loudly, no longer able to contain the breath. This is immediately followed by an involuntary intake of putrid air, and then a shaking, grumbling quiver of disgust rattles through his body, no doubt urging him to flee.

But Jason pushes on.

We hear him open a third window, and then the big window at the front of the trailer, followed by two more at the rear. When he emerges through the door a moment later, his face has a pasty, flaccid look to it, and though the temperature is near freezing, a sheen of sweat seems to lay upon his skin.

"Let's give it a few minutes to air out," he croaks.

Ten minutes later the trailer still stinks, but there's nothing to be done about it. Jimmy has his kit with him—a bag containing essentials for any investigation—so he digs around in the bottom and finds a small vial of peppermint oil. Measuring out a single drop on the tip of his finger, he rubs it under his nose and hands the bottle off to me. After doing the same, I offer the vial to Nate, and then snap on a double set of gloves.

The garbage smell is still present when I step up into the trailer, but the peppermint does a good job of masking it, or at least taking the edge off the pungent stench. Jimmy moves to the front of the trailer, which I suppose you could classify as the bedroom, so I begin my search in the kitchenette, opening cupboards and drawers.

Moving to the small refrigerator, I say a silent prayer that there are no body parts inside, and then jerk the door open. Bottles rattle and clank together on the door shelves, and I find that the fridge is mostly full, but there's nothing foul inside except two moldy pieces of old pizza and a jug of expired milk . . . and maybe the Chinese food.

Nate is at the back of the trailer and I notice in my peripheral vision that he seems immobile, as if rooted in place. Casting a glance his way, I note that he's standing with his hands on his hips in front of the table and bench seats that seem to serve as both dining room and living room. He's staring at the clustered piles of clothing and junk that obscure the table's dated Formica surface, perhaps wondering where to begin.

"What a sty," I hear him grumble.

The bench seats on the left and right of the table are stacked almost to the ceiling with a nonsensical collection of randomness: clothes, keyboards, a box of empty wine bottles, books on biology, electronics, and physics, at least five ping-pong paddles, an ant farm—thankfully empty— and dozens of newspapers.

And that's just the outer layer.

The table itself is filled at the back with several feet of the same, as if the piles from the left and the right had just spilled over, but the front of the table is relatively clear, leaving room for what appears to be a makeshift workstation.

A partially disassembled PlayStation 3 rests in this space. Its case has been cracked open and the power supply and disk drive have been removed and set to the side, leaving the green motherboard exposed. A set of miniature screwdrivers, a heat gun, a multimeter, several jumper wires with crocodile clips, and a tube of thermal paste are scattered around the project.

The small workstation is the only spot in the trailer that shows any sign of thoughtful placement or cleanliness. It's the eye of the hurricane, the calm in a storm of disorder, an oddity. One might even say it was an accident if not for the single folding metal chair that occupies the spot directly in front of the station. Despite the clutter under and around the table, Murphy managed to leave enough room to push the chair all the way in. Out of the way, yet always there for him.

Nate stands silently, surveying the mess and snapping absently at the latex of his gloves, perhaps wondering if two layers are enough—or if any number of layers would be enough for such a toxic dump. Bracing up, he gives a heavy sigh and starts picking at the pile.

With the trailer's limited space, Jan and Jason remain outside, busying themselves by checking the hatches and storage compartments accessible from the exterior. These yield nothing of interest, though Jason swears he saw a rat in one of them.

With their inspection of the storage compartments complete, Jason meanders around the backyard shining the powerful LED beam of his police-grade flashlight into various nooks and crannies, and behind a collection of old washers and dryers. He even lifts a piece of rotting plywood to make sure it doesn't conceal a trapdoor. When he catches Jan watching him, he just shrugs, saying, "You never know."

Five minutes into the search, Nate is still sifting through the first layer of nastiness on the back part of the table when he suddenly exclaims, "Geez! What the—!" and leaps backward.

My first thought is that he stumbled upon the body parts I'd expected to find in the fridge. Stepping to the side, I let Jimmy hurry past. He cocks his head to the side as his eyes search for the cause of the outburst.

"Right there," Nate says, pointing accusingly toward a large rectangular lump that's completely covered by the remnants of a tattered yellow bedsheet that used to be white.

Lifting the edge of the sheet a few inches, Jimmy peers inside a moment, and then peels the cover back, exposing a three-foot-long wire cage like those used for guinea pigs, hamsters, and, well . . . rats.

"Freak show!" Nate says, gesticulating wildly toward the cage. "That's not normal, right? I mean, what the hell's the guy thinking?"

Grasping the wire handle at the top of the cage, Jimmy gently jostles it free from the pile of debris, careful not to dislodge or jumble the contents, and then walks backward several paces before turning and setting it on the kitchen counter.

The cage itself is unremarkable. It's old and beat-up and has a metal base that shows as much rust as paint. The wire sides are distorted by years of abuse, and the latch that holds the door closed looks like it hasn't been used in years.

Despite the neglect, it's not the cage that concerns us; it's the contents.

Inside are the carcasses of seven desiccated rats, each one posed in a different position, as if they were stop-motion characters caught between photos. One is on the hamster wheel, its chin lifted high as its left front leg and right back leg are frozen in midstride. Another is reclining in a Barbie chair, its dead fingers folded around a miniature plastic bottle. The other five are scattered throughout the cage, each in a different pose more reminiscent of human activity than rodent, except for a juvenile rat who appears to be drinking from the empty water bottle.

As I stand behind Jimmy, looking around him at the strange diorama, it's not the rats that draw my attention, nor the odd, humanlike poses they've been placed in, but something far more bizarre. For a moment my head swims with the surreal image, trying to make sense of it—and then all at once the puzzle snaps together, and I realize what Murphy has done.

At first glance, each rat appears to be wearing a white helmet fitted over its head as if it were a piece of armor and they were gladiators in a rodent arena. As I look more closely at the rat on the hamster wheel, I begin to notice the lines and shapes, the distinct impressions, the texture of hair.

"It's a mask," I whisper.

More disturbingly, it's a mask that takes in every detail from the nose to the ears. It looks like it was made of ordinary white plaster, and since there are no tool marks to indicate it was carved I can only assume that Murphy made a mold of the rat's face and then used it to cast the mask.

Two short lengths of cotton string are attached to the macabre veil through tiny holes on either side. These, in turn, are tied together under the rat's lower jaw to secure the mask in place. The plaster perfectly captures the bulging eyes, erect ears, and whiskered nose of the dead creature.

"Jimmy?" I whisper. It's both a question and a horrified exclamation.

Nate is still flustered, and the longer he stares at the display, the more animated he becomes. Shifting his weight back and forth from one foot to the other, he waves his arm intermittently and without words until finally turning squarely on Jimmy and saying, "That's not normal. Even in your world, that's not normal, right?"

"*My* world?" Jimmy replies with a tepid smile.

"You know what I mean," Nate shoots back in an apologetic tone, waving away the inferred insult. "You guys run into a lot of serial killers and sickos doing what you do." He points to the cage. "Is that the kind of stuff you see, or is this guy just . . . special?"

Jimmy starts to shake his head, but then thinks better of it and transitions to a hesitant nod, saying, "It's always different, but, yes, this is the kind of stuff we run into." He spends a moment explaining to Nate some of the horrors we've seen, things far worse than dead rats. "This"—he waves a hand over the display—"is nothing."

Pulling his cell phone from his pocket, Jimmy takes at least a dozen photos of the cage and the individual rats with their individual rat masks.

When he finishes, I move in closer, so that my face is barely a foot from the cage. I'd noticed something while Jimmy was taking his evidence photos. Now, up close, I see that my suspicions are correct.

"The masks are different," I say.

Jimmy just looks at me and shrugs indifferently.

"It's a lot of work to make a mold," I persist. "Why wouldn't he just make multiple masks from the same mold?"

"You're saying he made a mold from each rat?" Nate interjects.

"Looks like it."

Jimmy is suddenly interested and leans in for closer inspection. He doesn't say anything for a full minute as he turns the cage this way and that, vying for a better view. "Why would he do that?" he finally whispers to no one in particular.

"That was *my* question," I mutter, knowing his words are rhetorical.

Jimmy turns to Nate, who's now keeping his distance. "We need to book this into evidence. It's probably just an oddity and unrelated to the investigation, but we can't be certain."

"Book it into evidence?" Nate asks incredulously.

"Yes."

"You're serious?"

"Yes," Jimmy repeats, a bit more forcefully this time.

Nate knows the drill, even if he's not thrilled with the rats. With heavy shoulders, he pinches the oblong metal handle at the top of the cage and lifts it from the counter. Maneuvering its awkward bulk through the trailer, he steps out into the brisk winter air and moves quickly toward Jan's patrol car.

Criminal investigations are a bit like playing ping-pong in the dark with marshmallows: no one ever knows the score and you spend half your time searching for the marshmallow.

Cases that aren't solved quickly soon become a crossroad of evidence, obstacles, deception, and data, all spilling upon the ground in a great heap so that it's hard to tell what's true, what's false, what's made up, and what's solid.

Making sense of this pile is what solves the case, but it can just as easily bury you.

It's often said that a good detective chases the lie, but in my experience a good detective also eliminates possibilities, winnowing down the pile. An investigation may tease you a hundred times with a promising new clue, a suspicious comment, or an alleged eyewitness, building hope and then dashing it to pieces.

The promising new clue isn't promising after all; the suspicious comment was misheard; and the eyewitness was drunk and only repeated what he heard from his friend. Detectives may suffer a hundred such disappointments before they finally get their first hallelujah. But that's how cases get solved: one disappointment at a time. It's this elimination process that's the undulating pulse of the investigation: sometimes slow and unrevealing, other times frenetic.

It's how cases get solved—and why they go cold.

Disappointments carry weight. Sometimes this weight builds up and bears down. The hallelujah never comes.

When it comes to evidence, the general practice during a search is to take anything that might be connected to the case, even if the link is still a bit murky. Sometimes the clue is obvious: a recently fired .357 Magnum lying on the ground at a gun-related homicide would be a good example; it's a no-brainer. Even then, you don't know if it's the suspect's gun or the victim's.

Other times, the supposed evidence is less solid, less sure.

A fingerprint recovered from a stolen truck may belong to the suspect, or it may belong to a long list of others who have been in the vehicle: the owner, the owner's friend, a coworker, a valet, a relative, even the guy who last changed the oil.

Every law enforcement agency has a secure space where they keep evidence items, whether it be a broken synthetic fingernail or a dump truck. In some cases it's a single room, but for larger agencies it could be a giant warehouse. The expensive items—drugs, cash, high-end jewelry—often go into a safe within the evidence room, and firearms may have a separate spot all to themselves, but everything else, including wire cages filled with dead rats, belongs in the common area. Bigger items are tagged; smaller items often go into a box or even an envelope.

Everything is tracked and audited.

Thank God for bar codes.

We finish the search just after midnight. By this time, everyone has had a go at the nasty pile festering in the back of the trailer, but nothing else of note is discovered. For the last twenty minutes, Mrs. Cotton has been hovering just outside her back door, alternating between puffing on her cigarette and glaring at us.

Clearly, we've worn out our welcome.

Retrieving our gear and locking the door to the fifth-wheel, we start for the car, exhausted and smelling a bit like old garbage. A moment later, I realize that Jimmy's not with us, and turn to see him talking to Mrs. Cotton. I don't hear the words, but she shakes his offered hand and they part on good terms. She even waves and smiles as he jogs to catch up.

That's Jimmy: always trying to leave on a good note.

Jason holds the gate open for me as I approach, and I'm just about to go through it—I really am—when I stop cold and turn my gaze to the left . . . to the row of coin-operated gaming machines lined up like parked cars against the fence; *seven* gaming machines, to be precise.

Seven victims; seven dead rats; seven machines.

Each one large enough to conceal a body.

The wiser me, the one I never listen to, tells me to keep walking, that we've already wasted too much time at Murphy's, but the gaming machines are problematic. They're problematic because their sum is a coincidence, *seven* is a coincidence, and I don't generally believe in coincidences.

As Jimmy comes up beside me, no doubt wondering why I'm lingering, I tip my head at the games and say, "There are seven. . . ."

It only takes a moment for my meaning to register.

As I take a few hesitant steps toward the machines, Jimmy follows. Then Nate sees what we're up to, and Jason and Jan, and soon they're circled behind us as I fiddle with the front panel on the first machine—some game called *Gorf*—and try rattling the piece loose. It doesn't budge.

"Help me turn this," I say to Jimmy.

Together we twist the machine away from the fence, turning it a good ninety degrees so we can access the back panel. "It's certainly heavy enough to hold a body," Jimmy grumbles as the unit comes to rest.

"Probably just waterlogged," I say. "Who knows how long it's been sitting here?"

This time it's Jimmy who tries accessing the inside of the machine. Gripping the pressboard panel that covers most of the back, he begins to pull gently and looks up in surprise when the board crumbles in his hand. The next attempt meets with the same results, and now we have a pretty good view into the interior.

A sweep of my flashlight reveals nothing unusual; it's just an arcade game.

"One more?" I suggest, and Jimmy gives a wordless nod.

Next in line is a *Galaga* machine. Of the seven machines in the sad line along the fence, this is the only one that looks remotely familiar. Perhaps I placed some quarters in one just like it at some distant point in time, perhaps it was this very machine. I vaguely remember visiting a few arcades as a kid, back in the day when they were still a thing, before Xbox and PlayStation reinvented the concept.

Galaga proves to be just as heavy as *Gorf,* but we manage to get it turned away from the fence without bulging any vertebrae. Jimmy grasps the back panel as before, and it crumbles in his hands as before. The seven arcade machines were probably worth thousands when they were placed alongside the fence too many years ago. Now they're worth the value of their scrap, which isn't much.

When I shine my flashlight into the innards of the second machine, we can see that it's just as empty as the first. "Worth a shot," I mutter, trying not to sound disappointed.

Jimmy insists that we turn both machines back the way we found them. This is probably because Mrs. Cotton is at the back door again, glaring once more. I'm too tired to argue, so the gaming consoles get turned to their original positions, no one gets a hernia, and Jimmy gives a cordial wave to Mrs. Cotton as he hurries us along.

Aside from a cage of dead rats, the evening's been a bust.

I don't know why I'm disappointed. Murphy obviously has some serious mental issues and probably doesn't know what's real and what isn't. Still, we listened when he told us Charice Qian was number eight, and Charice certainly believed him when he told her that seven other women were waiting for her to join them. We listened, and we believed, not just because Murphy was compelling, but because the case was just that bizarre. The idea of seven other victims seemed to fit.

Things may have played out differently if Murphy had been operating by himself. His rambling, semi-coherent statements would have been easier to disregard—another mental imagining impossible things.

Anyone listening to him could have easily written him off, and probably would have if not for Charice Qian. The petite brunette was adamant that she hadn't seen Murphy until that morning, and that it was another man who had kidnapped and held her. That made Murphy part of something bigger, something more sinister.

Faceman and the Onion King: two suspects who've never met.

That's a new one.

We're feeling a bit beaten and deflated as the four of us toss around ideas during the short flight back to Port Angeles. Nate keeps sniffing at the funk coming off his clothes, while Jimmy tries to talk some enthusiasm back into us.

"We know that Charice was kidnapped at her home in Tumwater," he says. "We know that she was held in a cell for days if not weeks, and then she was handed off to Murphy in the woods, probably at a preselected drop location or—" He suddenly freezes, and for a moment he looks like he's contemplating a particularly difficult puzzle. He turns to Nate. "Where's the backpack?"

"What backpack?"

"Murphy's backpack; the one he stashed in the cabin."

"I gave it to one of the deputies," Nate replies. "We were tied up with Murphy and the ambulance, so I asked him to book it into evidence."

Jimmy nods. "We need it back."

CHAPTER ELEVEN

Monday, December 15

The two-story farmhouse rests at the edge of an open field that looks like it's been raked with a giant comb. Long rows run east to west in perfect symmetry, each exactly four feet from peak to peak, filling the rectangular forty-acre field with ordered precision. It's hard to tell what crop the even rows will yield come spring, and the vegetation that lingers at the crest of each row is covered in frost, blurring it into a white haze.

A large barn with faded red paint occupies a spot perhaps two hundred feet from the house, and a long driveway connects the homestead to the nearest paved road. Little traffic interrupts the bucolic setting, and if one were to take a black-and-white photo of the farm, they might easily pass it off as an image from the 1930s or '40s.

We saw none of this last night, in the dark.

It was one A.M. when we arrived back in Port Angeles. Normally we would have dropped Nate and Jason at the airport and continued on to Bellingham, but there's more work to be done here. What was the point of flying all the way home, only to return in the morning?

Nate made the choice easy, offering to let us rack out at his place. He even extended the invitation to Les and Marty, but they'd already checked into a motel in Port Angeles that afternoon. Nate assured us that he had plenty of room, which seemed dubious considering his status as a bachelor. I was imagining a one-bedroom apartment with a love seat, a La-Z-Boy recliner in the corner, and room for two sleeping bags on the floor near the kitchen.

The farmhouse was a surprise.

Bachelor or not, Nate wasn't kidding when he said he had room: five fully furnished bedrooms, plus a living room and family room, both with large fold-out sofas. It may not be the Hilton, but it's a refreshing change from our normal routine.

"Fresh-brewed," Nate offers, hoisting a mug of coffee into the air as I shuffle into the kitchen still half asleep, with my hair pointing in thirteen different directions.

"I'm not much of a coffee person," I manage. "Don't suppose you have any orange juice?"

"Will grapefruit juice do?"

"It will."

Pointing to a plate on the counter next to the toaster, he says, "We also have English muffins. You look like a butter-and-strawberry-jam kind of guy, but there's also grape jam, honey, and Nutella. If none of that works for you, feel free to dig through the pantry."

Somehow that seems like too many choices this early in the morning, but then I realize it's not early at all, it just feels that way. It was early in the morning when we went to bed; now it's the same morning, only later. We haven't even transitioned into the next part of the day. It almost seems cruel.

Jimmy is standing at the dining room window with a mug of coffee in his hands. He looks as beat-down as I feel, sipping intermittently—almost dutifully—at the coffee, letting the steady infusion of caffeine work its way through his system. Ten minutes from now he'll be raring to go, and I'll still be wiping sleep from my eyes. I've tried to like coffee, I really have. At times like this, I wish I'd tried harder.

"What do you grow?" Jimmy asks, glancing at Nate and motioning out the window.

"Lavender."

"Really?"

Nate grins and nods; it's obviously not the first time he's gotten that reaction. "The farm belongs to my grandparents. I just maintain the field, help with the harvesting, that sort of thing."

"Is there any money in it?"

"Oh, yeah!" Nate replies enthusiastically. "Most of what we grow gets wholesaled, but there are farms half this size, even smaller, that are grossing a million-plus a year. 'Course, they're turning their harvest into soap, essential oil, bath salts, tincture, facial cream—stuff like that. Once you start making your own products, your margins go through the roof. I mean, it's not like pulling gold from the ground, but it'll give you a comfortable living."

Jimmy cocks his head and gives an impressed lift of his eyes. After a few minutes of lavender-flavored small talk, he goes back to his coffee as he flips through his messages.

My English muffin pops out of the toaster as Jimmy makes a call to Les and Marty and asks them to fly Murphy Cotton's laptop to the computer forensics lab at the FBI's Seattle Field Office. He tells them where to pick it up and who to ask for, and then tells them to call if they run into any problems.

Haiden Webber, one of the Bureau's most accomplished computer forensics experts, has agreed to give the laptop his immediate attention. Considering that Haiden's work-load is usually scheduled out weeks in advance, we caught a lucky break.

Then again, he knows that we always have the most in-teresting cases.

At nine forty-five, Jason arrives in a gray Ford Focus. The detective sergeant walks through the front door without knocking, carrying himself with the ease and air of some-one accustomed to the house and those within; someone not required to pause at the sill or rap at the door.

Holding a sealed plastic evidence bag aloft as if it were a trophy, Jason tosses it gently onto the kitchen counter and pulls a folding knife from his pocket. With one smooth mo-tion, he slices along the upper edge of the bag and upends it, letting a yellow-and-black Garmin GPS drop into his hand. It's the GPS from Murphy's backpack.

"Where's the on button?" he wonders aloud, but then finds it.

The GPS screen comes to life a moment later, displaying a zoomed-in view of nothing: no marked roads, no buildings, nothing. Jason hands the unit to Jimmy, sheepishly admit-ting that his knowledge of the device ended at the power button.

Zooming out slowly, Jimmy watches as roads begin to appear, first one, and then another, and then a main road running through a small town. On the other side of the road is water. Road names pop out at him, but it's not until he zooms out a little further that he finds what he's looking for.

"Where's Brinnon?" he asks.

CHAPTER TWELVE

"The Onion King," I whisper to no one.

The words seem to fall out of my mouth, clutching at my gut momentarily as they tumble to the ground and break. Vanished forever is the faint hope that the Onion King was just an imaginary bogeyman hatched in the unfathomable darkness of Murphy's broken mind.

The GPS shows that we're three or four miles west of Brinnon, high in the hills and on the cusp of the Olympic National Forest. Winding roads, then logging roads, and finally a rutted simulation of a road brought us close. The last couple hundred feet we hiked, finding ourselves standing around a young fir tree with fresh remnants of duct tape lying about.

The spot is isolated and remote, yet the ground around us is trounced and trampled by Murphy's pimpled gray shine. That's not all. A collection of amethyst footprints glow around the tree, each one strikingly marbled with burnt orange: the Onion King.

His texture is almost reptilian—somewhere between

crocodile and lizard. Combined with the violet hue of ame-thyst and the probing veins of orange, it's both hideous and beautiful in the same glance, like the hide of some psyche-delic swamp creature.

The Onion King took his own path to the tree, coming in from a slightly different direction than Murphy. Their com-bined shine cuts a wedge in the forest, like a piece of pie ending at the tree.

"I've got a trail," I call out, giving Jimmy a subtle cue that I hope he picks up on.

He does.

"Can you collect the duct tape and any other evidence?" he asks Nate and Jason as he hands over his kit. "I'll follow Steps and see if there's anything else. We can meet back at the car."

"Don't get turned around in these woods," Jason warns as we start off. "The mountains will swallow you whole and that's the last anyone will hear of Steps and Jimmy."

"No worries," Jimmy says, flashing him a smile. "I brought my own tracker."

I think he's talking about me, but then he holds up the GPS.

When we're out of earshot, I tell Jimmy that Charice may have walked out under her own power, but she didn't walk in. The Onion King must have carried her. "It's just his track," I explain. "One set of prints in, one set out." Pausing next to the winter remnant of some unidentified deciduous bush, I point out where Charice's drooping arm or leg must have brushed against the exposed branches, splashing her shine across the twigs.

Jimmy looks where I point, studies what he cannot see, and then takes a long breath. "She told Angie that before she woke in the woods, tied to the tree, the Onion King injected her with something." He isn't speaking to me so much as he's talking the problem through. "The single track fits," he continues.

A minute later we find ourselves back on the rutted semblance of a road. My eyes scan the ground, recognizing patterns I've seen too many times before. "Small car," I say. "Looks like he had her in the trunk. They always stick them in the trunk," I add in a small voice.

Jason's car is clearly visible two hundred feet to our south, so we start ambling in that direction, our movement slowed by contemplation.

When Jimmy next speaks, he counts out each statement on the fingers of his right hand. I'm not sure why he does this, since they're not really steps—at least not the type you'd check off a list, like laundry or dishes or homework.

"The Onion King picks the victims," he muses, counting the first statement out with his index finger, "he abducts the victims, he holds them for a couple weeks, he leaves them in the woods for Murphy to find . . . and then he starts all over."

He holds the five splayed fingers near his belly, contemplating them.

"Does that tell us anything?" I ask.

The answer is slow in coming.

"He's meticulous. He doesn't like loose ends," Jimmy finally says, though the words come out as if he's still trying to convince himself. "But he also doesn't like killing."

"Which is why he needs Murphy to take them and do whatever he does."

"Exactly," Jimmy replies. "Murphy's the perfect henchman: a psychotic who's malleable. And if he got caught"—Jimmy shrugs—"who's going to believe him?"

"You honestly think Murphy's the fall guy in all this—the scapegoat?"

"You don't?"

The question comes back at me like a ricochet and I have to grudgingly admit that the idea has merit. I don't *like* making such an admission, because it's almost like giving kudos to the Onion King for being clever.

"The planning that went into this . . ." Jimmy says, letting the words settle as he shakes his head slowly. "This guy is dangerous."

A tense ball suddenly knots in my belly and I can almost hear a voice in my head whispering, *Hurry! Hurry! Hurry!*

CHAPTER THIRTEEN

When Diane calls for an update, Jimmy asks her to dig deeper into Gloria Cotton and her son. "Public records, social media, everything," he says. "If Murphy *does* have seven other victims, we need to find out where he's keeping them, and we need to do that today."

Jimmy pauses, so I add my own request to the list. "When you're checking social media, Diane, can you keep an eye out for any reference to the Onion King? He's the other half of this equation. I'm guessing he's not going to show up as one of Murphy's Facebook friends, but you never know."

"Onion King?"

"Yeah, welcome to our world," I reply dryly. "At first I was thinking the Onion King might be a character from an online role-playing game, maybe even another player, but we didn't see anything in Murphy's trailer that suggests he's a serious gamer. Whoever he is, Murphy has an almost worshipful admiration for him, kept going on about how smart he is, and how he's the king of Onionland, and—"

"Onionland!" Diane says sharply.

"Yeah, does that mean something?"

"It should," she replies. "Onionland is another name for the dark web."

"The part of the web that's not indexed?" I ask.

"No, that's the deep web."

"What's the difference?" Jimmy asks.

"The deep web is all the stuff that's accessible online but not directly indexed by search engines, usually because it's contained within a password-protected database or page. Your bank account information is a good example. It's available online, but you won't find your balance by searching Google."

"How's that different from the dark web?"

"The dark web is about anonymity. It's about preventing people from tracking your online activity and the sites you visit. It also allows access to sites that are blocked, and no one, not even law enforcement, can identify your physical location. You could be down the street or in New Delhi and they wouldn't be the wiser.

"Think of the deep web as the ocean: you can't see what's below the surface, but there's a lot there, including your bank accounts, tax records, email, and everything else that's locked in a database behind a password or not indexed by the search engines. Now, within that vast ocean is a single submarine filled with pirates: that's the dark web."

I can hear her tapping her pen against the desk. "There's a whole underworld on the dark web," she continues in a slower, more contemplative tone. "Some of the stuff that goes on is legit, other activity includes things like pirated music, books, and movies, but then things get darker: drugs, prostitution, pedophilia, even murder for hire. It's part of the reason that supposedly untraceable digital currencies like bitcoin have become the currency of the realm in Onionland."

"There it is again," I mutter. "Why do they call it that?"

"Because most people access the dark web through the TOR browser," Diane explains, "which uses anonymizing software that bounces communications around the world on a network of relays. TOR stands for The Onion Router, named so because it buries your activity under layers of re- lays. You've seen *Shrek*, right?"

She knows we have. Jimmy's six-year-old son, Petey, will sometimes hang out with us at Hangar 7, our office, so we keep a supply of kids' movies on hand, *Shrek* being one of them.

"Uh-huh," Jimmy replies.

"Remember when Shrek tells Donkey that ogres are like onions because they both have layers? Well, it's the same thing with the Onion Router, only these are layers that no one can peel away."

Nate turns in his seat and watches as we digest Diane's words. "I'm guessing there's no king of Onionland?" Jimmy eventually says.

"No."

"So, who's the Onion King?"

"Someone with an overinflated opinion of his computer skills," Diane proposes, and then adds, "It's probably just a username. And before you ask, remember what I said about the dark web being untraceable. I'll do some checking, but unless he posted something using his real name or home- town, I'm probably not going to be able to provide much."

"Is that kind of search safe?" I ask. "I thought the dark web was filled with hackers and identity thieves. If you start snooping around, it seems a bit like walking into a lion's den with a pork chop dangling from your neck."

Diane shrugs off the concern. "Anonymity goes both ways."

"Uh-huh. I *knew* you were a hacker."

CHAPTER FOURTEEN

Haiden Webber is an anomaly.

In a world where coding and hacking is dominated by teens and twentysomethings, he remains one of the most competent computer forensics experts the FBI employs despite being several years beyond retirement eligibility. If anyone can hack Murphy's laptop, he's the guy.

Was it extravagant delivering a piece of evidence by jet?

Perhaps.

We debated the wisdom of spending both fuel and air time on the delivery, especially since other options were available. We could have overnighted it, or driven the laptop to Seattle, and under most circumstances either choice would have been a reasonable option.

But we're still not sure what we're dealing with.

What if Murphy is telling the truth? Half his ramblings are nonsensical, but what if the crazy bastard really *is* holding seven other women? By now they've been without food and water, perhaps even air, for at least a day. That gives us maybe two more days to find them before the situation turns dire.

Jet fuel seemed the least of our concerns at the time.

We're on our way back from Brinnon when Haiden calls.

Jimmy puts the phone on speaker and Haiden launches into what sounds like a long string of ancient Aramaic, or maybe just some version of geek-speak with an American accent. We can't make heads or tails of it, and Nate starts quietly mimicking one of those old Japanese movies where the soundtrack doesn't match the lip movements.

"Haiden," Jimmy says, trying to interrupt. Then, in a louder voice, he again says, "Haiden!" That seems to do the trick.

"What?"

"Can you start over," Jimmy asks in the kindest way imaginable, "and this time pretend you're speaking to a car filled with a bunch of computer illiterates?"

The computer forensics guru chuckles at that.

"Sorry. That's why they don't let me out of the office much." Pausing, as if having difficulty finding the right words, he finally begins.

"When you erase a file from your computer, two things happen: first, the master reference for that file, which is like an address that tells the operating system where to find it, is removed from the hard drive so the computer can no longer find the file; second, the space occupied by the file is reclassified as open memory, so new files and programs can be written to it. Following me so far?"

Four voices join together into some semblance of affirmation.

"Good," Haiden says, sounding almost relieved. "Now, most people think that by deleting a file and emptying their garbage can, the file is gone, but that's simply not the case. The data itself hasn't moved or changed. Sure, the space it occupied has been freed up, but until someone overwrites it with new data, the file info is still there. And that's where I come in. With the right software, I can pull all the data off a hard drive even after the master reference has been removed. Sometimes the data doesn't make much sense because it's been partially overwritten, but a lot of times I can extract the complete file, whether that's a Word document, an email, or even an image."

"And that's what you did to Murphy's hard drive?" I ask hopefully.

"That's what I *tried* to do," Haiden corrects, "but your suspect is smarter than most. It looks like he's been using some version of file shredder." Before I can ask the obvious question, he continues. "A shredder program acts just like a paper shredder but for digital files. It removes the reference file, frees up the space on the hard drive, but then overwrites it with gibberish so that every bit of the original data is replaced and unrecoverable."

"So we've got nothing," Jimmy surmises.

"I didn't say that," Haiden replies smugly. "I spent some time snooping around and noticed that his Mozilla Thunderbird email program was set up but never used, which is a bit out of the ordinary."

"Because everyone uses email," Jimmy states in a matter-of-fact tone.

"Exactly! So I tried some of the free online email services: Hotmail, Gmail, Yahoo Mail, and a few others, figuring he might have used one of them instead, but still found nothing. Then, on a whim, I tried Yandex Mail. It's a Russian company, but the mail program is in English. Sure enough, as soon as the page popped up I could see that the log-in data was auto-filled with his username and password." In a voice dripping with disdain, he says, "All I had to do was click the log-in button and I had full access."

"Why would Murphy go to extra lengths to protect the

information on his computer," I wonder aloud, "but leave his email unprotected? That's a bit like locking all the windows in your house but leaving the front door standing open, isn't it?"

"That's one way of putting it," Haiden replies. "I guess he underestimated us."

"Any interesting emails we should know about?" Jimmy asks.

"Just one," Haiden says cheerfully. "At first it stumped me, but then I remembered a conference I attended a few years ago on antiterrorism. See, your guy Murphy never sent a single email from this account, nor did he ever receive one." Haiden lets that hang in the air for a minute until I take the bait.

"Then why have the account?"

"They were using the draft file," he says, as if that explains everything.

When none of us reply, our silence heralding our confusion, he gives a disappointed huff and continues. "It's like the dead drops used by Cold War spies: someplace to leave a message where it won't be found, though these days it's mostly terrorists and criminals who communicate this way. Suppose you want to get a message to your partner in crime, but you're paranoid that the government might be monitoring your email activity—"

"Probably because they are," I interject.

"Probably because they are," Haiden parrots. "So, you set up an email account and make sure that both you and your buddy have the log-in information. Then, when you want to send some sensitive info to your opposite, you just log into the email account, write a message, and save it as a draft. Now your partner can log in and read the message in the draft file. He can add to it, delete it, or create a whole new message and save it as another draft. The point is, no one ever hits the send button. If nothing is transmitted, nothing can be intercepted." He pauses. "It's brilliant, if you think about it."

"And you said there was just the one email in the draft file," Jimmy observes, "so that means they were adding to the same file as they went?"

"No, not adding to it. They were erasing the last entry and replacing it with the new one. That way, even if someone figured it out and got into their email account, the only thing they'd find was the last message."

"Speaking of which . . ." Jimmy lets the words hang.

"Right," Haiden replies briskly. "Got a pen? You'll need to write this down."

Jimmy fishes in his pocket a moment and then says, "Fire away."

"Okay, it's a string of numbers." Slowly, he begins to read them off: "Four . . . seven . . . six . . . seven . . . one . . . three—"

"Hold on a second," Jimmy interrupts suddenly. He pushes his bag aside and glances around as if he's lost something.

"What, that's not slow enough for you?" Haiden chides through the phone's inadequate speaker. "I thought you special agents were supposed to be . . . you know . . . special."

"It's not that," Jimmy says distractedly. It takes him a moment to find what he's looking for, but then he says, "Okay, go ahead with the rest." And as Haiden reads off the remainder of the two number strings, Jimmy holds his pen in hand but doesn't write a single number. Instead, his eyes are fixed on the object in his hand, and when Haiden finishes, he turns it toward me.

The screen on Murphy's GPS displays the same numbers digit for digit.

"What is it?" Nate asks, craning his neck.

"You just read off the coordinates we found on Murphy's GPS," Jimmy tells Haiden, "the latitude and longitude where the Onion King left Charice."

The expletive from Haiden is recognized by its tone rather than the word itself, which comes out garbled and half swallowed.

From the driver's seat, Jason lets out a low whistle. "That's how Murphy knew where to find her." It's hard to tell if he's impressed or horrified.

When Haiden speaks next, his voice is level and controlled. "I'm guessing there were other messages exchanged in this manner, probably a lot of them. Unfortunately, this is the only one we can see."

"What if the Onion King is expecting a reply?" I suddenly ask.

Jimmy, Nate, and Jason shift uncomfortably at the suggestion.

"Murphy was on the run shortly after he picked up Charice," I continue. "It's not like he had time to draft a message"—and then I realize my mistake. "In fact, we *know* he didn't draft a message, don't we, since the message Haiden found was the last one saved."

"Should we send something?" Nate asks, looking from face to face.

"That's a dangerous game," Jason cautions.

Jimmy seems to agree. "Let's just wait and see what happens. Haiden," he says, raising his voice a bit and addressing the phone, "can you leave the mail program open and monitor it?"

"If I leave it open, your suspect won't be able to access it from his end."

"You're sure?"

"Pretty sure." There's a shuffling sound from his side, and when his voice comes again, it's a bit louder, as if he's closer to the mic. "How about if I log in every hour or so and see if there's anything new?"

Jimmy nods to himself. "That'll work. We're heading back to the sheriff's office. Keep us posted."

CHAPTER FIFTEEN

The theme song from *The Pink Panther* begins to emanate from Jimmy's cell phone shortly after we pass Sequim, northbound on U.S. 101 toward Port Angeles. It's Diane's distinct ringtone, and Jimmy puts the call on speaker. "Find anything?" he asks bluntly, forgoing any attempt at preamble or greeting.

"Nice to talk to you too," Diane replies. "And as a matter of fact, I did." Her voice goes quiet and one might suspect that the call was dropped. I know better. Jimmy should too, but his head is bent around this case so tightly that he doesn't pick up on it.

After allowing the silence to marinate a moment—and giving Jimmy every opportunity—I blurt, "Hi, Diane," in a stupendously cheery voice I reserve for just such occasions. "How are things at the office?"

"Hi, Steps," Diane coos, enjoying the game. "It's pretty quiet on this end; just doing that analysis thing; turning water into wine and performing other miracles. You know how it is."

By this time Jimmy is rolling his eyes as Nate and Jason smirk and grin.

"Well, if anyone can perform miracles, it's you," I say, laying it on thick.

"Oh, you're good," she replies appreciatively.

I chuckle. "I bet you're calling because you found something interesting?"

"You would be right," Diane replies, and just that quickly she's all business. "In the interest of time, and because I know neither of you care, I'll spare you the details about how I linked Gloria Cotton to her great-uncle's widow, who's been in a nursing home in Poulsbo for the last four years, one of those places that specializes in Alzheimer's patients. That same widow still owns several properties in Kitsap, Jefferson, and Clallam Counties, but the one that piqued my interest is not far from where Murphy wrecked the car."

"How far is not far?"

"Maybe six miles to the southeast."

I raise my eyebrows and exchange a hopeful glance with Jimmy. At the same moment, Jason begins jockeying the Ford toward the median to make a quick U-turn. The location on Palo Alto Road where Murphy wrecked the stolen car is already a good ten miles behind us.

"Are we talking empty land, or are there buildings on this property?" Jimmy asks, leaning toward the phone.

"The assessor's website indicates that it's forestry land, no structures, but Google Earth shows what could be a cabin not far off the road."

"What about an address?"

"This isn't the kind of place that has an address," Diane replies. There's a pause as she works the mouse on her computer, and then she says, "Write this down . . ." and proceeds to read off two strings of numbers. "That's the latitude and longitude for the property—and that's according to Google, so if you end up in banjo country, take it up with them."

"Where do we turn?" Jimmy asks.

"Stay on U.S. 101 eastbound for about three miles past Palo Alto Road until you reach Chicken Coop Road."

"Chicken Coop Road . . . ?" Jimmy replies skeptically, wondering if Diane is messing with him.

"It's legit," Nate says from the front seat. He turns halfway around so that he's talking over his left shoulder. "One of our mentals lives near the end of the road. She calls us once or twice a week because the aliens keep dissecting her cows." He shrugs. "Apparently they put them back together when they're done, because the cows are always standing there chewing their cud and staring at us when we respond." He makes a dubious face.

"Invasion of the Cow Snatchers," Jason chimes in from the driver's seat, and from Nate's chortling response you can tell it's not the first time the idea has been bounced around the office.

"So this is what passes for work while you're away," Diane says, feigning disapproval.

Some people say you can tell the expression on someone's face just by the tone of their words. I don't know if this is true, but Jimmy's trying really hard not to grin when he continues. "Okay, so we get on this Chicken Coop Road . . . and then what?"

Diane is working from internet maps and Google imagery, which at best shows a primitive road leading off into the hills. "About a half mile up Chicken Coop Road, you want to stay to the right. You'll have a three- or four-mile drive, best as I can guess, most of which is logging roads, so I recommend a four-by-four."

Jason gives his nearly new department-issued Ford Fusion an appraising once-over from the driver's seat, and then shrugs. "Murphy was in a car," he says. "The roads can't be that bad."

"Murphy was in a *stolen* car," Nate reminds him. "I don't think he was worried about the undercarriage."

Diane finishes deciphering the maps, adding a few more caveats and disclaimers, and then waits for any questions or comments from Jimmy.

"All right," he finally says after scratching some notes. "I'll call if we find anything. Cell reception might be spotty, so if we go missing you know where to start looking."

When he says the last, I realize he's only half kidding.

We soon come upon the south campus of the Jamestown S'Klallam Tribe, with its totem poles, art galleries, and amazing views to the left and right of U.S. 101. Before we have a moment to fully appreciate these sights, we find ourselves angling off onto Chicken Coop Road, just as Diane promised.

Our visit with the quaintly named county road is brief; a half mile later it wanders absently off to the left, heading to better destinations, while we keep to the right and enter a much more difficult stretch of road—if that's what we're still calling it. Gone is the chip seal surface with its layers of tar and gravel built up into a relatively smooth byway. Instead, we find ourselves on a mix of dirt and gravel, with the inevitable army of potholes, ruts, high spots, and gullies that accompany such.

"Maybe we should turn back and get a four-by-four," I hear Jason mutter from behind the wheel. Yet despite these misgivings, he continues on.

The second turn that Diane suggested leads to a dead end at a clear-cut. The stumps of harvested trees are stacked in great piles, ready for disposal, and the ruts created by the logging trucks have reached epic proportions. The Ford bottoms out several times as Jason turns around, and just when I think we're out of the worst of it, the vehicle comes to a shuddering stop.

A string of expletives bursts from the driver's seat, and then Jason states the obvious: "We're high-centered."

Just like that, Jimmy and Nate open their doors and step out of the car. Jimmy pauses to give me a penetrating stare before closing his door: apparently it's time to push.

It doesn't matter that it's cold, wet, and muddy outside. My feelings on the matter became irrelevant as soon as the car gave its ugly convulsion and came to an abrupt stop. Complaining about it will only make things worse.

Jimmy is always quick to remind me that working for the FBI entails a lot of collateral duties that aren't necessarily spelled out in the job description. Tracking shine through impossible terrain is a good example. Same with examining body parts, washing the smell of decomp out of my hair with baking soda and vinegar, and having a serial killer take a potshot at me with a shotgun—twice.

All things considered, I suppose pushing a stuck car from the mud in the middle of Sasquatch country isn't so bad.

Jason's still revving the engine and spinning the front tires as we move to the rear of the vehicle and brace up against the trunk. Not wanting to be outdone, I give it my all, only to realize that Jimmy and Nate have no intention of being outdone, either. Straining against the trunk and bumper in synchronized spurts that set the car to rocking back and forth, we expect it to break loose at any moment, yet none of us are prepared when the wheels actually grab and drag the Ford's low-slung belly from its perch.

All three of us go down at the same time.

Jimmy and Nate are on their feet almost as soon as their hands and knees hit the ground. They grumble over their misfortune, but the complaints cease when they look over and see me spitting brown muck and rising slowly to my feet, like some drunkard who was just mowed down by the bulls at Pamplona. I wait for the laughs, but to their credit they keep it bottled up—for now. Every ounce of me knows that I'm going to hear about this later.

"What happened to you?" Jason asks as I open the back door and retrieve my backpack.

"Bodysurfing," I reply flatly, and close the door a little too hard.

I was never a Boy Scout or even a Cub Scout, but years of fieldwork have taught me to appreciate the organization's motto: Be Prepared! As such, my backpack—or go-bag—is equipped for scores of unusual situations and emergencies. Falling into the mud isn't one of them. Still, I find a pair of clean socks and a container of antibacterial wipes, which I use to clean the mud from my face and hands. After sealing the soiled socks and wipes inside a gallon Ziploc bag, I go to work scrubbing my coat and jeans, using up the remainder of the wipes.

When all is said and done, my face and hands are almost clean, but the state of my coat and jeans leaves a lot to be desired.

Jason finally manages to find a clean towel in the vastness of his cluttered trunk. He folds it in half and places it on my seat so I won't taint the new upholstery. The gesture is innocent and understandable, but for a moment I find myself empathizing with lepers.

Once we're all back in the warmth of the car, Nate turns around and studies me from his perch on the front passenger seat. He glances up and down, taking in my filthy clothes, and in a perfectly serious voice asks, "Did you find any tracks while you were down there?"

And so it begins.

———

Backtracking a few hundred feet to the main logging road, we continue southbound and then take the next offshoot to the left. This one seems to do the trick and the GPS mark on Jimmy's phone once again draws nearer.

Our speed is ten miles an hour at best, so it takes six minutes to cover the next mile. The road is just turning to the right, leading west and deeper into the hills, when Jimmy calls out. "Hold up a minute." He zooms his screen and studies the map, turning the phone to the left and then the right to align the road and the map.

"We're close," he says, "but now we're starting to move away from the GPS coordinates. Did we miss a road back there?"

"No roads," I say, "but there were two or three sets of tracks leading off into the trees. They looked more like ATV and four-by-four paths."

"Let's check them out."

Jason pulls ahead until he has room to turn the Ford around, and then starts back the way we came, moving slowly as all eyes scan the edge of the logging road for signs of passage.

"Here," Nate calls a moment later, spotting the first impressions. It's not much, just parallel ruts worn into the earth on the right side of the road. The primitive path leads away to the east—or what I'm assuming is the east. I haven't had my bearings since we left Chicken Coop Road, and the weak, intermittent sun gives none of its shadowy clues.

My eyes follow the ruts along the downward-sloping terrain until a wall of prickly green forest rises up and swallows the diminishing tracks, leaving no clue to their destination. From our vantage point, the hills rise and fall in every direction. This area hasn't been logged yet and is blanketed in trees so completely that one might imagine it's all one giant rolling sea of green, if not for the fact that some of the peaks are grander than others. Snow crowns the tallest of these, adding the illusion of whitecaps to the mix.

Jason eyes the deplorable dirt path hesitantly. "How far do you think it goes?"

"A couple hundred feet to the trees," Jimmy guesses. "After that . . ." He shrugs.

"Why don't we do this part on foot?" Jason suggests.

Nate grins. "*Now* he's worried about the car."

As I step out and close the door behind me, I nonchalantly pull my lead-crystal glasses off and make a show of wiping the lenses with the bottom of my shirt, all while taking an unfiltered peek at the path and the logging road. My disappointment increases the more I glance around, until I give up altogether and slip the spectacles back in place.

When I look up, Jimmy's watching me.

I lock eyes with him and give a barely perceptible shake of my head, disguising it by taking a few intentionally jolty steps away from the car. Murphy's shine is nowhere to be seen, either fresh or old. Much as I hate to admit it, he's never set foot on this ground. It doesn't bode well for our present course, and with the clock ticking on seven potential victims, we can't be wasting our time on dead ends.

If it were just me and Jimmy, we'd probably skip over this dirt path and move to the next one. But we have baggage today in the form of two Clallam County detectives, and illusions must be maintained.

The air is crisp with winter when we set out—just enough chill to give our exhaled breath a misty hue that lingers a moment and then vanishes; angel's breath, my mother calls it. Had I known this was going to be the last pleasant moment of the day, I might have walked more slowly and breathed more deeply . . . had I known.

CHAPTER SIXTEEN

Two hundred feet into the forest, the trees part before us, revealing a makeshift structure of perhaps nine hundred square feet that resembles a third-world shack. The most logical elements of the cabin are the four curtained windows we notice as we approach—*logical* because they actually look like windows and contain real glass.

Everything else about the cabin is a hodgepodge.

It's as if a Home Depot store exploded next to a recycling center and the resulting mess landed here in the forest. I half expect to see the legs of some wicked witch sticking out from under the house, ruby slippers and all.

"Well, that's something you don't see every day," Nate mutters.

"Great! Another hunter's shack," Jason observes, pointing to part of the structure that looks older and more weather-worn. "The rest has been added more recently."

"How do you know that?" I ask.

"Look at the porch." He gestures at a collection of pallets that have been set directly on the ground in front of the cabin and hammered together into something that resembles neither a porch nor a thing masquerading as a porch.

"What about it?"

"That's pretty cheap lumber, and it's resting right on the ground. I doubt it would take more than a couple years for it to start rotting."

"You think this has all been done in the last few years?" Jimmy says with a hint of urgency. "You're sure?"

Jason lifts a shoulder in a half shrug. "Pretty sure."

Jimmy's eyes find me again, but I'm already pulling my glasses off. Immediately my gut goes to butterflies as I take in the incredible wash of pimpled gray.

Murphy is everywhere: on the ground, against the trees, and on the porch, the walls, and the windows. His shine is present everywhere one would have touched, pushed, held, or lifted in order to convert the old hunting shack into an ugly and confused cabin.

The shock of this revelation elicits an unusual sound from my lips: a cross between a gasp, a moan, and a laugh. Unfortunately, it's loud enough to draw the unwanted attention of Nate and Jason, who look at me with puzzled expressions.

Thinking quickly, I say, "Sorry . . . excited utterance."

My choice of words is intentional, since an excited utterance is the legal term for a statement made while a subject is still under stress after a startling event. It's an exception to the hearsay rule, and admissible as evidence. Cops love a good excited utterance because it can convict a suspect with his own words. Usually it's something like, "He had it coming," or "I didn't mean to hit her so hard."

While my gasp wasn't exactly a statement, my explanation is immediately understood, and both Nate and Jason grin as if I'd just told a joke . . . which I kind of did.

Nate walks up onto the so-called porch and knocks on the door. It's clear he doesn't expect an answer because he immediately rattles the door handle and finds it locked. As he moves to the large window to the left of the door and presses his face to the glass, cupping his hands to block the light, Jimmy and Jason move to opposite corners of the cabin to watch for any unexpected exits. Their handguns are still holstered, but I know they'll come out in a startling blur at the first hint of activity.

"Can't make anything out," Nate says. "There's a crack in the curtain, but . . ." He pauses and retrieves his flashlight. "That's a little better. Looks like a living room. There's a coffee table and a lamp, and I can make out part of a bicycle wheel. There's some clutter—" A startled cry and a spasm of movement erupt from the front of the house. A loud *crack* rings out.

Nate goes down.

I watch in confusion as he falls backward onto the pallets, unable to stop his fall or even turn and stretch his arms out. He hits hard and the wind leaves him in a *woomp* of sound that carries away and dies in the trees.

He tries to scramble back from the house, but his body is demanding oxygen his empty lungs can't give. The jolt from the fall and his inability to catch a breath leaves his efforts weak and flailing, but it's clear he wants to put distance between himself and the cabin.

Jason has his Glock in hand and moves to a cover position with the barrel pointing at the dark window. Rushing forward, Jimmy and I grab the downed detective under both arms and try to drag him to safety. Nate can't cry out in pain, but the look on his face and the sudden cringe of his body warns us to stop pulling.

Then I see it: his foot is wedged sideways in one of the pallets.

The loud and ominous crack was nothing more than old wood giving way. In his sudden and spasmodic rush to flee the window, his heel had landed hard on the pallet porch and pushed through one of the boards, snapping it like dry bone.

Freeing the foot quickly, Jimmy and I lift Nate until he's close to standing, and then drag him to the security of a nearby tree cluster. Jason falls in behind, his aim never leaving the window.

A cursory and somewhat rough inspection of Nate finds no obvious injuries, and when the detective finally catches his breath, his lungs are like a reluctant engine finally sputtering to life. Each breath is stronger than the last, and less gasping.

It's not long before he's able to speak again, and the first thing out of his mouth is a string of sharp expletives that flow like water from a bursting dam. The explosion of profanity lasts mere seconds, but its effect seems to compose him, as if the excess adrenaline in his system had somehow attached itself to each hurtled syllable and flushed the fight-or-flight hormone from his system.

In a calmer voice, Nate says, "There's someone inside—just sitting there! Scared the crap out of me!" As soon as he says it, another thought occurs to him. "Or it's a body."

"Did you see movement?" Jimmy asks.

He shakes his head sharply and wipes his face with his hand.

"Where in the house?"

Nate flails his hand loosely in the direction of the window. "There's a chair, or a couch. It's pushed up against the window. Only the left end of it is visible through the gap in the curtain, but you can tell someone's sitting there."

"Male or female?"

"I don't know," he stammers, and then blurts: "Female, I suppose. All I saw was her arm." He sweeps his hand up and down his own arm by way of explanation. "It looked like a woman's arm. You know, thin with no bicep. She had it resting on the arm of the couch. The upper arm disappeared to the right, but you could tell it was rising to her shoulder." He shakes his head. "She's just sitting there."

"Was she bound in any way?" I ask.

"No. Not that I saw."

"Sedated?"

"How the hell should I know that?" Nate snaps, and then immediately apologizes.

We stand in silence for a long moment, each of us working this development over in our heads as we decide the next course of action . . . or so I think. Then I realize I'm the *only* one thinking about what comes next. Everyone else is standing perfectly still and listening: listening for movement inside the cabin, for the soft pleas for help uttered through a gag, for the slow telltale scrape of feet upon the wooden floor.

Even the forest seems to hold its breath.

"We need to get in there," Jimmy says after what seems like minutes.

"Exigent circumstances?" Jason suggests.

"Sounds right to me. We have seven women that are supposedly missing, one of whom appears to be immobilized inside a shack owned by Murphy's great-aunt. I think that qualifies."

"And if it's the Onion King?" Nate asks.

Jimmy looks my way and I give him a furtive shake of my head. The Onion King has never been here, of that I'm certain.

"That's a chance we'll have to take," Jimmy replies.

With his Glock in hand, Jimmy moves swiftly to the front of the cabin and pounds on the door three times, announcing, "FBI!" while Nate covers the window from a safe distance and Jason positions himself along the side of the house. I rarely pack my Walther P22 when we're working a case, so I pull back and watch the opposite end of the house, just in case someone pops out through a window and goes rabbit.

"FBI!" Jimmy calls again, rattling the door with his fist. When he gets no answer, he tries the door handle and finds that the latch is loose in the strike plate. Applying pressure to it, he works the handle back and forth, but it doesn't give.

"Jason!" he calls, jerking his head to summon him over.

The detective sergeant knows what's needed before he reaches the porch, and quickly fishes the lock-pick set from his pocket. Inserting the tension wrench into the lock, he uses the rake to bounce the pins. A moment later the pins are set, and he turns the tension wrench and rake like a key. Giving Jimmy a nod, he pockets the tool kit and returns to his position on the side of the house.

"Last chance," Jimmy calls into the house. "This is the FBI and we're coming in. Keep your hands where we can see them and don't make any sudden moves."

With his flashlight in his left hand and his Glock in his right, he toes the door open and stands to the right of the opening as he does a quick sweep of the left side of the room, using the outside wall as cover.

"Freeze!" Jimmy suddenly shouts, tensing up and drawing down on a target in the corner of the room. His gun then dances to a second target . . . and a third, moving back and forth between them.

Jason rushes forward and takes up position on the opposite side of the door opening, covering the other half of the house so that no one can move up on Jimmy and blindside him.

As soon as the beam from his flashlight cuts the darkness, Jason yells, "Freeze! Clallam County Sheriff's Office!" Like Jimmy, his gun floats between multiple targets, only these are on the other side, meaning there are at least four or five subjects in the house.

Then, inexplicably and without a word, Jimmy and

Jason lower their guns simultaneously and step through the opening.

I glance over at Nate and he just gives me an exaggerated shrug; apparently he's as puzzled as I am. Jimmy and Jason are just inside the open door, shining their flashlights this way and that. When I can't take it any longer, I yell, "What?" in my loudest voice.

Jimmy glances out but doesn't seem to be in that big of a hurry to reply. "I could tell you," he finally says, "or you can come over and see for yourself."

We do, and as Nate and I approach, Jason pulls open the front curtain. Moving to the back of the cabin, he parts a second set of curtains, and then a third. The tepid light of the winter sun flows through the cabin like a spring flood. Corners that were once dark are now illuminated; shadows that once menaced are dissolved.

Placing my feet carefully on the pallet porch, I make my way toward the front door, pausing for just a moment at the front window to glance inside. In that instant, much is explained. And then I notice something else: an abundance of recent shine. Murphy's stands prominent, but it's the others that I'm interested in.

With my glasses in hand I move forward, passing through the open door as if it were a portal into a surreal world of neon color and horror. Separating out the distinct shines in my head, I count them as I go.

"Oh, no," I whisper when I finish.

CHAPTER SEVENTEEN

A lot of things unfold quickly when a crime scene is discovered: CSIs are called out, detectives and deputies hurry to the location, the sheriff is notified, and the beginnings of a perimeter are set—and that's all in the first few minutes.

After clearing the house, Jimmy asks me to do a walk-through to get my impressions. He then steps outside, consults with Jason a moment, and then places a call to Sheriff Eccles.

Since Clallam County has only four detectives—and half of them are already on scene—Jason calls Detective Mike Hopkins, who's working a case in Sequim, and asks him to gather up any bodies that patrol can spare and respond to the cabin.

Next, he calls Detective Tony Halsted, who's writing a polygraph report at the office. Based on what we found in the cabin, it's clear that exigent circumstances no longer apply, and everything we do from here on out has to be meticulous.

"Tony, I need a search warrant," the detective sergeant says without preamble.

"Sure, boss. Whatcha got?"

Jason spends several minutes detailing the case, the reason for the search, and what they hope to find—the basic elements of a search warrant affidavit. Tony takes notes at a breathtaking pace. Earlier in his career he'd signed up for a shorthand course thinking it would be useful when making notes in the field and during interviews. That was before they switched over to tape recorders.

In just a few minutes, and with little repetition or clarification from Jason, Tony has everything he needs to prepare a search warrant affidavit.

"I'll give the prosecutor's office a heads-up," Tony says. "We should have it in front of a judge in the next hour."

"That'll work," Jason tells him. "It'll be a few hours before the cavalry arrives."

"Cavalry?"

"You'll see when you get here," Jason replies. He thanks Tony and ends the call.

Jimmy and I have worked enough major crime scenes to know that this one is well beyond the scope of Clallam County. It's not that they don't have good people ready to dive into the investigation; they just don't have enough of them. When Jimmy calls Sheriff Eccles and explains what we've found, she quickly agrees and requests FBI assistance in processing the scene.

Most of what the Special Tracking Unit deals with does not fall under federal jurisdiction, so contrary to popular belief the FBI can't just sweep in and take over an investigation. Almost every case we work is at the request and invitation of a local agency. Sometimes there's resentment on the part of one or two detectives who think we're there to flex the FBI muscle and steal their case away. More than once I've heard a sarcastically muttered, "I'm from the government and I'm here to help."

I don't take it personally.

One of the things Jimmy tells investigators the first time we meet is, "We work for you." The words are easily said but he means them, and our actions back them up. It probably helps that we have no interest in being in the media spotlight, holding press conferences, or taking any credit for solving the case. Mostly we prefer to just fly in, help as much as we can, and fly home without ever being referenced in the press or, when possible, case reports.

This is our fifth investigation with the Clallam County Sheriff's Office, which explains the camaraderie and trust: We've already proven ourselves. There are no bridges to build or egos to soothe. It also explains the sheriff's unflinching willingness to bring in specialized help.

The FBI has 141 highly trained Evidence Response Teams, or ERTs, attached to fifty-six field offices throughout the United States. Each team is led by a special agent, but most of the members are non-sworn professionals who are meticulous about evidence collection and up-to-date on all the latest techniques.

Whether it's ultraviolet photography, DNA, fingerprint analysis, gas chromatography, or digital information recovery, the ERTs have the personnel, the training, and the equipment to glean the maximum amount of evidence from a crime scene.

They're ideal for complex cases, so the decision is a no-brainer.

After getting an official request from Sheriff Eccles, Jimmy makes the call. "Here we go," he says under his breath.

The phone begins to ring.

CHAPTER EIGHTEEN

The cabin is an unintentional caricature.

The rustic simplicity of the interior is accented here and there by freakish splashes of some pretend reality, and I have to admit that I'm a little creeped out at being left alone inside. Still, the seven occupants seem harmless enough, so I suck it up and move through each room methodically.

The layout is fairly straightforward. To the right is what I would call a kitchen, though there are no appliances and the sink appears to be for show, since there's no running water and the drainpipe isn't connected. Inside the sink, however, is a plastic shopping bag with several empty candy wrappers, two empty Coke cans, and other miscellaneous garbage. Among this refuse I find the empty packaging of something else I recognize. I leave it in place but make a mental note to point it out to CSI.

Stretching across the top of several dilapidated waist-high cabinets between the kitchen and living room is a countertop that seems to serve as a breakfast bar and includes two high-backed metal stools.

One is occupied.

Her elbows are on the counter and she's leaning forward, as if talking to another occupant who's standing in the kitchen with a towel in her hand. The seated figure is dressed in dark blue sweats and white sneakers. The one with the towel is wearing a pair of jeans and a T-shirt.

Behind the kitchen, in the back-right corner of the house, is a space occupied by a single dominant feature: a barber chair. It's not one of the old collectible barber chairs, but something more recent, less appealing. Against the wall are three cardboard file boxes, the type used by law firms and sold at office supply stores.

I learned long ago how to move through a building without tainting evidence. Crime scene investigators tend to be touchy about where you walk, what you touch, and what direction you sneeze. So, as I crouch to examine the first of the three boxes, the first thing I do is snap on a pair of latex gloves. Using both hands, I lift the cardboard lid straight up and keep it horizontal as I move it to the left, exposing the contents.

What greets me would have been somewhat surprising, even shocking, if I hadn't already expected to find it somewhere in the cabin. Replacing the lid, I repeat the process with box two and box three, finding similar contents. I don't have to count them; I already know they number seven, each with their own unique shine.

Something Murphy said comes back to me now, something about the soul residing in the face. That part, at least, is starting to make sense.

Moving to the living room, I ignore the three silent occupants and make a mental note of the old seventies-style console TV, the cheap exercise bike, the sofa, the two chairs, the four throwaway paintings on the wall.

The two tiny bedrooms to the left of the living room are equally devoid of evidence, except for their occupants and a single paperback book on one of the beds. Each space holds a twin mattress and box spring that rests atop a frame rail, as well as one nightstand and one picture on the wall—as if everything was purchased in pairs and then divided between the rooms.

Exiting out the front door, my mind still digesting everything I've seen, I pull my gloves absently from my hands. Jimmy joins me near the porch.

"How bad?" he asks in a low voice, expecting the worst. He saw my reaction when I first walked into the cabin, saw me glance around and take it all in, heard my utterance. I think he knew then, at that moment.

"It's like Murphy said," I reply heavily. "Seven victims."

"Dead?"

I just nod. That's the funny thing about shine: when someone dies, it ceases to pulse and glow, as if all the energy that once powered it had fled.

There's a long pause as Jimmy looks over my shoulder at the cabin, and then glances around at the small clearing and at the trees beyond.

"Then where are their bodies?" he finally asks.

Where are the bodies?

It's a good question; a logical question, considering what we found in the house. As soon as the words are out of Jimmy's mouth, I motion for him to follow with my index finger, and move away from the cabin at a ninety-degree angle. When I think we're fifty or sixty feet from the front door, I start walking a slow circle around the structure. It's a three-hundred-foot circumference, mostly through trees and rough terrain, but it's necessary.

Murphy's shine is condensed in and around the cabin, almost all of it within twenty or thirty feet of the building. By putting some distance between myself and the cabin, and then walking a circle around it, I'll be able to determine if he ever walked off into the woods or made his way to a nearby clearing.

As I walk, the ugly truth begins to settle on me: I'm looking for a graveyard.

It's the only place this can end.

The victims were here, in the cabin. Their shine is on the floor and in the barber chair, and if Murphy took the trouble to bring them here, why would he take them elsewhere for disposal? He wouldn't. What would be the point? It's unlikely he'd find a place more secluded . . . unless he hiked them farther into the mountains, and that's just not practical.

That means we're close.

Somewhere out here is a shine-imbued trail leading off to who knows where. At its end, I expect to find a place of bones.

Minutes into my track, I glance to the left and note that the back wall of the cabin is visible through the trees—meaning we're halfway through our search. A dozen potential paths have already presented themselves, only to quickly peter out as we followed them to their truncated ends. After each of these false starts, we return to the circumference and continue on.

When the trail finally comes into view, I immediately know it's the right one. I know this because it's heavily traveled by Murphy, whose shine paves a wide swath through the trees. Back and forth his feet march, as if he were building a rock wall at the destination and carrying the stones in one at a time.

"This is it," I say to Jimmy, my words all but a whisper.

The stream of color leads away from the cabin, heading south along an old game trail. I can tell by the lack of footprints that the victims never walked this way. That they came this way is a certainty, but they were never under their own power. Murphy had carried them in his arms or slung them over his shoulder in a fireman's carry. Their shine marks the trees that he brushed past and the ground where he set them down when he needed to rest.

As we follow the trail, it's not long before I've accounted for all seven unique shines, all seven victims. And, arriving at our destination, Jimmy and I stare in rising horror as the slow realization of what we've found settles upon us. After a moment, he drags a toe through the dead earth at his feet, revealing the truth of it.

"Are they here?" he asks quietly.

I simply nod, speechless.

"Good God," he mutters.

CHAPTER NINETEEN

The days are short, and darkness comes early to the Pacific Northwest in winter. When the four Clallam County police utility vehicles, or PUVs, turn off the logging road and bump their way along the rutted path toward the cabin, it's their headlights that herald their arrival.

The vehicles come to a stop just short of the cabin and all the doors open at once, giving the column the odd appearance of some sort of mechanical land beast with gills. Four deputies step from their respective driver's seats, while the eleven-member Evidence Response Team from the FBI's Seattle field office pours out and begins unloading equipment from the back.

They made good time from Seattle.

Jimmy placed the call just four hours ago, and the first two of that would have been spent pulling the team together and getting ready for deployment. The rest of the transit time was spent driving to Seattle-Tacoma International Airport, where they hopped onto Betsy—courtesy of the Special Tracking Unit—and flew to Port Angeles. From

there it was easy: the impromptu Clallam County convoy picked them up, and they made short work of the drive to the cabin, even without the benefit of lights and sirens.

Emerging from the front passenger seat of the lead vehicle, Special Agent Darren Rossiter stretches his arms out and then twists at the waist, working the miles out of his body. Spotting Jimmy, he smiles broadly and begins to saunter over. Jimmy meets him halfway and they greet each other with a warm handshake and comfortable familiarity.

In addition to the seven lab technicians and forensic scientists on the team, there are four special agents, with Darren serving as the special agent in charge. In his mind this doesn't mean much, and he often refers to himself as the chief cat herder.

Years ago, several of his good-humored teammates started calling him cowboy—on account of the herding reference—until someone decided that he looked more like a shepherd. It's doubtful any of them had ever seen an *actual* shepherd, but the reference stuck and quickly became a nickname. These days it's no longer Special Agent Darren Rossiter, it's just Shepherd, or sometimes just Shep. Even his no-nonsense boss compromises and calls him Special Agent Shepherd, making sure to include his full title.

Turning my way, Shepherd says, "Nice to see you, Steps." He takes my outstretched hand and claps me on the shoulder.

Jimmy introduces Jason and Nate, and then Detectives Tony Halsted and Mike Hopkins, who joined us earlier in the afternoon and brought along three Clallam County deputies who they borrowed from day shift. Two of the deputies are cross-trained as crime scene investigators. They'll be needed in the hours ahead. Even if they hadn't been invited, it would have been hard to keep them away.

Counting the eleven-member Evidence Response Team, and the four additional deputies who picked them up at the airport and drove them here, we now have twenty-two law

enforcement professionals to work the two crime scenes. Their depth of knowledge may vary, but they're all well versed in evidence preservation.

The plan is to have the four detectives, the two CSI-trained deputies, and the members of the Evidence Response Team split into two groups, one for the disposal site in the woods, and a larger element for the cabin, which deputies have already dubbed "Murphy's Misery."

I've always suspected that those in law enforcement are a bit more imaginative than the average person. After all, they see more, are challenged to believe more, and often have to put their imagination to work when trying to figure out a crime.

Imagination is like any other skill: the more you practice, the better you get. Still, much as I'd like to give credit to the first deputies on scene, Murphy's Misery was not conceived during a moment of imaginative eureka. Rather, it was so named because the only book in the shack happens to be a copy of Stephen King's *Misery*. The much-used paperback was found at the foot of the mattress in the bedroom to the left, next to one of the occupants.

A bookmark juts from page 102.

That a book about a guy confined to bed in a remote cabin in the woods should be found next to, well, next to the occupant of a bed in a remote cabin in the woods is . . . ironic. That both cabins are ruled over by raging psychotics is downright alarming. Whether Murphy is sending a message with the book, having a little fun, or completely oblivious to the parallels of the story and the reality he created is anyone's guess. I'm hoping he's oblivious, because any other possibility is truly frightening.

There's no book at the disposal area in the woods, so it's simply called site two.

While the ERT, CSIs, and detectives work Murphy's Misery and site two, the remaining deputies will be handed the

thankless but necessary task of providing site security. This includes not just the two crime scenes, but also the command vehicle, which is parked on the logging road next to a large fifth-wheel trailer that Detective Halsted brought with him.

After hearing what we'd discovered, Tony correctly figured this was going to be an all-nighter—possibly even a multiday evidence recovery. He thought it would be nice to have a place where team members can rack out for a few hours, if needed. And while the command vehicle has a small bathroom and a mini-fridge, Halsted's luxury fifth-wheel sleeps eight, has a full kitchenette, a living room, and a respectable bathroom with a massage shower—which hopefully won't be needed.

All in all, it's a pretty sweet setup.

The two CSI deputies will be split between the sites and answer directly to the Evidence Response Team. They can learn a great deal working with the best the FBI has to offer, and the skills they'll learn and practice in the coming hours will pay dividends for years to come.

Big-city homicide detectives may work dozens upon dozens of murders a year, but in most of the United States the homicide rate is low, and a police department or sheriff's office might see a single case every year or two. This is good for the general public but does little to hone the skills of investigators tasked with solving those crimes.

Lights from the command vehicle illuminate a wide area around the logging road, and the extension cords running off the outside outlets funnel power to four lights dispersed along the path between the road and the cabin.

Once their gear is unpacked, Jimmy leads the ERT to the small clearing at the front of Murphy's Misery. The low hum of a generator grows louder as they draw near. The portable power unit is necessary because even the industrial extension cords from the command vehicle won't reach this far. A red-and-black five-thousand-watt generator sits to the side of the cabin with enough extension cords sprouting from it to send a fire marshal into cardiac arrest.

Its twin, equally festooned, is at site two.

A circular array of lights is set back from the crime scene, illuminating it from seven different elevated positions. The practiced placement of the array diffuses the light so that it's not blinding—unless you look right at one—yet it covers the area in an overlapping pattern that diminishes shadow and presents an almost pleasant work environment.

Additional lights have been set up inside Murphy's Misery, covering the two small bedrooms, the living room, the pretend kitchen, and the macabre room now known as Sweeney Todd's.

Another nickname coined by deputies—on account of the barber chair.

Introductions are made all around, no small task considering the number of investigators on scene. Despite the small crowd, Detective Sergeant Jason Sturman handles the meet and greet like a pro and seems to commit every name to memory with flawless precision.

Once again, my inability to remember names returns to haunt me. Of the eleven members on the Evidence Response Team, I manage to recall that one is named something Chatman, and another is something Jenkins. I manage this stupendous feat only because I've worked with Chatman and Jenkins in the past.

"Special Agent Jimmy Donovan is going to take a few minutes and provide a rundown on the case to this point," Jason says when the introductions are complete. "If you have questions, please wait until he's done, that way we can get through this quickly and get to work. I don't have to tell you it's going to be a long night." Nodding to Jimmy, he says, "They're all yours."

If anyone had asked me what the "rundown" on the case was, my answer would have dripped with pessimism, perhaps even dismay. Jimmy says I can be overly dramatic, but that's because my emotional range is broader than his.

With everyone gathered around, some crouching, some standing, and others sitting on equipment cases, Jimmy spends the next ten minutes bringing them up to speed, starting with the vehicle chase yesterday morning with state patrol, the pursuit of Murphy Cotton, the revelations about the Onion King, and, finally, our discovery of the macabre cabin and the grisly secrets it implies.

"Any questions?" Jimmy asks when he's done.

There are.

Despite their eagerness to get started, nearly every team member has at least one question, and between Jimmy, Jason, Nate, and I, we answer each one in turn. As this process finally draws down, the mood seems to shift. The air suddenly feels electric, as if the stored static of an impending lightning strike had been captured and contained in the area around the cabin.

It's about to get real.

Waving me out front and center, Jimmy says, "I've asked my partner, Steps, to explain what we found in the cabin and in the woods nearby." He gives me a nod, and I feel the sudden heat of all those eyes upon me.

It would be an understatement to say that I don't like being the center of attention, so the "hi" that escapes my mouth is exceeded in its brilliance only by the awkward half wave I give with my right hand.

"Uh, so—" I swallow hard and brace up, reminding myself that I'm the expert. Sometimes it works, sometimes it doesn't. "Detective Sergeant Sturman and Special Agent Donovan made initial entry through the front door," I say, "which opens into the living room on the left and a kitchen area on the right. In the living room, they observed what they initially mistook for three unknown subjects. One was seated on a love seat, another was on an extremely old exercise bike, and the third was in a broken lounge chair with a blanket over her lap."

One of the techs raises her hand and I immediately acknowledge her.

"You said you mistook them for unknown subjects," she says, "so does that mean they *were* known?"

"No, it means they weren't subjects at all . . . they were mannequins." I let that settle in for a moment before continuing. "We found two more in the kitchen, and one in each bedroom, for a total of seven. They were all posed, as if we'd walked in on their daily routine. Since we had information from Murphy Cotton that there were seven victims—or *patients,* as he calls them—this discovery was, well, disturbing."

An agreeable murmur courses through the group.

"The mannequins are dressed in clothing that I believe comes from the victims. Several of them wear coordinated outfits, and two of them are in workout gear with matching tops and bottoms. Obviously, without knowing who the victims are, we can't compare this against missing person reports to find out what they were last wearing."

Chatman starts to raise her hand, but then forgoes the gesture and says, "He could have picked the clothes up at a yard sale, or Goodwill, for that matter." Her words are steeped in skepticism. "What makes you think they came from the victims? For that matter, how do you know there *are* victims? All you have is the statements of this Murphy Cotton, who, for all we know, is talking about the mannequins. Maybe he thinks they're people."

"Oh, trust me," I say, "the victims are real." The words come out cold and flat, and Chatman seems to recoil apprehensively as I speak them. That was not my intent. Forcing a deep breath, I say, "It's an educated guess. We found . . . well, we found something else." I shake my head, as if even I can't believe what's about to be revealed.

"Rather than explaining it to you, why don't you all follow me inside and you can see for yourself? It'll probably be a little crowded, but it can't be helped."

Their curiosity is palpable as they surge forward, and I have to pause and caution them about the sketchy pallet-porch. The last thing we need out here is a broken ankle.

As the first member of the ERT steps through the front door behind me, she gasps and nearly backs out again before being jostled forward by those coming behind her. There are more gasps, murmurs, and exclamations, and in a few cases utter silence and bewilderment as the entire team makes its way inside.

"As you can see," I continue, "the mannequins are wearing inch-thick masks cast in plaster." I approach the mannequin sitting at the bar and use my pen to point out the hole on the right side of the mask. "Two holes have been drilled into each mask, one on each side. Through these, Murphy has tied two lengths of ribbon, which he used to secure the mask in place, almost like a cheap Halloween costume. We're confident the mask material is plaster because of the color, and because we found an open bag in the next room."

I hesitate, but the words finally come: "These are death masks."

Murmurs and puzzled looks once more sweep through the team, and a young male tech who looks like he should be in high school says, "Are you sure? Just because he made impressions of their faces doesn't mean they're dead, right?"

Their shine is flat, I don't say. *There's no energy left in their mortal residue,* I want to explain to the young technician . . . but I don't. Even if I just didn't care anymore and decided to reveal the phenomenon of shine, these are mostly scientists standing before me. Not one of them would believe a word of it because it would challenge other elements of their lock-step dogma. These days, the truth of science seems to depend on either consensus or where the grant money comes from.

Galileo had it easy by comparison.

"I'm sorry, what was your name again?"

"George."

I wave him forward fifteen paces and point to the barber chair in the corner of the house behind the kitchen. "Do you have a barber chair in your house, George?"

"No."

"Me either, which is why I found it a bit odd that Murphy would drag this thing all the way out here to the middle of nowhere. It's not like he was sitting in it and watching TV, right?" It's a rhetorical question, so I forgo the pause. "Notice all the footprints around the chair?" I ask, pointing for emphasis. "It seems when you mix plaster it gets dust all over the place, and Murphy wasn't much of a housekeeper. These prints around the chair are all his; when we came through here during our sweep, we were careful to limit our tracks to the edges." Looking at George, I ask, "Notice anything about the prints?"

It only takes him a moment.

"They're mostly around the head of the chair."

"Exactly! I'm guessing this is where he made the molds."

It's a solid statement, but leaves some room for doubt, meaning it's still an open question. The seven distinct shines on the chair tell me everything I need to know, but I've found that it's sometimes better to present an investigator with a possibility they can prove, rather than a fact they can only support.

"There are three boxes there on the floor," I say, pointing to the cardboard legal boxes. "Inside, you'll find the original mold for each victim." George takes this in, as do the others, who are hanging on every word of our exchange. "Do you have gloves?"

George holds up a pair of blue latex gloves and then snaps them on. He knows exactly what I want. Opening the nearest box, he gingerly removes one of the molds and holds it up high, so everyone can get a look. The back side of the mold is rough and undefined, but as he turns it around, the concave impression of a woman's face presents itself. The detail is breathtaking; a moment frozen in time with such precision that even her eyebrows show definition.

"You asked how I know they're dead," I say to George in a sobering tone. Tipping my head toward the mold, I ask, "Do you see any holes for the mouth or nose?"

This realization and its meaning sends a shudder through the room. There's a long moment of quiet. At length, George kneels and places the mold back into the box, as if afraid to hold it any longer. He composes himself quickly and asks, "What type of material is that?"

"We think it's an alginate impression material used by dentists, something called Mirror Image. It's the stuff they use to make a mold of your tooth when they're preparing a crown or a replacement. It's also popular with crafters because it captures every detail. There was an unopened container of it in Murphy's backpack when we captured him yesterday. At the time, we had no idea what he was using it for." I glance around the interior of the room. "Now we do." Gesturing toward the kitchen, I add, "There's an empty package in the sink that I flagged."

"If the masks are plaster, why not make the molds of the same material?" someone asks from the back of the group. "Wouldn't that be easier?"

"You're looking for logical actions from an illogical mind," Jimmy explains. "Murphy believes he found some way of saving broken women; he told us as much. Maybe the type of mold-making material is important to that process, we just don't know. But I guarantee you this, these masks and the mannequins on which they're displayed are all part of it. They all play a role, at least in Murphy's distorted reality."

"How messed up is this guy?" another voice interjects.

Jimmy gives a resigned nod. "He's a barely functioning psychotic."

Glancing at the older woman who asked the question, then at the others, he adds, "We plan on having another talk with Murphy Cotton first thing tomorrow morning. It'll be interesting to hear his explanation for all this." He waves his hand around the room, as if to encompass it.

When Jimmy steps back a single pace, I take it as my cue to continue.

"Obviously, there are parallels between these death masks and those found on the rats Jimmy mentioned earlier, the ones in Murphy's fifth-wheel," I say. "In his mind, he probably perfected his system experimenting on the rats, and then applied it to the victims. How much of this was influenced or directed by the Onion King is speculation. He's the wild card in all this."

Walking slowly through the living room, I pause near the front door. "Now we're going to take a short walk through the woods," I say, "to the . . . to the place. . . ."

I don't know how it happens or why, but the words escape me. It's not like I haven't seen my share of nastiness during my time with the Special Tracking Unit. I've been witness to every manner of horror the human mind can conjure, the images of which still come to me in nightmares.

Yet this is different.

It's downright sterile in comparison. Perhaps that's why it bothers me to my core. Murphy's victims haven't just been killed, they've been erased.

"Let me show you something," I finish in a quiet voice.

CHAPTER TWENTY

The bail bond agency on South Lincoln Street in downtown Port Angeles is housed in a run-down storefront that was once a music shop, a barbershop, a video store, and a sandwich shop. There were more failed ventures before that, but who's counting?

The cleanest, or perhaps just the brightest part of the building is the neon BAIL BONDS sign over the front window, and the equally neon OPEN sign next to the door. The inside doesn't look much better than the outside. The ancient wallpaper is peeling from a dozen locations, and the layers of mildew around the front window give the place a grimy look that seems perfectly in sync with many of its customers.

If the dingy office were a worn-out left shoe, the forty-something woman behind the desk would make it a pair. Her mottled complexion matches the wallpaper and her frayed hair complements the worn shag carpet. Like the room, she smells of cigarette smoke, is in desperate need of a makeover, and looks twenty years older than her true age.

"Bail was set at two thousand dollars," Jill Carver says

into her cell phone. "Our fee is a straight ten percent, so two hundred." She listens for a moment as the person on the other end grouses about the cost. "That's industry standard," she replies a moment later, not really caring what the guy thinks. "It's either that or you can post the full two thousand in cash. Sure, you'll get it all back—eventually, as long as your friend shows up for court."

She listens a moment. "If he doesn't, the court keeps your money." There's another pause, and then she says, "That's what I thought," and picks up a pen. "Will that be Visa or Mastercard?"

In the United States, the legal practice of releasing someone on bail dates back to the colonies and was based on English law. Simply stated, it allows a person to surrender money or other property to the court to secure their release from custody while they await their trial. This money or property guarantees that they'll show up, because if they abscond— also known as bail jumping—the court keeps every dime.

Not such a big deal if the bail is five hundred dollars for shoplifting, but if it's twenty thousand for burglary you're talking some real money. Only the most serious of crimes creep into six- and seven-figure territory. These are reserved for serial rapists, bank robbers, major drug dealers, murderers, and other hard-core criminals.

In forty-six of the fifty United States, a commercial bail bondsman can post bail on behalf of an individual—for a nonrefundable fee, of course. By doing so, the bondsman is on the hook for the full amount of the bond if the subject doesn't show up on the appointed date.

Interestingly, the business of posting bail on behalf of another is illegal in the rest of the world.

As Jill Carver punches in Arthur Bedlington's Visa number, she's not worried about his friend showing up for court.

Almost all do, mostly because they might need her services again in the future. That's one bridge you don't want to burn.

For those who skip bail, well, Jill has a few special friends who are adept at tracking down those who don't want to be found. The modern term for them is bail enforcement agent, or just bail agent, but most people still call them bounty hunters.

"Okay, Mr. Bedlington. I've processed your payment and verified your friend's bail amount with the jail. These things take up to an hour, but I'll try to expedite this for you." She listens a moment. "No, if you're picking him up you can head over to the jail now. . . . That's correct. . . . As I said, I'll try to expedite things on my end."

She has no intention of expediting anything, but Mr. Bedlington doesn't know that, nor does his incarcerated friend. As far as Jill is concerned, the process takes however long the process takes, and if you don't like it, don't break the law.

The path to site two is illuminated by three light stands that are spaced about forty feet apart. Each has four adjustable lights that can be pointed up or down and rotate 360 degrees. Power is provided by the second generator, the hum of which grows louder as we make our way along the lit path.

Earlier in the afternoon, while the winter sun was still with us, we cleared the path of branches, broken limbs, and other debris as we anticipated the coming darkness and the long night ahead. One of the deputies showed up with a small chain saw and spent the better part of an hour clearing away the larger obstructions. The result is a walkway free of hazards, even in the dark.

Other hazards are not so easily mitigated.

For this reason, the Evidence Response Team routinely travels with a large assortment of containers that store the various items they may need while in the field. One of these containers is devoted to nothing but safety clothing and biohazard gear, everything from disposable coveralls and shoe covers to high-end encapsulated suits made of PVC.

An opaque plastic fifty-five-gallon barrel stands alone at site two.

Here is the final element of Murphy's so-called "fix," and as the truth of this place becomes shockingly apparent to all those gathered around, you can see the expressions on their faces begin to change.

"We've all seen body dumps before," I say. "This is . . . no different."

Even as I say the words I know it's a lie. The bodies of those who die violently are subject to the atrocious imaginations of their killers, but this usually means a shallow grave or a dumpster or a secluded spot under a pile of brush in the forest.

This *is* different.

Murphy is nothing if not efficient, and there's nothing quite as efficient when it comes to body disposal as dumping the remains in a barrel and then dissolving them with lye, provided you know how to safely handle corrosive chemicals and have a good place to dispose of the resulting sludge.

"Careful where you step," I say quietly, pointing to the ground.

The team members are so intensely fixated on the plastic fifty-five-gallon barrel that they haven't bothered to look where they're stepping—a cardinal sin for crime scene investigators. Still, you can hardly blame them. Only now, with the quiet prompting of my cautionary words, do they look down for the first time, staring with little comprehension at first, but then you see recognition in their eyes; finally, they understand.

Before them is a place of death.

As I watch them, I know exactly what they're feeling, for the same overwhelming sense of horror swept over me when I first cast eyes upon the scene. It's here that our seven victims ceased being human, their forms corrupted and washed away. The manner of their disposal seems to have affected everything around us, so that even the earth has a withered and spent look. The ferns that once flourished have long since vanished, and the place carries with it an odd smell—not necessarily of death, but neither is it life. It's a pungent in-between, the smell of purgatory.

Murphy's Misery, it seems, touches all things.

In the light from the LED lamps, the members of the Evidence Recovery Team take in the small patch of choked earth before them. The ground is littered generously with small bits of white here and there—a wash of scattered stones, or so it seems. Most are not much bigger than a kernel of corn . . . only these are no kernels, nor are they stones.

"He dumped the sludge here on the ground," I say. "By then, all that was left was calcium from the teeth and small bits of bone." Turning, I walk over to the fifty-five-gallon drum and stand to its side. Even now, in the artificial light, one can see through the opaque drum and tell that it's filled nearly to the top with a brownish liquid, as if a barrel of weak coffee has been brewed up and now awaits approval.

I gesture toward the plastic drum, careful not to touch it. "We're assuming victim number seven is still inside. As you know, sodium hydroxide, better known as lye, dissolves a body fairly efficiently. Unfortunately, it also means we won't get any DNA from the teeth or bone, so we'll have to rely on swabs from the face molds and the clothes."

What I don't tell them is that I can see the shine of all seven victims around the upper lip of the barrel. No doubt Murphy struggled to get them into the container. A dead body is an awkward thing, and moving one around takes patience and strength. After carrying them from the cabin, he would have been tired, and most likely he laid them on the edge of the barrel before repositioning and pushing them the rest of the way in.

The barrel would have been empty as he did this.

It's simply too dangerous to drop a hundred-and-thirty-pound corpse directly into a ready-made mix of lye and water; the splash it would create could be disastrous. Murphy would have known this, since he obviously did his homework; he would have known that one misjudged splash could burn or even blind him.

Every recipe has its order, and for human tea, that order calls for a body first, followed by a few gallons of sodium hydroxide, which is readily available in any hardware store in the form of ordinary household drain cleaner. After that, all Murphy had to do was top off the barrel with water and let simmer.

With both crime scenes examined and explained, we divide the group into two teams based on the special skills required at each site. Shepherd takes lead on the division of labor. He knows the capabilities of each member of his crew in shocking and comprehensive detail and has already assessed the requirements of each crime scene and the best person for each task. With little fanfare, he calls out names and team assignments with such prompt efficiency that in less than two minutes everyone knows exactly where they need to be and what they'll be doing.

And that's it.

The serious business of evidence collection commences,

and a new mood settles over the forest. As I walk back to the cabin, it occurs to me that I'm now the fifth wheel. The gathering has suddenly evolved into a double date: two forensics teams, and two crime scenes. It's unlikely that anyone will need a tracker at this point.

I'll make myself available, of course. If I can help, I'll help, but it's unlikely that I'll be much good to either team. Besides, anything I could have learned or discovered has already been identified. I had four hours to explore the area while we waited for the Evidence Response Team to arrive. There's nothing left for me to find.

Just as this discouraging thought begins to beat me over the head, a sudden revelation dances across my brainpan, something that will help us identify the victims, even if we don't manage to extract any usable DNA. Hurrying up the path, I spot the back of the young lab tech's head.

"George!" I call out. And when he pauses and turns, I hurry to close the distance. Grabbing him firmly by the elbow, I guide him forward, saying in a quiet voice, "You're in charge of crime scene photography at the cabin, right?"

He gives me a puzzled look. "Yeah; why?"

"Just grab your camera and meet me inside."

"Dude, I can't just grab my camera. I've got diffusers, light meters, measurement scales, a variety of lenses and filters, an electronic flash, tripods, and an angle-finder. On top of that, I've got to log every image—"

"Yeah-yeah-yeah," I say impatiently. "Just get it and meet me inside."

CHAPTER TWENTY-ONE

Tuesday, December 16

Jimmy is in a mood when we start the drive to Port Angeles the next morning.

I could blame it on exhaustion, but we've had worse—and we did manage to grab a few hours of sleep in Halsted's fifth-wheel. Still, the quality of one's sleep is just as important as the quantity, and if Jimmy's dreams were anything like mine, they included the recurring image of a melting woman crawling out of a fifty-five-gallon drum.

Not exactly the lullaby to a restful night.

"Hope this is worth it," Jimmy says from the driver's seat.

It's just the two of us. Jason was gracious enough to loan us his Ford for the interview with Murphy Cotton. The overnight search at the cabin turned up nothing new—if that were the case, a forty-five-minute drive to Port Angeles to see a mentally unstable suspect would be the last thing on our to-do list.

Jimmy is optimistic about a second interview with Murphy, but Jason doesn't share his enthusiasm. With the activity at the cabin still in full swing, he and Nate decided that they needed to stay at the crime scene and see things through.

"It's just gas and time," Jimmy mutters to the steering wheel.

The words aren't really meant for me, and seem to have no meaning or origin, since we weren't talking about gas *or* time. In fact, we weren't talking about much of anything. Perhaps he's running scenarios through his head, playing them out, trying to figure out the best way to crack open the nut that is Murphy Cotton.

"It's just gas and time," I echo.

The words stir something in Jimmy, and he glances over at me, as if emerging from a trance. "Murphy's just half our problem," he says with hard resolve. "If we don't figure out who the Onion King is—if we don't stop him—we'll have more of what we saw yesterday. He'll find someone else to do his bidding and we'll be right back where we started. That's why it's important that we get through to Murphy, get him talking." He throws his hands in the air. "I just don't know if we can."

"What's your gut tell you?"

Jimmy waits at a stop sign and then turns northbound on U.S. 101 before answering. "My gut? Well, I suppose if he's really suffering from grandiose delusional disorder, he wants to talk. He can probably barely contain himself. It would be like Einstein discovering the theory of relativity, and then not telling anyone. It's just not conceivable. I think the only thing that's keeping him from talking is the Onion King. Somehow, he's convinced Murphy that the secret *must* be protected, at least for now." He strums the steering wheel for a moment, deep in thought.

"I'll bet that's it," he says a moment later. "I'll bet the Onion King promised him something or said there'd be *more* recognition if the timing was right, if he waited until given the go-ahead."

"What if the Onion King helped Murphy perfect this so-called fix?" I ask. "Wouldn't that make him a coinventor? And if that was the case, he'd have some say in when they made the big announcement. The way Murphy idolizes him it wouldn't have been hard to control him."

And then a darker thought occurs to me.

"What if it was his idea to dissolve the bodies?"

Jimmy and I tend to do a lot of brainstorming in the field, and that's all my comment was meant to be. But as soon as I say it, I can see the idea settling heavily on my partner. "Somehow it seemed better when we thought Murphy came up with that," he says quietly.

We ride in silence for a few minutes, but all the while there's another thought nibbling at the corner of my mind. It's a question that first raised its head the day before yesterday, after Jimmy's first interview with Murphy. Now it's back, and this time it won't be ignored.

I look sideways at Jimmy long enough for him to notice, and when he gives me a questioning look, I say, "Why are we so sure they've never met in person?"

"Murphy said so," he replies. "Why? You think they have?"

"I don't know, but I don't want to ignore a possible lead. What if the Onion King is just as psychotic as Murphy? And if that's the case, wouldn't it be possible that they met at a treatment center somewhere?"

Jimmy chews this over and then states what I've been thinking. "You want to get a warrant for his medical records."

I shrug. "Diane's been mostly left out of this one, and she's probably champing at the bit right now. It would be nice if we could give her something to work with. Besides, at some point we have to go home. You know how cranky she gets when she doesn't get to play."

"Yeah," Jimmy replies with a snort and a good-natured

grin, "just slightly crankier than she is on any other given day—birthdays and holidays included."

"You can pick your friends," I reply, "but you can't pick your family and coworkers."

"Uh-huh. Remind me again, which one is she?"

Several months ago, I began writing letters to my girlfriend, Heather. It's not that she lives in France or some other far shore, it's just that our jobs keep us apart far too often. Heather is the owner, president, HTML coder, CEO, and head blogger at a website that specializes in crime stories, which is how we met.

Right now she's in Chicago researching a murder case that may have ties to Russian organized crime. Not exactly the type of case you want your girlfriend sticking her nose into, but if I mentioned this concern she'd start with her left hand and list all the serial killers I've helped chase down. And when she ran out of fingers, she'd switch to toes . . . and keep going until they were almost gone.

In any case, I write Heather letters so that she knows that I've been thinking of her during our time apart. Most of it is pointless observations, dreams, thoughts on the next first edition I want to add to my collection, and my feelings regarding the taste and texture of bok choy. The content is really irrelevant; it's the letter itself, the handwritten words, and the sentiment behind them that matter. When I'm traveling and she's not, often my letter doesn't even arrive in the mail until I'm home, but this too is irrelevant. Heather is like a schoolgirl whenever she gets one. I'm sure the thrill will wear off with time, though she denies this could ever happen.

The road is fairly smooth along this section of U.S. 101, so I break out my folder and retrieve a pen from the clip on the side. The exposed page on the right side has two paragraphs at the top, which I wrote on Sunday. Reading them quickly, I pick up right where I left off.

The words come easily.

I'm almost to the bottom of the page when Jimmy breaks his brooding silence. "I forgot Jane's birthday yesterday."

The words come as if in answer to a question I didn't ask, and it's clear that he's been chewing this over for some time, letting it gnaw at him and fester until he just couldn't take it any longer. That's the funny thing about Jimmy: just when you think you have him sorted out—you don't.

See, I thought he was quiet and withdrawn because he was thinking about the upcoming interview with Murphy. Turns out he's worried about something entirely different— and Jimmy can be pretty hard on himself, particularly when it comes to his family. Birthdays, holidays, school events, date nights—at some point he's missed them all . . . and more than once.

"I called her last night," he continues, "but the signal was weak, so I tried to keep it short. We talked for just a minute, and then she put Petey on. I think she was probably trying to get even with me for leaving her alone with him. The kid has completely lost his mind, and the closer we get to Christmas the worse it gets."

I chuckle at this, only because I've seen Petey when he's excited and I don't think there's an auctioneer on the planet who could outtalk him.

"Yeah, go ahead and laugh," Jimmy grumbles. "He's always been excited about the presents, but now that he's six I think he has a whole new understanding of Santa. His wish list last year included a Nerf gun and a Play-Doh press that makes dinosaurs. Take a guess what the number one thing on his list is this year."

"I have no idea—" I begin to answer, but Jimmy talks right over me.

"One of those Phantom drones, the ones that cost over fourteen hundred bucks—like I'm going to give my six-year-old a drone in the first place." He hesitates, and in a more subdued voice says, "When did Christmas get so complicated?"

"Since you made a little miniature of yourself," I reply with a clever smile.

He grimaces at me, but then relents and returns the smile. "Careful. Someday you're going to be in my shoes," he warns. The wicked grin that follows suggests that the Ghost of Christmas Future visited him last night and gave him some special insights.

"Anyway," he continues, "after talking to Petey, I completely forgot to say happy birthday to Jane." He shakes his head. "We were supposed to go to Anthony's for dinner, and she's been bugging me to take her to the Upfront Theatre."

"So, what you're saying is that you'd give up girls-in-a-barrel and Murphy's house of horrors just to go to dinner with your wife at Anthony's, followed by some comedy show?"

"Absolutely!"

I smile at the force behind his answer. "Well, it's a lucky thing you're married to the most understanding woman in the world. You could miss a hundred birthdays because of this job and she'd tell you not to give it a second thought."

Jimmy's quiet a moment. He knows it's true, but it still doesn't sit well with him. "That doesn't make it right," he finally replies.

I can't argue with that, so I don't.

We arrive at the Clallam County Jail at nine.

Sergeant Martin Thomas greets us and, after verifying our credentials and securing Jimmy's Glock, buzzes us through the security door into the facility. He pauses on the other side, waiting for the hydraulically loaded door to slowly close. When it finally seals into its casing and locks with a loud metallic clunk, it's as if a tomb were closing—only this tomb has lights.

With a wry smile, Sergeant Thomas presses a second button and the tomb begins to open on the other end, letting the world back in, only this world is vastly different from the one we just left.

The sparse intake hall is occupied by two inmates who are cuffed to separate steel benches, each irrevocably bolted to the floor.

"If you don't mind hanging out here a moment, I'll see if one of the interview rooms is free," the sergeant says. "We're a bit short-staffed, so things aren't movin' and shakin' as silky-smooth as we like, but we'll find a spot for you. If you call ahead, we can usually have things ready when you arrive."

"I should have thought of that," Jimmy replies. "It was a long night."

"Tell me about it," the sergeant replies, giving a weary sigh as he wheels around and wanders off in search of a vacant interview room.

Jimmy leans against the wall and watches him go. Pulling out his phone, he starts checking his messages and emails. I envy him. He's always been comfortable wherever he finds himself, but it's a little maddening that he can be so relaxed standing in the intake hall of a county jail with two inmates seated fifteen feet away.

I'm the exact opposite.

Just standing here I feel ill at ease. It's nowhere near as bad as being in the woods, which gives me anxiety that's often hard to manage, but the confined nature of a jail is so . . . confining. If I ever find myself on the wrong side of the bars, I'll be the first one lining up to cut a deal or snitch on my cellmate—whatever it took to get out.

I'd probably get shivved in the shower for my trouble.

"All right, sorry about that," Sergeant Thomas says, bustling back a moment later. "Looks like you lucked out. One of the public defenders just finished in room three. This way." He motions for us to follow.

I fall in behind Jimmy and march down a perpendicular hall and through another controlled door. Three doors down on the left, Sergeant Thomas deposits us in a sterile room with a metal table in the middle that's bolted to the floor. "That was a Mr. Murphy that you wanted to talk to, right?" he says from the doorway.

"No, his first name is Murphy, Murphy Cotton."

"Cotton—right." Something clicks in his head, and he asks, "Is he the one who had the girl in his trunk?"

"That's him."

"What was that all about? Ex-girlfriend or something?"

"No," Jimmy replies. "A little more complicated than that."

Sergeant Thomas accepts this and doesn't press further. "Give me a couple minutes and I'll round him up for you." Before closing the door, he asks, "Can I get either of you something to drink? Water, soda, maybe some orange juice?"

Jimmy declines, but an orange juice sounds good to me right about now and the sergeant seems happy to oblige.

A few minutes go by . . . then five . . . then ten.

We hear the footsteps before we see him; just one set of feet. Sergeant Thomas opens the door and steps halfway in, letting the door continue swinging open, as if preparing an exit for us. "Did this Murphy guy know you were coming?" he asks.

"No," Jimmy replies. I can't tell if it's concern or impatience that I hear in his voice. My first guess is that Murphy is with his lawyer, which could mean we're going to be here awhile. It could also mean that Murphy will follow the advice of said lawyer and refuse to speak to us. That's his constitutional right, of course, but that doesn't make it any less disappointing when you're sitting on my side of the table.

"Is he with someone?" I ask.

"Might be," Sergeant Thomas replies. When he doesn't elaborate, I shoot him a piercing stare that somehow reconnects his brain to his tongue. "What I mean to say is that if he *is* with someone I wouldn't have any way of knowing." He opens both palms to heaven in a supplicating gesture. "He's not here."

"What do you mean, he's not here?" Jimmy snaps.

"He made bail last night."

"How's that possible? The judge set bail at a million dollars, and there's no way he's had a bail reduction hearing in the time since."

Sergeant Thomas is shaking his head. "Bail was two thousand; I just looked it up. He posted through one of the local bond agencies."

Jimmy's stupefied. "What the hell's going on?" he practically spits. "The guy's a serial killer and you let him walk out the front door!"

The sergeant is taken aback. "No one said anything about him being a serial killer," he snaps in return. "And it wouldn't have mattered if they did. We've never had a mixup on bail amounts. If the computer says bail is two thousand, bail is two thousand."

Jimmy takes in a long, deep breath and lets it settle through his system. "You're right," he says a moment later in a much calmer voice. "Sorry for yelling. This is just—"

"Frustrating," I finish.

Jimmy points a finger at me in acknowledgment. Rising from his chair, he gathers his things. "Can you contact the sheriff immediately and let her know that Murphy is out? After that, contact whoever handles your information technology—"

"That would be the county IT division," Sergeant Thomas replies quickly.

Jimmy just nods. "Tell them we need a complete history of the bail record on Murphy: when it was entered, when changes were made, everything, and we need it in the next hour. Finally, get a hard copy of the arraignment document setting bail, and any updates, as well as the bail transaction details. Call the bonding agency and find out everything you can."

"Where do I contact you?"

"Not me," Jimmy replies, "Detective Sergeant Jason Sturman. You know him?"

He nods, and then says, "It's a small county."

As we exit the door and start up the hall, he calls after us. "Where are you going?"

"To catch a serial killer," I reply.

"Again," Jimmy adds in a low voice.

CHAPTER TWENTY-TWO

Meetings are hell.

I know this because when I was fifteen I read *Inferno* by Italian poet Dante Alighieri. In the book-length poem, Dante recounts his journey through Hell in the company of one of ancient Rome's greatest poets, Publius Vergilius Maro, better known as Virgil. His imaginative descriptions of the nine circles of Hell have stuck with me, and in recent years I've found myself applying them to meetings, of which I'm no fan.

As it turns out, Limbo is the First Circle of Hell. It comes from the Latin *limbus*, meaning edge or border, and, in Dante's masterpiece, represented the edge or border of Hell. Over time, limbo has come to represent a state of waiting or oblivion and is also regarded as an imaginary place to which forgotten or unwanted things and people are relegated.

It may be just me, but I find it an apt description for most meetings.

Inferno is also where we get the phrase, *Abandon all hope, ye who enter here.* As Dante and Virgil pass through the gates of Hell, the disquieting statement is inscribed above, as if perched like some eager vulture eyeing the newcomers.

The phrase is often presented as a warning, but it's not. A warning implies you have a choice, as if you arrive at the gate, see the ABANDON ALL HOPE sign, and say, *Eh, I think I'll go somewhere else.*

There's no escaping Hell.

Another thing meetings and the fiery abyss have in common.

I'd like to say that the meeting Jimmy and I walk in on at the sheriff's office is a First-Circle-of-Hell-type meeting, but that would be a stretch. Pitched words slam into us as we walk through the conference room door, propelled this way and that by at least three different voices all speaking at once and talking over one another in increasingly louder intonations.

I study the room quickly, knowing that Jimmy's doing the same.

Sheriff Angela Eccles is sitting quietly at the head of the table; I can't tell if she's angry or just disappointed. To her left is a bald man in his midfifties who I recognize as Undersheriff Warren.

On the other side of Angie sits Detective Sergeant Jason Sturman. If Angie's face is ambiguous, Jason's is very clear: he wants someone's head on a platter, perhaps garnished with a kidney. Nate is seated beside him, but he's clearly intent on keeping his mouth shut and presenting as low a profile in his chair as he can manage without actually sitting on the floor.

At the opposite end of the table is a bespectacled woman in her forties who is flanked by three associates who even without identification badges or pocket protectors would be readily recognized as IT-types. The IT boss, Becky, seems like a nice enough person, but what comes out of her mouth dispels that silly notion in less than three seconds.

Clustered on both sides of the table between these opposing forces sit ranking members of the Clallam County Jail, including the chief, two lieutenants, and the unfortunate Sergeant Thomas, who looks like he'd rather get a root canal or a colonoscopy than sit in this room any longer than absolutely necessary.

When Angie sees us, she motions to a pair of empty chairs next to Nate. The room grows suddenly and inexplicably quiet as Jimmy and I move around the table and take a seat. I don't like being at the center of attention, so as every eye in the room follows us across the carpet and into our respective chairs, my anxiety rises up like bad tequila.

"This is FBI Special Agent James Donovan and Operations Specialist Magnus Craig," Angie says by way of introduction. "They're the ones who led the hunt that resulted in the capture of Murphy Cotton."

She looks around the room, taking advantage of the temporary cease-fire. "Before we start assigning blame, I suggest we go through what we know. Everyone seems to have a different piece of the puzzle that explains how Murphy was released, so let's put it all together before we decide who to lynch." She looks directly at Becky and asks, "Does that sound like a plan?"

The head of IT gives a slow, unrepentant nod.

The truth of Murphy's jailbreak is more troubling than we imagined. It was no mere clerical error that set him free, but a sophisticated attack on the county's mainframe.

The county's secure network had been breached first, which gave the hacker indirect access to the jail system. At 4:53 P.M. the previous afternoon, Murphy's bail was changed from one million dollars to a paltry two thousand dollars—a sum usually demanded for crimes like drunk driving or punching a guy in the face.

Roughly an hour later, at 5:57 P.M., the True Bond bail agency in Port Angeles posted bail for Murphy after receiving a Mastercard payment from Mr. Arthur Bedlington of Seattle. This was all news to Mr. Bedlington when Detective Sergeant Sturman called him an hour ago. He stated quite emphatically that he didn't know anyone named Murphy Cotton, had never called a bail bond agency in this life, let alone the previous day, nor had he authorized the use of his credit card to post bail.

While Jason was on the phone with him, Bedlington checked his account information and confirmed that two hundred dollars had indeed been charged to his account by the True Bond bail agency in Port Angeles—the ten percent fee required to post the bail. After this discovery, it was impossible to get anything else out of him. He just wanted to call his bank and cancel his card before more charges popped up, as if having his account used to secure the release of a serial killer was the least of his concerns.

It's now Sergeant Thomas's turn.

Holding up two unlabeled DVDs in individual plastic cases, he states that they contain video of the jail parking lot. He then goes into some detail explaining how he came up with the idea to check the video—like that had never been done before—and no one was more surprised than he to see Murphy strolling across the parking lot and getting into a car.

Using his department-issued laptop and a borrowed Epson projector, he plays the video against the pull-down screen at the front of the conference room. The video is awful. It's everything I've come to expect from video surveillance.

You can tell the car is a silver four-door—most likely an

import. It pulls up to the sidewalk right as Murphy reaches the curb and seems to startle him. He hesitates and then stoops to look through the passenger window, as if talking to someone. A moment later, Murphy opens the door and gets into the car. Then, like a cart on rails, the silver sedan zips through the parking lot and disappears off-screen.

The only good news is you can see the front, side, and back of the car at various points as it stops for Murphy and then hurries from the lot. The images may be horrible, but I can see the general configuration of the taillights, the position of the license plate, the location of the third brake light, and other identifying features. To most, these points would be useless.

"Can I get one of those?" I ask, gesturing toward the duplicate DVDs.

When the sergeant hesitates, Jason snaps, "Give him one of the damn DVDs!" He flings his hand at the sergeant in an irritated manner. "They can do more with it than we can."

That's only partly true.

I'll be passing the video on to Dexter Allen at the Whatcom County Sheriff's Office back in Bellingham. He has a special program he developed over several years that allows him to analyze vehicle images based on different criteria. In some cases, he can identify a car right down to the make, model, and exact year of production. This information, when cross-referenced against the state's Department of Licensing database, has helped identify a significant number of suspect vehicles.

After everyone has finally said their piece, Angie looks across the long table at Becky and asks the one question yet to be answered: "So, how'd they get in?"

"We're efforting that as we speak," Becky replies, sounding for a moment like one of the NASA technicians out of the movie *Armageddon*.

"Meaning you don't know."

"Meaning whoever hacked us is very good," Becky shoots back with all the venom of a pissed-off pit viper, "and they obviously found a vulnerability in our system that we weren't aware of."

"That's just great," Jason mutters.

"You have something to say?" Becky snaps.

Her dislike of the detective sergeant is clear as soon as the words escape her lips. Perhaps this is simply because she dislikes *all* cops, or it could be that she feels herself way above his pay grade and in a position where she shouldn't have to tolerate any disparaging remarks he might throw her way. Wasn't it bad enough that she had to put up with the sheriff?

"Oh, I have a few things to say," Jason begins, but then checks himself and glances at Angie for the briefest of moments. When she makes no effort to restrain him, he continues.

"We've been saying for years that we need a server that's separate from the county," he growls. "Instead, you continue to lump us in with road maintenance, human resources, and all the other noncritical county departments. I mean, really: Who gives a crap if the Parks Department gets hacked?" He gives an exaggerated shrug to emphasize the point.

"The sheriff's office, the courts, and the jail all deal with confidential information. I'm talking about records and court proceedings that can either deprive people of their freedom or set them free."

He glances around the table. "We just let a serial killer walk out the jail door," he says, his tone suggesting that he still can't believe it himself. "I don't even want to *think* what's going to happen when the press and the public find out about this—and they will. If I have to tell them myself, they will."

Tapping straight down onto the tabletop with his rigid index finger, he says, "We need a dedicated system maintained by personnel who answer to the sheriff's office, not IT. That means personnel who can pass the same polygraph exam and background investigation that all our deputies and support personnel are required to pass." He locks eyes with Becky, letting the full weight of his words press upon her.

The year before, she'd been arrested for driving under the influence. After a search of her pockets during booking, deputies found a baggie of eighty-milligram OxyContin pills, a frequently abused prescription painkiller. She worked a plea deal that included treatment, and managed to keep her job, but this didn't sit well with the sheriff's office, which expressed legitimate concerns about someone with a drug history having access to every aspect of the criminal justice computer system.

It takes Becky but a moment to digest Jason's meaning, and then all hell breaks loose, and the room reverberates once more with the echoes of raised voices, shouts, and accusations.

Just like that, we're back in the *Inferno*.

The room is still loud and oppressive five minutes later when Jimmy's phone rings. Checking the caller ID, he elbows me and tips his head toward the door. The phone is on its fourth ring by the time we make it to the relative quiet of the hallway, and Jimmy quickly answers on speakerphone before the call disconnects.

"Haiden," he says by way of greeting. "I've got you on speaker. What's up?"

"Hey, Jimmy," the FBI computer forensics expert replies in a voice that somehow manages to simultaneously convey alarm, surprise, excitement, and fear. "Remember how you asked me to keep an eye on that draft document in Murphy's email account?"

"Yeah, why? Did something change?"

"The numbers," Haiden Webber replies. "I checked the account a couple minutes ago and the numbers looked . . . different. At first I thought maybe I was remembering them wrong, but since I'd written the two original strings of numbers on a Post-it note and stuck it to the screen, I was able to compare them against the draft." He takes a deep and audible breath. "The beginning of each number is the same, but the last half has changed."

"New coordinates!" Jimmy utters the words as if they're a curse.

"What's that mean," Haiden presses, "another victim?"

"That would be my guess. Any idea how recently the draft was changed?"

"It was sometime in the last two hours. I've been trying to check at least every hour during the day, and every four hours in the evening and at night, but it's hit-or-miss. We had a staff meeting that ran long and I just checked it when I got back a few minutes ago."

Jimmy sighs. "Well, we've had some changes on this end as well. Murphy made bail last night. He's been in the wind for almost eighteen hours and we just found out this morning. Do you think he has access to that email account through another computer or device?"

"I'd almost guarantee it," Haiden replies. He has more questions, of course, many more questions, but right now there's just no time.

Jimmy promises to call later and fill him in, and then asks Haiden to text the new coordinates to his phone. When he hangs up a few seconds later, we stare at each other for a long and dreadful moment, and then he pockets the phone and, at a fast walk, leads the way back into the conference room.

With an urgent swipe of his hand, he motions for Jason and Nate to join us. They pop from their chairs as if the cushions were spring-loaded and hurry around the table.

When Sheriff Eccles looks at Jimmy with a concerned expression on her face, a pained visage that begs for good news rather than bad, he simply says, "The coordinates in Murphy's email account were just changed." She immediately understands the implications.

No more words are necessary, but Jimmy says them anyway: "We need to get there before Murphy does."

CHAPTER TWENTY-THREE

The town of Quilcene, Washington, population 596, is an isolated cluster of buildings around U.S. 101 that one might miss entirely if they happened to glance down to change the radio while driving by. Located on the Hood Canal, a fifty-mile stretch of natural waterway that defines the eastern edge of the Olympic Peninsula and separates it from the much smaller Kitsap Peninsula, it's a place of natural beauty and horrifying forests.

In fairness to the town, almost everyone on the planet would find the forests and endless march of trees absolutely delightful. I'm not one of them. Hypothermia and death have a way of anchoring such opinions.

The town was named for the Quilcene, the saltwater people who originally inhabited the area. They were one of nine groups of Coast Salish peoples, collectively known as Twana, who once lived along the length of the canal.

Of the nine, only the Skokomish remain.

I blame the trees.

Like Quilcene, the Falls View waterfall is easy to miss but not hard to find. Those who seek it need only travel along U.S. 101 to the Falls View Campground just four miles southwest of Quilcene. It's a magnificent waterfall, though it lacks the volume of its bigger brothers—and dries up completely four or five months out of each year.

We neither sought the waterfall nor stumbled upon it by accident. Rather, we were led here by a digital marker on a GPS, a location dictated by a latitude and longitude entered into a draft email in a psychotic's personal email account.

As we hike into the area, I can't help thinking that the coordinates are bait, and we're the eager rats walking into a trap. Perhaps like the rats we found in Murphy's fifth-wheel, their dissected corpses wearing miniature plaster masks just like the mannequins at Murphy's Misery.

Even under normal conditions I'm anxious among the trees. This sudden, paranoid thought about traps and creepy rats sends my anxiety into overdrive and I find my eyes casting about, my six senses trying to take in everything at once and absorbing nothing.

That's why I don't see it right away.

I'm ten feet behind Jimmy and Detective Halsted, and just stepping around Nate, when I realize the group has stopped. Seven sets of eyes are staring ahead and to the left, and when my gaze follows, I see what fixes their attention so firmly. With a sharp, involuntary gasp, I take several stumbling steps backward.

The base of the waterfall is just a stone's throw away—so close I can feel its mist upon my face. Like a shimmering white-and-silver ribbon, it stretches from the overhang two hundred feet above, down to the plunge pool below.

Its movement is like a ballet of water, mist, and fleeting rainbows—an undulating dance to music that only the water can hear . . . but it's not the waterfall that captures my attention.

Instead, my eyes are drawn to a spot ten feet off the trail where a body sits with its back up against a Douglas fir. The body hears no music, sees no waterfall, feels no condolences. It sits facing us, as if contemplating our purpose. A bullet hole the size of a pea is drilled into its forehead just to the left of dead center.

"You've got to be kidding me," I hear Nate mutter.

"Secure the scene," Jason says in a quiet but solid voice. Without another word, the four Clallam County detectives begin searching the area for evidence while the two Jefferson County patrol deputies who joined us in Quilcene start stringing yellow police tape.

Crouching in front of the body, I stare into the dead eyes. One of them is slightly misshapen, a result of trauma inside the skull caused by the violent entry of the bullet. Based on the size of the hole and the fact that the skull is otherwise intact, I suspect the killer used a .22-caliber handgun.

There's stippling around the wound, so this was up close.

The eyes bother me. You would expect that most people would die with their eyes closed, as if they'd gone to sleep. In my experience that's not the case. That said, my opinion on this matter may be slightly skewed, since most of the bodies I see died suddenly or violently. I suppose there's something about a bullet penetrating your skull that pops your eyes open and keeps them there. Still, it's disquieting when you look into them and no one looks back.

"Clouded over," I say to Jimmy, gesturing at the eyes.

"So, death was at least three hours ago," he replies.

Aside from the pupils dilating upon death, the potassium in red blood cells begins to break down, causing the eyes to cloud over. This process takes about three hours and is sometimes a better indicator of time of death than rigor mortis or livor mortis.

Standing, I brush the leaves and dirt from my knees. "Didn't you say that the Onion King was squeamish about doing his own killing? I thought that's why he brought Murphy into his little freak show and helped him perfect his *fix*." I put the word in air quotes.

"It's not the first time I've been wrong," Jimmy replies. He glances over at me. "Probably won't be the last."

"So . . . where does this leave us?"

Jimmy wipes his hands on the bottom of his jacket and sighs. "I suppose it's a race now, only we have no idea where the finish line is or even what direction we're supposed to run. We've got a serial rapist out there who just decided to do his own killing."

Pulling his jacket tight against the chill, he adds, "I'm afraid he might grow to like it." Looking down at the empty husk that was Murphy Cotton, he turns and walks away.

CHAPTER TWENTY-FOUR

Betsy is finishing her climb to ten thousand feet, cutting through the sky in a northeasterly direction that will take us back to Bellingham and a much-needed reprieve from the simmering nightmare wrought by Murphy Cotton and the Onion King.

The Gulfstream G100 is configured to seat eight passengers. When Jimmy wants to rest or be left alone he'll take one of the seats at the tail of the plane, but normally we're seated as we are now, near the middle of the fuselage in chairs facing each other with a small table between us.

Jimmy didn't say much on the drive north to Port Angeles, so when we boarded Betsy at the airport I was a bit surprised that he took the seat opposite me; I just assumed he'd want to be left alone.

"Something's bothering you," I say when he remains silent.

He looks up . . . and in that look and that moment I realize how understated the words are. There are a million things about this case that would give one pause, but the killing of Murphy Cotton has affected Jimmy in a way I've rarely seen.

He shakes his head and mutters, "Dark wolf rising."

"Say again?"

He looks away, his eyes finding the window and the angry sky beyond. "It's something a friend used to say," he finally replies, his eyes still on the window: "Dark wolf rising—the perpetual struggle between good and evil."

I wait for him to continue and prod him when he doesn't. "What's that mean?"

He looks at me now, a blank stare on a whitewashed face. After a few seconds, he seems to return to himself and sighs deeply, saying, "Sorry. This case . . ."

"I know."

He just nods. "Did I ever tell you about my friend Danny Bear Cloud? We served together in the 460th Security Forces Squadron in Aurora, Colorado."

"Yeah, wasn't he Cheyenne or something? Taught you a few things about tracking before you knew where it would lead you?"

"Crow, actually, out of Montana. And the tracking he taught me was limited to animals. It was Danny who first got me interested in hiking and camping, among other things. More importantly, he was a good storyteller; around the campfire, in the office, in the car, it didn't really matter where you were, it seemed he had a story or legend for just about any occasion."

Jimmy smiles, but it's a small smile, a distracted smile, the expression of one whose thoughts are still a thousand miles away. "Danny always took special pleasure in educating the *yellow eyes* about Indian ways."

"Yellow eyes?"

"*Mah-ish-ta-schee-da*," Jimmy says, pronouncing every syllable fully. "The literal translation is *eyes yellow*. It's what the Crow called the whites—never *white man* like you see in the movies, just *yellow eyes*. The name supposedly goes back to the first meeting of the two races; whether they were a trapping party or explorers, I don't know. One or more of them may have had jaundice, or at least that's the going theory for the reference."

"Okay. That's kind of cool," I say with an approving nod.

Jimmy smiles now. "Danny taught me at least a hundred Crow words, and of all these it's *mah-ish-ta-schee-da* that I remember. Whenever I didn't learn something quickly enough, or if I made a mistake identifying a track, Danny would throw his hands up and call me *yellow eyes* in the flowing language of the Crow—always with a subtle smile on his face, though.

"His way of motivating me was to say that little Crow children could do this or that by the time they could walk. This only made me try harder—which was the point, I suppose. Still, no matter how good I got, I was always *mah-ish-ta-schee-da*."

"And what did Danny mean by the dark wolf thing?" I ask, bringing the conversation back around to the original question.

Jimmy nods. "The Security Forces Squadron is the Air Force equivalent of military police, so Danny and I saw our share of assaults, bar fights, and the usual idiots bumping chests and getting in each other's faces. On occasion we'd respond to a situation that really got out of hand, more than the usual bloody noses and scraped knuckles. It's after these that I'd often hear Danny mutter, 'Dark wolf rising,' and shake his head the way he did when disapproving of something.

"I heard him say it three or four times in the first few months we worked together. I didn't know him well at that point, so it took a while before I asked him what he was talking about. Turns out it's an old Cherokee legend about the two wolves that reside within each of us: a dark wolf that is evil, and a light wolf that is good. The dark wolf feeds on anger, envy, lies, sorrow, greed, arrogance, and all the negative traits we display. The light wolf is just the opposite, and feeds on joy, peace, love, hope, understanding, truth, and compassion. These wolves are constantly at war with each other, one trying to gain dominance over the other. In the legend, a young Cherokee boy asks his grandfather which wolf will eventually win. The old Cherokee simply replies, 'The one you feed.'

"When Danny saw people arguing or fighting, he didn't view it the way you or I would. He saw it with different eyes, as if he could actually see them feeding the dark wolf . . . and the dark wolf rising, growing stronger, becoming more dominant."

Jimmy shakes his head slowly. "The Onion King didn't want to do his own killing, which is why he recruited Murphy. In the meantime, he's been feeding his dark wolf, which has grown stronger. Now he finds that he *can* kill; maybe he even likes it. I don't think he'll need a disposal guy after this." Looking at me, he says, "Dark wolf rising," in a whispery voice that borders on the ominous.

I want to tell him I understand, but the words don't come. He sees it on my face and in my eyes nonetheless. Pushing back in my chair, I contemplate his words as he starts reviewing case notes.

Before dropping us off at the airport, Jason had handed me a manila envelope that contained a copy of the only real surprise discovered during the search of Murphy's cabin. It's a thirty-two-page document that was shoved up underneath one of the cabinet drawers in the kitchen. It's handwritten in Murphy's messy scrawl. I glanced at it briefly when he handed it to me, and then dropped it into my backpack.

As Jimmy starts pounding away on his laptop, getting a

head start on the case report, which is going to be extensive, it seems I have about thirty minutes of flight time to kill before we land in Bellingham; I can't stand the thought of sitting idle, so I open my backpack and find the manila envelope. Sliding the thirty-two-page document free, I lay it on the table and start at the beginning.

By page three my mind is reeling.

By page ten I can contain myself no longer. "Are you sure Murphy had this . . . what did you call it? Delusional disorder?"

Jimmy looks up from his keyboard. "Grandiose delusional disorder," he replies. "And no, I'm not even close to sure. That would have required extensive tests and interviews, which obviously we can't do now."

"Because he's room temperature."

"Exactly."

"But if you had to guess, you'd stick with grandiose delusional disorder?"

Jimmy thinks about the question a moment before answering. "I'm not sure. I think that's part of it, but after finding the cabin and the barrels, I can't help wondering if something else was going on. It's not uncommon for someone with mental illness to have multiple disorders."

"Like what?"

Jimmy shifts thoughtfully in his seat. "Well, to paraphrase a commercial, I don't always diagnose people with mental disorders, but when I do, I prefer the *DSM-5*."

The *Diagnostic and Statistical Manual of Mental Disorders*, or *DSM*, is the American Psychiatric Association's go-to reference for thousands of mental disorders, from the benign to the extreme. The manual is generally referred to by edition, and since the version released in 2013 is the fifth update, it's simply called *DSM-5*.

Jimmy has the ebook version on his laptop.

I've never really taken the time to look through it, mostly

because Jimmy's the one with the master's degree in psychology and I defer to his judgment in such matters. Also, I have enough trouble keeping ahead of my own phobias; I don't need to spend time exploring the peculiarities of others.

"Have you checked to see if Murphy fits into any other categories?"

"No," Jimmy replies soberly. "It's pointless now, don't you think?"

I give him a surrendering shrug.

"Why the sudden interest?" he asks.

I pick up the left-hand stack of papers from the document and hold them aloft. "There's some pretty crazy stuff in here. He talks about transcending his victims, whatever that means. There's a lot of the same blather about the face being the place of the soul, and about the necessity to destroy the corruption if the soul is to be free. I'm assuming that's why he dissolved the bodies."

"Any mention of the Onion King?"

"Over and over again," I reply, "and always in glowing terms. It's like he worshipped the guy, which, in a way, I guess he did. He certainly laid down some sacrifices at his feet."

"Any clues as to who he is?"

"Nothing," I reply. "I think Murphy was telling the truth when he said he'd never met him in the . . . what did he call it? The three-dimensional?"

"Yeah, that one's a keeper; we should probably write it down."

Leafing through the stack of papers, I find one with a dog-ear. "I marked a couple pages where the Onion King discussed mental health issues with Murphy. Kind of reminds me of some of the things that come out of your mouth." I nod when he glances my way. "Makes me think the Onion King might be in the mental health profession."

"Like a psychiatrist?"

"Probably not, but remember what I told you when I first learned you had a degree in psychology?"

Jimmy screws up his face and tries to look indignant. "Yeah, that most of the people who get a degree in psychology do so by accident."

"Uh-huh. By taking classes they think will help them sort out their own issues," I finish, flashing him a good-natured grin, which he can't help returning.

Picking up the Pilot G2 gel pen from beside his laptop, he rolls it back and forth between his thumb and index finger as he ponders the idea. "I suppose that makes sense. It seems to me that *most* people with phobias, compulsions, and other disorders spend at least some time researching the subject." He looks me up and down in an appraising manner. "Take you, for example."

"Me? Why me?"

"Because you're afraid of forests."

"So! Lots of people are afraid of forests."

"True, but most people are just spooked or a bit anxious in the woods. Your anxiety is more extreme, and it hasn't gotten better over the years, though you mask it well. More to the point, when you realized you had this unreasonable fear of forests, you took the time to research it and learned that it's called hylophobia. You claim it was triggered when you were eight years old and froze to death in the forest, but I think part of it may be genetic, considering how superstitious and anxiety-ridden your mother is."

I can't argue with the point, so I don't.

"You're also afraid of Styrofoam," Jimmy continues, "which is a bit odd, but you recently told me that a good number of Americans suffer from it. How many was it?"

"About a quarter million."

"And you know this how?"

"I looked it up," I reply grudgingly.

Jimmy smiles at the admission. "My point is that you don't have to be a psychologist to know some of the terminology. For all we know, the Onion King is a self-indulgent computer geek in his mom's basement who likes raping women and gets off on manipulating those who suffer with real mental illness."

The stack of pages marked up with Murphy's sloppy scrawl are still in my hand and I place them back on the table, making the document complete.

"Well, whether he's a psychiatrist or just a psycho, you need to read this," I say, gesturing at the document. "Maybe you can pick up on something I missed."

Tipping his chin at the document, Jimmy says, "Flag anything you think I need to see and I promise I'll take a look when we get home." With that he seems to refocus on his laptop and the lengthy report waiting to be written.

A moment later, after I've turned my own eyes back to Murphy's manifesto, Jimmy offers a final thought: "Did you know that caffeine withdrawal is now classified as a psychiatric disorder in the *DSM*?"

And then it hits me: he hasn't had a cup of coffee all day.

Murderous rampages have started for less.

Twenty minutes later we're beginning our descent into Bellingham International Airport when a question occurs to me. It's not case-related, nor is it relevant to anything else we're doing, but it's one of those questions that pops up and won't go away.

"What ever happened to Danny Bear Cloud?" I ask, genuinely interested. "Do you still keep in touch?"

Jimmy shifts in his seat and it's a full ten seconds before he answers.

"He's gone."

"Gone?"

"Dead," Jimmy clarifies.

For a moment I feel like someone took a sledgehammer to my chest. "Sorry," I practically whisper, and then I say it a second time without knowing why: "Sorry, Jimmy." The how of it still hangs between us unanswered, and I can't help but press.

"He was killed in a terrorist attack on Bagram Airfield in Afghanistan." He pauses for a long moment, his eyes looking past me at nothing. When he continues, the words come slowly, each one strained, as if it were a scab ripped from his soul. "I was with his family at the Billings airport when he came home."

He falls quiet then, and I embrace the low rumble of the engine, willing it to wrap me in white noise and hide me away, willing it to take back the question and the memory it stirred.

CHAPTER TWENTY-FIVE

Wednesday, December 17

I'm a perpendicular.

By this I mean that while most people work, act, and think in parallel with one another, I often find myself heading ninety degrees away from them. Not in the contrarian or devil's advocate sort of way, which can be both obstinate and confrontational, but rather in a way that's dictated by how I look at the world, and how I go about solving problems.

One of the benefits of being a perpendicular is that I can't be bullied into an opinion: I either believe it or I don't . . . and when I don't, I at least try to be diplomatic about it—most of the time. Peer pressure means nothing to me, yet vexes me with hints of disapproval. I'm the least likely to jump off a cliff simply because my friends do, yet at the same time I'm terribly concerned about how people look at me, and how they think of me.

I realize that almost everyone suffers to one degree or another from that sense that all eyes are upon them, watching, waiting for them to trip or make a mistake. For some it's so bad that they dare not leave the house, building for themselves a prison that only their mind can see. The laughable truth is that the people we think are judging us are too busy worrying about us judging them to even notice us.

That's what I call irony.

When it comes to perpendiculars, there have always been those who aren't, yet who try to claim the mantle simply by being contrary. In the sixties they cried, "Peace, love, dope!" and burned their bras and their draft cards. In the seventies it was disco and bell-bottoms—seriously, what were they thinking? The more they tried to be perpendicular, the more they found that others were suddenly traveling in the same direction, and pretty soon they were all parallel again.

None of this made them perpendiculars, it just made them nonconformist.

A true perpendicular *thinks* differently than others. Not always, but often.

In my case, I suppose I could blame this on my accident, the mishap in the woods, the little episode that killed me and brought me back . . . well, different. But that seems too simplistic, almost like a cop-out. The more logical explanation is that I was always this way, and the eight-year-old version of me just didn't realize it at the time.

Dexter Allen is also a perpendicular.

The crime analyst for the Whatcom County Sheriff's Office is the type of guy who would tip a room thirty degrees to starboard if he could, just to see it from a different angle. He once told me that when he works on jigsaw puzzles he'll alternate between looking at the developing picture straight on and looking at it upside down. He says it helps him see what he might otherwise miss.

I tried it once.

I saw an upside-down puzzle.

———

As I pull into the Starbucks on Bakerview Road, I spot Dex's crappy old car shoved dismissively into a spot at the end of the parking lot. He's like Jimmy when it comes to transportation: if it still goes down the road, it's still worth driving, but there's no love between car and driver.

It's Wednesday morning, which means the intel group is meeting.

It's not what I or anyone else would call an *official* meeting, but rather a once-weekly excuse to binge on coffee and unplug from the constant demands of law enforcement, even if it's only for an hour. The fact that cases have been advanced and a few even solved at these meetings is just frosting on the cake.

And while much of the discussion relates to law enforcement in one way or another, there are no rules or limitations. One week they might be opining on the lunacy of North Korea's leadership, and the next, the lunacy of social media. Lunacy always seems to make an appearance in one form or another.

No topic is off-limits and anything that even smells of political correctness is soundly beaten and sent scurrying from the premises.

The size of the group might change from week to week, but there are three regulars you can pretty much count on. Aside from Dex, there's Kevin, a longtime detective with the Whatcom County Sheriff's Office, and Thom, a special agent with Homeland Security Investigations.

Other detectives often join the mix, and it's never dull.

I've known Kevin almost as long as I've known Dex. He's the lead detective on the Jess Parker cold case, which has been a pet project of mine since before I started at the Special Tracking Unit. Jimmy and I have always referred to it as the Leonardo case because the killer posed Jess like Leonardo da Vinci's Vitruvian Man. The cops on scene only saw her feet pointing south, and her arms spread wide pointing to the east and west. Her shine told a different story. I saw where he first splayed her legs and raised her arms, and where the sick bastard walked a nearly perfect circle around the body.

The Vitruvian Man.

Dex and Kevin only recently learned of this peculiarity.

Jess Parker's was the first in a string of murders that began eleven years ago—or at least we *think* she was the first. The truth is we don't really know. I was sixteen when she was abducted, and though I'd already been using shine to find the missing for several years, hers was the first homicide case I was asked to assist with, brief though my involvement was.

Between Dex, Kevin, and Thom, the intel group has close to eighty years of combined law enforcement experience, and when you get the three of them together at one table it makes for a lively discussion and some pretty amazing insights.

That's what I'm hoping for this morning: insights.

Much as I enjoy their company, right now I need the group's wisdom more than their wit and war stories.

In my pocket I have a thumb drive of the pictures that George, the young ERT tech, took for me Monday night at Murphy's Misery. That was just a day and a half ago, yet with all that's happened since, it feels more like a week.

It's just a thought—perhaps a crazy thought—but these images may provide a way of speeding up the victim identification process. It's something I've never attempted before, so I'm keeping my optimism in check. Still, succeed or fail, we have nothing to lose by trying, and I'm hoping Dex can help me with that.

Aside from the thumb drive, I have a DVD that contains surveillance video from the jail parking lot. I'm fairly certain

Dex will be able to examine the images of the fleeing sedan and narrow down the make and model.

Several years ago, frustrated with the poor quality of video surveillance, he developed a process called forensic vehicle analysis. It uses more than fifty identifiable criteria, or markers, that are often visible even on the most deplorable of images. I've sat next to Dex a dozen times as he's studied grainy images and somehow extracted details that others would miss, details that helped lead to the identification of the vehicle and, in some cases, the driver.

The warmth of the coffee shop envelopes me as I step through the door and shake off the cold. The fireplace in the corner burns brightly and the smell of coffee and pastry washes over me, presenting an altogether pleasing sensation. Though I'm no fan of coffee as a drink, I find the smell pleasing, even invigorating.

Glancing to my right, I spot the intel group immediately.

It's no surprise where I find them. The table where they sit may as well be branded with their names, because on Wednesday mornings they own it.

Dex calls out my name as I approach, prompting similar calls from Kevin and Thom. The ruckus raises a few heads around us, but the other patrons quickly return to their own conversations and coffee, finding me of little account.

Thom steals a chair from a neighboring table before I'm halfway across the room, placing it between himself and Kevin.

After a few minutes of catching up, which includes the latest on a recent murder-for-hire that didn't go so well for the suspect, Dex notices the DVD in my hand and lifts his chin toward it.

"Is that a Christmas present?" he asks with a grin.

"Only if you're a masochist," I reply, handing the disk

across to him. Over the next ten minutes I lay everything out for them, starting with the police chase and ending with the discovery of Murphy's body at Falls View.

"Now, that's a case!" Thom says in a sober voice when I finish. The words seem to capture the sentiment of the entire group.

"The disk holds video and some stills from the jail parking lot," I tell Dex. "It's pretty far away and grainy, but I was hoping you could do your magic and give me an idea of what kind of vehicle I'm looking for." As I speak, I dig into my pocket and extract the thumb drive, which I place in the center of the table.

"Well, this gets more interesting by the moment," Kevin says, shifting his gaze from the thumb drive, to me, and then back at the thumb drive.

"More vehicle images?" Dex guesses.

"Photos of the death masks," I reply.

He gives me an odd look, so I quickly explain.

"A while back, you mentioned that the Department of Licensing had just purchased facial recognition software, which they can run against millions of images in their system."

Dex nods. "Anyone with a driver's license or ID card issued by the state. We had some success with it last month on a fraud case, but"—he pauses to look at me—"you seriously want to run photos of death masks through facial recognition?"

"Why not?"

He shakes his head but doesn't seem to have a good answer. Eventually he shrugs. "I guess it might work. The software uses an algorithm that analyzes the size, shape, and relative position of facial features. As long as the lighting isn't skewed and there's no excessive emotion or exaggerated expression on the face—"

"*Is* there an emotion for dead?" Thom asks, only half serious.

"I've seen emotion on dead faces," Kevin chimes in. "Most of the time you can't really tell what they were feeling, but other times . . ." He shakes his head. "I've seen fear, shock, anger, even peace—frozen right there on their faces clear as a winter's day." He taps the table. "I had a suicide a couple months ago where the guy hanged himself from a beam in the garage with an extension cord. I just remember the stubborn look on his face, like he was absolutely determined to be dead."

"Sounds like he got his wish," Thom quips.

"He did. Unfortunately, it was his kids who found him."

Thom shakes his head and clicks his tongue, saying, "That's just wrong."

"I don't know about all that," I say, "but Murphy Cotton sure seemed surprised to find a bullet hole in his forehead."

"There you go," Kevin says, as if I just proved his point.

"As far as the facial expressions and lighting," I say, turning my attention back to Dex, "they mostly have slack looks on their faces with their mouths mostly closed. We had the Evidence Response Team with us, and it was one of their guys who took the photos, so they should be good images."

Dex nods, seeming more comfortable with the idea. "Facial recognition has advanced a lot in the last few years," he explains, "especially with companies like Google and Facebook jumping into the game—not to mention the banks and security firms."

As he continues to speak, the words take on the reflective tone of internal dialogue, and for a moment it appears as if his mind has wandered down a side alley and left the rest of us behind. "The nodal points *are* based on rigid bone and tissue areas like the eye sockets, the nose, and the chin," he mutters, "all features that a death mask would capture. If the images are straight-on, that is." His expression is briefly troubled, but then he continues. "Though the FBI photographer would have made sure of that . . . that's what they train for."

He lets the words linger, and then seems to come to a conclusion. His mind returns from wherever it had strayed, and he fixes me with a thoughtful gaze. "All things considered, the likelihood of a positive recognition should be pretty good."

"Which is all we need," I reply. "We might get a DNA hit off the clothing, we might not. I just want to have other options."

"I don't know," Kevin says, setting his iced latte on the table and then wiping the condensation from the side with a napkin. "If they've been missing more than a couple months there's a chance their DNA will be in CODIS."

"Provided someone reported them missing," I agree.

He nods his understanding. "You think they're the type that doesn't get reported."

"It's just a hunch," I say. "Murphy kept saying they were broken, but never explained how or why. When you think about the victimology and the serial nature of the crimes, my guess is they're mostly prostitutes."

"What about the one from the trunk?" Dex asks.

"Charice Qian," I say. "Diane found some minor arrests for shoplifting, possession of stolen property, and theft, but she's also been arrested for heroin. Worked a drug court plea on the first arrest and did twelve months on the second. I wouldn't have pegged her for a heroin user, at least not a regular user. She's not hollowed out like your typical addict."

"Maybe she's been on the wagon and recently slipped," Thom suggests, drawing a unified murmur of agreement. It's something they've all seen a hundred times before. You don't have to work in law enforcement long before you come to understand that addiction consumes one's resolve like fire takes to paper. It's a truth that becomes gospel with repetition.

When the thought has marinated long enough, Thom brings forth another truth: "Thieves and druggies tend to run in the same circles as prostitutes," he says, "and let's face it, prostitutes rarely get booked."

"Well, we should have DNA profiles from the clothes later today. Either we get a CODIS hit or we don't. In the meantime . . ." I tip my head toward the thumb drive in the middle of the table.

Reaching out, Dex picks up the small drive and weighs it in his hand, as if the gigabytes within hold the actual plaster masks and not just their images. "We'll need a subpoena," he says at length.

"I can have one in a few hours."

Dex hesitates only a moment. "Okay, let's give it a try."

CHAPTER TWENTY-SIX

Janet Burlingame is an eleven-year veteran of the FBI's DNA Casework Unit, based in Quantico, Virginia. In my five years with the Special Tracking Unit I've met her in person twice: once right after the unit was formed, and then again three years later while we were working on a case west of Quantico.

In her mid to late thirties with striking red hair, stylish glasses, and a trim, athletic build, she's naturally attractive, yet wickedly dangerous. As Jimmy tells it, she has black belts in three different forms of martial arts. I never found out which ones because, honestly, when someone can kill you seven hundred different ways, does it really matter?

Needless to say, my conversations with Janet are always cordial.

When the call comes early in the afternoon, Diane transfers it to the conference room and then joins us as we greet Janet over the speakerphone. After some friendly banter, she says, "So, some good news and some bad."

"Give us the bad first," Jimmy says, ever the pragmatist.

"Well, they kind of go hand in hand," Janet replies. "We came up with seven distinct female profiles from the clothes, as you suspected, but only one of them was in CODIS, a woman by the name of Erin Clare Yarborough. Her DNA is associated with the sixth mannequin. We got a match on both the mask mold and the clothing."

"The one in the bedroom with the paperback copy of *Misery*," I say to Jimmy, and then realize that it doesn't really matter where she was found, leastwise not to Janet. Still, for some reason it's important to me. I suppose it makes them more real, and right now I need them to be real.

Murphy did something far more insidious than simply destroying the women's bodies, he supplanted them with mannequins dressed in their clothes and wearing their faces.

"What do we know about Miss Yarborough?" Jimmy asks.

"She was entered into NCIC two years ago after she went missing in Seattle," Janet replies. "The only reason we have her DNA is thanks to her sister. Apparently Erin made a number of suicidal threats, which escalated to an actual attempt when she took a fistful of pills and washed them down with whiskey. Paramedics got to her just in time. Anyway, it was after this last incident that her sister picked a bloody bandage out of the trash after Erin tossed it away. You know—just in case."

"Yeah, just in case," Jimmy echoes in a somber tone.

"Where there's smoke there's usually fire," Janet continues, "so I imagine there's more to the story, but with HIPAA rules being what they are, we don't have ready access to her medical records."

"Do you know which hospital she was taken to for the overdose?"

We hear papers shuffling, and then Janet says, "Harbor-view Medical Center."

As we speak, Diane is already logging into LInX, the Law Enforcement Information Exchange, to run more in-depth analysis of Erin Yarborough.

Created by the Naval Criminal Investigative Service (NCIS), LInX allows jurisdictions to share access to their databases. In this case, it'll give us access to the records of almost all the police departments and county sheriff's offices that Erin may have come in contact with.

"Can you make sure the unidentified DNA gets linked to our case number?" Jimmy says as the conversation winds down. Janet assures him it's already done and then calls out a cheerful goodbye before ending the call.

Pushing his chair to the right with his feet, Jimmy scoots up next to Diane and peers at the laptop screen over her shoulder.

"Contacts begin about four years ago," Diane says without looking up, "mostly with her as a victim or contact. There are a few local arrests where she was cited and released, plus those Janet mentioned, the ones where she was booked." She does a quick count in her head: "Seventeen incidents in all."

"Any others that might be suicide attempts, overdoses—"

"Prostitution," I suggest.

Jimmy points his index finger at me, as if to underscore the word.

"There's a suspicious circumstance where she was contacted in the car of a known pimp. She claimed not to know his real name, only that he went by Stain, and Stain was nice enough to give her a ride so she could meet her uncle."

"That's nice," I say in a singsong voice. Then, elbowing Jimmy, I say, "That's nice, right? Stain sounds like a great guy, giving her a ride to meet her uncle like that. And they say there are no more nice guys."

Jimmy just snorts, and Diane ignores me outright.

"The officer noted that she was dressed the part—of the hooker, that is, not the adoring niece—and that they were idling in a casino parking lot." She says the last words slowly and with more emphasis, as if Jimmy and I don't know that casinos are havens for prostitution, even in the Pacific Northwest.

Diane continues to open the seventeen reports linked to Erin Yarborough, finding additional incidents of possible overdose, suicidal actions, and drugs. The casino incident was the only one that hinted at prostitution, though it wasn't the streetwalking variety, the type most vulnerable to predators.

When Diane finally gets tired of us peering over her shoulders, she shoos us from the conference room like farmyard chickens, and then locks the door behind us. She'll spend the better part of the next hour crafting a comprehensive report on the young woman once known as Erin Yarborough. Her life story will be told not in pictures of vacations and baby showers and family gatherings, but in police case numbers and mug shots. Her relatives will be presented not as a concerned sister or worried parents, but as next of kin. Their phone numbers and addresses will be attached for notification purposes.

As Diane reclaims her seat in the conference room, I watch her through the glass wall and wonder about Erin Yarborough, about the person she was before she started down the road of bad decisions.

Will she be missed?

In the end, I suppose that depends on how much damage she did before she went missing, how many lives she disrupted and overturned. Exactly how many bridges do you have to burn before no one cares?

I don't think anyone has the answer.

CHAPTER TWENTY-SEVEN

"Dex—talk to me," I say, answering the call on the first ring.

"Hey, Steps. I suppose I should congratulate you," the crime analyst begins. "The facial recognition paid off in a big way—better than I would have imagined. Helped that you have straight-on images of the faces; usually we get shots of the subject looking one way or the other and it's more difficult to match points."

"How many matches?"

"Nineteen possible hits," he replies, "but the details get a bit complicated, so let me start with the easy part, because I also finished the analysis on your suspect vehicle."

"And you know what it is?"

"Without a doubt," he replies. "It's a seventh-generation Honda Accord, which was manufactured for model years 2003 through 2007. Now, the thing about Honda is they like to swap out the taillights on their vehicles every couple of years. In this case, the change came for the 2006 model year, where the taillights are significantly different from the 2005 and earlier models. That means you're looking for a 2006 or a 2007."

"That's great," I say.

"Not really," Dex replies hesitantly.

My face sours, and Jimmy leans closer to the phone, asking, "Why's that?"

"Sorry to say, but Hondas are a dime a dozen—particularly the silver ones. If I ever take to a life of crime, I'll drive a silver Honda," he quips.

Jimmy purses his lips and then gives a quick nod. "What about the facial recognition?"

"Right," Dex says, shifting gears. "We have nineteen possible matches on the seven masks. None of them are a hundred percent, but we have some that are in the high nineties. I just sent a PDF with names, dates of birth, and photos to your email."

"Any hits on mask six?" Jimmy asks.

We hear pages turning, and then Dex says, "Three hits."

"Is one of them Erin Yarborough?"

It takes a second, but then Dex's voice returns with a mystified, "Yes, she's here," followed by, "How did you know?"

"DNA," Jimmy replies. "We got the results back a couple hours ago. Unfortunately, Erin is the only one we were able to match."

"The good news," I say, "is that the facial recognition obviously works, since it picked her as a possible match from the database. That means we should have luck with the rest of the list. We just need to separate the proverbial wheat from the chaff."

"Meaning we separate the missing from the living," Dex observes.

"Exactly."

"Need any help with that?"

"Yes," I reply immediately, "but if we don't let Diane have a crack at it first, she's liable to skin us both alive."

"Well, if Diane's on it, you probably won't need my help," the crime analyst replies. "But you know where I am." With that he ends the call.

With Diane on a late lunch break, Jimmy and I take it on ourselves to print out three copies of the PDF and then try to open the digital version on Diane's laptop, which is still in the conference room. Neither of us is surprised to find the computer password-protected, and we're so engrossed trying to guess her password that we don't notice when her silhouette appears and then lingers in the doorway.

Jimmy has already guessed macadamia, Hawaii, and Outlander—her favorite food, place, and series of books. I've guessed Einstein and Gabaldon, the latter being the author of the Outlander series.

None of them work, of course, because they're the kind of passwords Jimmy or I would use, not Diane. She's spent too much time working with and around hackers to go light on security. Most likely it's a seventeen-digit combination of letters, numbers, and special characters that have no relevance to one another, an impossible jumble no one would guess.

The figure in the doorway clears her throat.

"Heyyy," I say, drawing the word out as I move away from the laptop.

"Umm," Jimmy says, pointing meekly at the keyboard. "We were trying to pull up the facial recognition report on your . . . computer."

Diane gives Jimmy the stare-down before turning her disapproving gaze my way. After a penetrating moment that leaves me feeling slightly violated, she turns her eyes back to Jimmy. "Try Steps and Jimmy, all run together as one word, all lowercase."

Jimmy thinks she's toying with him, but types it in anyway. A moment later, the screen comes to life and he quickly opens the PDF and links the laptop to the large-screen TV on the wall.

With arms crossed, I study the screen as Jimmy starts to scroll through. Diane moves up beside us and I say in a low voice, "Really—Steps and Jimmy?"

"Better than Lord Humungus," she whispers.

"It's a *Mad Max* reference," I say defensively. Though the thing I should really be concerned about is how she knows my password.

"Sure thing," Diane replies, sounding anything but convinced.

We give her the same spiel that Dex gave us. "Minus the three possible matches that are linked to Erin Yarborough," Jimmy says, "there are sixteen candidates for the other six victims."

Diane takes control of the mouse and starts scanning through the list, letting the names and images flash by as she absorbs everything. After a few minutes she pauses to give her first impressions.

"A few of these we can almost eliminate right now. One lives in Spokane, the other in Walla Walla. It's unlikely this so-called Onion King is targeting women that far away."

"What makes you so sure?" I ask.

"Charice Qian is from Tumwater, Erin Yarborough is from Everett. He's hunting in the greater Seattle-Tacoma area. I'm guessing the other victims won't be much more than an hour's drive from either location."

Her logic is hard to argue with, and the fact that she came to this conclusion after one scan of the report—and without making any notes—is both frightening and inspiring.

"Give me a couple hours," she says, her eyes never leaving the screen. When we don't move right away, she turns and says, "Go . . . go . . . go!"

Hard to argue with that kind of diplomacy.

Two hours pass, and Diane barely stirs from her seat.

From the conference room, she has access to NCIC, LInX, CLEAR, DAPS, and a slew of other law enforcement databases, all of them providing individual bits and pieces of a more sweeping picture.

Jimmy and I entertain ourselves to the best of our ability and are engaged in a heated round of foosball on the hangar floor when, at a quarter after five, we hear the pointed *tap-tap-tap* of metal striking glass. Glancing around, we see Diane standing at the conference room's glass wall, rapping on it with the obnoxious gold ring on her right hand. Even after she *knows* we see her, she continues to tap away, and then gives us an evil grin as she motions impatiently for us to join her.

No longer is the hastily constructed facial recognition report on display. Instead, the flat-screen hosts a meticulously crafted PDF that, at first glance, seems to lay out our possible victims by the mannequin number assigned to them a few nights earlier. Each number has names, addresses, and other data attached to it, and rather than trying to make heads or tails of it, we wait for Diane to explain. After all, that's her favorite part.

"As you can see, I've added some order to our data," she says as she slides gracefully into the chair next to the laptop, takes the mouse in hand, and scrolls to the top of the report. "Of the nineteen possible matches, we've already eliminated three of them with the DNA identification of number six—"

"Erin Yarborough," I say.

"Of course, Erin Yarborough. That leaves sixteen. We have four possible matches from facial recognition for the first mannequin. One of these is living in Walla Walla, as previously mentioned, another is an accountant in Redmond, who, coincidentally, posted several new photos on Facebook yesterday, so I'm guessing she's alive and well. If we eliminate those two, that leaves Toni Greer of Fife and Abitha Jones of Beacon Hill. Both have criminal history, though if we're keeping score, Abitha is the clear winner."

"When were their last arrests?" Jimmy asks.

"Abitha was booked for drugs a year and a half ago; Toni was booked for trespass six months ago. Since we don't know the abduction date for number one—"

"Don't . . . do that," I say through clenched teeth.

"What?"

"Don't call them numbers. That's what Murphy did; it's just . . . wrong." I catch myself halfway through the sentence and try to soften the last words, but the damage has already been done. Diane has a startled look on her face, as if I'd slapped her, and I instantly regret both my words and their delivery. "Sorry," I mutter.

Jimmy catches Diane's eye and in a quiet voice explains what I can't.

"Murphy was clinical about how he viewed the victims," he says. "Charice Qian was just number eight; he never called her by name and we don't know if he even knew her name. It didn't matter to him. He kept saying Eight is broken, and Eight needs to be fixed. They were just projects to him, tasks to be completed."

Glancing at me, Jimmy adds, "I'm sure Steps doesn't mean to be short, but you didn't see what we saw. You didn't see the mannequins dressed in their clothes, or the barrel." He sweeps his hand over the table as if casting seeds. "You didn't see the fragments of teeth and bone scattered on the forest floor. It was medieval."

Diane is quiet for a moment, and if I didn't know better I'd say her eyes had teared up a bit. When she finally speaks, it's in a subdued voice halfway between hurt and ashamed. "I'm sorry, Steps. I sometimes forget that the pictures I see are very real for you and Jimmy. To me they're just images. Like Murphy, I suppose I view them as a task to be performed."

She gives an almost imperceptible shudder. "It's how I cope with what I see, how I endure it. I imagine it's a very different experience when you're standing there surrounded by the sights and smells of it." She hesitates. "It's not something I want to experience."

"You shouldn't have to," Jimmy says in a consoling voice.

Standing up, I'm rather startled to find myself moving over to Diane's chair, leaning over, and giving her a hug. When I rise back up, she wipes at the corner of her eye and says, "That's sexual harassment, you know?" and turns her attention back to the screen.

Jimmy grins at me, and I just flop back down in my chair.

Our little drama lasts just over a minute.

Her voice carries a slight quaver when she begins again, but in a moment it's gone and she's ramrodding the report our way as fast as we can chew and digest. "Our second grouping," she says, choosing her words more carefully, "includes two possible subjects, one of whom is dead." Scrolling down, she stops when she gets to two driver's license photos placed side by side on the page. With her pointing stick, which she loves to wave about, she aims at the young woman on the left, a stern brunette with only a hint of smile. "Since we're looking for the dead, and she is, I didn't rule her out immediately. But then I learned that she died from a fall."

"Mountain climbing?" Jimmy guesses.

"Ladder," Diane replies, cocking her head. "Did you know that three hundred people die from ladder falls each year? I had no idea." Shrugging, she continues. "That leaves just Gabriella Paden. CLEAR shows her at an address in Tukwila for the last five years, so she should be easy to track down, though I have to say she doesn't fit the profile of the others."

"No criminal history?" I ask.

"None."

The third grouping also has two possible matches. After scrolling their images into view, Diane taps the one on the right, saying, "This is Jennifer Holt of Everett. She's your best bet for number—I mean, grouping three. Last known address was her grandmother's place about a year and a half ago. It seems the two of them got into a bit of a donnybrook."

"Punching?" I say in surprise.

"More like mutual screaming and pinching. Jennifer was the primary aggressor, so she got hooked up and spent a few days in jail. The whole thing blew up because she'd stolen some of her grandmother's back meds. The report out of Everett PD didn't specify, but I'm guessing it was Oxys," she says, referring to the potent pain reliever OxyContin. "She had plenty of other contacts before that, and an overdose a month later, but nothing since."

"What about her?" I ask, pointing to the woman on the left.

"Elane," Diane replies, shaking her head. "Highly unlikely; she's the one who lives in Spokane. Our suspect seems comfortable moving up and down the I-5 corridor between Tacoma and Everett, but nothing I've seen suggests he'd be willing to undertake a six-hundred-mile round-trip journey for one victim, especially since she'd be in the trunk for half that mileage. The risks aren't worth the reward. Not to mention that she renewed her vehicle registration three weeks ago using the Spokane address." With a toss of her head, she concludes, "I think we can eliminate her."

The minute hand on the clock drags itself fifteen more clicks clockwise in the time it takes Diane to scroll through the rest of the report.

Debra Mata, it seems, is our likely victim from group four. Her visage is sharp and angular, with cheekbones that look like they could cut meat. Her pallid skin seems to emphasize this, pulling tight in places where it should hang loose. All in all, it's a dead face—as dead as the mask it created. The only flicker of life is in her haunted eyes, which stare out from the two sunken recesses under her brow.

Debra was reported missing almost two and a half years ago, which means she may be the Onion King's first victim. There's a lot that can be learned from the first. A killer is more likely to make mistakes early on, before they have a chance to perfect their skills.

For group five we once again draw a lucky card—though I cringe to use the word when speaking of the dead. Of the three possible matches spit out by the facial recognition software, Sheryl Dorsey stands alone because of the simple fact that she was reported missing out of Tacoma just five months ago.

That brings us to group six, which has already been whittled down to Erin Yarborough, and group seven, where we find two names: Amber Bartlett of Burien, which is near Seattle-Tacoma International Airport, and Chelsea Younger of Covington, which is ten miles to the southeast.

Their police records suggest that one is just as likely to be dead as the other, and as I ponder this, I feel the hair rise up slightly on the back of my neck; ghost fingers, some might say, playing at the base of my skull. It's a sensation I've grown accustomed to over the years, though it still sends a shiver down my spine.

"So, even without eliminating the extras," Jimmy says, tapping the PDF in front of him, "we seem to have a pretty solid profile on our victim type."

"Yeah, half are mentals or druggies," I say. Jimmy gives me a disapproving look, and I return the favor by rolling my eyes—like speaking the truth suddenly became uncouth.

"Someone going through a mental crisis is far different

from someone dealing with mental illness. Anyone can be led to the point of suicide given enough provocation." He lowers his tone. "You of all people should understand mental anguish."

Diane knits her brows at that and tilts her head the way she does when something strikes her as odd. Recognizing his blunder, Jimmy quickly steers his comments back to the victims. "The point is we're well on our way to identifying the Onion King. We just need to find the common denominator between these names. There's an abnormal level of suicide attempts and drug overdoses among these women, and that's what we need to focus on."

"What better victim . . ." I say, letting the words trail off.

"How so?" Jimmy asks, though he has a pretty good idea what I mean.

"Who do serial killers prey on?" I ask. "It's usually the invisible. Mostly that means prostitutes, but if a drug addict with a history of overdose goes missing, how hard do you think police are going to look for her? If a missing person report is even filed, they'll just assume she overdosed someplace and just hasn't been found; same thing with suicides."

Sweeping my right arm as if to take in the entirety of Whatcom County's two thousand square miles in one brushstroke, I say, "Even here the sheriff's office will occasionally find bodies that have been in the woods for months or even years. Sometimes the victim was reported missing, sometimes they weren't."

I shake my head. "Places like Seattle and Tacoma have so many transient and troubled people that a thousand of them could walk off into the sea and no one would notice."

"That's a bit harsh," Diane says quietly.

I look at her without reply and then stare at my hands.

The slow drumming of Jimmy's fingers begins to play against the table. It's one of his tics, something he does when he's conflicted or thinking.

I like to pace; he strums.

At length he looks across at Diane and says, "He's right. Let's put out a request for information on any missing person reports involving women between the ages of, say, sixteen and thirty. Include a line or two emphasizing the possible drug and suicide angles. I also want to know about any attempted abductions or suspicious circumstance reports. If someone sees a woman getting stuffed into a car too roughly, I want to know about it."

Diane nods. "It'll go out within the hour."

Jimmy turns his gaze on me. "Are you up for a drive tomorrow?"

"Seattle?"

There's a smile on his face, but it's not humor that I see reflected, it's resolve. "Seattle, Everett, Tacoma . . . a few others," he says. "I'll pick you up at seven."

"Heather *just* got back . . ." I say imploringly.

He sighs, and then nods. "Make it nine."

When I exit through the steel-reinforced door separating Hangar 7 from our small parking lot, I pause momentarily and close my eyes, drinking deeply the crisp winter air. Standing there, my face to the sky, I feel the brush of something small and wet against my cheek. I imagine for a moment that fantasy worlds are real, and that a kindly, clever pixie has just kissed me on the cheek for good luck.

Of course, it's not so, and when I open my eyes I behold the first flakes of winter—or at least the first for Bellingham. And then there are dozens, scores, hundreds emerging from the blackness above, until the dark sky grows light with them.

Heather wants a white Christmas.

She may get her wish.

CHAPTER TWENTY-EIGHT

My home is called Big Perch.

It's nestled on the side of Chuckanut Mountain and enjoys sweeping views of the Puget Sound to the west, with unbelievable sunsets over the San Juan Islands and the Olympic Peninsula beyond. At twenty-four hundred square feet, most of it on the main level, Big Perch has more space than I'll ever need, which is why my brother, Jens, is living with me while he finishes his studies at Western Washington University.

Jens is determined to get his doctorate in anthropology, and as he's months away from finishing his master's, it seems a goal he'll achieve . . . not that there was any doubt. When I told him several years ago that there's no money in anthropology, he said he didn't need money, he had me.

It's hard to argue with logic like that.

Surrounding Big Perch on the north, south, and west—mostly the west—is a massive deck with square footage that almost rivals the house's. There's an outdoor fireplace, a hot tub, random seating for twenty, and, in the summer, sporadic herbal gardens growing from collections of containers here and there.

I also own the adjoining home to the south, which is a mirror image of Big Perch, only smaller. At thirteen hundred square feet, the appropriately named Little Perch is now home to Ellis Stockwell, the former owner, designer, and builder of both homes.

It's an odd journey that brought us to this arrangement. Suffice it to say that Ellis is a retired Customs and Border Protection officer whose successful start-up company took a sudden nosedive that cost him millions and ended his short tenure as a business executive. The tragic part of the story is that none of this was due to any fault or mismanagement on his part—unless allowing your wife access to the business bank accounts is considered mismanagement.

Ellis's wife pilfered the money and relocated with her much younger boyfriend, forcing Ellis into foreclosure and ruin. It was clear he loved the houses, so when I closed on the property I struck a deal with the old man that I've never regretted: in exchange for tending the grounds he gets to stay in Little Perch rent-free.

His duties have expanded considerably since then—his doing, not mine.

Both Jens and I like Ellis tremendously, but he's an odd duck who puts on an English accent most of the time, sunbathes in the nude, and is never without a hat—even during said sunbathing. Despite all that, he's now a member of our family. Whether that makes him a brother, a grandfather, or a quirky uncle, I'm still not sure, but it doesn't really matter. On nights when Jens and I both find ourselves at home for dinner, he joins us. And on many occasions, we've worn away the longest hours of night listening to his stories, never knowing which to believe and which to take with a healthy dose of skepticism.

I've laughed with him, called him a liar, and been pulled to tears by his tales.

He's my kind of family.

After we enjoy some long-overdue home cooking, Jens and Ellis shoo Heather and me from the kitchen and insist on doing the dishes. We don't argue. Heather grabs the quilt off the back of the couch and, taking my hand, leads me out onto the deck. Steering me toward the porch swing at the north end, she wraps the massive quilt around the both of us before we sit so that the warmth completely engulfs us. The coverage is so complete that it's as if we're hiding at the back of a small, soft cave, looking out from our warm place into the wind and chill of a winter's night.

A moment later, Christmas music begins to issue from the deck speakers.

I'm too comfortable to peer out and see who's responsible, but it's almost certainly Ellis. This time of year, you can always hear Christmas music issuing from his home, his car, his lips. There's no other music he takes to so completely.

For him, only the classics count. He has little patience for songs that seem to make light of the holiday or exploit the season, which means no grandmas getting mowed down by errant reindeer, no cats meowing "Jingle Bells," and no John Denver singing, "Please Daddy (Don't Get Drunk This Christmas)."

Ellis is a traditionalist, which means he wants his music draped in nostalgia.

He wants to feel the joy of the season, as he did when he was a boy. I've watched him in past years as he closed his eyes and let the music flow through him, allowing it to play with his soul. Ellis is the type who feels the ache of each chord, each word, embracing them with joy or melancholic quiet, depending on the song.

Such nostalgia cannot be manufactured or replicated; so, for Ellis, only the songs of Perry Como, Ella Fitzgerald, Bing Crosby, and Glenn Miller will do. There are others, of course, but those are a few of his favorites.

As I sink comfortably into the blanket with Heather's head on my chest, I feel a gentle euphoria settle upon me. Ellis's chesty baritone soon joins Frank Sinatra as he sings "White Christmas," and I can't help wondering if this is one of those rare moments when the seed of nostalgia is planted. Thirty years from now, will I listen to "White Christmas" and ache for this moment, remembering Heather in my arms, and the crisp winter air, and the sounds of my brother and Ellis goofing off in the kitchen?

I hope so. What is life but a long string of memories, and those steeped in nostalgia are the best of these.

As Ellis continues to sing, accentuating every word for Jens's benefit, I notice a slight taint to the occasional word. Recognizing what my eccentric neighbor is doing, I say, "Leave it to Ellis," and shake my head gently.

I glance at Heather under the hooded quilt, and she anticipates my words. "He's singing with a British accent," we say in unison. She starts to laugh and then covers her mouth and buries her face in my chest.

CHAPTER TWENTY-NINE

Biscuits Bar & Grill was the last place Melinda Gaines wanted to be on a Wednesday night, particularly with a busy workday ahead, but the evening turned out to be quite enjoyable. She hadn't seen Trish and Alice in a month, and the desire to share time with them and catch up proved greater than her fear of the place.

Fear may be a strong word.

Alcohol was once Melinda's favorite poison, her self-medication of choice, but she hasn't touched the stuff in ages. In fact, the last time she had anything stronger than coffee was six months ago when she drank an entire bottle of room-temperature merlot and slit her wrists in a warm bath.

They say it doesn't hurt when you do it that way, but that's just not true.

It was Alice who saw the Facebook post; Alice who called the cops; Alice who knew all too well that Melinda had been struggling for years with the unimaginable mood swings brought on by bipolar disorder.

The bathtub incident wasn't the first time she had tried to end it. Just two months earlier she'd swallowed enough pills to take down a bull elephant. It should have killed her, but her sister had one of her *feelings*, and stopped by Melinda's apartment to find her passed out at the kitchen table with the empty prescription bottle at her side.

They pumped her stomach and she tried to live again . . . or she lived to try again; they both amounted to the same thing: a sharp blade and red water.

But that's all behind her now.

"You sure you don't want a ride home?" Trish asks, fumbling for her keys.

"It's two blocks," Melinda replies with a smile, flicking her wrist up the well-lit street for emphasis. "Besides, I can use the air."

There's a round of goodbyes and a round of hugs and a round of promises to get together again soon, and then Trish and Alice start across the parking lot. As Melinda turns to make her way home, she hears the chirp of a car door unlocking and the suddenly raucous laughter from Trish, who had a few drinks beyond her limit.

Thank God Alice is driving, Melinda thinks, and then smiles.

As the cheer of her friends diminishes behind her, Melinda tucks her head deeper into her coat, warding off the cold. And so she doesn't immediately notice the man rounding the corner up ahead. If she had, she would have paid little notice. It was a well-lit street near a popular bar, and just minutes from home.

Like Melinda, the man's eyes are to the ground as he moves briskly along the sidewalk, hustled on by the cold and the wind. As the distance between them dissolves, Melinda recognizes him from the bar—John or Jim, something with a J. Lowering her head and looking away quickly, she prays he doesn't look up, but when they're just ten feet apart he seems to realize someone else is there and pulls up short, stopping dead in his tracks.

"Oh, hey," he says. "Melinda, right?"

"Yeah," she replies hesitantly, glancing around at the deserted street.

When she doesn't seem to remember his name, he says, "Jeff," and puts a finger on his chest. Then he gives an exaggerated shrug, like it's no big deal.

She nods, as if she knew that. "Are you going back to Biscuits?" she asks, trying to keep the encounter short but polite.

"Meeting a friend in an hour," he replies, looking at his watch before realizing he's not wearing one. "How about you?"

"Home," she replies. "I've got work in the morning."

"You're not walking, are you? It's freezing."

"It's not far," Melinda replies, not wanting to divulge too much. While the man is somewhat handsome—maybe a seven on a scale from one to ten—he makes her uneasy. And the fact that she can't explain this unease is even more troubling.

When he sat next to her at the bar earlier in the evening, she swore that he leaned in close on two occasions and . . . smelled her. When she turned to look at him after the first instance, he'd been staring down at his cell phone, so she dismissed it and blamed her imagination. Then it happened again—or she thought it happened again. When she turned and looked at him he was leaned over trying to get something out of his coat pocket, his wallet, she presumed, because he left shortly after.

Had he sniffed her?

Her gut told her yes.

Even so, she might have excused it as curiosity or even appreciation if she'd been wearing perfume or a scented body lotion, but she barely had on makeup. Her intent that evening was to catch up with old friends, not meet new ones, particularly the kind who would sniff at you like a dog.

Now here he was again.

"I've got time to kill," he says. "Why don't I make sure you get home safely?"

"No, that's very nice of you, but I've walked it a hundred times."

He looks at her a moment and in a low voice replies, "As you wish."

It's not so much what he says or how he says it that chills her, but rather the way he looks at her as he does so, as if he's sniffing and smelling her all over again, only this time with his eyes. With a nod and a pinched smile, she moves past him, casting a wary look back a moment later, perhaps to make sure he doesn't follow.

She quickens her pace.

Halfway up the next block—her block—she feels a sudden prick in her neck and reaches up with her hand. Almost instantly the world goes swimmingly woozy and she falls sideways, landing not on the frozen concrete, but against something soft that clutches her and seems to suspend her in midair. A face floats before her, or what seems like a face. There's a blur of eyes and nostrils and teeth, but they seem set against the night, suspended in blackness.

It's a puzzle how those teeth manage to stay suspended, and she thinks hard on it until a moment of clarity seeps through the fog and she almost laughs. Her last thought is one of chastisement as she realizes the eyes and teeth aren't suspended in blackness, they're peeking out from behind a black ski mask.

Funny, she thinks . . . and then the darkness takes her.

CHAPTER THIRTY

Thursday, December 18

As the town of Marysville looms before us, Jimmy yawns widely and says he needs coffee, a proclamation that's neither surprising nor unexpected. It's been at least twenty-five minutes since he announced with utter disgust that his travel mug was empty—as if it were the mug's responsibility to keep itself full. Or worse, that the mug had poured itself out upon the floor just to spite him. Twenty-five minutes is an abhorrent length of time for the caffeine-deprived.

"Has Jane talked to you about your coffee consumption?" I ask.

"I'm allowed one vice," he replies. "Out of all the possible vices in the universe, I chose coffee. It could have been alcohol, cigarettes, women, drugs, food, shoes—"

"Shoes!" I laugh.

"The point is, I could have chosen something a lot worse than coffee, so in answer to your question, no, Jane has *not* talked to me. She's perfectly fine with it."

His earlier dose of caffeine is clearly wearing off, so I decide to leave it alone . . . for the better part of twenty seconds, but then I can't help myself. "Shoes?" I say. "Is there rehab for that, or are you condemned to a life of back-alley sneaker deals?"

Jimmy doesn't miss a beat: "It's a twelve-step program."

Before I can reply to the pun, he jerks the wheel to the right and shoots the black Ford Expedition across two lanes of traffic and down the off-ramp at exit 199. Turning left, we find two Starbucks within a half mile of each other. They're like caffeine pimps staking out their own corners.

I order my usual: a twenty-ounce single decaf mocha with one-percent milk and no whip. Half the time I can count on a playful comment from the barista when I place my order: something like, *Why bother?* or *Do you want some coffee with your coffee?* or *Here's your cocoa.* This time the caffeine dealer leaves me alone and I retreat to a round table in the corner, spreading the target files out before me.

Diane prepared profiles on our remaining subjects. They all live—or lived—in either Snohomish, King, or Pierce County, a stretch of land that accounts for the greater Everett-Seattle-Tacoma area. Efficient as always, Diane ordered them from north to south, making our work easier.

Our cover story is that we're going to do some knock-and-talks, see if we can learn more about our subjects, maybe talk to some family members and see if we can get a toothbrush or comb—something that'll yield DNA.

A good cover story is a constant but necessary burden. Diane—being Diane—is endlessly and relentlessly curious. And since she knows nothing about shine, Jimmy and I find ourselves constantly walking the razor's edge between fact and fiction.

Like all our cover stories, this one tends to be *mostly* true. We'll definitely be knocking on some doors and talking to some relatives, but only if I see shine that matches one of our victims.

"Who's first on our list?" Jimmy asks, slipping into the chair opposite me and setting his hot coffee on the table. After situating himself, he reaches out and clutches the cup with both hands, as if it might fly away.

"Jennifer Holt," I reply.

"What's her story?"

"Juvenile runaway, busted for pot at fourteen, meth by sixteen, in and out of the system. Her favorite poison before she went missing seems to have been heroin, and by then she was both using and dealing. Snohomish County had a pretty good case against her, but then she ups and vanishes. It's not surprising that they didn't take it seriously when her grandmother reported her missing; probably figured she skipped the state to avoid arrest."

"What were the charges?"

"They had probable cause to arrest her on three controlled buys, but when they couldn't find her it went to warrant. It's still in NCIC, but no one has come across her to make the arrest."

"Well, she fits the victimology," Jimmy observes.

"Pretty close," I say, scanning the report. "Last known address was with Grandma on Fulton Street in Everett. That's about ten minutes from here."

Jimmy drags the report across the table and spends a minute reading it from beginning to end. "Same old story," he says. "Dysfunctional or absent parents, no discipline, no supervision, lousy friends and worse acquaintances, drugs, and now death." He pushes the folder away in disgust. "Remind me again why we're killing ourselves to help people who couldn't tell a good decision from a bad one if it slapped them in the face?"

"Because life is a vast wilderness where it's easy to get lost," I suggest with a humble smile.

"Yeah," he snorts, "but it's only a vast wilderness if you ignore the giant signs that say STAY ON PATH." He flicks a wrist at me. "Aren't you the one who always says we get what we deserve in life, good or bad?"

"No, that's my mom."

"Same difference," Jimmy says, forcing a smile. He tips his head in my direction and waits for an argument but gets none. "Generally speaking," he says after a long moment, "I agree with you—and your mom. There are exceptions, of course, as with everything, but for the most part our present circumstance is predicated on the decisions, actions, and in-actions we took over the years leading up to this point."

For a moment he sounds less like my mom and more like my high school counselor.

Leaning back, he places his hands on the table, one on each side of the coffee cup. "Suppose two boys grow up on the same block," he says, "and upon entering high school, one begins cutting class to play Xbox and smoke dope while the other takes advanced placement classes. By gradua-tion, one has moved on to harder drugs and dropped out of school, the other has already completed two years of com-munity college because he enrolled in a Running Start pro-gram and spent the last half of high school taking college classes.

"As the years go by, one will complain about how unfair it is that the other lives in a nice house, drives a fancy car, and goes on vacation twice a year. It'll be a conspiracy of the rich against the poor, the lucky versus the unlucky, the haves versus the have-nots. And neither of them is likely to step back and look at the diverging paths that led them to these very different places."

"Yeah, I don't know," I say with a hint of skepticism. "These days it seems a lot of people have smoked *a lot* of dope and somehow still managed to get an education and a somewhat decent job. In Silicon Valley they're microdosing mescaline because they claim it enhances their creativity." I'm just playing devil's advocate with Jimmy, having never tried drugs myself. I've got enough weirdness in my head without adding pharmaceuticals to the mix.

"So why do some end up going down a bad road and others don't?" I ask.

Jimmy twists his mouth up and gives a one-shoulder shrug. "I'm not saying that cutting class and getting high is guaranteed to send your future into a death spiral," he concedes, "but bad decisions are like compound interest: after a while it starts to add up."

He takes a long pull from the coffee, letting the dark nectar placate his nerves as it works its way through his body. Setting the cup back down with a contented sigh, he shakes his head thoughtfully. "If people only realized the power they have to redirect their lives . . . it's like the needle of a compass: It shows you exactly where you're going, and at any time you can turn one way or another. If the needle remains fixed in the wrong direction, it's not hard to guess at the general position of one's life in five, ten, or even twenty years."

"Provided you're still alive," I add.

"There's that," Jimmy concedes, raising his coffee cup as if to toast me before taking another drink.

"But the needle on the compass *can* change," I say, and as the words escape me I find myself wondering if this is really true, or just another misguided hope.

"It can," Jimmy replies slowly, "and does . . . but rarely." He's quiet for a moment, and then smiles. "Imagine what the world would be like if one day everyone woke up and took charge of their own destiny, if they took responsibility for their lives and their mistakes and set out on a different course."

He sighs. "Wishful thinking, I suppose. Too many are willing to accept their circumstances, bleak as they are.

Worse yet, they won't give up their crutches, whether that's heroin, alcohol, or the zombified stupor of mindless entertainment."

I'm quiet for a moment. "I kind of like mindless entertainment."

Jimmy just shrugs. "Everything in moderation."

"Except coffee," I say.

"Except coffee."

CHAPTER THIRTY-ONE

Jennifer Holt's last known residence is on Fulton Street, which begins near the heart of the city and runs north into a dated residential area with tired homes and subdued alleys. A mile to the west lies Naval Station Everett, which is home to five guided-missile destroyers, several Coast Guard vessels, and, on occasion, an aircraft carrier.

When Jimmy pulls to the curb in front of the side-gabled bungalow, I note how the house seems to hunch over its foundation, like a beast too weak to rise. If I had to guess, I'd say it was built sometime shortly after World War II and was last updated in the seventies. The faded paint is likely lead-based, and the whole sorry heap is wrapped in asbestos siding.

Morning frost is still on the hibernating lawn, mixing its winter-white with the pale greens left over from summer. Weeds mingle with the grass, and there are bare patches of earth here and there where the tiny blades have perished, never to be reseeded. This semblance of a lawn butts up to a concrete sidewalk that's as timeworn as the house.

I take all this in with a glance, and then slip my special glasses from my face, fold them, and place them in their case. When I look again, I behold a different world . . . and yet the same. It's a world splashed in paint, as if Jackson Pollock had a go at it and didn't know when to stop.

Thousands of unique shines lie on the street, the sidewalks, the lawns, and the porches of Fulton Street. Decades of comings and goings have stacked the colors one upon the other and condensed them into a rich kaleidoscope that reaches back through the decades to when the sidewalks were first poured, the porches first built, and the lawns first seeded.

As I glance about, I spot a familiar almond glow and the cracked texture of dried mud. It flows in a river of footprints up and down the sidewalk, in and out of the house, and around the yard in patterns that indicate both play and lawn mowing.

Jennifer Holt is mannequin number three.

"This is it," I say, and without waiting for a response, I open my door and step out onto Fulton Street. Rather than immediately approaching the front door, I walk to the south for a half block, and then, with Jimmy watching me but not saying a word, I walk to the north an equal distance. The simple exercise doesn't disappoint: I find the Onion King in three locations.

"He's been here," I tell Jimmy as I return to the SUV. "He never approached the house, but he walked up and down both sides of the street on different occasions, and another time he seems to have stepped out of his car for a moment, and then immediately left. Who knows how many times he was here and never exited the car?"

"But he never approached the house?" Jimmy confirms.

"Not from this side; we'll have to check the alley."

"Well, all right." Jimmy nods. "One down and five to go. How about we go talk to Grandma and see what she knows?"

I fall in behind him as he makes his way to the door, noticing several ceramic gnomes in the flower beds as we pass. I can't help thinking how sad they look, worn by sun, wind, and rain, their paint faded to chalky-hued pastels. The sharp black eyes that once graced each face have worn away to cataracts, and the once-bright clothes have weathered, looking no better than the garments one might find on a neglected scarecrow.

If my mother were here she'd probably wipe their faces with a damp handkerchief and bless them for good luck.

Jimmy knocks three times on the aluminum screen door, and presently a squat woman in her mid to late fifties opens the inner door and stares out at us with impatient eyes. Her fleshy skin is blemished by both years and abuse, but it's her unkempt hair that gives her the appearance of a rag doll at the end of its useful life.

The woman opens her mouth at the sight of us, but before she can say she doesn't want any magazine subscriptions, can't afford to paint the house, and already loves Jesus, Jimmy assaults her with a barrage of words that stops her cold.

"Good morning, Mrs. Holt," he says, flashing his FBI credentials. "I'm Special Agent James Donovan with the FBI, and this is my partner, Operations Specialist Magnus Craig. I was hoping we could ask you a few questions about your granddaughter, Jennifer Holt?"

She looks for a moment like a woman who just took an ill-advised sip from a fire hose. "Jennifer?" She looks us up and down. "And you're with the Federal Bureau of Investigators—"

"Investigation," Jimmy corrects. "You *are* Jean Holt, aren't you?"

"Jeannie," she replies. "No one calls me Jean, leastwise not since my mom died."

"And Jennifer Holt is your granddaughter?"

"Yeah, sure. She's my son's kid, but I kind of raised her."

"May we come in?" Jimmy asks. "It'll only take ten minutes."

She hesitates a moment, but then pushes open the screen door.

Leading us to the living room, Jeannie offers something to drink, but Jimmy and I both decline. It's always a loaded proposition when someone offers you food or drink during an investigation. You want to be polite, but at the same time you have to trust your instincts. It usually comes down to what you see, smell, and sense. To say that Jeannie Holt's living room doesn't meet the standard of our culinary feng shui would be an understatement.

The place isn't clean, it's just . . . not filthy.

It's a turn of the screw before filthy, a notch below.

I question the wisdom of even sitting, but when Jimmy clears the cats off the sofa and assaults me with his eyes, silently commanding me to plop down, I have no choice.

"She's dead, isn't she?" Jeannie blurts as soon as she settles into the chair opposite us. "I mean, she's been missing over a year now—people just don't go missing, especially when they have *her* kind of history." She tips her head up and lifts an eyebrow, as if we're all in on some secret understanding of just *who* Jennifer Holt was.

"We're investigating some leads," Jimmy explains softly, "but yes, we believe she may be a victim of homicide." He delivers the last part of the statement with compassion and with the hesitation that always comes when delivering such news.

Everyone reacts differently to death.

The variations are as numerous as the people on the planet, but the range is fairly well established. On one end of the scale is jubilation, a silent jig in honor of a departed ex-spouse or despised parent, though we rarely see this reaction because most people are smart enough to recognize how guilty it makes them appear—even when they're innocent.

Further down the scale we find the accepting nod, the handshake, and the "Thanks for letting me know." This is someone who expected the news and prepared for it, or who just doesn't care one way or the other. At the far end of the scale we find shrieking and fainting. This is either an Oscar-worthy thespian, or someone truly devastated by the loss. Mostly it's the latter.

Jeannie Holt is near the middle of the range.

You can see the loss on her face, but the emotion behind it is subdued. I realize she's been expecting this visit for some time now, perhaps even hoping for it, to end the waiting and wondering, though she'd done little of either.

"So, you think she might be dead, but you're not sure?"

Jimmy gives her the watered-down version of DNA analysis and she dutifully retrieves some of Jennifer's belongings, including two brushes, one for hair and one for teeth. Jimmy seals the items in small brown paper bags with red-and-white tape that has the word EVIDENCE printed in a repeating pattern. He scrawls his signature in the white section of the tape on both bags so that any tampering will be immediately evident. When he finishes, he leaves the bags sitting on the coffee table.

They stand like brown tombstones between him and Jeannie.

"I understand Jennifer was taken to the hospital for an overdose shortly before she went missing," Jimmy says.

"Hmm," Jeannie grunts. "I heard about that, but I kicked her out about a month before. Wasn't the first time she overdosed. There were two other times that weren't reported, and another time—like three or four years ago—when her drug buddies rolled her out of the car at the emergency room and took off." She snaps her finger, as if remembering something. "And the time they hauled her out of that drug house in Seattle." She wipes her nose with her thumb and index finger and then brushes them off on her pants.

"Mostly they'd just give her that narc stuff and she'd be fine," she says, referring to the emergency medication Narcan, which, due to America's ongoing opioid epidemic, has become standard in most ambulances.

"Do you remember which hospital she went to?" Jimmy asks.

"Would have been Providence, I suppose, except when she overdosed in Seattle. That would have been Harborview."

Jimmy writes the names down.

"Any history of suicide attempts," I ask, "even if it was just a threat?"

Jeannie gives a snort. "What do you call heroin?"

"I was thinking more like guns, knives, or intentional overdoses."

"She never actually tried anything, leastwise not as far as I know. The police took her to the hospital once or twice when she was saying she wanted to hurt herself, but she never did. The counselor helped a little, at least when she was clean."

"She was seeing a therapist?"

"Yeah, I drove her there a few times. They got an office downtown with three or four doctors, but she mostly saw the one. Don't remember what his name was, but he's the one that said she's got the bipolar thing." Raising an index finger pensively, she pushes herself from her chair and says, "Hang on."

Shuffling to the kitchen, her slippers never seeming to fully leave the floor, she rummages through the cabinets, opening and closing drawers and slamming doors. A moment later we hear a satisfied grunt and she returns to the living room and hands me a worn business card.

"BrightPath Wellness," I read aloud.

"That's them," Jeannie says, clearly pleased with herself. "The receptionist is a cranky old sea hag, but the rest of them are nice enough."

The business card is like any other. It has a logo that shows a footpath leading toward a bright horizon, under which is the address, phone number, web page, Facebook address, Instagram name, and Twitter account. Among all this is the name Dr. Arthur Hemming.

"Dr. Hemming?" I read aloud. "Is he the one Jennifer was seeing?"

"Yep, that's him."

"When was the last time you took her to see him?"

She exhales hard, letting her lips flap with the releasing air. "It must have been a couple weeks before we had our little falling-out." She leans forward in her chair. "She was stealing my pills. I got back problems and when they flare up, it's bad. I go to get a pill one day, just after I got my prescription filled, and the bottle is near empty. Well, that was just it, the last straw; I couldn't take it no more."

Her eyes find Jimmy.

"I s'pose there's stuff you're not telling me because you're trying to spare me, but you don't need to bother," she tells him. "I figured that girl was dead long ago—hell, I figured she was dead when she was still living with me, she just didn't know it yet." Her eyes drift to the corner of the ceiling, as if seeking meaning and purpose among the cobwebs. Despite her brave front I can see the water in her eyes.

"They got a copy of her dental records when she went missing," she says at length, her voice suddenly aged and tired. "I don't know much about police stuff, but I've seen enough shows to know that you don't ask for DNA if you have dental records and teeth to compare them to, so I guess I'm just wondering if there's going to be enough of my Jennifer to bury?"

Jimmy glances at me and then moves closer to Jeannie,

placing a consoling hand on her shoulder. "We'll try to get you something," he says, "but . . ." He pauses, unsure how to finish such a statement. How do you tell a woman that her granddaughter was dissolved in lye and dumped out on the forest floor, the remains of her teeth and bones becoming small pebbles in the landscape?

"It's okay," Jeannie says, stiffening her chin. Inhaling deeply and then breathing out in one long breath, she repeats, "It's okay," as if the words make it so.

"I'm sorry for your loss," Jimmy says.

Jeannie shakes her head as if utterly defeated, and in that moment a great, solitary tear runs down her left cheek, dragging with it all the sorrow and heartache of too many years. Sorrow not just for the loss of Jennifer, but for the loss of the *potential* of Jennifer: all the things she could have been and wasn't; all the things she could have done and didn't.

Jimmy and I sit with Jeannie a good while, letting her talk, letting her cry. She shows us old photo albums of Jennifer when she was a baby, and the box of pictures she'd drawn through the years, first in crayon, and later with charcoal and pencil. The last of these was a pencil drawing on a standard sheet of paper that she'd signed and dated when she was thirteen, about the time she'd started getting into trouble. The image is exquisite and shows Christ on the cross, but instead of Jesus, the figure is that of a young Jennifer, her face turned down as if the weight of the world were upon her. I suppose when you're thirteen that's how it sometimes feels.

There were no more drawings after that.

CHAPTER THIRTY-TWO

Our next stop is Lynnwood.

We're looking for the shine associated with mannequin number four, but so far, we're having no luck. After knocking on Emily Cantu's front door, we find her alive and well . . . and a bit curious why the FBI is checking on her. Jimmy quickly explains that it's a simple case of mistaken identity and assures her that all is well and she has nothing to fear.

When we reach the curb, Jimmy pulls the list from his pocket and scans down. Crossing off Emily Cantu's name with three swipes of his pen, he looks at the remaining names. "That means mannequin number four has to be either Debra Mata of Seattle or Cheryl Kaffe of Olympia."

"Or neither," I suggest.

"Or neither," he says with a sigh.

After grabbing a belated lunch at Panera Bread, we make our way into the heart of Seattle, to Yesler Way, and the last known address of Debra Mata. We're still rolling into the neighborhood when I recognize her distinct shine, and that of another: amethyst with burnt orange marbling, the shine of the Onion King.

"It's her," I say with words clipped short by a rush of adrenaline. "He's been here too." I point to an empty parking spot along the right side of the road, and then at another one farther up the street on the left.

"Does he approach the house?"

"No; it's just like before. He's watching. I'll bet he doesn't come near any of the houses, he just waits and watches, learns their routine, follows them. That way he can grab them elsewhere, someplace he won't be seen."

Jimmy nods. "Counting Erin Yarborough and Jennifer Holt, that's three so far."

"It'll be seven by the end of the day," I reply confidently. As the words leave my lips, I have no idea just how right and wrong I am, and both at the same time.

If Kristin Mata is surprised to find two FBI agents on her porch asking about her sister-in-law, she hides it well and greets us with a welcoming smile, the smile you give to a longtime friend or a good neighbor. When we explain our purpose, she invites us in and offers something to drink, without specifying anything in particular. We decline, hoping to make this a quick visit so we can be on to the next.

"I'm sorry Ken isn't here," Kristin says, motioning for us to sit. "He should be home from work by six if you want to come back. Debra is his younger sister by about ten years, but they don't talk. I don't think we've seen her for about three years now."

Kristin's manner of speech reminds me a bit of a bull-fight. There's some initial hesitation and ground-pawing, followed by a rapidly accelerating charge of words that end in something akin to a crescendo. After this there's a lull, a sort of repositioning for the next charge, and then it's all hooves and red capes again.

As she finishes her preamble, she seems to almost shudder, and then hurriedly takes a seat opposite from us. "I really do think it would best if you talked to Ken directly—I just feel funny talking about his sister when he's not here. Know what I mean?"

"We're not looking for anything salacious," Jimmy assures her. "We're just trying to figure out where she might have gone and maybe who some of her associates are."

Kristin snorts. "Associates!" She says the word as if it's a public joke or a private profanity. "Toward the end, before Ken told her to leave and never come back, the only time we saw her with her so-called *associates* was when they showed up here looking for money—though I suspect her real purpose was to check and see if we were away, so they could sneak in and rob us blind."

Her voice suddenly rises sharply. "Five times!" she says, holding up the splayed fingers of her right hand. "That's how many times we were broken into in the six months after Ken told her not to come back. We had to harden all the doors and windows and install a monitored security system before it finally stopped." She seems to realize that her voice has risen and turned sharp, so she forces a deep breath and then brushes out the nonexistent wrinkles in her slacks.

"I'd like to say I miss her, but I don't," she says with a bitter edge. "It hurts Ken, though, especially during the holidays and around her birthday. He still remembers when she was little, before she got caught up in all that—that nonsense."

She sighs. "God knows where she's living or what she's doing with herself. Whenever I'm downtown I'm afraid I'm going to see her on the street, panhandling or strung out or . . . or prostituting herself." She grows quiet, and then adds, "That's Ken's biggest fear. I tell him she wouldn't do that, but I know better. That's part of the lifestyle, isn't it?"

"Not always," Jimmy replies softly, "but often."

Kristin nods.

She assures us that she has nothing of Debra's that might contain DNA but promises to ask Ken if he'll speak to his mother. She might have old clothes or toiletries, but Kristin can't be sure. From our standpoint, the lack of DNA isn't critical. With the facial recognition, the fresh knowledge that Debra fits the same pattern as the others, and the fact that she's missing, it's enough.

"Was Debra ever admitted to the hospital?" Jimmy asks as we wrap up the brief interview.

"Sure, at least twice that I know of."

"Which hospital?"

"Harborview—both times."

"And was it for illness or overdose or something else?"

"The first time she wouldn't say, but I suspect it was overdose or something close to it. The second time it was because Ken called the police after she threatened to kill herself. They took her for a mental health examination, one of the ones where they hold you for a couple days."

"Did she ever actually *attempt* suicide?"

Kristin shakes her head slowly. "She'd talk about swimming out into the middle of the Puget Sound and just letting herself sink to the bottom, but she was too afraid of the octopuses."

"Octopuses?"

"Under the Tacoma Narrows Bridge," Kristin clarifies, "though I suppose they're all over the Puget Sound, it's just the under-the-bridge part that you always hear about. They say they have tentacles twenty feet long."

"Giant Pacific octopus," I say, leaning close to Jimmy, as if the information is somehow confidential. When he gives me an odd look, I shrug. "Marty is always going on and on about them, like they're sacred or something."

He stares at me a moment and then turns back to Kristin.

"So, she never actually swam out into the sound, she just talked about it," he summarizes. "Did she ever try anything else? Pills, cutting, anything like that?"

Kristin purses her lips and shakes her head.

"Was she ever in counseling?"

"Off and on, I think, but only when it was court-ordered."

"Do you remember who she saw?"

"It was a long time ago," she replies in a weary voice.

Jimmy nods his understanding, and I can tell he's disappointed at the lack of concrete information. He wraps up the interview and we say our goodbyes, leaving Kristin standing on the porch with a sad, troubled expression on her face, perhaps wondering what, if anything, she should tell her husband.

As Jimmy and I make our way south, going from neighborhood to neighborhood, from house to house, it becomes clear that the women we seek all suffered the same fate because they suffered the same symptoms: addiction, mental illness, suicidal thoughts, despair. How much of this can be blamed on them, or on their circumstances, or on the abuse they endured at the hands of others is now irrelevant. To Murphy, they were broken, and he had a fix; to the Onion King they were vulnerable and easily lost to the world.

The only thing I'm certain of at the moment is that more victims will follow. The only way to stop it is to find the Onion King.

Jimmy says that Murphy was just as much a victim of the Onion King as Charice and the others, but it's hard to see him in that part, at least not the way most view victims. His fate was determined by his decisions, even though those decisions were tainted by mental illness and twisted by the cunning manipulations of a psychopath. He was a true believer, but his faith was misplaced.

Murphy used the word *transmogrified* in his manifesto.

If you'd asked me the meaning I could only say that it had something to do with change or transition. It turns out that transmogrified refers to someone or something that's been *transformed, especially in a surprising or magical manner.*

The fact that Murphy underlined the word several times is downright chilling. He had transmogrified seven living and breathing women into plastic and plaster representations of themselves. And despite his use of the word, there was nothing magical about their transmogrification, no frogs turning into princes or pumpkins blossoming into coaches.

With sudden realization—stained by dark humor—it occurs to me how ironic it is that Murphy died as he did. The man who reveled in the glory of transmogrification had himself been transformed into a limp bag of skin filled with dead tissue. The magic was provided by chemistry: the rapid combustion of nitrocellulose pushing a copper-lined chunk of lead through Murphy's forehead at eighteen hundred feet per second.

There was no spoken spell, just the sudden clap of thunder and the aftertaste of burnt air as the three-dimensional Murphy crumbled to the forest floor.

In a few years he'll be rendered to bone, and eventually nothing; the three-dimensional will become non-dimensional.

Just like magic.

We're southbound on I-5, moving away from downtown Seattle and toward the suburban sprawl of Beacon Hill, when Jimmy's phone rings. He answers and puts it on speaker.

"Hey, Jimmy. It's me," Haiden Webber announces.

"Haiden," Jimmy says, "please tell me you've got something for us."

"Yes and no," the computer forensics expert replies. "I've run everything I have against the hard drive, but Murphy's shredder program was used on every file he's deleted in the last two years, so those are gone for good. That said, I was able to find some old files from before he started using the shredder. These were also deleted, but fortunately Murphy doesn't use a lot of disk space, so they were never overwritten—well, mostly. I lost a few chunks of data, but the documents are mostly complete."

"Please tell me they're not poems or letters to the editor," Jimmy says.

"No—well, yeah, most of it was garbage, but I found several documents that make for good reading. One is a download from Silk Road 2.0, from a vendor known only as Trash Can Mike. It's a how-to guide on body disposal, including step-by-step instructions on how to dissolve human remains in lye. Murphy paid for it with bitcoin."

The look I give Jimmy is one of bewilderment, and he stares at me a moment before turning his eyes back to the road. "Haiden, I think Steps has a question for you."

"Shoot," the computer tech replies.

Leaning closer to the in-vehicle speaker, I say, "Isn't the dark web supposed to be anonymous? I mean, that's the whole point, right? So how do you know this document is from this Trash Can Mike and that it was sold on Silk Road 2.0?"

Haiden chuckles. "Well, the cover page says Trash Can Mike, Silk Road 2.0 Edition. I'm not a tracker-slash-investigator, but isn't that what you guys call a clue?"

Haiden then gives us the rundown on the other documents, which are less nefarious than the guide to body disposal. One describes various ways to enter and hot-wire a car, another is a guide to mold-making.

"I don't think we're going to find much more," the computer scientist says. "I know you were hoping for an address or some kind of smoking gun, but we both know that was wishful thinking."

"I suppose so," Jimmy concedes. They chat another minute, and before going, Haiden promises to forward the dark web reports to Diane.

After Jimmy disconnects the call, we ride in silence, the road noise rumbling beneath us like some primordial asphalt beast. "So," I finally say, "I guess wishful thinking is no longer approved law enforcement policy?"

"It is in my book," Jimmy replies.

CHAPTER THIRTY-THREE

Melinda Gaines woke disoriented that morning when the overhead lights burst to life abruptly and without the subtleties of dawn. The light surrounded her and filled her small world with the warm yellow glow of five incandescent bulbs. It was a familiar feeling, waking and not knowing where she was, how she got there, or what time of night or day it was, despite the silent pronouncements of the light. Hers was the morning grogginess of an accomplished drinker—and then she remembered: she hadn't had a drink in six months. So, what was this?

Her eyes found the clock.

It was sitting on the small nightstand next to the bed, and as she picked it up and stared incomprehensibly at the glowing numbers it finally came to her: eight o'clock. She was going to be late for work.

As she sprang from bed, she glanced around . . . and froze. She couldn't have been more frozen if she were lying naked on a lake of ice. A cold finger of fear traced its way along her bony spine, spreading to every nerve and pore. Her breath caught in her throat. And then she stopped breathing altogether.

Time stood still.

Only when her body screamed for oxygen did she finally take the air of the room into her lungs, pulling it down in great staggering gulps. With trembling legs, she sat back on the edge of the bed, a bed that wasn't hers, in a room she'd never seen, in a place she feared she'd never leave.

The wall of heavy prison bars opposite the bed told her she was in trouble. This was no county jail or state prison. And so, she sat; she sat for the better part of an hour trying to remember the night before and the circumstances that landed her here . . . wherever *here* was.

She fought for every recollection, every scrap of remembrance: a table with three barstools pulled around; Trish and Alice; a grungy bathroom smelling of beer and perfume. Eventually she remembered Biscuits Bar & Grill. She remembered dancing sober with Trish and Alice, a threesome on the dance floor, shaking and singing along to Elle King as she bellowed out "Ex's & Oh's."

And then an image came rushing back to her, as if the winds of her mind had lifted it off a poster and flung it against her face. It was the man from the bar: James—no, Jeff! The guy who smelled her when she wasn't looking and then offered to walk her home after what was supposed to be a chance encounter on the sidewalk.

But she'd said no, thank you, and good night and left him behind. He hadn't followed her, at least not as far as she could tell. Or had he?

Was he responsible for this?

She strained to remember, striking her forehead with the palm of her hand, as if self-abuse were going to knock the rust from her mental gears. It didn't. Instead, her brain began to throb as a headache took root and began to strobe behind her left eye.

She should have memories of arriving home, petting her cat, reading several chapters of *All the Light We Cannot See*, and perhaps eating some ice cream before finally tucking in for the night, but there was nothing.

Her mind was a void.

Yet voids exist in shadow, and as she let herself wander into this darkness, embracing it, something finally came to her, flitting like a bat just beyond reach. It started as a nebulous haze, wispy puffs of smoke resembling distant, dirty clouds; an abstract of an abstract.

As she continued to probe her memory, the abstract became suddenly concrete, and there it was before her, where it had been all along. The blackness remained but peering from behind this veil were two eyes and a mouth.

The black ski mask!

And then she remembered the prick in her neck and the soft fall into nothing. With renewed vigor, fear coursed through her and she heard the desperate beat of her own heart drumming in her ears.

She spent the rest of the morning waiting for the inevitable sound of approaching footsteps. The sudden eruption of light that woke her at eight that morning should have heralded the arrival of her captor, perhaps to gloat or appraise or partake, but she soon spotted the small box mounted next to the light switch on the wall beyond the bars. The lights were on a timer, and as she would learn in the coming days, they came on at eight A.M. and went off at ten P.M.

The wall beyond the bars was artificially three-dimensional, an effect produced by a floor-to-ceiling mural of trees—a rich green forest made mysterious by morning mist. It stretched twelve feet along the opposite wall, a picture of tranquility meant to—what? Calm her? Put her at ease?

The idea was laughable.

Yet the same sentiment was displayed in the warmly painted walls of the cell, the plush carpet on the floor, and the scattered furnishings, which included a small but comfortable twin bed with a thick quilt and high-end sheets, a recliner, an elegant nightstand, and a diminutive bookshelf that held dozens of the latest paperback titles, their spines facing out and ordered alphabetically. Among these is *All the Light We Cannot See*, the same book that sits half read on her nightstand at home.

Had he known?

Had he been in her house and seen the book next to her bed, or followed her through the bookstore when she bought it a week earlier? The possibilities sent a chill through her.

The comfort of the cell was interrupted only by stark necessity. Opposite the bed and tucked into the corner of the eight-by-twelve-foot space, looking like prison surplus, was a small curtained shower, a toilet, and a sink.

There is no beauty in these items, just utilitarian simplicity, and yet Melinda takes comfort in their presence.

The passage outside her cell goes to the right and to the left, with destinations that couldn't be more different. To the right, just a few feet beyond the end of her cell, was a steel door painted in the same warm, earthy tones as her cell. The handle was thick and overbuilt, part of an extensive latching system that probably included a built-in cipher lock. She'd seen such locks at the various hospitals and treatment centers where she'd been a guest, both voluntarily and involuntarily. She had no doubt that the passage door would be difficult to breach without special equipment, even if she could get out of the cell.

That was the other problem.

The cell door had a large, heavily reinforced lockbox with no keyhole. One of the first things she'd done was to feel around all six surfaces of the box looking for a hole, a button, a lever—anything that might allow her to pick the lock or access the box.

It was solid steel all the way around.

As far as she could tell, the only opening was the hole where the locking bolt engaged the doorframe, meaning it was remotely activated. She guessed it was wireless because without a keyhole or wires there was no other way to explain the operation of the mechanism.

Of all the places her eyes wandered that morning, and of all the things she studied and tried to make sense of, it was the long passage to the left of her cell that kept drawing her back. The mysterious corridor wandered away for twenty feet before it narrowed and continued on into unfathomable darkness. Where it went she couldn't guess, but the dark maw troubled her, both from its blackness and from the small noises that occasionally issued from its depths—scraping and scuttering and, every once in a while, heavier sounds that were less defined.

She screams for the better part of an hour at noon, finally collapsing onto the bed and sobbing herself into exhausted, troubled sleep. It's a tiny sound that wakes her some time later; a different sound.

She glances at the digital clock on the nightstand and sees that it's exactly two o'clock in the afternoon. The sound in her ears is disorienting at first, but as she comes fully awake and gets her bearings, she recognizes that it doesn't come from the black maw of the endless narrow passage to the left, but from beyond the steel door to her right. It's the sound of hard-heeled shoes clicking against stone tile, and it's growing louder, more pronounced. A moment later, the sound stops on the other side of the door. There's the quiet rattle of something being set aside, perhaps on the floor or a low table, followed by the steady *tink tink tink* of . . . what?

Is it a spoon stirring the contents of a glass?

Is he poisoning her? Drugging her?

What other explanation could there be? It's the same

sound her glass makes when she stirs chocolate syrup into her milk, or vitamin C powder into water. *Tink tink tink*. He's going to drug her; she's sure of it now.

When the door finally opens and her captor enters, she's disappointed to find his features hidden behind the same black ski mask that plays at the edge of her memory. With rising fury, she wants to scream at him, to call him a coward for hiding his face, but the words won't form in her throat. Instead, she finds herself pressing against the back wall of the cell, trembling, despite her best efforts to hide the toxic mix of anger and fear.

Wordlessly, the mask takes the tray of food he carries and slides it through a horizontal slot welded into the bars of the makeshift prison. He holds it there silently, waiting for her to step forward and take it. When she doesn't, he whispers, "Take it or starve."

I'm already starving, she thinks.

Peeling herself from the wall, Melinda moves forward by inches, one shaking hand outstretched before her. When the tips of her fingers brush the edge of the tray, she quickly swings her other hand up and grabs hold, jerking the tray into the cell with enough force to spill some of the orange juice from the heavy glass mug.

Taking the juice, she walks to the sink and is about to pour it down the drain. Guessing correctly, the mask whispers, "It's only vitamins." Holding up an empty packet of vitamin powder, he waves it in front of her as proof. "I have a hundred ways to render you unconscious, and a thousand ways to kill you," the mask continues. "I don't need to play games by spiking your food or drink."

Whether Melinda believes him or not, she slowly sets the glass back down and then shuffles over to the edge of the bed and sits with the tray on her knees. Picking up a wedge of avocado, she begins to raise it to her lips, but then drops her hand back to her lap. She wonders at the ambiguous nature of hunger, that she could be so famished and yet have no appetite. It's as preposterous as matter and antimatter occupying the same space, but as long as the mask leers at her from the other side of the bars, she finds herself unable to eat. Even the thought of it churns her stomach, and she feels the bile rising unbidden.

The hole at the bottom of the mask twists into a broad, toothy smile, as if he feels her discomfort, as if he were a kindly man smiling away her distrust.

The man stands at the bars a moment longer and Melinda hears a soft sniffing from under the mask, like someone with a cold who's trying to hide it.

He's doing it again, she realizes with growing dread.

He's sniffing the air of the cell the same way one might a container of food from the fridge, checking for freshness. The snuffling and sniffing might have gone unnoticed if not for the memory of Jeff leaning in close to her in the bar and then again on the street, taking her in by clandestine whiffs and sniffs.

It's him; she's sure of it now.

Part of her wants to call him by name, to strip away the mask and the anonymity he so easily presumes. But for all she knows, Jeff isn't even his name. She knows his face, though. Even if the name is a lie, the face is truth, and she swears to herself in that moment that she'll spend her waking hours remembering his face, the shape of his body, the way he walks, even the nearly indecipherable whisper he uses to disguise his voice.

She vows to remember it; all of it.

CHAPTER THIRTY-FOUR

When we arrive in Beacon Hill at the last known address of Abitha Jones, the single-story home at the end of a forgotten cul-de-sac looks vacant and ill-used. Garbage lines the collapsing fence on the west side of the house, and most of the windows are boarded up.

The remnants of tape and paper hang from the front door where various notices had been repeatedly posted and torn down; perhaps eviction notices or foreclosure announcements or just ordinance violations issued by the county or city. It doesn't really matter, since all were equally ignored.

Exiting the black Ford Expedition, I study the sidewalk and surrounding street. The shine is there, but it's old, perhaps three years old, well before she went missing, and there's no sign of the Onion King.

"Abitha is mannequin number one," I inform Jimmy.

He nods and studies the old house. "When was she last here?"

"Two to three years ago, though I'm leaning toward three."

"And when was she last arrested?"

I lean into the Ford through the open door and flip through the notes in my folder. "She was booked for drugs by Seattle PD a year and a half ago, and then nothing. No hits in CLEAR, no new driver's license or registered vehicles, no parking tickets."

"Meaning she was grabbed shortly after her last arrest," Jimmy summarizes. "At least we can put a date range on her disappearance."

If we didn't already know she was dead, we'd consider her disappearing trick rather remarkable. Abitha was a frequent flier, someone who was contacted by law enforcement with such regularity that the only way they'd possibly drop off the map is if they died, relocated, went to prison, or changed their ways, and Abitha showed no inclination for the latter.

Fishing in his pocket, Jimmy extracts his phone and speed-dials Diane. When she answers, he passes on our predicament in two short sentences and asks her to dig deeper. "She must have a mom or dad someplace, right? Maybe a brother or sister?"

I can't hear the other side of the conversation, but I can imagine Diane assuring him that yes, she's almost certain that *everyone* has a mother and father, whether they know them or not.

Or perhaps she saves that kind of sarcasm just for me.

The twelve-mile drive from Beacon Hill to Burien takes twenty-five minutes as the Seattle-area traffic thickens and begins to congeal. When we finally turn onto Amber Bartlett's street, I pull my glasses down an inch and study the terrain for just a moment before pushing them back up and crossing Chelsea Younger of Covington off the list. I circle Amber's name four times in slow, encompassing circles, marking her among the dead.

"Amber Bartlett is mannequin number seven," I say to Jimmy, feeling the heaviness of my words as they leave me.

During our brief discussion with Amber's mother, who reportéd her missing a year ago, we learn about her history of schizophrenic episodes, which began when she was nineteen, and the various antics that landed her in trouble with the police. On several of these occasions she'd been hospitalized on a seventy-two-hour hold, something referred to as an involuntary, or by its longer name: involuntary mental health evaluation. Either way you say it, the key word is *involuntary*. It's like jail without the bars.

"She's fine when she takes her meds," her mother assures us.

The problem with Amber was that she frequently refused her meds, claiming they made her light-headed or sick, or that they gave her constipation. And during those times when she did follow her prescription, it was only until she started feeling better, at which point she'd declare that she felt fine and no longer needed the pills. It was a vicious circle of meltdown, medication, normalcy, rejection, and back to meltdown.

In the year before her disappearance, Amber spent several months at Western State Hospital, an inpatient psychiatric facility in Lakewood. She was also attending regular therapy sessions.

"A place called BrightPath something," Mrs. Bartlett says. "They have an office on Glover Street, not far from here. That's where I'd take Amber for her visits. It was the only way I could be sure she'd go; I'd take her there and read magazines in the waiting room until she finished."

When Jimmy asks for the address, the woman just shakes her head. "Couldn't tell you that, but it's next to a two-story dental office that's god-awful blue. You'd have to be blind to miss it."

———

"Notice a pattern forming?" I say to Jimmy as we pull away from the curb.

"If you mean mental illness and drug addiction, I'd have to say yes."

"Don't forget BrightPath Wellness."

Jimmy nods. "I wouldn't put too much stock in that, at least not yet. They own a whole chain of clinics, so it's hardly unusual if two of our seven victims have been treated by them. And let's not forget that Jennifer Holt was treated at a BrightPath clinic in Everett, which is over an hour away in *good* traffic."

"And Seattle traffic is never good," I chime in, seeing his point. Still, I'm not ready to concede just yet. "Glover Street is just two miles west of here," I suggest. "It wouldn't take long to do a quick drive-by."

Jimmy rolls slowly up to the stop sign at the intersection just south of Amber's house, the SUV's left blinker flashing and ticking. He pauses, starts to make the turn, and then abruptly flips the turn signal all the way up so that the right blinker begins to pulse.

When I grin at him, he mutters, "I just don't want to listen to you complain all the way to Tacoma." But then his face melts into a small grin, confirming what I already knew. It's always the same with Jimmy: he's just as curious as I am, but it takes longer to settle in his bones.

When we roll onto Glover Street, I spot the god-awful blue from a block away and can't help thinking that this amalgam of dentists either hired the world's worst decorator or there was an emergency clearance sale of God-Awful Blue at the hardware store. The only other explanation is that they want to shock their patients into numbness *before* they enter the clinic.

It saves on lidocaine.

"BrightPath," I say, my finger pointing to a modest building just north of god-awful. By comparison, the mental health facility is a marvelous two-story with wonderful aesthetics and ample parking on all sides.

Somewhere between turning onto Glover and pulling into the parking lot at the clinic, my special glasses leave my face and I find myself holding them in my right hand as a world of shine fills my vision. Filtering through perhaps a million different footsteps and colors, I quickly find Amber's pleasing yellow-green. I look for Debra Mata next, but she's nowhere to be seen. It's the same with Erin Yarborough, Sheryl Dorsey, and Jennifer Holt. It's only when I get to Abitha Jones that I find another match.

"How about mannequins two and five?" Jimmy asks after I pass on my findings.

We're pretty sure mannequin number five is going to be Sheryl Dorsey, since she was reported missing five months ago. As for number two, we're hoping— No! That's the wrong word. We're *expecting* that it's going to be Gabriella Paden of Tukwila, only because the other candidate is dead.

Scanning the lot and sidewalks thoroughly, and then doing it once more for good measure, I glance at him and say, "They're not here."

Jimmy nods. "As I said, it's not unusual to have—"

Like a shot, my left hand finds his forearm and clamps on, squeezing until he winces. He digs at my fingers to pry them loose, but I'm oblivious. It's an involuntary spasm, as if my soul suddenly convulsed with some celestial epilepsy.

"It's him!" I finally manage. "It's the Onion King."

CHAPTER THIRTY-FIVE

"You know perfectly well they're not going to give out that kind of information," Diane argues. "You could tell them Ted Bundy just returned from the grave and is stalking their clients, and they'd yawn and tell you the same thing I'm telling you: get a warrant. The HIPAA laws are clear when it comes to medical privacy, and they don't make exceptions, even for the likes of Jimmy and Steps."

"Yeah-yeah-yeah," Jimmy blurts, tired of the lecture. "We'll wait until we have the last two names and then request a warrant, but in the meantime, get hold of Jason or Nate and see if Charice Qian is still at the hospital. We need to know if she ever went to one of the BrightPath Wellness clinics, and if so, where?"

"I talked to Angie Eccles this morning," Diane replies in a softer tone. "Charice is being released tomorrow morning. So, yes, she's still at the hospital, and, yes, I'll call Detective Sturman and pass on your request. The sheriff also asked me to pass on the lab results from Charice's blood work."

Jimmy readies his pen. "Go ahead."

"She had two different drugs in her system; one of them you may have already guessed, and that's propofol. The other is sevoflurane."

"Never heard of it," Jimmy mutters.

Diane continues. "They think she was first injected with the propofol, which is fast-acting and would have rendered her unconscious in seconds. The effects of an injection are short-lived, maybe ten or fifteen minutes, as I'm sure you know. The point is that the abductions would have been quick and the propofol would have given him time to move the women to a vehicle or other location where he could administer the sevoflurane."

"Why not just use the fluoride stuff from the start?" Jimmy asks.

"Se-vo-flu-rane," Diane corrects, enunciating every syllable the way she does when reading Doctor Seuss to her grandkids. "Because it has to be inhaled," she explains patiently, "and I can't imagine Mr. Onionhead bogeyman rolling a canister of gas down the street asking his intended victims to take a sniff, can you?"

I raise my eyebrows at Jimmy, mostly in appreciation of the sarcasm, but also because she's right.

"Point taken," Jimmy concedes. "Call us when you have the information on Charice." Before Diane can reply, he disconnects the call.

I stare at him with widening eyes, which quickly drop to the silent phone, and then back to his set and stoic features. Sucking a long and intentionally slurpy breath through my clenched teeth, I say, "Dude, you hung up on *Diane*."

"Mm-hmm," he hums, looking at me without an ounce of care or concern, as if he really means it, as if saying, *You want some too?*

I shake my head in disbelief and mutter, "Your funeral."

It's a short drive from Burien to Tukwila, where we discover that Gabriella Paden is alive and well and living in suburban splendor. That eliminates our second and final candidate for mannequin number two, which means we have an official Jane Doe on our hands. I don't let it bother me, and I don't think Jimmy is concerned either. These things have a way of working themselves out as an investigation progresses.

Swinging back onto I-5, Jimmy is just getting the Ford up to traffic speed, the nose pointed south to Tacoma, when his phone rings. He glances at the caller ID before answering, expecting Diane. It's not.

"Nate! How are you?"

"Doing good," the detective replies. "Diane called about twenty minutes ago and filled me in. Sounds like you guys are having some luck out there."

"Not bad," Jimmy says, playing it down, as usual. "We just struck out at Gabriella Paden's place—which is good for her because it means she's alive, but we have no other candidates for number two—mannequin number two," he quickly corrects, likely sensing my head swiveling his way. "Did Diane tell you what we're up against?"

"That depends. Do you mean the part where you have your panties in a knot, or the part where you need to ask Charice about her therapy sessions?"

"The latter."

Nate chuckles. "Yeah, she filled me in. It's a short drive from the office, so rather than calling Charice, I came to the hospital. I'm with her now, just let me switch to speakerphone."

"Perfect," Jimmy says. Reaching for his notepad, he tosses it into my lap and makes head motions that I'm supposed to take notes.

Nate's voice sounds hollow when next he speaks, like we're all ten years old and talking through tin cans connected by string. We obviously sound just as bad to him, because he apologizes for his cheap phone.

"Okay, go ahead," Nate says.

"Hi, Charice," Jimmy begins. "How are you feeling?"

"Better," she replies in an airy voice. "Still a bit sore, but I'm not complaining. That first day, the doctors were trying to decide whether they should amputate two of my toes. I guess I had frostbite." She gives a humorless laugh. "I didn't even care; I was just worried that my shoes might not fit. Weird, huh?"

"Not so weird," Jimmy says, and even though she can't see him, he has a consoling smile on his face. "I take it they saved the toes."

"Yep. Still got my ten little piggies."

"That's good. You had a close call all the way around." He hesitates a moment, and then plunges on. "I was hoping I could ask you something . . . about before? I don't want to pry, but we need your help if we're going to catch the guy who did this to you."

"No, sure. What do you need?"

"I understand you had some issues with heroin. . . ."

"Yeah." Her voice is resigned, ashamed.

"Did you ever go to counseling, either for the drugs or other issues?"

She sighs, and this time her voice is more withdrawn. "Yeah. It didn't take. I went through rehab a couple times, but as soon as I'd finish, I'd hook up with my old friends and be right back where I started from."

"Where was the rehab?"

"One was in Spokane, the other was in Portland."

"What about other counseling, maybe something closer to home?"

She laughs that same humorless laugh. "Sure. I've got all the usual demons. Depression, anxiety, paranoia, and some anger issues—or at least that's what they tell me. I'll admit to the first three, but I never thought of myself as angry."

"Why do you think they said that?"

You can almost hear her shrug on the other end. "I took a baseball bat to a vending machine after it ate my money." She quickly adds, "Everyone gets mad once in a while; that doesn't mean you have *anger issues*."

"That's true. Sometimes burning off anger is better than bottling it up."

"So my baseball bat wasn't such a bad thing?"

"Well, I wouldn't say that," Jimmy replies, and then quickly changes the subject. "So, where did you go for therapy?"

"It was a clinic in Olympia."

"Do you remember the name?"

"Yeah, it was the Bright Path, or something like that."

Jimmy and I exchange a look, our minds dissecting the odds and possibilities. We're silent so long that Charice eventually says, "Hello?"

"Sorry," Jimmy apologizes. "We're still here; just . . . processing." His gaze never leaves me—or should I say his gaze never leaves whatever is just *beyond* me. He has a habit of doing that; staring and not staring all at the same time. I don't know if it's something he picked up in the military, or if it's just Jimmy. Maybe it's the thousand-yard stare you always hear about in the movies. In any case, he's focused on something or nothing that resides on the other side of my head.

"Was there one particular counselor you worked with, or was it just whoever was available?"

"I almost always worked with Thomas Chambers, well, Dr. Chambers, but he had everyone call him Thomas."

I scribble the name down in Jimmy's notepad as he says, "That's great; that's all we need. Thanks for your help, Charice. And I was glad to hear you get to go home tomorrow. Just make sure you keep up with your counseling. It helps."

"Thanks." The word comes out as if others were meant to

follow but somehow got lost on the way to her mouth. Then she spits them out, late, but all accounted for: "I hope you get him."

"We will." He lets the sentiment settle, says goodbye, and then asks Nate to pick up.

We hear the phone switch off speaker and Nate's voice suddenly booms crisp and clear. "Yeah, Jimmy, whatcha got?"

He quickly fills Nate in on the other two victims linked to BrightPath, though the story loses a lot of its potency since we can't tell him the clinic we just left is swimming in the Onion King's shine. Then he updates Nate on our progress with the facial recognition list.

"Four confirmed matches, one Jane Doe, and one unconfirmed match. The latter is Abitha Jones," he explains. "She wasn't at her last known address, so Diane is working on a better location. We're pretty sure she's going to be a match."

By "pretty sure" he means we know it for a fact, but we can't tell Nate that.

"At this point we just need some DNA to compare against." He pauses, reaches over, and yanks his notepad from my hands. Resting it on his lap, he flips through three pages of notes before finding what he's after. "The last name on the list is Sheryl Dorsey in Tacoma. We're heading there now." He finishes with Nate and disconnects the call.

Jimmy has a thing about pens, so after he so unrighteously yanked the notepad from my hands, I make a big show of clicking the ballpoint closed—*his* ballpoint—and placing it in my pocket.

He scowls at me, eyes darting wordlessly between my face and my pocket, until finally saying, "That's my pen."

I don't say a thing. I just turn and look out the passenger window, letting myself sink into the hum and rhythm of the road noise as I watch the tree-lined berm alongside the highway. The mound follows us, never leaving our side. It's like when you were a kid and the moon followed you on the ride home. Only the moon never changed or wavered, whereas the berm rises and falls and morphs so that it could be just one horizon or a thousand, and all the while it hides the ugliness of industrial sprawl on the other side.

My urban meditation is broken by four insistent words that make me smile: "Steps, that's my pen. . . ."

CHAPTER THIRTY-SIX

I'm not a fan of labeling neighborhoods as good or bad based on first impressions, mostly because I've been to a lot of villages, towns, and cities during my time with the Special Tracking Unit and have found that there are plenty of good people living in allegedly bad places, and a healthy dose of bad people living in good places.

So, when we turn onto Gardner Street and roll up to the residence of Peggy Camp, the mother of Sheryl Dorsey, I don't judge her, nor do I judge the neighborhood . . . but the two sketchy dudes leaning against the fender of a 1980s-era Caprice parked in the center of the front lawn give me pause. The unrestrained bellowing of some song by Five Finger Death Punch doesn't help. The thundering music pulses from every corner of the property, but nowhere in particular.

I imagine the speakers are the size of steamer trunks— stolen, most likely.

When Jimmy pulls to the curb, the doper dudes quickly douse their cigarettes and slink into the house, heads down and hoodies up so we can't get a good look at their faces; all the usual mannerisms of upstanding, law-abiding citizens.

"Tweaker city," Jimmy mutters as he puts the Expedition in park. "Got your little gun?"

My "little gun" is a Walther P22 semiautomatic. I like it because it fits nicely in the palm of my hand and the holster isn't too bulky. It may only fire .22-caliber rounds, but with the right load it can be devastating. Jimmy likes to make fun of it because it doesn't spew cannonballs and blast doors off their hinges like his Glock. He doesn't kid me about it as much as he used to, not since I shot and killed Pat McCourt.

Another memory I wish I could erase.

"No," I say, without elaborating.

He nods, unconcerned and unsurprised. Generally, I only pack if things start getting dicey, and, frankly, I didn't think visiting the relatives of murder victims would qualify as dicey. Who knew? In any case, my little gun is tucked away in a pistol safe next to my bed.

Slipping my glasses off, I start my routine—and immediately stiffen in my seat, my pulse quickening. Sheryl Dorsey is here; her shine is all around the house and in the street and on the sidewalk, but it's old. She was reported missing five months ago, so that part fits.

It's what *doesn't* fit that has me on high alert, and what doesn't fit is the Onion King's shine. I'm not surprised to find it here, but I am surprised that it's fresh, left sometime during the last few days—maybe even today.

It's not his first visit either. His shine is everywhere, and it dates back at least a year, probably longer. As my head swivels about, I see his tracks in the street, around the house, on the porch, alongside the house, and even at the mailbox, like the guy lives here. These are the tracks not of someone doing reconnaissance, but of a frequent guest or sometime resident.

As I relay this to Jimmy, he briskly pulls a large folding

map of Clallam County from the side pocket of the door and unfolds it across his steering wheel. Then he holds it up between his two hands, blocking out half the windshield.

"What are you doing?"

He grins at me from behind the map, the map of a county two hours away. "We're just two old-school Feds without GPS," he says in a twangy country-boy voice.

I nod. "Who pulled over to check the map."

"Exactly. If they think we're lost, they won't think we're here for them."

Playing along, I lean over and point to a location on the map. It's no place in particular, just a random spot my finger lands on. "You know we're in Pierce County, right?"

"It's the only map I have."

Neither of us appears to give the house or neighborhood a second thought, but my eyes are screwed into the corners of their sockets first left, then right, watching for any runners, any weapons or threats.

After a moment, Jimmy makes a big show of folding the map and then points down the road and makes an indication of a left turn with his hand, all above the dash and visible to anyone peering out from the house or watching us from one of the three surveillance cameras I've spotted so far.

"What's the plan?" I ask Jimmy as we pull away from the curb.

"Knock-and-talk," he replies, "but I don't want to go in light, especially with you unarmed. We'll see if Tacoma PD can spare a couple uniforms."

Parking at an intersection two blocks down and one block over, Jimmy places a call to Tacoma's finest while I call Diane. I confirm that Sheryl Dorsey is one of our victims and ask her to get started on the BrightPath Wellness warrant. We need to know how many of them received counseling or other services from the chain of clinics, and if so, where.

Diane reads off the list: "Abitha Jones, Jennifer Holt,

Debra Mata, Sheryl Dorsey, Erin Yarborough, and Amber Bartlett."

As an afterthought, I add one more name to the list.

"Why?" she asks.

And so I start to explain, but she understands before I'm halfway through. "Make sure they know it's urgent," I say before ending the call.

Four minutes later the first patrol unit arrives, followed a minute later by a second. Each is a two-man car, and as we brief the four cops at the bumper of the Expedition, they seem more than familiar with the house on Gardner Street. More importantly, they're eager to have a crack at it.

When we converge on the home again, one of the doper dudes has returned to his post at the side of the Caprice, meaning he's either a three-pack-a-day smoker or a lookout. I'm betting on the latter.

When the guy turns our way, you can tell the moment of recognition because he suddenly bolts upright. The Expedition's massive engine roars to life as Jimmy mashes the pedal to the floor. Clearing the last block, he comes to a skidding stop in front of the house, leaving black marks on the road and shedding whiffs of smoke off the smoldering tires.

It's all for show.

The rapid approach, roaring engine, and tortured tires are meant to draw attention to the front of the house while Tacoma PD rolls unnoticed into the alley behind, the two marked units coming from different directions.

It works beautifully.

Rather than making for the front door, doper dude runs down the side of the house, making for the alley and a quick escape. When he bursts through the back gate, he's looking over his shoulder at Jimmy and me as we pour from the SUV.

He should have been looking where he was going.

With a neat thud he plows headlong into the side of one of the patrol cars and skids halfway across the hood. Not in the cool way, either—the well-choreographed skid where some Fonzie wannabe flawlessly slides his ass across the hood of a car and lands perfectly on the other side. Doper dude does it face-first and at the wrong angle, so instead of landing like the Fonz, the windshield stops him—hard.

We don't hear it from our vantage point, but I imagine there's a crunching sound as his nose gives way, and the obligatory grunt and whimper of pain.

Once the Fonz is detained, three of the officers spread out across the back of the property and cover the sides, while the fourth moves to a cover position at the front right corner of the house.

Watching for any movement in the windows, we make our way to the porch and Jimmy presses the doorbell. It jiggles, loosens from its setting, and then falls and clatters onto the painted concrete. We stare at it a moment, not really surprised, and then Jimmy switches to knocking.

There are different types of knocks one uses when contacting a residence on law enforcement business. This isn't something taught at the academy or codified in some knocking policy; rather, it's something one picks up on the job after knocking on a lot of doors and learning what works and what doesn't, and which to use in each particular situation. Jimmy's knock isn't the aggressive *bam bam bam* that he might hammer out if we were executing a warrant and getting ready to boot the door. Instead, it's more of a hey-I'm-your-new-neighbor kind of knock, or a here's-your-mail, the-postman-put-it-in-the-wrong-box-again knock.

It doesn't work. Apparently neighbors and postal carriers aren't well regarded in this neighborhood.

Meanwhile, the house has become eerily quiet, intentionally quiet, like a big church on Monday morning. No one peeks out through the dirty blinds, no footsteps creak across

the old floor, and no hushed voices seep from the walls and windows. Even the shattering sound waves of Five Finger Death Punch have lapsed into silence.

Jimmy smiles and shakes his head.

It really is predictable and a bit funny how criminals re- act when 5-0 shows up on their doorstep. It doesn't matter if it's Tacoma on a Thursday afternoon or Tampa in the sum- mer. They all hunker down and pretend they're little mice, hoping the cops will go away. The problem is they often get their wish.

Without a warrant, we don't have enough to enter the house. It doesn't matter that the Onion King is a serial kid- napper and rapist; the only thing we have linking him to this property is shine, which we can't exactly talk about, not unless I want my own court-appointed mental health ses- sions at BrightPath Wellness.

So we knock.

If we want to find out why the Onion King has been com- ing and going from this residence, we need to talk our way in somehow. We need to convince Peggy Camp that it's in her best interest to open the door and let us in. So far, it's not going so well.

"FBI," Jimmy calls out, banging a bit louder, more of an upset-neighbor knock. "Mrs. Camp, you're not in trouble. We need to speak with you about your daughter."

The "not in trouble" part usually helps.

The house continues its state of utter quiet for a few more moments, and then things begin to shift. The hiss of urgent whispering rises beyond the door, perhaps an argument over how to proceed, or if to proceed. They may just be fighting over who gets to hide in the attic and who has to use the tight, spider-ridden crawl space.

"If you'd prefer, I can apply for a warrant," Jimmy adds.

It's a bluff. If we had enough for a warrant, we wouldn't be talking.

It wasn't long ago that you could tell a suspect that you were getting a warrant and they'd figure the jig is up. *Getting* a warrant implies that it's a done deal. Sure, you'll have to fill out some paperwork and talk to a judge, but you're *getting* that warrant, no doubt about it.

These days you have to say you're *applying* for a warrant. The word *applying* leaves a lot of gray area; maybe you'll get it, maybe you won't. Someone in the halls of justice decided that saying you're *getting* a warrant is just too misleading, that it's unfair to the criminals. These are the types of rules we play by. I sometimes wonder how we manage to arrest and convict anyone.

Regardless, the bluff works, though not as expected.

The occupants must have heard the word *warrant* and not much else, because the next moment the front door yanks open, imploding with a violent pull. This is followed by an explosion of arms and legs and faces as three subjects seem to fill the empty doorframe simultaneously, fighting for position in their scramble to get away. Like steam from a ruptured pipe, they shoot from the house, bolting for the yard or the street or anywhere without cops.

It happens so fast and with such energy that the first guy in line bowls Jimmy over and knocks him onto the concrete porch hard enough to elicit an unhealthy *Umphf.* I'm next in line, and with no time to think, all I can do is brace and grab. In a tangled heap we go down, limbs flailing. It's hard to tell who tackles who, but I find myself rolling around on the cold hard ground with some toothless tweaker's face inches from my own. His breath stinks of chemicals, smoke, and bile. He's sweating profusely, despite the cold, and his body reeks of cat urine—only it's not cat urine, it's the smell of meth seeping from his pores.

As we struggle, I gain a quick advantage because he's fighting with just one hand. That's fine by me until I feel his other hand groping around at my belt. He's searching for the gun I'm not wearing. It should be on my right hip, but there's nothing there.

Now I'm pissed.

Jimmy has taught me a lot of cool moves over the years, most of which I've only practiced and never actually used because, let's face it: I'm not a special agent. I'm not supposed to be scrapping with the bad guys. That's Jimmy's job. And the problem with practice is that you have to do a lot of it before it becomes instinct. I've only had *some* practice, and *some* practice is a long country mile from *a lot* of practice.

The one thing that Jimmy drilled into me was that the eyes, nose, throat, and solar plexus are the weak points, and it's these four areas that I remember now, when it counts. Using my elbow in place of my fist, I smash it hard into the tweaker's nose. A satisfying *crunch* sends him reeling up and back, dazed and bloody.

He punches wildly, unable to see through the tears and disorientation. Lunging, he claws at my face, leaving a fingernail gash along my left cheek. Now would be a good time to shove my thumbs into the guy's eye sockets, but the thought of it grosses me out. Jimmy says that attitude and the willingness to use total force is what separates the living from the dead in a street fight.

I don't care. I'm not sticking my fingers in the dude's mushy sockets.

Instead, I punch him hard in the solar plexus, number four on Jimmy's must-crush strike zones. It's the soft spot right below the rib cage that'll turn someone into jelly faster than a dog can scarf down dropped food.

I hear the air leave him as he crumples into a heap on his side.

His name is Devon, assuming the wallet in his pocket isn't stolen. He's not a very talkative fella, at least not at the moment. I try to make him more comfortable by applying a pair of borrowed handcuffs, and it works wonders. I immediately feel more comfortable.

Jimmy's tweaker fared much better than mine, despite knocking my partner down in his haste to exit the house. Jimmy has ways of twisting someone around, backward, and upside down until they don't know if they're coming or going, only to discover that they're not going anywhere because their arm is bent halfway up their back and handcuffs are being applied to their wrists. The look on the guy's face tells me he's hallucinating badly, or he's still trying to figure out what just happened.

Maybe it's a little bit of both.

I was too busy with toothless Devon to see what happened to the third runner, but Jimmy tells me he ran back inside when he saw the officer coming at him from the corner of the house. Jimmy was still fighting the first guy at the time but managed to grab the runner by the leg as he passed. This caused him to fall, but then he kicked his leg free, bloodying Jimmy's nose in the process.

That's actually a good thing.

The guy just assaulted a law enforcement officer and fled into the house. That gives us probable cause not just for his arrest, but also for a warrant to enter and search the house. Most judges don't look kindly on people who thump on cops, and in Washington State that's assault third, a Class C felony.

Jimmy's nose is still bleeding, so I try not to sound *too* happy.

Sergeant Brice Johnson with Tacoma PD handles the warrant application, and after being sworn in telephonically and testifying before a judge, the warrant is issued forty-five minutes later without having to break perimeter.

The warrant allows us to enter the residence and search for an unknown subject tentatively identified as John Doe and arrest him for assault third of a law enforcement officer.

Because we're looking for a person, we can only look in places where a person might fit, so closets, attics, bathroom showers, and under beds are all a go, but sock drawers and medicine cabinets are a no-go. There is some reasonable flexibility in this, since there are documented cases of subjects hiding inside couches, clothes dryers, cabinets, and other places the average person wouldn't consider.

Search warrants can be amended, of course, so while we're checking under a mountain of dirty clothes in the bedroom, if we happen to come across a bag of meth or some obviously stolen property or firearms in a home occupied by convicted felons, the warrant can be modified to allow a broader search.

By the time we're ready to make entry, a dozen officers are on hand.

From the porch, Sergeant Johnson announces the warrant in a loud voice several times and then tries again over the PA system in his car, but the mice are all quiet and huddled in their holes, hoping we'll go away.

After knocking and announcing and waiting an extremely generous period of time, Sergeant Johnson boots the door open with a kick so dainty it would barely rouse a drunk from his barstool. It's not the first or even the fifth time the door has been booted, and the frame and catch are so obviously battered that if you breathed on the door heavily it would fly from its rest.

Everyone rushes in.

The air explodes with shouts and commands and the thump of something big hitting the floor . . . and then the real commotion begins.

CHAPTER THIRTY-SEVEN

The ruckus inside the house continues for several minutes and then subsides to quieter voices and only the occasional shout or exclamation. Five minutes after breaching the door, Jimmy exits the house onto the front porch and holsters his Glock. Waving me forward from the lawn, where I've been relegated because of my lack of a weapon, he gives me a quick rundown.

"One female and four male subjects detained," he says. "Three have active felony warrants, and all of them have misdemeanor warrants of one flavor or another—driving suspended, shoplifting, loitering, vehicle prowl, that sort of thing."

"What about the mom?" I ask.

"Peggy Camp decided to resist," Jimmy says slowly. "I'm not sure she's going to be too cooperative. It took three of us to escort her to the ground, and four to cuff her."

"Four?"

He shrugs. "She's a big woman. Six-foot at least, and maybe three hundred pounds. I've never wrestled a Clydesdale, but after that I have a pretty good idea what it might be like." He grins and then tips his head at the house. "Tacoma is still sweeping the upstairs, but we can get started on the first floor. Watch where you step and where you put your hands; there's drug paraphernalia everywhere, including used needles."

I follow him back into the house and pause in the living room, where two of the detainees, one of them being Peggy Camp, are still laid out facedown on the ratty carpet. The other three have already been helped to seats, hands cuffed behind their backs.

As I follow the Onion King's trail through the downstairs, I study every chair he sat in, every cupboard or closet he opened, every wall he walked up to. I honestly don't know what I'm expecting to find, but I look anyway. There's no way he left anything of value in a drug house, that's a given, but his movements may give a clue as to what he was doing here.

Working my way through the fruitless search, one thing becomes clear: the Onion King may have visited often, but he never slept here. That in itself is telling. He was an associate of the dopers, but he wasn't one of them. He wasn't the type to sleep on a dirty mattress with needles strewn about. Mostly he just showed up, came into the house, occasionally sat, and then left.

The big question is, why?

The even bigger question is, does it have anything to do with the women?

I'm guessing not.

Tacoma PD finishes with the second floor and finds two more subjects. They clearly had better hidey-holes than the first five. One, an emaciated female, was folded up inside a large hamper. She's probably eighteen or nineteen years old but looks a hard thirty. The sores on her face and arms are raw and red, and she picks at them even as they try to cuff her, the drugs muddling her mind so that she believes bugs are crawling under her skin.

She can't get them out, no matter how hard she picks.

The second detainee is Hector . . . who was found in a wall.

At some point long before our visit, he'd managed to carve out a section of drywall and make a little niche for himself. It was in a section that was double-walled with two-by-sixes, and since Hector is rail-thin it hid him well. The hole was covered with a large, vertically hung Mexican flag in such a way that you'd never know what was behind it. If he hadn't started whispering to himself, they might not have found him.

As they hustle Hector down the stairs, he's complaining that the small baggie of meth in his pants pocket isn't his. When one of the Tacoma officers asks what it was doing in his pocket, Hector doesn't miss a beat, stating, "These aren't my pants."

Apparently—or at least according to Hector—the pants belong to his friend "Bob." He can't remember Bob's last name, his phone number, his address, or where he might be right now, but he's absolutely certain those are Bob's pants.

The officers are familiar with Bob. They contact people all the time who are wearing Bob's pants or Bob's coat or Bob's shirt. One or two guys have even been known to wear Bob's underwear.

Bob's got a lot of clothes.

And if it's not Bob, it's Jim, or John, or Steve. There's always some nebulous friend getting his buddies in trouble, intentionally or otherwise. If Bob was real, no one would associate with him because of all the trouble he causes.

Bob's an ass.

I climb the stairs to the second floor and quickly scout the three bedrooms. The Onion King was here, but long ago. There's no fresh shine. We spend a few minutes looking around, pause in Hector's room to admire his hole-in-the-wall, and then return to the first floor.

Sergeant Johnson is sifting through a battered twelve-by-twelve cardboard box at the kitchen table, picking at the items inside. As we approach, he upends the box onto the table and what must be two hundred credit cards, passports, and driver's licenses pour out in a heap.

"What do you make of this?" Johnson asks.

"Car prowls, thefts, and burglaries," Jimmy replies.

"Yeah, but why keep them? Credit cards have a limited life expectancy after they're stolen, usually less than a day, depending on when the victim discovers the theft and reports it. Passports and driver's licenses are good if you're into identity theft, but this group"—he looks behind him at those gathered in the living room—"they don't look smart enough for that."

"I don't know," I reply. "We've come across some pretty clever crooks. It's amazing how much work someone will do to avoid . . . you know, work."

Johnson snorts, turning up the corner of his mouth into a smile. "I suppose, but these guys are traveling far and wide." He picks up a license. "This one is from Seattle." Grabbing another, and then another, he reads them off. "Olympia, Gig Harbor, Tukwila, Enumclaw, Kent, Renton, Bellevue—one out of ten is from Tacoma, the rest are from places an hour or two away."

"Maybe *she* can explain," I say, dipping my head in Peggy Camp's direction.

"We need to talk to her anyway," Jimmy tells the sergeant. "We'll add this to our list of questions."

Escorting Peggy from the living room to what might once have passed for a family room, we sit her down in a shredded recliner that stinks of cat urine—real cat urine this time, not meth. She's too large for a single set of handcuffs, so the officers had double-cuffed her. Jimmy checks the handcuffs after she's seated to make sure they're not poking into her back.

"How's that?" he asks, but she just glares at him.

We choose not to sit, because . . . well . . . it's a drug house. Instead, I move away and lean against the wall while Jimmy crouches in front of Peggy, close but not close enough that she can catch him with a swift kick.

When Jimmy starts in on his questions, I'm encouraged. She seems to want to talk after all, vigorously telling him where to go and what to do with himself and what he can do to her. Jimmy seems receptive to her suggestions, nodding and smiling at her like she just told a funny story about her stinky cat.

This just pisses her off and she reminds him where he can go and offers new suggestions on what he can do once he gets there.

"She don't live here!" Peggy finally barks.

A long string of accomplished profanity escapes her chapped, depleted lips, while Jimmy just stares at her, a tired look replacing the dutiful smile on his face. There's disdain in the subtle way he shakes his head.

When her tirade reverberates to its ultimate end, she takes a couple deep breaths, slumps her shoulders in resignation, and asks, "What did the little whore do now?"

"She got herself into a bit of trouble," Jimmy replies. It's not exactly the truth, but neither is it a lie. He can't tell her she's dead, mostly because she'll shut down and we won't get a thing out of her, but also because we have no proof that she's dead.

"She had some squatters, you know?" Peggy offers up.

"Squatters?"

She tries to lift her hand but is quickly reminded of the cuffs. "In her head. She had voices talking to her, other

people living in her head who didn't belong; squatters."
She shifts her bulk in the chair and adds, "Least she wasn't
lonely," and then laughs at her own joke.

Jimmy watches her in disgusted silence for a long moment. "Was she being treated for it?" he finally asks.

Peggy exhales brusquely through her lips, like he just
told a whopper. "Treated? Yeah, she was being treated for it;
treated like the crazy little bitch she is. She had some quack-
jack doctor downtown, last I knew."

"And when was that?"

"A year ago; maybe longer. She'd get a prescription and
then sell the pills, though I don't know who would want to
buy psycho pills, but people will crush and snort just about
anything these days."

"Did you know that her boyfriend reported her missing?"

"He *said* she was missing, came around here about five,
six months ago pretending to look for her, but she ain't
missing. He just said that because I was pissed when she
stole seventeen dollars and some"—she pauses—"when she
stole seventeen dollars from my purse. You want to find her,
just go ask around and see who she's whoring with."

She's calmer now, watching Jimmy as he makes a few
notes. I notice her posture changes and she shifts herself
into a bit of a slanted lean in the chair, extending her ample
legs and then crossing them at the knees.

"You're a handsome one," she says as Jimmy continues to
write. "Are all FBI special agents so . . . special?" She shunts
her head to the side and rolls one shoulder down, searching
for sexy but failing at every curve. She's twenty years, seven
teeth, and two hundred pounds past average, so sexy is a
hard goal to hit.

Jimmy ignores the overture; it's not the first time he's
been propositioned by someone in cuffs. "Do you have anything that might contain her DNA?"

"Like what, honey, blood or something?"

"No, a toothbrush would do—or a hairbrush that has strands of her hair present."

"I got none of that." She gives Jimmy a how-am-I-doing look, and asks, "So, you married? I see the wedding ring, but I figure you wear that to keep the women away, right? Not that it would matter if you were. Know what I mean?"

Jimmy smiles at her, if for no other reason than to keep her talking. "Would you mind if we get your DNA?" He produces what looks like a giant Q-tip inside a clear plastic tube, sealed inside a sterile plastic envelope.

"What you want my DNA for?" Peggy asks, suddenly defensive. "I haven't done nothing." The sexy pose is suddenly gone, and her eyes dart around trying to figure a way out of this. "You want to link me to some crime I didn't commit. I seen that stuff on TV."

"It doesn't work that way," Jimmy assures her. "We'll be testing your mitochondrial DNA. That's different from the DNA they use to identify suspects. Mothers and daughters share the same mitochondrial DNA, but it can't be used to identify a specific person." He gives her the layman's version of DNA, dumbing it down and stripping out all the technical jargon.

"So, they can't use it to convict me of nothing?"

Or something, I want to say, but I keep my mouth shut.

"Correct," Jimmy replies, forcing a smile.

Peggy remains unconvinced, and as she opens her mouth— I'm sure to say no—Jimmy cuts her off. "Your daughter has landed herself in some real trouble, Mrs. Camp—"

"Miss Camp," she corrects.

Jimmy nods. "We need this sample to help her," he continues. "Now, it sounds like you two aren't on the best of terms, but she's still your daughter. Before you say yes or no, I want you to think back to when she was first born, to her first birthday, or the day she first called you Mom. Ask yourself what you would be willing to do for *that* Sheryl."

The statement carries weight; visions of better days with a different little girl. And as Peggy Camp thinks back to the girl that, for a time, was her daughter and best friend, the one who was her only comfort and joy through some very rough times, her eyes fill and she lowers her head, giving a slight, affirming nod.

Before she can change her mind, Jimmy opens the buccal swab and asks her to look up. "I'm just going to rub this up and down on the inside of your cheek," he explains.

"What is it?"

"It's called a buccal swab."

"Like a belt buckle?"

Jimmy smiles at her. "They only sound the same. This one is just for cheeks." He prompts her to open her mouth and then scrapes the cotton tip up and down on the inside of her left cheek and repeats it on the right. Extracting the swab, he pulls the end of the stick and retracts the cotton tip back into the plastic container without touching it, and then seals the end.

It's after six when we leave the Tacoma house. One of the K-9 units uncovered a substantial stash of both meth and heroin hidden in the floorboards. With all the drug residue and paraphernalia throughout the house, it's a miracle the dog could pinpoint a single, specific location, but somehow he managed.

Since this was initially our show, our soup sandwich, we couldn't just head home and leave the Tacoma guys with all the work. Sergeant Johnson was happy for the help, and if we ever have reason to come back to Tacoma, I have no doubt he'll be right there in our corner.

We're just passing through Seattle when Jimmy's phone rings.

It's Nate.

Though Jimmy doesn't bother to put it on speaker, I can tell something's wrong. They talk briefly, and he asks Nate to forward everything he has to Diane. Tells him we'll be in touch in the morning.

"What?" I say as he disconnects.

A dreadful mask clouds Jimmy's face as he shifts uncomfortably in the driver's seat. He stares straight ahead, a hard look weaving his mouth, nose, and eyes together, like one struggling with difficult emotions and losing.

"We've got another missing girl," he finally says.

I hear the words.

I hear the silence that follows.

I hear a countdown clock start ticking in my head.

CHAPTER THIRTY-EIGHT

Friday, December 19

Jimmy and I somehow arrive at Hangar 7 the next morning before Diane—unusual for her as she's almost always the first to arrive and the last to leave. Her absence leaves the place feeling a bit hollow, or out of tune, like a radio with the channel not dialed in quite right.

The long mahogany table in the conference room is entirely covered by reports, photos, and other case information, so Jimmy and I start poking through it. We're careful to replace each page or folder exactly where we found it so as not to disrupt Diane's system . . . which is a good way of ensuring we don't disrupt Diane.

"Looks like BrightPath paid off," Jimmy says, hoisting a manila folder aloft and then laying it open in his hands as he begins to sift through. We have time to skim a handful of reports before the hangar door opens and we see Diane scurrying in our direction, her purse in one hand and yet another stack of folders in her other.

She makes for the stairs to her office, but then sees us through the glass wall of the conference room. With a look of surprise mingled with embarrassment, she changes direction in mid-pace and blows into the room like a northeaster.

"Good morning," Jimmy and I say, our greetings overlapping and echoing.

"Sorry I'm late," Diane blusters. "I was up late going over the files. The alarm clock went off, but I must not have heard it."

"Did you get enough sleep?" Jimmy asks, looking her up and down.

She gives him a searing stare and then glances at her watch, only to realize she left it on the vanity at home. "What time is it?"

"Eight forty-five."

"Then I got about five hours," she replies tersely. "More than enough."

It doesn't look like enough, but neither Jimmy nor I are stupid enough to put the thought into words. If she saw herself right now she'd probably flip, so we'll keep her away from mirrors until she's finished with the briefing.

"You could have slept a little longer," Jimmy says. "A few hours aren't going to hurt the investigation."

She waves off the concern with a flick of her hand. "I'm fine. I couldn't sleep if I wanted to. Besides, all the heavy thinking should be behind us."

Jimmy and I exchange a hopeful glance, but before we can ask her for the Onion King's home address, she plows on. "I see you've been perusing the stacks. Would you like to continue, or do you want the CliffsNotes version?"

"CliffsNotes," we say in unison.

With words and images, Diane introduces us to twenty-six-year-old Melinda Gaines, who parted with friends on Wednesday night and hasn't been seen since. A copy of the

Tacoma police report lies unopened on the table before her as she recites the details of the skimpy file. "SPD believes it was well organized, precise, and swift in its execution."

"And they know that how?" Jimmy asks.

"Because she walked home from a place just blocks from her home on a well-lit street, yet no one saw or heard anything. From what the police report says, this is a neighborhood where people look out the window if a door slams too hard or a car backfires, so if she'd gotten off a scream, someone would have noticed. But like I said, no one saw or heard anything."

"Where was she coming from?"

"A place called Biscuits. She was meeting a couple friends. They've both been interviewed and said it was just a normal evening. A couple guys asked them to dance, but they weren't interested. Melinda drank Sprite and was happy and stone sober when she left."

"And just vanished," I add.

Diane lifts an eyebrow and nods.

"Nothing else?" I say. "No creepers hanging around, guys eyeballing them, or getting offended if they wouldn't dance?"

"No," she replies, glancing at her notes. "The girls said one guy was a sniffer, but that's about it."

"Sniffer?"

She nods. "He was talking to Melinda at the bar, before they moved to a table, and when she looked away he leaned over and smelled her. It's not uncommon, I suppose, though usually they're looking at you when they do it and follow it up with a compliment on your perfume."

"Odd, though, right?"

"It's odd only because, according to her friends, Melinda wasn't wearing perfume; though I suppose he could have gotten a whiff of body lotion, hair spray, dryer sheets—who knows?"

Standing suddenly, I start sifting through the piles, knocking two of them over and making a mess of the third before Diane grabs both my hands and demands, "What are you looking for?"

"The Charice Qian report."

Releasing me, she holds up a finger, looking for a moment like my mother, and moves down the table to a folder near the end. "Charice Qian," she says as she hands it to me.

It takes me a couple minutes, but I find what I'm looking for in the transcript of Charice's second interview. Diane and Jimmy have moved on without me by this time, so I place the open folder in front of Jimmy, underlining a passage with my finger.

He reads the sentence and then the paragraph. Then he backtracks and starts two paragraphs up, rereads it just to make sure he hasn't missed something, and then reads the relevant sentences aloud: "I was on the ground and he pulled me toward him by the leg, dragging me right up to the bars on the cell. Holding me at the ankle and under the knee, he smelled my leg. He smelled down the whole length of my lower leg, the way you do to see if meat has gone bad."

I cross my arms and lean back against the glass wall. "So maybe he's not just a sniffer—at least a normal sniffer, if there is such a thing."

"Well, he's not a cannibal," Diane replies.

"That's not what I'm saying. But there's something else going on that we're not seeing. Charice said that she was raped once—and that was the day before he dumped her in the woods. So why would he keep her almost two weeks and then rape her once and discard her? The abduction-rapists that we've dealt with before have all raped their victims repeatedly throughout their captivity. So why's this guy different?"

"And you think smell has something to do with it?" Jimmy confirms.

"I do. Charice says she was fed well while she was held, but it was always fruits and vegetables. No meats, not even fish."

"Please don't say he's vegan," Diane practically groans.

I shake my head. "That's not what I'm saying. But what if there's a certain smell he's going for—or one he's trying to eliminate? If we were able to talk to the other victims, I bet they'd tell us the same thing, that they were fed a special diet and held for a week or two before being raped and dumped in the woods for Murphy to find."

"The guy's a freak," Jimmy says impatiently. "How does that help us catch him?"

I hesitate and then grudgingly admit, "It doesn't."

Jimmy studies me a moment and then motions for Diane to continue with her review—and then something occurs to me: "It means we have time," I interrupt. Turning on Diane, I ask, "When was Melinda taken?"

"Wednesday night or early Thursday morning."

"Don't you see? If he repeats the same ritual with Melinda as he did with Charice, he'll keep her a week or two before killing her or handing her off to another Murphy Cotton."

"So, she's alive, but maybe only for another five or six days," Jimmy says.

I'd like to say for certain that she's still alive, but I haven't seen her shine yet. Nonetheless, I'm sure the theory is correct, so I nod my head, and with as much conviction as I can muster, I say, "She's alive."

The discussion about Melinda Gaines is downright depressing, but the meeting takes on a different tone as Diane starts detailing the BrightPath Wellness data. It turns out that all the victims except Sheryl Dorsey had been treated by BrightPath.

We can't tell Diane that we're not surprised, that we figured she'd be different. We can't tell her the Onion King was a frequent guest at Sheryl's house, because how would we explain that? Instead, we just nod at the interesting deviation and tell her to keep looking for a link.

The problem with the BrightPath Wellness connection is that most of the women used separate clinics, some of them hours apart. There are two exceptions.

"Debra Mata and Erin Yarborough went to the same clinic in Seattle," Diane says, "and during the same general time frame. I couldn't find any overlapping appointments, so it's unlikely they ever met, but they did share the same counselor, a Dr. Jeffrey Mills."

"Jeffrey?" Jimmy says, looking up sharply. "Didn't Nate say that Melinda's friends thought the sniffer introduced himself as Jeff?"

Diane scans the report quickly and confirms.

"Could it be that simple?" I ask.

"Why not?" Jimmy says. "BrightPath has seventeen clinics, but it's still only one company. They probably move staff around, just like any other business. That would explain the different locations. After all, we're talking about, what—a three-year period?"

"Six or seven different clinics," I say, shaking my head. "That's a lot of moving around, even over three years."

"And that's assuming it's him," Diane says. "I'm guessing the counselors aren't the only ones who move around and fill in for other employees."

Jimmy nods his understanding.

"What about that other name I gave you?" I ask Diane.

"I was wondering when you were going to ask about that." She pulls a stapled batch of pages from the back of the BrightPath folder and hands it to me.

"What other name?" Jimmy asks, leaning over and trying to peek at the pages.

"It was just a hunch," I tell him, "but it looks like it paid off." Realizing that I can either spend the next ten minutes reading the report or have Diane summarize, I hand the papers back to her and give her a nod.

"What name?" Jimmy says again, more irritated this time.

Before answering, Diane tucks the pages back into the manila folder and places it on the table in the exact spot she removed it from. Finally, agonizingly, she brushes her pants smooth and clasps her hands in front of her.

"I'm afraid your partner has outdone you on this one," she acknowledges, giving me a princess-like nod. "He figured out something that you missed."

"Yeah, what's that?"

"How the Onion King picked Murphy Cotton."

Jimmy is silent a moment, digesting the statement, and then it dawns on him. "He was a patient at BrightPath?"

"He was, but at the Port Orchard branch."

"But Murphy said he'd never met the Onion King; he was adamant about it, probably would have pissed himself if he had."

"I'm sure that's what Murphy believed," I say, "but what if they *had* met and he just didn't know it? What if the Onion King was his counselor, or a fellow patient, or—I don't know: the receptionist? The other option doesn't make sense."

"What other option?"

I rise from my seat and start pacing the floor. "The Onion King is smart, right? Or at least we think he's smart based on how he operates. So why would he recruit someone off the dark web, someone he hadn't vetted, and have him dispose of his victims? Seems kind of risky, don't you think? Wouldn't he want to know *everything* about Murphy before approaching him? In fact, he'd have to know Murphy pretty well if he wanted to tap into his—what did you call it— delusions of grandeur?"

"No, I think that was *Star Wars*."

"Right, but it was something like that."

"I can't diagnose Murphy—" Jimmy begins.

"Yeah, yeah, we know," I say, cutting him off. "But you thought he might have some rare type of mental illness."

"Grandiose delusional disorder."

"There it is," I say, as if I'd just extracted a bullet fragment from the depths of a four-hundred-pound cadaver. "So how did the Onion King know about Murphy's disorder?"

"You're assuming he did."

"He played into it pretty well. In fact, he pushed *all* the right buttons, didn't make a single misstep. How'd he do that without knowing Murphy's condition?"

Jimmy doesn't want to admit it, but it's starting to make sense.

"And if the Onion King is an employee, as we suspect, he had access to that kind of information—or at least he had ways of accessing it." My next words come out quiet, contemplative. "I guess breaking a few HIPAA laws doesn't mean much to a serial kidnapper and rapist."

When Jimmy raises his eyes again, his entire focus is on Diane. "This Dr. Jeff you were talking about, did he ever work at the Port Orchard branch?"

She presses her lips tightly together, perhaps thinking, and then shakes her head.

Diane takes another ten minutes to wrap up the presentation, and then we all sit around the table in silence, staring at each other. The eyes of the dead women peer out from the photos before us, silently demanding justice that has so far been denied.

One thing has become crystal clear in the last half hour: BrightPath Wellness is the key to this investigation.

We just don't know what door that key opens.

By ten A.M., Jimmy and I are preparing to head south once more, though with a different agenda this time. Extracting a Glock 26 from the gun locker in his office, Jimmy slaps in a loaded magazine and chambers a 9mm round. When he holds the Austrian-made handgun out to me, I grudgingly take it, hoping I won't have to use it. He hands me two spare magazines and then closes the locker.

Diane walks us out to the parking lot and tells us to be careful. The sight of Jimmy handing me a gun has her on edge, though she'll never admit it. She's still standing there as we pull out and head for I-5 south.

CHAPTER THIRTY-NINE

I'm a huge fan of Sherlock Holmes, and hold Sir Arthur Conan Doyle as a gifted and visionary writer. The observant and analytical detective he created was truly one of a kind, unassailable in his ability to outthink and outsolve any investigator from his day to ours. I can say this because I've met a lot of talented investigators and analysts over the years, but not one rose to the impossible standard of Sherlock Holmes.

Without the services of such a brilliant consulting detective, those of us in his shadow must plod along, solving crimes with the tried-and-true methods handed down through a hundred years of policing. In the end, every investigation comes down to two things: evidence and interviews.

In the case of the seven mannequins, the evidence part is almost complete, but the interviews, research, and polygraphs are still under way. It's said that detectives chase the lie, meaning they look for the blatant mistruths, the omissions, and the conflicting stories—any round peg that doesn't fit into the square hole opened by the investigation. It could be anything, but there's always something.

That *something*—whatever it may be—is like a big fat burrito to the detective, and once he wraps his fingers around it, good luck convincing him to let go.

Our brilliant but simple plan today is almost identical to the brilliant and simple plan we used yesterday: mainly, we're going to hit the pavement and investigate. The only difference between the two days is that today it's all about BrightPath Wellness.

Jimmy will chase the lie, while I chase the shine.

Starting in Everett with Jennifer Holt, we plan to work our way south. We don't need to stop at all seventeen BrightPath clinics, just the handful frequented by our victims. Seattle has two clinics, but we're only interested in the one in the Fremont neighborhood.

After Seattle, it's on to the clinic in Burien. It's there that I saw the Onion King's shine, though not enough of it to suggest he's a staff member. This time we'll be talking to the manager and employees. It'll be easy enough to eliminate them as suspects, but that won't help us determine if the Onion King is one of their patients.

Amber Bartlett and Abitha Jones attended counseling sessions there about a year and a half ago but missed each other by a month. Perhaps that's how the Onion King discovered them.

Tacoma will be our next stop.

Diane talked to Larry Gaines last night, the ex-husband of Melinda Gaines. Apparently they're still on good terms, and Melinda lives in a basement apartment attached to the house that Larry bought after their divorce. They talk often, and though we didn't learn about Melinda in time for the warrant, Larry confirmed that she has regular sessions at BrightPath. Her primary counselor is a Dr. Mariah Crawford.

If time permits, we'll visit Charice Qian's clinic in Olympia, and Murphy Cotton's clinic in Port Orchard.

That's the plan.

There's nothing sexy or Sherlock Holmes about it, it's just grunt police work. There's an unwritten recipe for solving crimes and it's pretty simple: collect the evidence, follow the leads, ask the questions, and peruse the shine. That's it in a nutshell. It's Crime 101.

Jimmy and I are feeling pretty good about our prospects when we pull off I-5 at Everett and work our way toward the Navy base. As the dot on the GPS draws closer to our destination, you can almost taste the adrenaline seeping out into the cab of the SUV. We're already amped up, almost walking on clouds.

The problem with walking on clouds, of course, is that they're illusions, just water vapor disguised as tangibles. They seem so much like mountains in the sky, yet they crumble in the wind and eventually weep themselves into oblivion. The fool who walks on clouds soon finds the earth, and it's not the fall that kills him, but the abrupt stop.

When the BrightPath theory suffers a setback at the Everett clinic, I feel this firsthand; my gut feels like I'm freefalling from ten thousand feet. Ironically, I'm staring down at the earth as this happens, because that's where the Onion King's shine should be but isn't.

He's never been here—ever.

Jennifer Holt's shine is abundant. It comes at the building from every angle, from parking spots along the street, to others in the adjacent lot. It leaves a crisscrossing network of tracks that reminds me of a poorly constructed spiderweb.

But there's no sign of the Onion King.

We walk around the clinic twice, checking and rechecking all the doors and windows for his distinct shine, but he's just not here. We stand in the parking lot and stare at the building, as if we were orphans staring into the warmth of a family home. There'll be no comfort for us here, and we don't bother going inside for a look around. What's the point?

Back in the familiar warmth of the SUV, Jimmy sits behind the wheel with his hands instinctively at the ten and two positions, even though he hasn't bothered to start the engine. He's leaning forward a little, his back straight, almost as if he's sitting at attention behind the wheel. His face looks like he just fell off a cloud and experienced an abrupt stop.

"We have a missing woman and we're wasting time," he mutters to himself.

He's no quitter, so the words surprise me.

"We've got nothing else to go on," I remind him. "Unless Haiden comes up with some brilliant new evidence from Murphy's hard drive, or Diane suddenly discovers that she missed something, which doesn't happen often, this is what we have to work with. That's just the way it is."

"Our whole point today is to confirm that the Onion King was present at the same clinics the women frequented," Jimmy replies. "If his shine isn't at Jennifer Holt's clinic, and she never attended any others, the theory falls apart."

"Theories are fluid," I remind him. "They change with discovery. If this particular theory is broken, let's see if we can modify it."

Jimmy and I often take turns playing cheerleader. If I'm feeling pessimistic about something, he's quick to dredge up some optimism; if he's beat-up and shuffling toward the chasm of hopelessness, I do my best to yank him back from the brink. This mutually assured nondestruction works pretty well . . . until it doesn't.

Then we have a problem.

Right now we can't afford a problem, not with so much

at stake. Instead of wallowing in the mire of my own inner dejection, I embrace Zeno and his philosophy of Stoicism, resigning myself to fate. I'm not going to tell Jimmy that I'm just as disappointed and washed-out as he is. Instead, I smile and pretend it's just a minor hiccup, something that'll make sense down the road.

And as I try to convince him of this, I try still harder to convince myself. I remind myself that we're still in the grunt-work phase of this investigation, and the thing about grunt work is that you keep at it until it's done. You leave no stone unturned, as tedious as that can be.

Despite his misgivings and my assurances, there's one thing we both know but won't say. I've felt it since yesterday, that tickle at the back of my brain telling me to open my eyes and look, open my brain and think.

We're missing something . . . something significant.

As Jimmy starts the Expedition and begins the return trip to I-5, the drooping gray sky comes to life. It casts down raindrops the size of cherry pits, which drum against the roof and windshield with relentless fury.

When we get to the interstate, to the stoplight where one sign points north to Bellingham and the other points south to Seattle, Jimmy takes a turn to the south. As we pick up speed and enter the freeway, I'm suddenly aware of the countdown clock in my head: *Tick,* it whispers; *tick,* it cries; *tick,* it screams.

We're running out of time.

The Fremont neighborhood in north Seattle is an eclectic hub of gentrification, replete with hipsters, quirky shops, and interesting architectural statements. Basically, everything you imagine when you think Seattle, but wrapped up in a smaller package.

The self-proclaimed "Center of the Universe," Fremont

is perhaps best known for the eighteen-foot troll under the Aurora Avenue Bridge, and the equally tall bronze statue of Communist leader Vladimir Lenin that stands at Fremont Place North and North Thirty-Sixth Street.

Fremont's motto is *Libertas Quirkas*: Freedom to be Peculiar.

It's a sentiment they indulge.

The BrightPath clinic is just three blocks from the Lenin statue, and we find it with little trouble. When I slip off my glasses, the Onion King's shine pops, looking like neon footsteps; hundreds, even thousands of footsteps. Oddly, the tracks are all clustered near the front door. As I look around, I can't find a single set of footprints leading in from the parking lot or the street.

All of the Onion King's activity seems to emanate from five parking spots directly in front of the building. This would make sense if he was an employee, but as we circle the building we find an employee parking lot in the back . . . and no sign of the Onion King.

"So, the Onion King is a client . . . ?" I say to Jimmy, unconvinced.

He just shakes his head and gives a hapless shrug.

After a few polite words at the front desk, an escort guides us through the building. There are eleven rooms in all, counting the employee break room and the large supply closet filled with shelves of pens, paper, toner, and other office necessities. The supply closet also houses a high-end modem mounted on the wall that feeds Wi-Fi to all the computers, printers, tablets, and other devices required of such a business.

The only thing *not* in the supply room is the Onion King's shine.

Six of the rooms we visit belong to counselors. Each is

and I have matching stress headaches, his from the drive, mine from his driving.

I'm not much of a drinker, but some nights it sure sounds appealing.

decorated in a similar fashion, right down to the inspirational pictures mounted on the walls. The framed images scream at you from every angle; things like, "What you do today can improve all your tomorrows," or "It's never too late to be what you might have been." The only thing not in psychological lockstep seems to be the desk and the wall of shelves in each office. The furniture is identical, but each has been adorned and personalized with trinkets, photos, collections of this or that, awards, books, and memorabilia.

As I walk through the building, observing everything, I'm presented with a conundrum: the Onion King isn't acting like a patient.

His shine is plentiful in every single office; an odd showing if he's just a patient. Even more peculiar is that in three of the rooms his shine is on the counselor's chair, on the desk, on the drawers, and, more importantly, on the keyboard and mouse.

Since it's hard to imagine a patient doing a Google search or watching YouTube on his counselor's office computer, the discovery brings us back to the likelihood that we're dealing with an employee—maybe.

Smiling at our guide, I ask, "Can you give us a minute?" and then pull Jimmy out of earshot. "His prints are all over the desk, the mouse, the keyboard, and the CPU," I tell him in a low tone. "We shouldn't have any trouble getting one or two with good ridge detail," I add, referring to the dermal ridges that give fingerprints their unique patterns.

"All we need is one," Jimmy whispers back. The corner of his mouth lifts slightly and I can see in his eyes a sense of relief. Turning back to our escort, he says, "We'd like to dust a couple of the computers for fingerprints, if you don't mind." The girl shifts uncomfortably.

"I'm afraid we'd have to run that by corporate . . . unless you have a warrant," she adds, almost hopefully.

"We didn't think we'd need one," Jimmy replies incredulously.

It's partly true. We didn't expect we'd need one, but we also have nothing to justify a warrant; nothing we can swear to before a judge.

"It's just . . . with HIPAA laws being what they are," the girl tries to explain, "and because we deal with mental illness, the company has a strict policy regarding what we can and can't share with law enforcement. Strictly speaking, I'm stretching the rules just letting you back here."

Jimmy nods and gives her a forced smile.

Me—I'm plunging toward the ground again from ten thousand feet.

By the time we make our way through the building we've seen all six counselors, a receptionist, and three other employees. None of them have the Onion King's amethyst and burnt orange shine.

"Is everyone here today?" I ask our guide as we start for the front door.

"Rachel is on vacation," she replies. "Other than her, everyone else is here. No one wants to miss the party."

"Party?"

"Yeah, we're closing early today for our annual Christmas party. That's when they hand out bonuses. No one wants to miss that."

"You get bonuses?"

She nods and grins. "They're usually pretty good. I got a couple thousand bucks last year, enough to go to Maui."

I steeple my eyebrows and glance at Jimmy, saying, "They get Christmas bonuses."

He doesn't reply, so I keep staring. I don't really expect a Christmas bonus, I just want to get his mind off the finger-

prints. Annoying him usually does the trick. As I continue to stare, he shakes his head and says, "We're government employees. We don't get Christmas bonuses."

I'm tempted to add a *Bah humbug*, but don't.

Our next stop is Burien.

Here we run into the same odd and conflicting patterns we found in Seattle: the tracks coming in from the parking spots nearest the door, computers accessed, and all the employees accounted for but not one with the Onion King's shine. We again ask if we can dust for prints, and again are turned down.

The rest of the day is a bust.

In Tacoma we find Melinda Gaines's shine, and Charice Qian's shine is at the clinic in Olympia. On the way back north, we veer left and cross the Tacoma Narrows Bridge into Mason County. We keep driving until we reach Kitsap County and the town of Port Orchard. Here we find Murphy Cotton's shine all over the clinic, the parking lot, and the nearby bus shelter. Apparently he was a longtime customer.

What we don't find is the Onion King; he's conspicuously absent from all three locations. And by the end of the day the question remains: Is he a patient or an employee? In those places where we *did* find him, he seems to wander about freely, accessing personal workspaces and computers at will.

Even with this knowledge, I have the overpowering sense that I'm missing something, a piece of the puzzle that dangles before me, just out of reach, like some forbidden fruit.

By the time we get back to Bellingham the sky is dark, wet, and dreary, the precipitation caught somewhere between rain and snow, as if unable to commit to either. Jimmy

CHAPTER FORTY

Saturday, December 20

"Orange juice?" Jimmy offers. He reaches into the fridge and extracts a half-full gallon jug, holds it up, and gives the contents a little shake and swirl.

"Sure. Thanks," I say. He pours a tall glass and hands it across the counter, then returns the jug to the fridge.

I'm glancing around, admiring the kitchen, when he leans on the counter, resting both forearms on the granite, his hands encircling his own orange juice.

"I still can't believe how well this kitchen turned out," I say.

"You sound surprised."

"No . . . well, yeah."

He grins. "Me too."

Back in September we gutted his kitchen in one day. We thought the remodel was going to be a job we could finish in a few days, but days turned to weeks, and weeks turned to months. Two and a half months, to be precise. We didn't finish until the week before Thanksgiving, and that's only because Jane put her foot down.

It's not like they didn't have appliances that whole time.

The new fridge was in the dining room, a little out of place but working; the microwave was on the dining room table; the stove was . . . well, the stove was still in its carton in the garage, but Jimmy's pellet-fueled barbecue is almost as good as a stove, and it was right outside the sliding glass door on the back deck. At least until the weather got nasty.

They ate off paper plates and used plastic utensils, and if they needed to wash some dishes there was always the tub sink in the laundry room.

All in all, it was a minor inconvenience, at least for me.

Jimmy takes another drink of orange juice and we make small talk as he waits patiently for me to get around to the point of my visit. Before parting last night, we'd agreed to take the weekend off. We're too close to the case; we need to step back and take a breather and come at it again with fresh eyes.

Still, it's hard to take time off knowing that Melinda Gaines is being held somewhere, subjected to God knows what. The clock is ticking, and her life depends on us finding her before it winds down.

"Jane and I are thinking about getting Petey a puppy for Christmas," Jimmy says, "I was thinking golden retriever, but she's always loved bull terriers."

"What's a bull terrier?"

"You know: Patton's dog."

"Patton's dog?"

"General Patton. Don't you remember the movie, his little dog?"

Then it comes to me. "The one with the funny-shaped head."

"Right," Jimmy says, raising his glass and pointing at me. "For some reason Jane thinks their funny-shaped heads are cute."

"Didn't Patton call his dog a coward?"

"I think so," Jimmy says with a shrug. "At least he didn't slap him."

We chuckle.

"Why not a cat? They're a lot less demanding."

Jimmy scoffs. "Every cat thinks it's the alpha. They think you're there to provide food, shelter, and affection on demand, and then dismiss you whenever they please. At least dogs know who the alpha is."

"What do you expect?" I say. "Cats are miniature lions and cougars. Genetically, they're predisposed toward being in charge. Just because they've gotten smaller doesn't make them less of a lion."

"Please," Jimmy says with a groan, drawing out the word.

"Miniature horses," I say, tipping my head as if that settles the argument.

"What about them?"

"Are they horses, or aren't they?"

Jimmy senses the trap. "That's different."

"A horse is a horse," I say.

"Of course, of course," he shoots back with a grin, pleased at the Mr. Ed reference. "I'll tell you what, you find a cat that fetches sticks, and I'll consider it."

We clink glasses at the détente, though I suspect I'm going to have a difficult time finding a cat breed renowned for its stick-fetching prowess. Still, I'm always up for a challenge.

Jane and Petey arrive home a half hour later, and I can only assume that the little guy saw my Mini Cooper, Gus, parked on the street. As soon as he comes bolting through the front door I hear him squeal, followed by the sound of his little feet thundering toward me.

I crouch at the last moment and grab him in a bear hug.

I've learned to crouch when Petey comes charging at me, because, well, I'd like to have children someday. The kid is all elbows and energy, and when he slams into you it's like Thomas the Tank Engine on steroids. I don't know much about football, but someone should be recruiting this kid now.

Without being asked, Jane smiles and says, "It's behind the couch."

Petey beats me to it. Racing around behind the couch, he drags out a large but shallow storage container, which he pulls into the center of the living room. Inside is a partially completed Lego *Millennium Falcon*, though at this stage it's only barely recognizable as such. We've been working on it off and on for six months now, a project just for Petey and his uncle Steps. Someday we'll finish it, but I'm in no hurry.

I had a lot of things on my mind when I drove out to Jimmy's this afternoon. I know he sensed it, but to his credit he never brought it up or asked what was troubling me. Instead, we just hung out together, two normal guys in a normal kitchen on a normal Saturday afternoon. Sometimes that's all it takes to get centered.

He was right about one thing: we're too close to this case.

Before leaving the Donovan residence, I decide to let the case of the seven mannequins slip away from me, if only for the weekend. I'll go home, have a nice dinner with Heather and Jens and Ellis—and whoever else is hanging out at my house. Diane introduced Heather to high tea at some little shop in Fairhaven, so maybe I'll take her there tomorrow. Afterward we can go to a movie; a regular date-day.

And as I drive home, picturing these things in all their pleasantness, another image begins to intrude on my thoughts. I push it back, but thoughts are sticky things, they tend to cling and not let go. And by the time I pull into the driveway at Big Perch, my imagination has taken a decidedly dark turn. The perfect weekend I was just picturing with Heather has morphed into something else.

I still envision Heather and me arm in arm as we window-shop through Fairhaven, sip tea, and then enjoy a movie. Yet always behind us, several paces or seats away, lurks the figure of Melinda Gaines, her expression vacant, as if she were already a ghost.

The image will haunt the rest of my weekend.

CHAPTER FORTY-ONE

Monday, December 22

Legend has it that the Greek mathematician Archimedes, upon stepping into a bathtub, suddenly realized that his body displaced water, and that the volume of that water must be equal to the volume of his own submerged body parts.

As simple as the concept is today, it was a great discovery for the ancients because it allowed them to precisely measure the volume of irregular objects—such as Archimedes's torso. It's a handy ability when trying to determine if gold is really gold, since an ounce of gold displaces a different volume than an ounce of silver or an ounce of lead. This was exactly the problem Archimedes was working on at the time, as too many disreputable people were coating inferior metals in gold and trying to pass them off as legitimate coins.

The old stories tell us that Archimedes was so excited at this discovery that he cried, "Eureka! Eureka!" and then jumped out of the bath and ran through the streets of Syracuse naked.

My eureka moment is less dramatic. It comes in the

shower on Monday morning just as I'm massaging shampoo into my scalp. And though the temptation is great, I decide against running through the streets naked. It's far too cold.

Dressing quickly and wolfing down some orange juice and a pastry, I'm halfway to my car when I pause, a cautionary thought rising up, as if to block my way. I shake it off and start toward the car again but find myself hesitating once more. Turning, I hurry back into the house, to my bedroom, and to the gun safe within. Extracting my Walther P22 and two extra magazines, I quickly load the gun and shove the extra magazines into my pocket.

Not exactly tactical, but it'll do.

My black Movado watch says 8:13 A.M. when I punch the code into the cipher lock on the south door and hurry into the hangar, hustled along by the cold and the wind. I race up the stairs to see if Jimmy is in his office, but the lights are out and his computer is off. Diane, however, is stretched back in her chair like she never left the place. The woman has no concept of evenings or weekends, but then, *she'd* say the same thing about us.

"What's got you in a tizzy?" she asks as I plop down in the chair opposite her desk and then immediately stand and walk back out to the mezzanine, leaning on the rail that overlooks the hangar floor. "Steps?" she calls after me, but before she can rise and follow, I'm back in her office.

"Has Jimmy called?"

"No."

"But he's on his way, right?"

"I'm sure he is," Diane says in a placating tone.

"He's usually here before me," I say absently. "What makes you so sure he's on his way?"

"Because on Friday he said, 'See you Monday morning.' And, well, it's Monday morning."

"But you're not sure?"

"Oh, for Pete's sake!" Diane barks, throwing an eraser at me that ricochets off my arm and lands in the corner. "I'm *sure* he's on his way," she says with far too much energy, and then asks, "How's that?" But instead of waiting for an answer, she orders me to take a seat and then says, "Spill. What's going on?"

But I *can't* spill; not yet.

"When Jimmy gets here," I say.

From the bottom drawer of her desk, Diane produces a bag of chocolate-covered macadamia nuts. She pulls out six of the nuts and places them on a napkin. Returning the bag to its not-so-secret hiding place, she picks up one of the morsels and puts it carefully in her mouth, the way one might place a fresh briquette on a barbeque. Small, satisfied noises issue from somewhere deep in her chest as the chocolate melts, and then she crunches down on the nut, savoring it with just as much gusto.

When half the nuts are polished off in this manner, she drags the napkin across her desk and brings it to rest right in front of me. Hesitantly, I start to reach for one of the nuts, but the old witch suddenly pulls the napkin back a few inches.

"Spill," she says again.

And I do—just like that. I would have held out longer if she beat me with a hard stick and strung me up by the ankles. The use of chocolate-covered anything is just wrong. I don't think either criminal law or the Geneva Convention cover the use of chocolate during interrogations, but they should. It's just unethical.

When Jimmy arrives twenty minutes later, I have to explain my revelation all over again, and then it's his turn to plop down in Diane's guest chair. "Our theory was wrong," he says, strumming his fingers incessantly on her desktop.

"The theory wasn't necessarily wrong," I say. "It was just . . . in progress."

Diane, of course, is trying to ignore us as she searches databases and begins to cross-reference the new information. Her task is made all the more difficult by my pacing, Jimmy's strumming, and the ceaseless barrage of words flying around the office as the two of us reexamine the case from a new perspective.

Once again, we have to be careful not to inadvertently mention shine. Even preoccupied as she is, Diane would pick up on the reference and demand to know what this *shine* was that we were talking about. She might even break out the chocolate-covered macadamia nuts.

Our discussion drags on, growing louder at times, and then more quiet and reflective at others, until Diane can take it no longer. Rising from behind her desk, she says, "Out, out, out!" as she herds us toward the stairs.

"Go to Valhalla," she orders. "I'll call you when I'm done."

Valhalla.

She has a way of saying it as if it's a curse, when, in fact, it's the name she herself recently assigned to the break room. During all the comings and goings last week, she found time to hang a four-foot sign on the west wall that reads VALHALLA in narrow, foot-high letters. It's an early Christmas present for me and Jimmy, and it's adorned with Viking knots and images from Norse mythology, including the Midgard Serpent.

"It's not a break room when you practically live here," Diane told us when she presented it. "I thought a more appropriate name was called for. Hope I'm not stepping on your *man territory*." She frames the last two words in air quotes— as if we'd staked a claim to the break room at some point.

Jimmy liked it, though.

"Valhalla," he'd said with an approving nod, "where warriors go to rest."

At that, Diane just rolled her eyes, but she's an old fraud. You could tell she was pleased by the crease at the corner of her mouth. I won't be surprised if other Viking-themed items find their way into Valhalla in the coming months.

And so Jimmy and I retreat to the break room now known as Valhalla.

We spend the next two hours watching *John Wick* for the ninth or tenth time, and when the movie is over we wander out onto the hangar floor, lean up against Betsy's wing, and stare up forlornly at Diane's office, once more playing the part of pitiable waifs. After a while, we make our way quietly back to Valhalla.

Noon arrives, and we're just discussing lunch options when we hear the distinct clump, clump, clump of Diane's heels on the stairs. She's in a hurry, and when she enters Valhalla, there's a satisfied glow in her eyes. Her hair is off-kilter again, but this time not from neglect. She has a habit of running her hands through it as she works.

When she pauses in the entrance, I realize I'm holding my breath.

"I think I found him," she says . . . and the air rushes from my body.

CHAPTER FORTY-TWO

Our original theory was flawed.

It supposed that the kidnapped women had all been patients at various BrightPath Wellness clinics, and that the Onion King was either an employee or a fellow patient. He would have had to work at or attend each of the clinics in question, but because the kidnappings were spread out over several years, this wasn't completely unreasonable.

The warrant return from BrightPath was incredibly accurate as to which clinics each woman attended, and on what date and time. The first problem was that Sheryl Dorsey wasn't on the list. She had plenty of mental and drug issues, but she'd never been a patient at BrightPath, not once. This can perhaps be explained away by what we found at her home in Tacoma.

Instead of sitting at a distance and studying his victim from afar, the Onion King knew this one, and was a frequent visitor to her home. He found out all he needed to know up close and personal, where he could watch her, study her . . . smell her.

The second flaw in our thinking—and the one that almost killed the theory—was the discovery that the Onion King had only been to a few of the locations. Without being present to *see* his intended victims and access their records, how was he picking them?

And that's where my shower comes in.

As the warm water washed over me this morning, I suddenly realized what seems so simple and obvious in hindsight: BrightPath Wellness uses an internet-based database. The Onion King doesn't have to visit individual clinics in person because he can do it online, but only if he has a logon and password.

That's where his unusual pattern of shine comes in.

The Onion King isn't an employee, nor is he a patient. He's part of the contract janitorial staff. His tracks were always near the front door because that's the logical place one would park if arriving after hours. He was in every office because it was part of his job. It also explains why his shine is on every garbage can, something I had mostly ignored. I just assumed he was searching the trash for any important information that might have been inadvertently tossed out. Who would have guessed that he was emptying the trash?

It's a magnificent ploy.

Coming in with the janitorial staff gives him access to every desk and every computer. And because the crew works after normal office hours, he has the luxury of time: time to rifle through the desks in search of a cheat sheet, a slip of paper with a username and password.

He would have tried to log onto their computers, testing the password and looking for the information he would need to spoof the system from a remote location, make the database think he was logging in from a specific IP address.

It fits.

Every part of it fits.

Diane loves putting on a good show.

Her presentations are usually well thought out and to the point, so we indulge her as much as possible, though she can be agonizingly slow in the telling. She calls it the great unfolding and seems to take pleasure from each new revelation she ladles out to us, as if we're naked and exposed.

"I had to go all the way up the corporate ladder to the CEO of BrightPath before I finally got an answer," she says as the great unfolding begins. "She said that they've used the same cleaning service for about three years, a company called Cepa Industrial. Since we assumed that the Onion King was part of the cleaning crew, my next step was going to be to contact Cepa Industrial's HR department for a list of employees."

She holds a stack of papers in her hands, which she now hugs to her chest. "I didn't do that," she continues. "And before you ask, I didn't do that because it would have tipped our hand to Lo—" She catches herself, giving us a devilish smile. "It would have tipped our hand to the Onion King," she says in a softer tone. "I have no doubt that he would have learned of the request within an hour . . . probably sooner."

"Who's Lo—?" I ask, choking off the last part of the word intentionally, as she had.

At the same time, Jimmy asks, "Why?"

Ignoring my question, Diane turns instead to Jimmy. "I think your guy likes word games," she says after a moment.

"Why?" Jimmy asks again; same word, different question.

"Because," Diane says with a smile, "*Cepa* is Latin for onion."

The room settles into eerie quiet—even Jimmy's strumming ceases.

After letting her words sink in, Diane says, "There's more. When I ran a check on all vehicles registered to Cepa Industrial, I found twenty-two work vans of different makes and models, none more than six or seven years old. These are obviously for the cleaning crews. Other than the fleet of vans, there was only one other vehicle on the report: a silver 2006 Honda Accord."

I smack Jimmy's upper arm with the back of my hand. "A silver Honda Accord," I say, as if he doesn't get the significance. "Just like Dex said."

"I know that," Jimmy replies slowly.

Diane ignores the exchange and continues. "I called their corporate office, which appears to be a warehouse in Fife. Don't worry," she adds quickly, "I played it off that I was with one of the toll authorities and that the car had gone through a toll station without a pass and without paying. The office manager said that she's not aware of any silver Hondas registered to Cepa Industrial, and she's the one who tracks all the mileage and the gas cards. I told her it was probably a mistake on our part and she seemed satisfied."

"So . . ." Jimmy says, forcing calm into his voice, "who owns Cepa Industrial?"

From a stack in her arms, Diane extracts a single sheet of paper and places it in the middle of the table. It contains a three-by-five photo and the printed data from a driver's license. "His name is Lorcan Child," she says. "Thirty-seven years of age, black hair, about six-foot, with a medium build."

"Lorcan Child," I say, contemplating the name.

"Criminal history?" Jimmy asks.

"One arrest when he was twenty. He was booked, but the charge was later dropped."

"What was the charge?"

"Rape," Diane replies. She doesn't elaborate immediately, but lets the word grip the presentation and drag it toward some dramatic end. "He was accused . . ." she finally says, drawing out the last word, "of slipping some flunitrazepam, also known as Rohypnol, and better known as a roofie, into the drink of a young woman he met at a bar."

"The date rape drug," Jimmy says with a sour look on his face. "What a scumbag."

"Indeed," Diane replies. "As often happens, the victim decided not to press charges, and Lorcan walked. After that, he worked for a number of tech firms, and then, out of the blue, he started Cepa Industrial about seven years ago. They now have a hundred and twenty-seven employees and cleaning contracts in four counties."

"So, he's successful?" I ask.

"I imagine he makes a comfortable living from his janitorial business, but nothing compared to his other business." She lets the statement linger a moment. "It seems that Lorcan is, among other things, a hacker and a highly paid computer security consultant."

Jimmy and I exchange a look, and then lean in closer to Diane, who's still standing with the stack of papers in her hand. "Does that mean he knows the dark web?"

"Like a tongue knows teeth," she replies with a nod. "And since a good number of hacking consultants got their start as hackers, there's no telling what he's been up to. It *does* support the database theory. With a username and password, someone like Lorcan could have free rein, regardless of HIPAA safeguards."

Diane lays another page on the table.

"This is his home on Grouse Way in Lakewood. The pictures were captured off Zillow. They're a bit dated, since he bought the house seven years ago, but I've compared them to those on the Pierce County assessor's site and nothing seems to have changed—at least externally."

Diane places additional images on the table: kitchen, living room, entry, master bedroom, master bath, each room more elegant than the one before.

"How much did he pay for this?"

"One-point-seven million dollars."

Jimmy lets out a low whistle. "I'm in the wrong line of work."

When Diane lays down the next image, we're confused.

"What's this?" I ask.

"His other house: same neighborhood, but three doors up the street. Nowhere near as magnificent as the first, but he only paid half as much."

"Which one does he live in?"

"Oh, he lives in the first one, to be sure. This," she says, tapping the picture, "is a rental."

"Maybe that's where he holds the women," I suggest. "It looks like it's got a basement; that's all he'd need."

"Right," Jimmy says, "but how does he get them from the car to the basement without being seen? The picture shows a garage, but it's detached and set at the back of the property."

"Well, you're both correct and you're both wrong," Diane says. "The house *does* have a basement, and the detached garage *is* set at the back of the property where it opens onto the alley—a nicer alley, I might add, than the actual road that runs in front of my house. Both your points are irrelevant, however, since the house has been occupied by the Hatanaka family for the last three years."

She reaches down and picks up her favorite mug, the one that encourages people to FEED THE ANALYST, and takes a swig of lukewarm coffee. "He's a computer engineer and she's a copyright lawyer," she continues after returning the mug to its place. "They have two boys, ages six and eight. None of this screams psycho the rapist to me."

I smile at the wordplay: *psychotherapist* divided into three parts is *psycho the rapist*. It's an unfortunate meshing of words that Jimmy and I have used and abused for years. Apparently Diane pays closer attention to our break-room talk than we've given her credit for.

The rest of the presentation deals mostly with Lorcan's business ventures, the possibility of shell companies, and the single incident he was arrested for when he was twenty. Though the charges were later dropped and Lorcan walked free, his prints are still in the system.

That bit of information is particularly frustrating, since his prints were all over the BrightPath offices. It's irrelevant now, I suppose. We wanted to identify him, and we have.

When Diane finishes, Jimmy has just one request. "Can you contact the BrightPath CEO again and ask her to run an audit on their client database? In particular, we're looking for any access that was after hours. I need to know how many files were accessed, because if we don't get to Melinda before he's finished with her, he's going to go after someone else on that list."

"Don't talk like that," I say with a shake of my head. "We know where he lives; we know where he gets his information. We'll get Melinda back."

Jimmy gives me a humorless smile and nods, but his heart is not in it. I know what he fears, and he's right: the odds that the Onion King is holding Melinda in his upscale home in his upscale neighborhood are remote . . . but we're one step closer.

As Diane gathers her things and then starts for her office, Jimmy calls after her. "Can you also call Les and Marty and tell them they're on standby—just in case?"

When she's gone, Jimmy turns to me and asks, "Are you up for a drive?"

"Lakewood?"

"Lakewood," he confirms.

CHAPTER FORTY-THREE

We make two minor detours on our way south: the first is to the Fremont office of BrightPath Wellness, and the second is to the Burien office—the one next to the god-awful-blue dental facility.

Our original plan was to ask the office managers to talk to each counselor and see if they have any passwords written down and stored in or around their desks. Between Bellingham and Seattle, however, reason caught up with us and we realized that no employee is going to admit that they're violating company policy by writing down passwords, not to mention the possible HIPAA violations related to computer security.

Instead, we ask to speak to each of the counselors in private. Since we're conducting an active criminal investigation, it's a reasonable request, and hardly one that the office manager or anyone else can object to. The strategy pays off, but the dividend is worthless.

Almost all of the counselors have cheat sheets, but not one of them contains the Onion King's shine. He's never picked them up—probably never even saw them. Which means we're back to the same old question: How's he getting access to the computer?

He *is* a hacker, so I suppose that's a possibility.

And then I remember that he's also a computer security consultant, but I dismiss this idea almost as soon as it comes to me. If Lorcan Child had ever contracted with BrightPath Wellness for any type of computer services, Diane would have discovered this during her research—one way or another. She's a bit of a hacker herself. Still, it's an intriguing thought.

The winter solstice passed by yesterday with little fanfare; and with its passing, the dreary trudge into shorter and darker days finally ended. It'll be a few months before the sun stretches its legs properly and brings us the longer days that we crave, but that time is coming.

When we roll into the Moors, the high-end neighborhood in Lakewood that Lorcan Child calls home, it's just before six o'clock and the darkness has been upon us for the better part of two hours. It's good that the darkness is with us, it's the great obfuscator, blurring shades of gray and black together so that nothing is clear, nothing is certain.

This is a benefit when you don't want to stand out, but also a liability. When one walks around in the dark, he's automatically more suspicious to others than if he went for a walk in the full light of day. People tend to take a second look in the dark, or hold their gaze a moment longer, wondering what nefarious deed draws you out into the gloom.

A summer walk at nine P.M. and a winter walk at nine P.M. may both take place at the same time on the clock, but they are as different as . . . well, night and day.

Jimmy and I do an initial sweep of the neighborhood by driving through at normal speed and noting the exact location of Lorcan's rental property, and then his primary residence. One is occupied; the other is dark and ominous. It huddles like a feral beast forty feet off the road.

The elusive and telltale amethyst and burnt orange shine I've been searching for is everywhere on the property, and on the surrounding sidewalks and street. Any doubt that Loran Child is our man is quickly dispelled.

"It's him," I say to Jimmy, my voice breathy and low. An involuntary shiver runs up my spine as the anticipation, the thrill, and the terror of the moment collide. "He doesn't seem shy about chatting with the neighbors," I add after a pause. "There's a steady stream of shine to and from every house on the block. The guy's a regular social butterfly."

Jimmy nods. "Making it even less likely that he keeps the women here," he says. "It would hardly be polite to visit a neighbor and not extend a reciprocal invitation. Hard to do that if you have someone tied up in the spare bedroom."

"Good point."

After swinging back through for a second look, I park Gus along the curb two houses north of the rental. From here we have a good view of both properties, but we're not close enough to draw any undue attention.

Jimmy wanted to drive his Expedition for our little recon, but I convinced him otherwise. The vehicle's red-and-blue wigwags might be hidden behind smoked windows, and the emergency lights in his grille might blend in, but the rig still screams law enforcement. You park that thing on a street and people are going to notice. Pretty soon you'll have residents approaching to ask if they should be worried. Mostly they just want to know what's going on, but that's the kind of attention we don't need right now.

In the end, Jimmy sucked it up and allowed me to drive. I made sure I did the speed limit and observed all the rules of the road, but he still seemed to find plenty of opportunities to grab the dash or throw his hands in front of him as if we were about to crash.

I pity his wife.

Before getting out of the Mini Cooper, I reach up and adjust the switch on the dome light, so it won't illuminate when the doors open. The heavy rain we experienced coming through Everett and Seattle has tapered off, and a light drizzle plays in the air. It's enough to get us damp, but not soaked, so we pull our coats tight and start down the sidewalk.

Walking south on Grouse Way, we come to the rental property first.

The lights are on throughout the house, and we slow and then stop on the sidewalk to get a better look. Mr. Hatanaka and his wife are at the dining room table with their two boys. Their conversation is lively and their laughter frequent, but for us it's like watching television with the mute engaged.

A magnificent Christmas tree stands framed in the large front window of the room to the left, and you can see other decorations throughout the house.

"Hard to believe Christmas is three days away," I say quietly.

"Two and a woo," Jimmy says, reverting to military slang for two days and a wake-up.

I didn't quite understand the term *wake-up* the first time he used it four or five years ago, but I guess in the military a day doesn't get full credit if the event you're waiting for is first thing in the morning. And since Christmas begins first thing in the morning, we don't have three days to wait, just two and a woo. It sounds so much closer that way.

"Seems like a nice little family," I say, watching the Hatanakas. "Which one do you think is Lorcan's accomplice?

My money is on the little guy at the end—youngest son and all that. Probably has mommy issues."

Jimmy chuckles from his gut, and it's good to hear.

"Yeah, I think we can cross them off the suspect list."

"Even Short Round?"

He looks at me in all seriousness. "The Hatanakas are Japanese."

"So?"

"Short Round was Chinese; you know that, right?"

"He was?"

"Short Round from Indiana Jones?" Jimmy asks by way of clarification.

"Yeah; the little kid."

"He was Chinese," Jimmy repeats. "He was a juvenile pickpocket on the streets of Shanghai when he met Indiana Jones."

"I don't remember *that* from the movie."

"It wasn't in the movie," Jimmy says. "I read it somewhere."

Now it's my turn to chuckle. "You're a bigger geek than *I* am."

We continue along the sidewalk, now making our way to the shadow-veiled house three doors south of the rental. The dark, hunched shape is an adumbration, a shadow within a shadow, and it sets my skin to crawling.

I suppose that's just the way of it: When you stare into darkness too long, it's hard not to shiver, wondering what might be staring back. And when you've seen the horrific things Jimmy and I have, the shivering part comes easy.

Our chatter dies away as we draw near, and though we try to look inconspicuous to any who might be watching, I notice that we're both staring intently, dissecting the house with our eyes. I don't know what Jimmy's looking for, but I'm sifting through shine, looking for any hint of Melinda . . . or Erin . . . or Debra. I'm looking for the shine of nine different women, seven of whom are already dead.

I find nothing.

Like the other homes in the community, this one sits on a half-acre lot. It's a distinctly modern home with a wide driveway not of poured concrete, but of individually placed tan pavers. The three-car garage at the left has doors that imitate those of a barn or stable. An aggregate walkway covered in shine branches off the driveway and leads to a front door, which is framed by sidelights and capped by an elaborate transom.

It's clear at a glance that the lawn and landscaping are tended by others.

Lorcan has rarely walked his lawn or stepped close to admire the exquisite flower beds. A cast-iron seat completely encircles the trunk of a glorious weeping willow in the front yard, and yet it's a bench where he's never sat, a tranquil spot never enjoyed.

A moment later, our feet carry us beyond the house. At the end of the block, we cross the street and turn north, coming by for another pass on the other side of the road, just two guys out for a walk in the middle of December . . . in the dark . . . in the rain.

When we get back to Gus, I start the engine and turn the heat all the way up. When the windows fog up I turn on the air-conditioning and in a few minutes we're both warm and the windows are clear.

"Let the waiting commence," I whisper into the quiet of the night.

In Hollywood, they make stakeouts fun, so much so that it's been the premise of entire movies. The problem is that Hollywood only shows the last one percent of a stakeout.

No, make that the last one percent of the last one percent. If they showed the whole thing, it would be one long and boring movie.

Jimmy and I have done our share of stakeouts, so we know what to expect. For the next two hours we sit and not much of anything happens. About every twenty minutes I fire up Gus and defog the windows. We listen to Christmas music on the radio and stare absently at the festive lights around the neighborhood, but mostly we wait.

The dash clock says 8:47 P.M. when a blue BMW SUV passes us by and then slows. It's the fourteenth vehicle we've seen in the last hour, and when I see it approaching in the rearview mirror, I whip off my glasses and try to catch a glimpse of the driver, just as I'd done thirteen times before.

"It's him," I say, staring after the vehicle.

The BMW turns into Lorcan's driveway at the same moment the right-hand garage door begins to roll open and a light comes on inside, giving us a good look at the interior. The distinctive shape of a black Toyota FJ is clearly visible in the far-left stall, while the middle sits empty. There's no silver Honda Accord. And then the BMW is inside and the door comes down.

We watch as the lights come on in the house . . . and we wait for the Onion King—Lorcan Child—to once more come into view. We wonder if Melinda Gaines is right in front of us and just beyond our reach.

"Let's just go in," I say with resolve, staring at the house.

Jimmy understands my frustration. "We could do that," he says patiently, "but without a warrant or probable cause, everything in the house becomes fruit of the poisonous tree, inadmissible as evidence. You know that. A guy like Lorcan, with his resources and computer skills, he could change his name, relocate anywhere in the world, and just keep doing what he's doing. Instead of ending this, we'd just condemn more women to the same."

He watches me a moment as I stare out the windshield. "Besides," he continues, "I hate lawsuits, and if we go in without probable cause, he's going to sue us for violating his civil rights, and he'll win."

"You're sure we don't have enough for a warrant?"

"Yes," he replies simply. "You and I know he's the guy, but that's only because of shine. Without that, what do we have? *Cepa* means onion, but so what? He could easily argue that it's an acronym for something. He has access to the computers at BrightPath Wellness, but again, so what? Everyone on the janitorial staff has access."

Jimmy repositions himself in the passenger seat, seemingly uncomfortable with the truth in his own words. "The strongest argument we could probably make relates to the hacking job at the Clallam County jail, and even that's weak. Still, with Lorcan's computer expertise, we could try to convince a judge that he adjusted Murphy Cotton's bail and then used a stolen or hacked credit card to pay the bail. The problem is that a guy like Lorcan doesn't leave a digital trail, so once again we have no actual proof."

He sighs in exasperation. "I was hoping you'd find his shine on one of those password lists. We probably could have convinced the staff to let us dust them for prints, especially if they thought they'd had a security breach."

"I thought you said we couldn't use any prints from the offices."

"Yes and no," Jimmy replies. "His cleaning duties allow him access to the office, the desk, the keyboard, the mouse—all the places you saw shine. But he's got no business *inside* the desks. That would have been a game-changer."

"What if BrightPath finds no evidence of after-hours access?"

Jimmy smiles. "They'll find it, trust me."

The burst of confidence is reassuring, but it doesn't do anything for us right now, and I'm still not ready to concede the night.

"What about exigent circumstance?" I suggest a few minutes later.

Jimmy shakes his head. "We don't even know where Melinda's being held. If we heard screaming coming from the house, or saw him dragging her past a window, we'd be golden, but we've got nothing."

We watch for another hour, mostly in silence, and then Jimmy says the words I've been dreading: "Let's head home."

I start Gus and buckle my seat belt. Then I just sit there, holding the wheel. "Are we really going to leave her . . . ?"

"She's probably not here," Jimmy tells me yet again, and I want to believe him, but as I roll by the big house I feel something drop in my stomach.

"Sorry," I whisper to the darkness.

I feel Jimmy's hand on my shoulder, but it doesn't help.

CHAPTER FORTY-FOUR

Tuesday, December 23

Tuesday morning passes in a haze of examination and re-examination. The reports and photos and pages of the case are once again laid out on the conference room table like a cascading horror show. Though the Onion King has finally been unmasked, we're left tiptoeing across the razor's edge between knowing something and being able to prove it to a jury.

To make matters worse, the hours have begun to stack one upon the other, growing into a pile that will soon be crowned with Melinda's death if we don't figure things out.

One new report has been added to the field of paper.

It's the confirmation that BrightPath Wellness's secure database had indeed been breached, and a request from the CEO to keep them in the loop as the investigation develops. As expected, the list of client files that were accessed over the last three years includes Murphy Cotton and eight of the nine victims. The only one missing from the list is Sheryl Dorsey.

The report should be good news, but it sets a dark mood.

In addition to the names we were looking for, we find another hundred and forty-seven client files that were accessed, all of them women, and all of them the same general age range.

Diane has already worked through the list, and none of the women have been reported missing. Most likely these are just potential victims, women who appealed to Lorcan, women who are now at risk.

The Onion King has been busier than any of us imagined.

Throughout the morning, Diane remains cloistered in her office, completely obsessed with Lorcan Child and determined to take him down, singlehandedly if need be. At eleven A.M. she emerges long enough to mention a possible shell company, this after finding something that piqued her interest on FinCEN, the Treasury Department's Financial Crimes Enforcement Network. Since then, she's been bottled up in her office.

Jimmy is reclining in a conference room chair, staring at the ceiling, when we finally hear the steady clump of Diane's shoes descending the stairs. Like dogs at feeding time, Jimmy and I are upright in our chairs and facing the door when Diane makes her entrance. Instead of throwing us a bone, she takes a seat between us and leans back in the chair, stretching her neck out and staring at the ceiling, just as Jimmy had been doing a moment earlier.

We don't say anything; we just watch, knowing that it's pointless to push.

"So," she says at length, "it looks like Lorcan has been laundering money through a shell company in Grand Cayman."

"Grand Cayman?" I ask.

"It's in the Caribbean," Jimmy explains, "south of Cuba."

"Correct," Diane says, "and it's notorious as a tax haven. The place has twice as many registered companies as it does people. Lorcan owns a condo in Grand Cayman, as well as assets in other locations, all registered to the shell company."

"This just gets stranger and stranger," Jimmy mutters.

Diane lifts her left eyebrow as if to acknowledge the fact. "I'll give him this, he's the most technologically sophisticated sociopath we've—" She stops in midsentence, as if suddenly struck by something. Tilting her head slowly to the side, she looks at me through narrowing eyes. The furrows rise on her forehead, as if they have questions. "You said you went back to BrightPath looking for a list of passwords—" she begins.

"It was a no-go," Jimmy interrupts.

We can't exactly tell Diane that the real reason we were looking for the lists was to see if the Onion King had handled them. Better to pretend we found nothing than have her asking too many questions about subjects we can't discuss.

"Fine," she says dismissively, "but did you look for a key logger?"

Jimmy and I stare at each other.

"A what?" he finally asks.

"A key logger," Diane repeats. "It looks a bit like a thumb drive, but it would have been on the back of the central processing unit, where everything plugs in."

"We didn't look on the back of the CPUs," Jimmy admits.

"What's a key logger?" I ask.

"Key loggers are used to steal passwords and other private information. They're small enough that you can plug them into one of the USB ports on the back of the CPU, and then all you have to do is plug the keyboard into the key logger and everything the user types is captured on flash memory." She shrugs. "Lorcan could have placed one in about ten seconds; then all he had to do was wait. He could have retrieved it the next night, or weeks later."

"And it logs everything that's typed?" Jimmy confirms.

"Usernames, passwords, case reports, emails—anything and everything."

Jimmy is out of his seat so fast it startles me.

"Where are you going?" I shout after him.

"Phone call," is all he says.

The office manager in Seattle is skeptical and barely cooperative when she answers the phone, but she does as Jimmy requests and checks the back of every computer, including those used by the support staff.

"Okay, thank you for checking," Jimmy says a few minutes later, disconnecting the call. He gives me a barely perceptible shake of his head and then dials the number for the Burien clinic.

The manager in Burien is about as receptive as the one in Seattle, but since Jimmy's request doesn't appear to violate HIPAA regulations, she goes through the motions. We hear her pull out the first CPU, her voice slightly strained as she crouches and looks for anything out of place.

"I don't see anything like what you're describing," she says, "but, honestly, I'm not a computer person. It could be right in front of me. . . ." She lets the implication trail off.

"Is there anyone there who knows their way around a computer?"

"Half the office is off for the holidays," she replies, not really answering the question. "What if I take a picture and send it to you?"

"Uh . . . sure," Jimmy says. "Are you going to send pictures of all the computers?"

"I suppose; if that's what you need."

He gives her his email address and then she puts him on hold.

After we listen to five minutes of Christmas instrumentals on the speakerphone, she picks up again. "Okay, I just sent them."

An empty message with no subject and twelve attachments pops up on Jimmy's screen. Keeping the office manager on the line, he scrolls through the images. Diane hovers behind him, which is odd, since we're usually the ones doing the hovering.

"Right there," she suddenly says, jabbing a finger at the screen and circling a small rectangular item plugged into one of the USB ports. It looks like a thumb drive, just like she said.

"Jemma," Jimmy says into the phone. "I need you to go take a look at the computer associated with the eighth photo." It takes her a minute to get to the CPU, and then Jimmy tells her exactly what she should be looking for.

"I see it," she says at last.

"Good. Without touching it, can you follow the cord from the keyboard and tell me if that's where it plugs in?"

The response is faster this time. "It does."

Jimmy lifts a fist in triumph and practically jumps out of his seat, but to Jemma he sounds perfectly calm. "That's excellent, Jemma. I'm going to call the FBI's Evidence Response Team and have them send someone over to collect it. If you need a warrant, we can get one, but technically speaking, the key logger doesn't belong to BrightPath, right? It *could* be considered lost property."

This seems to work for Jemma.

With the holiday traffic, it takes the Evidence Response Team almost two hours to drive from the FBI's Seattle Field

Office on Third Avenue to the clinic in Burien, retrieve the key logger, return to their office, and dust the miniature surveillance device for prints.

The last update from the ERT was a few minutes ago: one nearly complete print was recovered from the small device. They're running it for a match right now. Even Diane joins us as we huddle around Jimmy's cell phone in the conference room, waiting to pounce at the first ring, waiting for word.

I've watched the fingerprint analysis process a hundred times, so I can almost picture in my head what they're doing at the Seattle office: loading the print, beginning the query, waiting for the hit.

When Jimmy and I first started, a lot of agencies were still using AFIS, the Automated Fingerprint Identification System. Since then, the Next Generation Identification, or NGI, system has become standard. It houses over a hundred and twenty million criminal and civilian fingerprint records, including those of Lorcan Child, who was fingerprinted when he was booked for rape seventeen years ago. NGI is much faster and more accurate than its predecessor and can process a print in a fraction of the time it took AFIS. That's why I'm not surprised when the phone rings a few minutes later.

"Donovan," Jimmy says, answering before the first ring dies away.

A quiet, indecipherable voice on the other end of the phone makes static for a moment, and then Jimmy says, "Thank you," in a flat, disembodied voice. He ends the call and places the phone on the table before him.

My heart skips a beat.

I'm suddenly worried that the print might not belong to Lorcan at all. What if the Onion King is again one step ahead of us? What if the print belongs to another Murphy Cotton, some employee or worshipful disciple addled by mental illness? I try to push the thought down, but such ideas are hard to displace once they take root.

Jimmy turns to me with a stony, unrelenting expression that reminds me of the soldier monuments at Gettysburg. I feel the hope drain out the bottom of my shoes.

And then the bastard grins.

"We got him," he says.

CHAPTER FORTY-FIVE

Three efforts begin simultaneously.

First, Diane begins the warrant affidavit. Considering the nature of the crimes involved, our request will be broad, and will include Lorcan's home, any outbuildings, and all the vehicles on the property. We'll be searching for evidence of abduction, rape, and murder, as well as related computer crimes. In addition to the print match on the key logger, Diane will be including a list of the client files that were illegally accessed in the BrightPath database, with special emphasis on Lorcan's victims.

The second effort is a SWAT callout. Jimmy places a call to Danny Marchant, the FBI Special Weapons and Tactics commander in Seattle. The call burns up ten minutes while Jimmy walks Danny through the whole case. He needs to understand what he's up against, so he can fill out a risk assessment. Every deployment of SWAT is considered a heightened response and needs to be justified.

That means paperwork.

While Jimmy and Danny go over the details, I start effort number three: contacting Lakewood PD and the Pierce County Sheriff's Office to request an agency assist. It'll be at least four hours before the SWAT team is assembled, and I want eyes on Lorcan's residence while we're getting all our ducks in a row.

It's been almost a week since he grabbed Melinda off the street. I'm not sure I could handle it if we got this close and he chose tonight to drag her off to some tree in a cold and distant forest. Besides, we'll need extra bodies to help set up a robust perimeter when we move on the house. Don't want to take any chances and let Lorcan slip past.

Next, I call Haiden Webber, the FBI's computer forensics expert. It's after hours, but Haiden was never one to conform to a standard forty-hour workweek, so I take a shot and call his office. He picks up on the first ring.

"I was wondering if I was going to get a call," he says before I even announce myself. "I just heard a rumor that you two tracked down your elusive Onion King. Please tell me it's so."

"It is," I reply. "He's living the good life in Lakewood, and we just found the piece of evidence that gives us probable cause for a search warrant. As soon as we have the warrant in hand and SWAT in position, we're going to take the house down—"

"And you'd love to have me there to handle the computer forensics," Haiden finishes, astute as ever.

"This is your chance to study the lair of a world-class hacker," I say. "I figured you wouldn't want to miss the opportunity."

"You figured correctly," he replies with a note of glee. "And when does this grand adventure begin?"

"I'll call Les and Marty," I reply. "Provided they can get to the hangar quickly, we should be landing at Boeing Field within the hour. We'll need ground transportation, so I'll leave that to you."

As I end the call, Jimmy is still talking to Danny. Raising a finger, he gets my attention and then slips me a scribbled note.

Briefly scanning the torn slip of paper, I smile and give him a nod. Punching a number into the phone, I listen to it ring. A familiar voice answers.

"You don't call, you don't write," I say, a grin seeping into the words.

"Steps!" Detective Nate Critchlow practically shouts. He makes a few cracks about the Feds and unending holidays, chuckling at his own jokes, and then asks, "So, what's up?"

"Not much," I say, completely nonchalant. "Jimmy and I were just wondering if you and Jason want to help capture the Onion King? Provided you don't have other plans. . . ."

There's a loud hoot, and then I hear him screaming for Jason.

CHAPTER FORTY-SIX

The Moors look as they did the night before. The drizzling rain is the same, the Christmas lights are the same, and the hunched, predatory shadow of Lorcan's home is eerily the same.

Haiden cruises through the neighborhood slowly in the red Volvo V40 that he commandeered from the agency motor pool. Jimmy is in the front passenger seat directing him, while Jason, Nate, and I are crammed into the back.

It's a tight fit, but we make it work.

As one of the agency's undercover vehicles, the Volvo has no lights or push bars or markings to suggest law enforcement affiliation. Even the make was chosen with intent, since no Volvo was ever mistaken for a law enforcement vehicle—except perhaps in Sweden.

The car fits the neighborhood perfectly, even better than my Mini Cooper.

Past Lorcan's residence, we spot the two-man surveillance team from Pierce County. They're parked two blocks down in a gray Hyundai Sonata that's missing one of its hubcaps.

We can tell they're the surveillance unit because their faces are shadowed by stubble and they exude a thuggish presence. The look is great for undercover drug buys, but probably not an ideal choice for this neighborhood. Someone's liable to call them in as a couple suspicious characters. We nod subtly as we pass, and then loop back around and park in roughly the same spot we occupied the night before.

Danny Marchant and the SWAT team are still two hours out, but a dozen officers and deputies from Lakewood PD and the Pierce County Sheriff's Office are parked a mile away at the local elementary school, ready to deploy at a moment's notice.

Once more we wait. Ten minutes into what could be a long night, Haiden decides to thrill us with tales of hilarious computer coding errors and traumatic hardware failures, one of which nearly brings him to tears. Honestly, if I knew the difference between a bit and a byte, it might actually be funny.

Shortly after eight it begins to snow; big flakes that mean business.

Soon the ground is covered, and the Moors take on the look of a Christmas postcard, the holiday lights reflecting off a pristine blanket of cold white. The night is suddenly brighter. If we weren't parked up the street from a monster, I'd even say it was magical.

Like the Grinch arriving home with a sleigh of stolen presents, Lorcan's BMW drives past and pulls into the garage around eight-thirty, leaving tracks in the fresh snow and disrupting the magic of the Moors.

The lights come on in the big house and we watch him through the naked windows: a bathroom stop, two trips down the hall, a trip to the kitchen where he retrieves a beer from the fridge, and then to the living room where he turns on the television. He pulls up something prerecorded and then settles in for the duration.

I'm hoping that whatever he's watching is at least an hour long, because Danny Marchant and the SWAT team just left Seattle. With the new snow, it'll be the better part of an hour before they get to Lakewood. Longer if the snow starts to accumulate on I-5.

"Looks like *The X-Files,*" Haiden says, peering through our only pair of binoculars as he studies the distant television. "Who still watches *The X-Files*? I thought that went out with the nineties."

"Blasphemy!" I say. "*The X-Files* will never go out of style. It's like *The Twilight Zone* or *Kolchak: The Night Stalker.* They're immortal." As I say this, it occurs to me that *I* could be an *X-Files* episode. Hell, I could be a whole season.

"They're at the elementary school," Jimmy says after disconnecting the latest call from Danny Marchant. The team made good time from Seattle, covering the distance in forty minutes, and without benefit of lights and siren.

It's welcome news; I'm tired of waiting.

"Danny's going to give Lakewood and Pierce County a quick brief," Jimmy says, "and then they'll move the containment teams into place. We're about fifteen minutes from go."

"So . . . front door?" I ask.

"Yep; we have a no-knock warrant, so they'll go in fast and hard." He gives me a telling look. "We'll have to sit tight until he's in custody. Once we get the word, I want you in there"—he chooses his next words carefully—"doing your thing."

It's always more difficult with other ears around, but I understand him perfectly.

"What about me?" Haiden asks.

"You'll come in with us." Turning to look at Nate and Jason, he asks, "Can you stay with Haiden while he pulls what he can off the computer?" The detectives both nod, just happy to be part of the action.

"Right," Haiden says. "Until then we just . . . hang out here?"

"Hurry up and wait," Jimmy says with a grin.

Haiden doesn't think much of the military vernacular and puts the binoculars back to his eyes. "He's back in the kitchen, by the way; looks like he's cooking dinner."

"For one or two?" I ask.

He drops the binoculars and gives me a look like I just asked him to solve cold fusion. "How am I supposed to know that?"

I shrug. "Aren't you supposed to be some kind of genius?"

"With computers," he says, "not people—and certainly not food." He huffs and resumes his surveillance, but I can tell he liked the genius reference.

The official report will record 9:37 P.M. as go time.

We don't hear the command.

We barely see the SWAT van speeding in our direction. One moment the street is empty, the next a black mass is pulling up to the house and a flurry of figures seem to disgorge from every orifice. The team immediately stacks up and moves at a fast walk to the front door, looking like a giant black centipede bristling with weapons and the possibility of a nasty bite.

The lead man on the stack is armed with a pump shotgun, so I wait for the cacophonous blast of a twelve-gauge shredding the door latch. Instead, I'm greeted with the equally thunderous shouts of, "FBI," as the stack pours through the opening and sweeps into the house.

Apparently, Lorcan doesn't lock his doors.

While we wait for the all-clear from Danny, Jimmy has Haiden move the Volvo closer, so that we're parked at the curb right in front of the house. The windows are down, and we can still hear the occasional shout of, "FBI," or "Search warrant," but those aren't the words I'm waiting for. I want to hear the familiar bark of, "Show me your hands," or "Get on the ground."

The more time that passes without hearing those words, or the radio transmission, "One in custody," the more anxious I get.

Five minutes ago, Lorcan was still in the kitchen making something to eat. How far could he have gone? The snow on the ground proves to be a boon, because if he manages to exit a door or window, his tracks will be clearly visible in the fresh powder.

So far, there are no tracks.

Forty minutes after initial entry, Danny Marchant emerges from the open front door and makes a beeline for the SWAT van, his head down against the snow. At the last minute he looks up and spots the Volvo at the curb. Diverting, he approaches at a half run and stops at the open passenger window.

The sour expression on his face is not encouraging.

"We're going to check the attic with thermal," he explains, trying to drum up some optimism. "He's here someplace; he's just got himself one helluva hiding spot." He gives us the one-minute condensed version of the search, which includes the discovery of an impressive computer room, and stacks of banded cash lying here and there. Then he's at a half run back to the SWAT van, and its vast array of equipment tucked away in waterproof containers.

The hour mark passes . . . then an hour and a half.

At eleven-fifteen, Danny steps to the front door and

waves us in, a defeated look on his face. If they had Lorcan, we'd know it. The tone and tempo of a scene changes with success, and I'm not seeing or hearing that. Somehow the Onion King has eluded them, and this leaves a sinking feeling in my stomach.

"How's this possible!" I hiss at Jimmy as we exit the car.

"It's not."

We start by cutting through the living room and depositing Haiden, Nate, and Jason in the computer room. It's an impressive shrine to Lorcan's dark web prowess, and the first thing I notice is a large poster of an onion on the wall.

The room has five thirty-inch monitors mounted onto a massive curved steel frame with two monitors on top and three below. The desk is equally large and impressive. I'm not much for expensive office furniture, but this monstrosity must have set Lorcan back ten or twenty grand. It's fully ten feet across and shaped like a fat *C* or a futuristic wraparound cockpit.

As soon as Haiden enters the room, he catches sight of a large red button on the wall, covered by a clear plastic flip-up lid. At the sight of it, Haiden wails, "Oh, no, no, no!" and rushes over to the computer. Powering up the CPU, he waits on the edge of his seat for something—anything—to appear on the screen. And then his shoulders slump and he says, "He wiped the hard drive."

"W-wiped it!" I stammer. "How? He didn't have time."

"It only took a second," Haiden replies, pointing to the industrial button on the wall. "That's a kill switch, and this"—he points to a box next to the computer's central processing unit—"is an electromagnet. All he had to do was hit the switch and run. The electromagnet powered up and destroyed all the data on the hard drive."

"All of it?"

Haiden nods. "What wasn't erased outright was corrupted beyond—" He suddenly stops, a light of realization clicking on somewhere in his complicated brain, and then he starts searching through the desk drawers with the fervor of a madman. He finds several banded bundles of cash in the process, which he throws onto the floor like so much dirty laundry.

"What are you looking for?"

"A thumb drive," he replies, and then pulls the CPU out from its resting space and examines the USB ports on the back. Nothing.

"Why a thumb drive?" Jimmy asks, trying to track Haiden's logic. "Wouldn't that be erased too?"

Haiden shakes his head vigorously. "No, no. They use a floating gate transistor to store data, not the magnetic method used by hard disks. It's more resilient."

"So, if we find a thumb drive—"

"Then we might have something," Haiden finishes for him. He turns and waves at the elaborate computer setup that Lorcan Child used during his reign as the Onion King. "This," he says, "is all junk; useless."

Leaving Jason, Nate, and Haiden to tear the room apart looking for a thumb drive that they'll never find, Jimmy and I move to the garage and let the connecting door to the house close fully behind us. The garage and its vehicles have all been searched so there's no danger of Lorcan suddenly appearing and gunning us down.

We're alone—or as alone as you can be with fifteen people swarming through the house. For the first time since entering the house, I take off my glasses and turn my eyes to the patterns of shine on the garage floor.

"Debra Mata," I say, and the name comes out as a whisper. "Erin Yarborough," I add a moment later, this time in a stronger voice. Her shine is much older than Debra's, but the footprints are clear; distinct. Looking around for another match, I find nothing. I walk completely around both vehicles and into every corner of the garage, but there's no other shine. It's just the two of them.

When I tell Jimmy, he just sighs. "So, he brought two of them here, here to his home in this nice quiet neighborhood. Why would he do that?" He seems to sense my deeper concern. "Just because you only found evidence of Debra and Erin doesn't mean the others weren't here, including Melinda. It just means he may have carried them."

He's right, but it does little to ease my growing sense of dread.

"The tracks lead this way," I say, waving him to follow as I make my way back to the door and into the house. The footprints of both women lead across the living room without deviation, and down the hall to the first room on the right. It's an impeccably clean utility room that's the size of most bedrooms. There's a front-loading washer and a matching dryer, a pull-down ironing board, counters for folding, cabinets for storing, and ample room for a vacuum cleaner, mops, a stepladder, and more. There's also a massive stainless-steel freezer tucked up right into the corner.

The shine ends ominously at its door.

The discovery of things in freezers is usually cause for concern when hunting predators like Lorcan Child, so it's with considerable trepidation that I give Jimmy a dark look and—taking a deep breath—jerk the door open in a blur of motion. I remove bandages the same way; best to just do it quickly and get it over with.

Jimmy stares inside and says nothing, his expression puzzled. Craning my neck around the door for a look, I begin to understand why: The freezer is empty. And by empty, I mean devoid of everything; there aren't even any shelves. It's just a big box of nothing.

Except . . . there is something.

Debra Mata's shine is brushed up against the inside of

the freezer. And then I see Erin Yarborough, Charice Qian, Sheryl Dorsey—all of them. They're all here . . . plus one I don't recognize. It glows and pulses with the energy of the living.

"Melinda," I whisper, touching her impression with the tips of my fingers.

The shine of all nine women seems to concentrate on the lower half of the freezer—and then it strikes me: there are no footprints. There should be footprints from all of them, whether they were forced inside or just placed there unconscious. It's an oddity I can't make sense of until I notice that the large plastic piece covering the bottom of the freezer is almost completely free of shine.

Lorcan's shine is present around the edges, but not one of the women has ever touched the piece. And as I look closer, I see a wisp of the Onion King's shine standing up at the front of the base, as if a strand of his hair had fallen and now lay in a curl, barely visible to the naked eye.

Leaning in, I hook the wisp with my finger.

"It's fishing line," I say as I give the invisible string a gentle upward pull. My breath catches in my throat as the plastic floor of the freezer begins to tip up. "Jimmy," I hiss, though I needn't have bothered. He's watching my every move.

A moment later, the nearly weightless piece of plastic comes free and I lift it higher before pulling it out of the freezer and setting it against the wall.

The bottom of the freezer is gone.

In its place is a black hole large enough to pass a steamer trunk through. The smell that rises up to greet us is unexpected. It's not the earthy stink of a cellar or crawl space, or the rot and mildew one might expect from a hole in the ground. Instead, it smells . . . sterile. Like my parents' house after Mom gets carried away with the Pine-Sol.

"Danny!" Jimmy shouts, cupping his hands to project

the call down the hall. His voice carries an urgency I rarely hear, and it's not lost on the others. We hear the rush of booted feet heading our way as half the SWAT team bears down on us.

CHAPTER FORTY-SEVEN

The trapdoor is genius.

Without the benefit of shine, one would have been hard-pressed to find it. The removable plastic base appears to have been made by a large 3-D printer, and even the color is a near-perfect match to the off-white interior of the freezer.

I play the discovery off as dumb luck for the benefit of Danny and his team. They'd already looked inside the freezer two or three times during their search of the residence, and it doesn't sit well that they missed it.

SWAT guys don't like it when they miss things.

After moving everyone back, Danny takes his flashlight in one hand and his Glock in the other and lights up the hole. By this time I've been shuffled back behind three layers of tactically clad bodies, so I don't immediately see what greets the others.

I learn soon enough.

The hatch, as it turns out, opens onto a metal ladder that plunges down an eight-foot shaft onto a small concrete slab enclosed by cinder-block walls. It appears unoccupied.

Leading the way, Danny descends the ladder and quickly probes the walls and floor with his flashlight. The area is smaller than most bathrooms, barely four-by-six, and its main purpose seems to be to provide a transition from the ladder to a more substantial flight of industrial steel stairs that start their descent at the north edge of the room.

"There's an overhead light," Danny calls up. "See if you can find a switch."

They do. It's recessed into the wall next to the ladder and painted to match its surroundings, almost as if it were camouflaged. As the switch is activated, the room below lights up in the yellow glow of a single incandescent bulb, something at the lower end of the Kelvin scale.

Danny motions his guys down, and they descend quickly, only to then disappear one by one through the opening in the north wall. A minute passes and I notice that the blackness that swallowed them has suddenly given way to a lighter gloom. Probably another light switch farther in, I think, maybe at the bottom of the stairs.

Two minutes tick by slowly, and then we hear the return approach of boots on steel. Danny appears at the top of the stairs and waves us down. "This section is clear," he calls up. "Come on down."

This section?

The words give me pause. I mean, seriously, how many *sections* could there be? We're crawling down a ladder through a hollowed-out freezer. Whatever they discovered can't be much bigger than the room below. Such an excavation takes equipment, lights, and dirt removal; lots of dirt removal.

Jimmy is already halfway down the ladder when Nate turns to me and makes a gracious sweeping motion with his arm, saying, "After you."

"No, I insist," I reply, stepping aside to make room for him. "I always defer to people with better aim."

He chuckles and starts down. Jason follows, and I bring up the rear.

A minute later we're down the ladder, down the substantial flight of stairs, and standing in a twenty-by-thirty-foot room that's deep in the ground. It reminds me of a bunker, which, I suppose, is what it is. The walls are lined with shelves, and the shelves are lined with boxes and bags and cans of every size and configuration. The walls are painted and the floor is spotless. A dozen fluorescent bulbs hum overhead.

The room has one peculiar feature, and that's the dark hall leading again to the north. It ends abruptly thirty feet away, where a reinforced steel door stands blocking the way. The hair rises on the back of my neck as I realize the door has a small viewing hatch at eye level.

"Nothing creepy about that," I mutter to no one in particular.

Beside the door is a small table and on the table is a tray of uneaten food.

After moving in for a closer look, Jimmy touches the food with the back of his index finger and announces, "It's still a bit warm."

The tray is beautifully arranged, something you'd expect from a five-star restaurant. It contains a generous pile of green beans, some type of vegan-looking soup, a slice of bread—sourdough, by the look of it—a baked potato with real butter, sour cream, and chives, a banana, and a glass of white wine. A vintage silver knife, fork, and spoon rest on an expensive linen napkin and even the wine is served in a glass appropriate for its type.

Danny lifts the metal lever holding the viewing port in place and pulls it open. Sweeping the beam of his flashlight through the space beyond, he scans from right to left—and freezes. Cursing with an almost primal force, Danny leaps back and looks for a way in.

There's no lock on our side, and as he turns the handle and gives a brisk push, the door flies open and slams into the opposite wall, the force of it echoing in the chamber beyond. As he steps across the threshold, Danny searches the walls for the switch that he knows must be there. Finding it an instant later, he flicks it up.

Lights fill the room . . . and oh, what they reveal.

We're greeted by the surreal.

Our eyes are first drawn to the north as the tunnel continues once more into darkness. To the immediate left, the concrete wall opens up into a cell that's eight feet deep and twelve feet long. The floor is carpeted from end to end, the walls are painted, and the collection of furnishings within would leave one with the impression that it was a spare bedroom in Anyhouse, America.

The steel bars dispel this illusion.

They run the length of the opening from floor to ceiling, presenting an impossible barrier to all but the most robust of prying and cutting tools. At first glance they look like the bars you might find in any jail or prison, but closer inspection shows that they are homemade. The welds don't have the factory precision one would expect, and some of the cuts are not uniform. Despite these minor imperfections, they're effective and terrifying.

"What's with the wall mural?" Nate asks. They're the first words anyone has spoken since stepping through the door.

We all saw it, of course, the giant mural of a forest drifting off into the distance, the mist among the trees. We saw it, registered it, and turned our attention to the more horrifying aspects of our discovery. Now, as the entirety of the room settles upon us, several heads turn and take in the forest scene. It reminds me of a bone-and-tooth-littered spot where a fifty-five-gallon barrel stands ready to do its duty.

I shiver at the recollection.

Melinda was just here.

I know this because there are eight shines in the cell that I recognize, and one that I don't, the same one from the freezer. Her footprints are all over the interior of the cell, and then they lead off to the north, farther down the tunnel, her shine so fresh I can almost feel it. Lorcan Child was at her side, no doubt rushing her along as SWAT hunted for him in the house above.

Jimmy is inside the cell with Nate, Jason, and three of the SWAT members. He's so completely mesmerized by the discovery that no amount of arm-waving on my part is going to get his attention, so I walk up to the bars, reach in, and tap him on the shoulder.

I have to tap a second time.

When he finally looks my way, I lift my chin toward the north. After almost six years together, we're like an old married couple. He understands immediately.

"Come on," he says, "we can't be far behind them." He leads the way north, into the narrow and dark tunnel beyond, and no one questions him. Soon the clean walls and smooth floor give way to a rougher version of themselves, a work in progress. A hundred feet into the tunnel, the concrete walls cease altogether, and timber framing takes their place. The floor is now hard-packed dirt, but it's sloping upward at a slight angle, which is a good sign that we're nearing the end.

We continue on into unimaginable darkness, broken only by the beams of several flashlights against the shadows of timber and earth. If Lorcan is waiting ahead to ambush us, he won't have much trouble; we're lined up like tin soldiers. The unwelcome thought is terrifying. I push it aside, telling myself that he came this way to escape, not to shoot it out with the cops . . . though the thought of him escaping provides no comfort.

Jimmy and Danny are seven bodies ahead of me as we march single file through the narrowing tunnel. A few minutes pass and then the column comes to an abrupt stop. My first fear is that Lorcan has somehow blocked the tunnel ahead. When I hear the soft rasp of hushed words ahead— none of them decipherable—this fear begins to take root.

Shuffling left as far as the tunnel will allow, I peer around the men in front of me, trying for a better vantage point. I find nothing but disappointment. Even when I slip my glasses off, all that greets me is a line of shining bodies and darkness.

Then I hear it; the sound of boots on metal.

Danny is climbing a ladder.

CHAPTER FORTY-EIGHT

When it's my turn to climb out of the tunnel, I find myself emerging through the floor of a filthy boxlike room that's maybe twenty or twenty-five feet on each side. Storage bins and cardboard containers are stacked in one corner, and the walls show open studs. It reminds me of an unfinished garage . . . and then I notice the roll-up door.

It *is* a garage.

Exiting the man-door on the north wall of the building, we find ourselves standing in the backyard of Lorcan's rental. It doesn't take long to find the fresh tire tracks exiting the garage and turning north up the alley. And since both the rental and its detached garage are beyond the containment area, there was nothing to stop the Onion King from simply driving away.

Danny and Jimmy knock on the front door, which is answered almost immediately by Mr. Hatanaka—who insists that they call him Stu. Normally in such a situation, they'd ask if they could search the house to make sure Lorcan isn't hiding someplace inside or holding the family under duress.

The fresh snow eliminates this necessity, however, since the only tracks leading away from the garage are those of the car, and they run up the alley and away from the Moors.

Stu confirms what we suspect: He has no access to the garage. It was one of the conditions of the rental agreement, and one they didn't mind because the rent was four hundred dollars under market average. Lorcan told them he needed someplace to store business supplies.

"There are tire tracks . . . ?" Jimmy says, letting the statement settle into a question.

"He kept his Honda inside."

"A silver Honda?"

"Yeah," Stu replies, "an Accord. I had one in college."

We already have the license plate number of Lorcan's Honda, so after thanking Mr. Hatanaka we make our way back to the SWAT van, where Danny issues a statewide Watch-For. Border crossings are alerted, the ferry system is notified, and those few places with license plate readers are fed the plate number in the remote chance that Lorcan passes their way.

The ugly truth is that finding the silver Honda Accord is going to be like looking for a specific penny in a massive wishing well. Pennies, pennies everywhere, just not the one you're looking for.

While Jimmy brainstorms with Danny, Nate, and Jason, I call Diane. It's after midnight, but she picks up on the first ring. It's disheartening to say the words aloud, but I fill her in on our failure. The fact that Lorcan slipped past us and took Melinda with him is almost beyond bearing.

"If we don't find her soon . . . ," I say, letting the rest of the sentence wither and die.

"You'll find her," Diane says. "You'll find her because you must. You've done it before, you'll do it again."

I wish I had her faith, but the clock is ticking. We have

twenty-four hours, if we're lucky. After that, the odds of finding Melinda Gaines alive begin to drop precipitously.

"There's another shell company," Diane tells me. "I'm not sure if it'll give us anything useful, but I'll call once I get done sifting through the records. In the meantime, you need to focus on what you do best." She promises to redouble her efforts and is downright comforting by the time I disconnect the call.

Her soothing tone scares me more than anything.

CHAPTER FORTY-NINE

Wednesday, December 24

Sometimes it's good police work; sometimes you just get lucky.

This might be a little of both.

The Watch-For was issued around midnight, and just twenty minutes later, Jimmy gets a call from Gig Harbor police officer Triston Mendoza. At around ten-thirty this evening, he'd responded to the Gig Harbor marina for a reported assault. According to Triston, the unknown assailant arrived at the marina in Lorcan's silver Honda. The altercation began when he pulled a bound woman roughly from the backseat of the car and then strong-armed her down the pier. The victim, who lives aboard his boat at the marina, saw this and decided to intervene in what he assumed was a domestic issue. Without a word, Lorcan punched him three times in the face with an SAP glove—a leather glove with steel shot sewn into the knuckles—and knocked him out. When he woke, Lorcan was throwing off the mooring lines to a boat parked in a nearby berth.

The only other information Triston can provide is that

the boat was last seen heading north. This is no great revelation, however, since Gig Harbor lies at the south end of Puget Sound and any other direction quickly leads to a dead end.

Still, north could mean Seattle or Everett, or one of the hundreds of islands in the sound. It could even mean Bellingham . . . or Canada, which would be very bad.

We're three hours behind him; time is not on our side.

Before disconnecting the call, Triston tells Jimmy that he knows the marina manager, and despite the hour, he has no doubt that she'll rush down and dig up the hull number and description of the boat. He promises to call back in fifteen minutes.

We have two choices: Gig Harbor offered up their marine patrol boat, which can be quickly manned and is capable of eighty knots in calm seas. The problem is that it's late December and the sound is rarely calm in winter. Depending on the waves and the wind, we might be lucky to match the speed of Lorcan's boat, which means we lose.

Our other option is an air intercept. Betsy is parked at Boeing Field with Marty and Les, but she's designed for speed, not aerial reconnaissance. A Cessna or something similar would be more suited for what I have in mind.

I dial Les and he picks up on the first ring. After explaining the situation, I ask him if he has any ideas. Low voices on the other end shoot back and forth as he and Marty confer, though I can't make out what they're saying.

When he comes back on the line, Les has a slight chuckle in his voice. "What's your location?" he asks.

"Lakewood," Jimmy replies, and then gives him the name of the nearby school. "Haiden can drop us wherever you want," he adds. "We just need to know where to meet you."

"Don't worry, we're coming to you," Les says in his usual reserved manner. Before Jimmy has time to reply or ask for clarification, the line goes dead.

Triston calls back twenty minutes later with an update. The boat that Lorcan either owns or stole is a Sea Ray 260 Sundancer registered to LC Limited in Las Vegas, Nevada. It's a two-hundred-thousand-dollar boat that, according to the company's website, has a top speed of thirty-seven knots, or roughly forty-two miles per hour.

In this weather it'll be lucky to do twenty.

Once again, my first call is to Diane. I pass on the info about LC Limited, suspecting that it's another one of Lorcan's shell companies simply from the initials. For a presumed genius, the guy is surprisingly unimaginative.

I hear Diane's fingers begin to fly on the keyboard, and she says nothing for the better part of a minute. Then I lose her completely; not because of reception, but because she absently mumbles something that sounds vaguely like, "Call you back," and disconnects the call.

We're back to waiting.

Waiting for Les and Marty to tell us where to meet them; waiting for Diane to link LC Limited to a condo in Seattle, or a vehicle registration on the Olympic Peninsula; waiting for justice for nine women who, despite bad choices or bad luck, were still worthy of life and dignity.

Shortly after one A.M., Diane calls back, her voice strained but pleased. "I think I know where he's going," she says. "LC Limited owns a chunk of land on Vancouver Island. It's about halfway up the island and right on the water. The property records list it as undeveloped, but Google Earth shows a short pier and what might be a cabin."

"That's it," Jimmy says, as certain as snow on a mountain. Turning his mouth away from the phone, he yells at Danny, "We have a destination," and then turns his attention back to Diane. "Can you send the coordinates to my phone—and if you captured any images from Google, forward those as well so we know what we're walking into."

"Are you forgetting something?"

Jimmy hesitates. "Thank you . . . ?"

"No," Diane practically snaps. "Vancouver Island is in Canada. If he crosses into Canadian waters, he's out of our reach." She takes a breath, and in a softer tone adds, "In case you've forgotten, Canada is not very cooperative with extraditions that might carry the death penalty."

Jimmy nods, though Diane can't see this. He glances at me for ideas, but I just shrug. I've got nothing.

Lorcan has a three-and-a-half-hour head start. We've got to get ahead of him somehow, but he's probably halfway up the sound by now—as far as Everett, at least. An even more frightening proposition is that he could be a lot farther north than we imagine. It depends on how hard he's pushing the boat, how many risks he's taking.

"What about Utah?" I ask.

Utah is the call sign for the UH-60 Black Hawk helicopter assigned to Customs and Border Protection's Air and Marine Operations, or AMO, in Bellingham. It's stationed at the airport not far from Hangar 7 and has an array of border security equipment that includes night-vision goggles, FLIR Safire cameras, and, of course, a Nightsun spotlight that'll cut through the darkest of dark. All three will be a godsend on this snowy winter night.

Jimmy is intrigued, but asks, "How will they stop him?"

"They don't have to. You get Utah in the air and see if AMO can spare some boats. Then contact Naval Air Station Whidbey and see if their search-and-rescue helicopter is available—they owe us one, if I remember correctly. Also, the Coast Guard station in Bellingham might have assets they can deploy quickly."

"You want to throw up a blockade?"

"Well . . . yeah. It won't be much of a blockade, but if we get searchlights sweeping the water at all the chokepoints, we might drive him to ground. Maybe he'll hole up somewhere." I shake my head, as if all this is obvious. "It buys us more time."

Jimmy likes it. "Did you catch all that?" he says into the phone.

"Got it; working on it," Diane replies. "You want me to contact Canadian Border Services Agency and see if they have any boats out?"

"Do it," Jimmy replies. "And I think the sheriff's office has a marine patrol boat, so see if they want to play. Frankly, I don't care if it's deputies in their private boats with flashlights."

"Deputies . . . flashlights . . ." Diane says, as if writing it down.

"Need anything from me?" Jimmy asks.

"Nope," Diane says, and the line goes dead.

Ten minutes later the phone rings again. This time it's Marty.

"We'll meet you at the elementary school in five minutes," he says, his voice seeming to vibrate as he speaks.

"What's the plan?" Jimmy asks.

"No worries, man," Marty says in a horrible Jamaican accent. "We got you covered." We hear Les chuckling in the background. Normally, a chuckle from Les is like a belly laugh from anyone else, so I'm a little curious . . . and a bit concerned.

There are now twenty-seven officers, deputies, and special agents combing through Lorcan's house and the rooms and passages below. With no victims on the premises, their focus is now on locating anything that will help us find and convict the monster. Eight members of the FBI's Evidence Response Team arrived an hour ago. Five of the eight were with us at Murphy's cabin, but I only know one of them by name, and that's George, the young tech who helped me photograph the death masks.

The crime scene is in good hands, but it's still hard to leave.

Danny gives us a ride to the school in one of the FBI's ubiquitous black SUVs. As usual, Jimmy sits in front while Nate, Jason, and I pile into the back. It's considerably more comfortable than the Volvo.

The drive is short, and a minute later Danny pulls to the curb outside the dark school. The parking lot is deserted, with not a soul or vehicle in sight. After a few minutes, Jimmy starts checking his watch and glancing up the street.

I don't know when I first notice it. I suppose it's like dogs before an earthquake: they know something is coming, they just don't know what.

A minute later, the once-imperceptible sound takes voice, hailing its approach; a growl growing into a roar. There's a change in the air, a familiar pulse as the sound now comes on fast. As it draws near, it fills my senses: I see it, I feel it, I hear it.

We step out of the SUV and watch with boyish delight as the sound consumes us, throbbing in the night and reminding us that we're alive.

It's Marty.

Of course it's Marty.

And as he comes to rest in the middle of the parking lot, he throws open a door and waves at us, a foot-wide grin on his face. Despite my surprise and wonder, I can't help but notice the nicely painted logo on the panel behind him. It reads MICROSOFT.

"Oh, my God," I say. "He stole Bill Gates's helicopter."

CHAPTER FIFTY

We're in the air a minute later, racing north, not sure exactly where we're going, but knowing our best hope lies in this direction.

Marty is both offended and tickled that we think he stole Bill Gates's helicopter. He's offended that we think he's capable of such a thing—until we remind him of an incident in Colorado three years ago. Then he just grins and says, "Oh, yeah."

It turns out that Marty's old Army buddy, Scoot, now flies for Microsoft. After Marty called Scoot and quickly explained why he was waking him in the early morning hours, Scoot made a few calls of his own and pulled some strings with the executives. The guys in the suits were sympathetic to the dire circumstances and readily agreed to loan out one of their extremely fast and expensive corporate helicopters, provided the FBI took responsibility for any damage.

The fact that this might generate some great PR probably didn't hurt.

By the time we pass the Port of Everett, the blockade to the north starts paying off. Utah spots a boat running dark just north of the San Juan Islands. They light it up with the Nightsun, but it's not slowing or diverting. According to the last update, it's moving way too fast for the current conditions. Utah is concerned that it may founder.

Since leaving Lakewood, the wind has only increased, and the snow has grown heavy. Even before the first flake fell, news channels between Portland and Canada were calling it the storm of the decade. It's starting to look like they might be right. Glancing out the port window, I watch the waves of the Puget Sound pass below, looking like an endless herd of white-maned horses.

This is no weather for boats, or for helicopters.

As the situation to the north plays out, Marty feeds us updates. "There's a Coast Guard cutter racing south from Point Roberts," he advises. "Utah says they've ordered the boat to stop, but it's ignoring the command. They're going to try to get a bit closer and see if they can make out the hull number, just to make sure." A minute later he adds, "Coast Guard is ten minutes from intercept."

"Can they tell what type of boat?" I ask.

"When they first spotted it, they said it resembled our target, but . . ." He pauses and holds his hand to the headphone. "Gee-eez!" he suddenly exclaims.

"What?"

"They're running parallel to the boat," he says.

"So?"

"They're ten feet off the deck." The massive grin on his face suggests he'd like to be doing the same, which is absolutely frightening. "Uh—hang on." He puts his hand to the headphone again, pressing it to his ear. When he releases a moment later, the grin is gone. "No go," he says, suddenly serious. "The hull number doesn't match. Coast Guard advises that they're probably just smugglers. They're going to have one of their boats intercept and check it out."

I swear under my breath. The hope I felt a moment ago is gone, and we're back to desperately searching for a marble in a football stadium. At the moment, it feels like Lorcan's winning again.

Whidbey Island runs north and south in the Puget Sound, beginning in the Everett area to the south and ending halfway to Bellingham. We fly the channel between the island and the Olympic Peninsula, watching the lights of Port Townsend drift past through the port window.

We finally slip beyond the congested southern islands and peninsulas, and into the largest stretch of open water in the Puget Sound. To the west is the wide mouth of the Strait of Juan de Fuca, leading to Port Angeles and then out to the Pacific Ocean. Twenty miles north of us, the San Juan Islands wait, their low silhouettes shrouded by night.

It's this northern archipelago that presents our next challenge.

Nestled in the Puget Sound midway between Vancouver Island to the west, and the United States to the east, it's here that Lorcan can make his break and cut through Haro Strait into Canadian waters. The fact that we're this close and still haven't caught sight of his boat has me worried. Was our assumption wrong? Could Lorcan have ditched the boat near Seattle, or somewhere on the Olympic Peninsula?

If there's one thing we've learned about him, it's that he has resources and contingency plans—maybe we just latched onto the wrong contingency plan.

"Take a look," Marty says a moment later.

Unbuckling my seat belt, I lean up between him and

Les as he points to the northwest. In the distance, I see the powerful glow of a searchlight shining down on the water and sweeping from side to side. Then Marty points at other lights. "That's all Canadian territorial water west of the San Juans," he says. "The Navy helo is on our side of the line, but the other lights are Canadian Border Services. They've got two helicopters up, and three boats. Guess they don't like the idea of your Onion boy coming into their country."

My hopes rise once more, but with less elevation.

With all the lights and activity west of the San Juan Islands, the smart money is now betting that Lorcan cuts up through the islands, keeping closer to shore, or even swinging farther east and then north through Rosario Strait.

Then we see Utah.

The Black Hawk is sweeping the water with her spotlight between San Juan Island and Lopez Island. As we draw near, we see the bird suddenly lift its nose and pull a sharp turn to the north. Quickly picking up speed, she suddenly drops low and skims over the wave tops. My heart begins to race at the sight.

Marty gets the call a second later.

"They've got something," he confirms. "Another boat running dark. Looks like it's trying to slip through using the islands as cover. They're trying to get close enough for a hull number."

Marty extracts every last shred of speed from the Microsoft helicopter as he races to join Utah, still ten miles to the north. I glance at the air speed indicator, which displays in both knots and miles per hour, and note that the latter shows we're now doing over 170 miles per hour. At this rate we'll close with Utah in three or four minutes.

You can always count on Marty to properly herald great and terrible things. With the grace of a teenage boy, he starts jumping around in his seat and fist-pumping the air.

When he composes himself enough to speak, he announces, "We've got confirmation on the hull number." He turns around and grins at me, adding, "That's your boat."

The news washes over me, and in a single moment I relax and then tense up again. I relax because we found Lorcan; that means we found Melinda—unless he dumped her in the sound someplace between here and Gig Harbor. But I don't want to think about that right now.

I tense up because this game is nowhere near finished.

With that thought, my hand goes instinctively to my coat pocket and the comforting cold steel of the Glock that Jimmy insisted I carry. It's not my Walther P22, but it'll do.

As I continue to gaze through the windshield, it occurs to me that I should be sitting down and buckling up, but I can't take my eyes off the pursuit playing out before me. As we draw nearer, I can clearly see the boat lit up in Utah's spotlight. It looks like Lorcan has thrown caution to the proverbial wind as he attempts to elude the relentless Black Hawk. He can barely keep his balance as the boat skips across the waves, giving the hull a proper pounding as it slams into the next whitecap, and the next, and the next.

Jimmy joins me, the allure of the chase too much to resist. Behind him comes Nate, and over my left shoulder Jason's face presses forward. The only one not glued to the windshield is Danny. When I glance back at him, he gives me a tired smile and then goes back to checking his equipment, which includes a heavily modified AR-15 rifle.

"What are they doing?" Jimmy asks.

It's a good question.

From our vantage point, it looks like the Black Hawk has moved up and parked itself on top of the boat. The powerful downward blast from its blades is churning the already frothy water into airborne soup.

"They're trying to force him to stop," Marty says.

"Aren't they a bit low?"

He shrugs. "The skids aren't touching the boat yet, so I'm going to say no."

As the channel draws to its end and splits into a Y with Shaw Island looming directly ahead, I realize that Lorcan has two options: cut left and make a run for the international border just past Stuart Island, a twelve- or thirteen-mile run, or go right and continue to try to lose us in the islands.

The Onion King finds a third option. Cutting his speed to maybe twenty knots, he steers the boat due north toward Shaw Island.

"He's going to run it aground," Nate says sharply.

We watch the whole thing play out in the brilliant light provided by Utah, even as the Black Hawk quickly gains altitude to avoid any flying debris from what's about to happen. At the last possible moment, we see Lorcan throw himself to the deck, covering his head with his arms.

We don't hear the crash, but it's spectacular.

Rising from the water and cutting across the small expanse of beach in a fraction of a second, the bow of the boat jerks spasmodically skyward as it collides full speed with the driftwood logs lining the high-water mark.

The hull explodes.

Chunks of fiberglass shear off and fly in a hundred different directions, taking with them any strength and rigidity the boat still had. Sheer momentum carries the moving shipwreck up and over the logs and launches it twenty feet through the air. It lands like a broken accordion in the clearing beyond.

Nothing moves.

Wisps of smoke begin to issue from the back of the boat, growing thicker. A flame appears near the motor, licking the fiberglass as it flickers in the wind, growing stronger as it feeds on the gasoline seeping from the fuel line.

When I see Lorcan rise from the wreck, staggering to his

feet, he seems momentarily disoriented, but quickly gathers his wits. The fire seems to sober him, and he rushes to the cabin door. It must be twisted in its jamb from the force of the crash, because he heaves into it with his shoulder, and finally manages to force it open. Then he's gone from sight for ten or fifteen seconds, seconds that seem like minutes.

When he reemerges, a black handgun is held snug in his right hand, while his left is clamped around Melinda's upper arm. She's still bound, and even from this distance I can see the blood running down the side of her head. Limping badly, she staggers and falls as Lorcan drags her from the burning wreck and then forces her toward the nearby tree line.

Why he doesn't leave her is beyond me, though I suppose someone with his twisted mind doesn't believe in giving up his possessions.

"Utah can't find a good place to set down," Marty advises. "There's a field a half mile north of here, so they're going to keep the light on your guy until they lose him in the trees, then they'll land and come in from the north on foot."

"Are they armed?"

"I hope so."

"How about us?" Jimmy asks. "Can we land here, or are we too big?"

"See—here's the thing," Marty rumbles. "There's a burning boat occupying the only decent landing spot, so I'm going to kind of *hover* over the beach, with like half the rotor over the water and the other half over land. That way you guys can jump down, and we don't have to worry about tangling with any trees or getting blown up."

"How far of a jump?" I ask.

He grins. "Trust me."

True to his word, Marty positions the helicopter so that the door opens right near the high-water mark. And while

Jimmy illuminates the ground with a flashlight, we take turns scooting down to the skid, and then hopping to the ground just a foot below. Since I'm the last off, I feel the helicopter rock and shift as each body springs free.

As soon as I jump, I feel and hear the rotors pick up speed, and then Marty swings out toward the tree line, lighting our way.

Slipping off my glasses, I fold them and slip them first into their case, and then into my pocket. Since Lorcan is now armed, Danny insists on taking point.

Instinctively I want to argue, not because I relish the idea of putting myself downrange of Lorcan's gun, but because shine is better than any night-vision or thermal device yet invented. Even now I can see flickers of both Lorcan and Melinda as they move through the trees, looking for all the world like a pair of walking glow sticks.

It's one of the maddening things about this charade that Jimmy and I constantly contend with: knowing and not being able to say; seeing and not being able to show. So we let Danny take point, despite my misgivings, and the rest of us follow behind, waiting for him to wave us forward. Thankfully, the trees and underbrush are giving Lorcan considerable grief as he tries to negotiate his way through them in the dark. Melinda is also slowing him down as she staggers along beside him. I'm sure she's in shock at this point, and she appears to grow weaker with each passing minute.

I curse Lorcan for putting her through this. He's done; he just doesn't know it yet.

As we start across the uneven clearing, Nate clings to a darkened spotlight he commandeered from a locker under the seat he'd been sitting in. I don't know why Bill Gates *needs* a spotlight, but he's a genius, so who am I to question?

The presence of the spotlight, however, gives me a really

bad idea and I hiss at Danny, waving for him to return. Taking the light from Nate's hand, I look for the on switch, but don't flick it just yet.

"What is it?" Danny whispers as he crouches beside us, his body just a vague silhouette against the low glow of the burning boat.

"We can't come straight at him," I say quickly and quietly, feeling the urgency of the moment. "He'll just use Melinda as a shield."

"What's your plan?" Jimmy asks.

"You two," I say, pointing at him and Danny, "move off to the right and come at him from the southwest." Turning to Nate and Jason, I say, "You guys angle around and come in from the northwest. Keep the angles so you don't end up in a cross fire. I'll use the spotlight to keep him distracted."

"They're still moving," Danny argues. "We can't get in position when the position keeps changing. Let's just move up and confront him. He'll have to stop, and yes, he'll use her as a shield, but he'll have no choice but to negotiate."

I turn to Jimmy. "What are the odds he kills her and then himself?"

He bobs his head to the left and the right, and then firms it up into a shake. "It's a risk. I suppose it depends on his opinion of prison."

I continue to stare at him, my eyes demanding a better answer.

"Pretty high," he concedes.

That settles it for me and the others, and even Danny seems to back away from a straight-on confrontation. "We need to force him to hold position," he insists.

Glancing at the AR-15 slung at his side, I ask, "How's your aim?"

His mouth turns up at the corners. "Fair to middling," he replies.

Two things happen as we execute the plan: one is expected, the other isn't.

"Freeze, FBI!" Danny hollers as soon as I light Lorcan up with the spotlight. They're just words, but they're good to hear. They bring with them the elemental forces of fire and lightning, and the certainty of cause and purpose.

As the words cut through the frozen air and into the trees, Lorcan freezes for an instant and then wheels around. Holding his left arm up against the blinding light, he throws his gun hand wildly in our direction and pulls the trigger three times in rapid succession.

He's not even close.

A moment later, when the screaming .223 round from Danny's AR-15 slams into the tree trunk fifteen feet to Lorcan's left, striking the exact spot the SWAT commander intended, you can almost see the Onion King loosening his bowels. He springs behind the trunk of the thickest fir tree within leaping distance and tries to drag Melinda with him.

Sensing her moment, Melinda takes a roundhouse swing at him, misses, and then takes off running. She doesn't get three steps before he has her by the hair. As he jerks backward, knocking her off her feet, she screams in agony. With unrelenting will, she tries to knee him in the face when he bends to grab her arm.

This too fails.

Jerking her to her feet, he takes a hard swing. The sight of his fist is sickening as it connects with her face, and she instantly goes limp, crumpling to the ground. Crouching, and then using her as cover, he drags her rag-doll body behind the tree, his eyes peering over her like a feasting hyena.

I'm seething.

Part of me wants to just race into the bastard's clumsy

hail of bullets and end him up close and personal with the Glock. The image of his fist . . . the sight of Melinda going limp; as I play them over in my head, the evil and injustice of it is almost too much to bear.

I feel a hand on my shoulder and I jerk. It's Danny.

"Well, they're stopped," he says quietly, seeming to understand what I'm feeling. "Let's get this done." He nods at Jimmy, and the two of them slip off into the darkness to my right. Nate and Jason take that as their cue and move to the left.

As the teams melt into the night, I turn my attention back to Lorcan, calculating the distance between me and him, between me and the giant fir tree blocking him from my view. It's not too late. I could just run up and . . . put an end to him.

It's a nice way of saying *kill him,* I suppose.

The thought settles over me and after a moment I sigh. Who am I kidding? I killed Pat McCourt three years ago in self-defense and it haunts me still.

"Focus," I whisper to no one.

When the teams are fifty feet away and widening the gap, I call out toward the trees. "You've got nowhere to go, Lorcan," I yell. "We have a team to the north and another one just pulled up on the beach east of you." The lie comes easily. Any thought the Onion King had of making a run to the north or east just became more consequential. Right now he's weighing his options.

I don't think surrender is one of them.

"Talk to me, Lorcan," I shout. "How do we resolve this? You have to be cold and exhausted after that boat ride." Then, just because I can, I say, "Our helicopter ride was nice and warm, no bouncing up and down in the elements like you were doing. I'm perfectly comfortable staying out here all night if I have to."

I'm freezing my ass off.

If we don't wrap this up soon I'm going to have frostbite.

"Walk away or I kill her!" Lorcan yells. His voice is higher pitched than I imagined it would be. I don't know if it's out of desperation, or if that's just his voice.

Glancing to the right, I see that Jimmy and Danny have worked their way across the clearing to within a hundred feet of the fir tree. On the north side, Nate and Jason are almost as close.

Danny has a handheld night-vision monocular that he puts to his eye every minute or so to check the position of the other team. Marty continues to hover high overhead, the steady *wump wump wump* of the helicopter ever-present, but not distracting or deafening. It provides enough background noise that the teams can use their communications gear to coordinate in whispered voices as they draw closer to the target.

"Tell me, Lorcan," I call out, continuing my efforts to distract, "was it hard shooting Murphy Cotton? I mean, he was your wingman, right? The guy who did the dirty work that you didn't have the stomach for."

That pisses him off: I can tell from the sound of the bullet flying over my head.

Sure, it's twenty or thirty feet over my head, but I can sense the angst as it passes. The good news is Lorcan is a bad shot; he's demonstrated that twice now.

As the scene in the woods crawls toward a final confrontation, I spot something moving behind Lorcan—two somethings. Two glow sticks. Jimmy and Danny are still off to my right, Lorcan and Melinda are in the middle, and Nate and Jason are off to the left. There should be six bodies lit up with shine, but I count eight.

"Please don't be hunters, please don't be hunters," I whisper into the dark. The new arrivals grow larger as they approach, so I call out and distract Lorcan again, risking another lousy shot and high-flying bullet.

"So, what's the deal, Lorcan?" I yell. "Why do you *smell* your victims?" I stretch out the word *smell* until it's almost obscene. "That's a bit weird, don't you think? Kind of creeps girls out. Hard to get a date when you do stuff like that. But hey, who am I to judge? If that's your fetish—"

The next bullet is only ten feet over my head.

He's getting better; I guess practice does make perfect.

When I lift my head again, I see that the new arrivals are *right* behind Lorcan, maybe twenty feet away, though the distance is hard to judge from this angle. They're using a tree for cover, but I see them clearly in the light of the spotlight: it's the crew from Utah.

All Lorcan has to do is turn around and he'll see them, but he's too focused on me, expecting the threat to come from my direction.

It's perfect.

He's hemmed in on four sides. There are a thousand ways this can still go wrong, but one thing is now certain: the damn Onion King is not walking out of here a free man.

The air crew can't see the two teams converging on the target, but the teams see them in the glow of the spotlight. I glance over quickly as Danny and Jimmy close the distance.

There might be an opportunity here.

"Lorcan," I call again, "it's finished. This is it; last chance to walk out of here. Release Melinda and put your hands on the back of your head." As I speak, a member of the flight crew steps out a little farther from the tree, his gun leveled at Lorcan's back. As he places his right foot carefully on the snow, something changes.

I don't know if a branch snaps or leaves rustle or metal clinks on metal, but Lorcan hears something behind him that shouldn't be there. He wheels around with frightening speed, and his gun is extended at chest height when the shot rings out.

The night explodes in front of me.

A second shot; a third; a fourth, a fifth, a sixth.

Bodies drop.

Leaping to my feet, the spotlight in one hand and the Glock in the other, I race across the field and into the trees, closing the distance in seconds. To my left and right I sense movement but ignore it and push on.

The fresh white snow is stained red where Lorcan lies on the ground, thrashing about in agony. "Don't move!" I bark, leveling my gun at his head. It's all I can do not to kick him into oblivion.

He's bleeding from an exit wound high in the chest, high enough that it missed his heart and probably his lung, which is a shame. He's also bleeding from a gut wound, but again, the hole is in a place suggesting that vital organs were spared.

Some criminals are like cockroaches: they just won't die.

Jimmy and Danny are on him a moment later, checking for weapons and then rolling him over roughly so that he's facedown in the snow. When he's handcuffed, they roll him onto his side and Danny tends to him while Jimmy joins the flight crew.

The pilot—his name tag says HANSON—was the one stepping out when Lorcan whirled on him. He's bleeding from the thigh and is having difficulty catching his breath. Checking him for wounds, Jimmy finds a spent round flattened against his body armor. He's probably got a broken rib or two, but he's alive.

Without the vest, the shot would have been fatal.

They'll piece it all together later.

A gun check will show that Danny fired one shot, Lorcan fired three, and Hanson fired two: six shots for four wounds. As close-quartered as the gunfight was, it's amazing no one is dead.

We know that Danny fired the shot that staggered Lorcan as he was whirling around to shoot Hanson. The .223 round punched him hard in the upper back and dropped him to his knees. He still managed to fire off three rounds, hitting Hanson twice. Almost simultaneously, the air interdiction agent pulled his trigger twice as he watched Lorcan's gun rise up on him from a dozen feet away. One round hit Lorcan in the stomach and finished dropping him to the ground, but not before two of the killer's three rounds found Hanson.

Melinda lies motionless on the ground.

She's wearing nothing but a pair of denim jeans and a thin T-shirt, the clothes she'd been wearing when Lorcan snatched her from her cell and rushed her from his underground lair.

Kneeling next to her, I begin to search for wounds. Her face is so white I convince myself that she's bleeding internally, dying in front of me. My search becomes more frantic, but I find nothing. No punctured clothing, no gaping exit wounds, no wet fabric red with expiring life.

Her face is a mess, swollen and ugly where Lorcan punched her.

I check for a pulse first at the wrist, then at the neck. I start to panic—but then I find it, steady, but weak. Stripping my coat off, I wrap it around her freezing frame. Then, sitting next to her with my back propped up against the fir tree, I lift her off the cold hard ground and cradle her in my arms. If I could stand and hold her I would, but I just don't have the strength, so the frozen ground will have to do.

"Help is on the way," I whisper to her over and over again. "Help is on the way."

Waiting is the hard part.

I'm so cold.

It seeps into me until the world becomes a fog. I hear voices around me, but I can't tell which belongs to whom. The voices tell me that Navy search and rescue is on the way, so is the Coast Guard, Air Marine Operations, and the San Juan County Sheriff's Office. Pretty soon I find a blanket wrapped around me. It feels good. It helps.

A face floats in front of me and I realize that it's Marty. He tells me they landed when the shooting started, and something about finding an emergency kit, but not in Bill Gates's helicopter; apparently it was inside Utah.

My mind struggles with the words and I wonder what Bill Gates is doing in Utah.

They realize hypothermia is taking me when my teeth begin to chatter and my body shivers with such intensity that my bones start to ache. Still I hold Melinda, willing what warmth I have left into her limp body. I try to speak to Marty, but the words come out stilted and slurred. He has a grave look on his face now, and tells me to save my strength, that they'll have me out of here in no time.

Soon the trees begin to move darkly overhead; the world moves, passing me by. I'm lying on my back. Melinda was just here, but now she's gone. My mind drifts back to another snowy night so long ago, to a time when I got lost in a storm and died. They found my eight-year-old body and revived me, and I came back with . . . something. It's that something that found Melinda tonight.

Am I blessed or cursed?

In almost twenty years, I still haven't been able to answer that question. I suppose it's a little of both.

CHAPTER FIFTY-ONE

No one sleeps well in hospitals.

When they brought me in six hours ago, I was cold and lethargic. It should have been easy to sleep, but when someone's coming in every five minutes to check your fluids or your temperature, sleep becomes an impossible dream over a distant horizon.

Here's something I didn't know: it seems when you arrive at the hospital with hypothermia, they need to get your core temperature up before they can start warming the extremities. While I've had experience with hypothermia—the whole thing in the woods when I was eight—I don't remember anything about warming blankets or blood flow to the extremities. The fact that I was dead for part of that earlier episode probably plays a part in my faulty memory.

The important takeaway from all this is the *way* they measure your core temperature. No ordinary oral thermometer will do, because your *core* is basically your torso. That requires a rectal thermometer—or so they say. My rectal thermometer guy is Tug. I'm sure that's just a nickname . . . or he has cruel parents.

One moment Tug is making small talk, and then—*wham!*

They should have called him Push and Tug.

Heather finds it all amusing but has the courtesy to look away before each probe. When she slips off to the cafeteria for coffee, I try to recruit Jimmy to aid in my escape. A minor distraction is all I need, a couple minutes to grab my clothes and make a run for it. I'll text Heather and tell her I was just released—a minor lie in the larger scheme of lies—and to meet me out front. After that I'm home free.

It's a good plan, but Jimmy's not having any of it. He assures me that we'll be out of here soon enough. Easy to say when you're not lying in bed waiting for the next visit from Tug.

"Flash your badge and tell them it's a national security matter," I finally suggest.

"I'm not going to badge them," he says, giving me a disappointed look.

"Seriously, Jimmy, you've got to get me out of here. If Pokémon comes at me with that thermometer one more time, I'm going to make him eat it."

Jimmy chuckles at that, and then stands and stretches.

"Where are you going?"

"I just want to see if they're finished with surgery." He glances at his watch. "They should be out by now."

I wave him away as he abandons me to my misery.

When he returns a half hour later, Heather is back from the cafeteria and desperately trying to convince me that the green cubes in my cup are actually Jell-O.

"Lorcan made it through surgery," Jimmy announces, betraying neither joy nor sorrow.

I have to admit that the Onion King's short-term outlook had me torn. On the one hand, I wasn't going to shed a tear for the guy if he bought it on the operating table. It would be justice both earned and deserved. On the other hand, the thought of Lorcan rotting away in a federal prison for the rest of his life is rather enjoyable.

"It was touch-and-go with Melinda," Jimmy continues. "She's doing better now, but they're going to keep her for a few days. She wants to see you before you're released." He studies me for a moment, an odd look on his face—almost proud.

"What?" I ask, suddenly uncomfortable.

He glances at Heather and then back to me. "The doctor said she wouldn't have made it if you hadn't done what you did. She was already in the early stages of hypothermia when Lorcan dragged her off the boat." I feel Heather's hand on my arm, warm and caressing.

I don't do well with praise, so before he can say anything else, I ask, "How's the pilot?"

He nods and smiles, understanding the diversion.

"Hanson's doing better," he says after a moment. "No broken ribs, but he's got some blunt-force trauma to the chest that's going to hurt for the next week or two. He doesn't recommend getting shot at close range." Throwing a thumb over his shoulder, he says, "If you want to visit, he's just three rooms down."

"What about his leg?"

"Bullet went right through. There's some muscle damage, but all things considered, it patched up nicely. He's eating ice cream and watching football reruns."

"How can he eat ice cream?" I mutter, shivering at the mere thought.

"He wasn't sitting in the snow without a jacket," Jimmy reminds me.

We make small talk and enjoy quiet company as the sounds of the hospital drift up and down the halls. It's the end of the case, the end of a monster's reign, a new leaf for Melinda, a hero's welcome for Hanson. Such things bring their own warmth, create their own comfortable glow.

"So . . . we did it," I say at length, the words quiet and with an edge of wonder, the way one might speak after accomplishing the insurmountable.

Jimmy smiles and pats my arm.

The pleasant, gratifying moment lingers—only to be shattered by the sound of Tug laughing at some joke in the hall. In my mind, I imagine him waving the rectal thermometer playfully for the nurses and then pointing at my room.

Grabbing Jimmy by the collar, I hiss, "Seriously, get me out of here."

CHAPTER FIFTY-TWO

Christmas Eve

Life is often a double-edged sword.

On one side is the strength and happiness of a life well lived, and on the other is the sorrow and insecurity of too many poor decisions. The good news is that we choose the edge that represents our life—most of the time. We can choose the edge that garners love and respect, or the one that cuts deep and festers, rotting us from within.

Charice and Melinda have had plenty of the cutting and festering in their lives, but it's in their power to turn the sword. In a moment, they can find themselves on a different path, one that might be rocky at first, but which will lead them to a better place.

I think they'll choose a different path, a stronger path.

At least I hope so.

When I finally arrive back at Big Perch, Heather makes me tomato soup and a cheese and pepperoni sandwich for lunch. Eating slowly in a semi-reclined position on my couch, I taste each bite with deliberation, as if I've never eaten before nor will again.

Outside the living room's tall bay windows, my deck is covered in virgin snow. Beyond, the world is white and still. The wind has quieted since last night, and as I look down upon the Puget Sound I find calm waters. Gone are the heaving waves and the windswept whitecaps that hindered Lorcan's northbound journey. What remains is tranquil beauty, and it's this image that I carry with me when I finally drift off to sleep on the couch.

When Jimmy calls at four, I'm already awake.

"I thought you'd want an update," he says, sounding almost apologetic. When I assure him that an update is *exactly* what I want, he continues, his voice now buoyant.

"You remember the place in Tacoma; Sheryl Dorsey's house? Well, it's owned by one of Lorcan's shell companies. Apparently he had similar houses in Portland and Sacramento, and I'm guessing they'll find others by the time Haiden and Diane get through."

"Is it a rental?" I ask.

"Not even close," Jimmy replies. "It's more like a junkie boardinghouse, but with a twist. Instead of cash, they pay in stolen cards. A driver's license or credit card gets you one night's stay; a stolen Social Security number gets you three nights. The volume is staggering. Sometimes they'd have twenty people flopping there at the same time. All those credit cards, debit cards, passports, and driver's licenses we found when we raided the house were from just one week of activity."

"So it was all about identity theft?"

"In a big way," Jimmy replies. "There was more in Lorcan's house, I'm talking boxes and boxes, and he had a notebook completely filled with Social Security numbers. Haiden says he was either acting as an information broker or setting up bogus loans and credit lines."

"Probably a bit of both," I say.

None of this makes sense.

"Why would he risk that?" I ask. "He owned a business that employed over a hundred people, he was earning huge paydays as a computer security specialist, and he seemed to have more money than he knew what to do with."

"True, but the way Haiden tells it, he was making three to four times that selling information on the dark web. Besides," Jimmy adds after a pause, "maybe it wasn't about the money."

"What do you mean?"

"Lorcan was a hacker first, before anything. Maybe that's his heroin."

I think on that for a moment and then give a tired sigh. "People are funny."

I can almost feel Jimmy smiling on the other end of the phone. "Yes, they are," he says.

CHAPTER FIFTY-THREE

Christmas Day

Heather gets her wish.

It's a white and bright Christmas morning when we start out for my parents' place in mid-county. The road crews have had more than a day to plow and sand, so all the main roads are passable, as well as many of the secondary roads.

Jens and I always spend Christmas with my parents. And since we can't bear the thought of Ellis being alone at Little Perch on Christmas Day, we drag him along with us. He protests, as he does every year, but the true measure of his feelings will be in the quiet, thankful smile he'll have on his face this evening when we all sit around the large dining room table for Christmas dinner.

Tonight, he and my dad will probably get sloppy from too much eggnog, and no doubt a tear or two will be shed for all that came before and all that remains. Ellis is, after all, family; if not by blood, then by choice.

Heather is joining us this year, and from the moment she walks through the front door my mother can't get enough of her. It's not the first time they've met, it's not even the tenth time, but from the way she dotes on Heather you'd think they were the last two women on the West Coast.

Jens and I always suspected that Mom wanted a daughter; this just proves it.

After a sit-down breakfast of bacon, scrambled eggs, cinnamon rolls, and traditional Norwegian *sylte*—a pleasant name for headcheese—Dad stokes up a good fire in the living room and we gather around to open presents.

The wrapping paper on the two dozen gifts under the tree is quickly reduced to confetti as we take turns opening them, revealing two signed first editions for me, gift cards and clothing for Heather, a couple hats for Ellis, and a new Bluetooth stereo for Jens.

Mom and Dad score the real prize. Jens and I pooled our money and bought them a portable infrared sauna for the spare room. Mom likes to claim that cold is in her blood, that it's part of her heritage, but we've noticed she does a lot more complaining in the winter than she used to.

With the gifts unwrapped we all turn to our stockings.

Over the years, the tiny oddities, candies, and useful trinkets found in our stockings have become the highlight of Christmas morning. Each item is chosen for its unique nature, gourmand appeal, or shock value. Some past items have included coal from the *Titanic*, French truffles, edible chocolate-covered crickets, a watch made from the metal of a dismantled Soviet SS-22 nuclear missile, and a letter signed by Calvin Coolidge.

We all try to outdo one another, but ever since Mom learned how to shop online she's been the undisputed champion. I swear she spends half the year shopping for just the right items. It's an obsession.

This year I have her beat.

As Heather slowly empties her stocking, charmed by

everything she finds, her hand finally reaches the small wrapped box stuffed into the toe. I wait until she's finished removing the paper, and then, before she can open it, I step in front of her and take the box from her hand.

No one in the room knows what's coming, so when I drop to one knee I hear a single gasp behind me—my mother. When I open the box and reveal the engagement ring within, the whole room gasps. I say the words just the way I practiced them, looking up into Heather's loving face with my parents, my brother, and Ellis behind me.

The moment is perfect . . . I only wish Jimmy were here.

Heather's lips quiver as she stares at the ring. Tears begin to tumble from her eyes, and then she throws her arms around me and kisses my mouth, my cheeks, my forehead. I fall slowly backward onto the living room floor as the kisses keep coming and the room erupts with the sounds of joy and laughter.

When she pauses long enough to look into my eyes, I ask, "Is that a yes?"

EPILOGUE

Bend, Oregon—Monday, January 19

She lies where she died, a lump of still-warm broken flesh on the barren, cold summit of a nameless hill overlooking the semiarid scrub of middle Oregon.

The man sits on his haunches several feet away, occasionally bouncing lightly, as if perched on a spring. He stares with unconcerned eyes at her body, throwing pebbles at her outstretched leg with the measured frequency of a metronome and counting the times he can successfully bounce them off her dead thigh.

The things you do to kill time.

He waits and watches, his senses tuned to his surroundings: the sights, smells, vibrations, and sounds of this exact moment in time, so that he'll know instantly if something changes, but nothing does. It's just like before. As the minutes march on, he grows increasingly frustrated and the pebbles become larger and the throwing becomes harder.

Twelve times he's repeated the steps.

Twelve times he's failed.

He glances at his watch, a stainless-steel Casio synced

with the U.S. "atomic clock" in Boulder, Colorado. The digital readout is self-adjusting and flawlessly displays the day, month, year, hour, minute, and second. It's accurate down to one billionth of a second, or so the salesman told him when he purchased it three years ago.

Such precision, such accuracy, and yet the watch betrays him, neither moving forward nor back, but continuing to *tick tick tick* the time away, as if it were an ordinary watch and this was an ordinary day. He feels the urge to fling it from his wrist, but tosses another pebble instead, harder this time. The stone bounces off the abused thigh and lands almost in the same spot he'd plucked it from a moment before.

His failure makes no sense.

The codes had been difficult but decipherable, and the images, though obtuse, came into focus and started to make sense when you studied them long enough, stared at them long enough, screamed at them long enough. He was *certain* his interpretation was correct from the moment he discovered it, and he's certain now; it's the only thing that makes sense. And yet here he is again, having diligently followed the instructions of the codes and images, and nothing has changed.

His great result is no result.

The only thing different this time was the age of the catalyst. The others were in their late teens to early twenties—at the peak of their energy. This one is older; could that mean the difference between success and failure? Was that the one element that ruined the experiment?

He didn't think so.

He'd walked a circle around the body fifteen times; once for each year, just as before. He'd elevated the arms and then returned them, so they were perpendicular to the body, pointing east and west. And he'd spread the legs into a wide stance and then returned them so that they pointed south, just as before. He even used true north as his guide, expecting that Da Vinci would have done the same.

That was something he hadn't figured out until just recently.

His therapist had called his ideas *delusions*. He would have stopped going after the first such utterance if not for his mother, who insisted that he continue his treatment or forfeit access to his substantial trust fund.

The sessions were weekly, so he tolerated them.

Besides, he had bigger problems these days, mainly the report a few months earlier about the so-called "Leonardo" killer. The article itself was shruggable, the kind of story most would scan quickly before moving on, unless the deed happened in their hometown.

He knew about the article only because he keeps an eye out for such stories. His computer runs automated news searches for terms like *homicide* and *body*, but only when they match the names of the eleven—now twelve—towns and villages that he has scribbled down on a torn sheet of paper in his top drawer.

His therapist knew of his interest in Da Vinci, and particularly the Vitruvian Man. It was the main element of his so-called delusions, and it was only a matter of time before she too stumbled upon the article. She followed such things, and if the Leonardo story gained traction, she would put two and two together and arrive at him.

That's why she had to go, risky as it was. No doubt her patients would be high on the suspect list, but he'd seen to that, forcing her to delete all the files related to him. He also deleted her schedule and pulled his substantial file from her filing cabinet. It now smolders in his wood-burning stove.

The trail has been erased . . . mostly.

There were things about him that she never knew, never

imagined. Things that drove him crazy, true schizoid-nuts, the bang-your-head-on-the-wall type of stuff. It was the quest for Leonardo's secret that kept him on an even keel, that gave him hope, that kept him from putting a gun in his mouth.

Glancing down at Dr. Emma Nicholson as she cools on the frigid winter ground, he's struck once more by how beautiful she is. It was the one thing that made their sessions tolerable. He tosses another pebble at her thigh and finally accepts the failure.

Still, this could change everything.

Even if they find no link to him, the police will be all over Emma's history, her patients, where she lived, where she worked out, where she ate. He feared this most. And yet, it was Emma who had taught him to embrace his fears, to take power away from them.

A smile suddenly cracks across his frozen face and he rises. Walking ten paces to his backpack, he unzips the main compartment and digs around a moment before finding it. Closing the flap, he makes sure the backpack is zipped up tight before laying it back down and then walking back to Emma's prone form.

Kneeling, he hikes her shirt up until the bottom quarter of her breast is exposed. Twisting the cap off the red marker, he writes seven words on her belly in bold block letters, taking care not to smudge the ink before it dries. Pressing the cap back in place, he stands and studies the seven words, the grand revelation.

"Goodbye, Doc," he says, and as an afterthought, he reaches down and straightens her shirt, hiding the exposed belly and the contagious words. They'll find it soon enough, but it's a game now, and the pieces must be played one at a time.

He leaves the cold summit cloaked in the same indifference with which he arrived, though without the company of the beautiful and gifted Dr. Emma Nicholson. When he reaches the bottom of the hill he glances back, but only for a moment. There is no regret or remorse in the gesture, just the quiet discomforting knowledge that time marches on and nothing has changed.

When the wind kicks up later that afternoon, it comes from the south, a warm and steady breeze with occasional gusts that push the hastily smoothed shirt back up the torso of Emma Nicholson.

The exposed words look like a wound: red, raw, and open. To the casual observer they would mean little, just another clue among clues, something to be documented and entered into evidence. To the right eyes . . . well, those seven words will turn the world upside down.

Someone waits for those words.

They don't yet know that they wait for this revelation, but they wait nonetheless. He made sure that the words and those seeking them will find one another. The first four words—FBI DONOVAN AND CRAIG—read like a partial postcard address, as if Emma's body were the message and her death the cost of postage. The words perch on her belly, scratched there in letters two inches high.

If the first four words are the address, the last three are a warning. In other circumstances they would be fun words, the kind of words you say while cooing at a baby or playing hide-and-seek. Here, in this context, they're poignant and chilling.

I SEE YOU.